missing

'This is brilliant, utterly compelling, heart-wrenching writing. I was gripped and loved it.'
Peter James

'Full of twists and turns . . . this is a gripping and compelling read you won't want to put down.'
Heat

'An unputdownable thriller that is also a mesmerising study of a family facing their worst nightmare and realising that it is only the beginning. The characters and events will stay with you for a very long time.'
Elly Griffiths

'Sensitive and moving . . . but with a core of pure tension.'
Sunday Times

'*Found* is one of those rare finds – a page turner that is equally remarkable for the beauty and consideration given to the writing. It will suck you in and take you on a journey that stays with you.'
Jo Spain

Erin Kinsley is a full-time writer. She grew up in Yorkshire and currently lives in East Anglia.

Also by Erin Kinsley:

Found
Innocent

missing

erin kinsley

HEADLINE

The right of Erin Kinsley to be identified as the Author of
the Work has been asserted by her in accordance with the
Copyright, Designs and Patents Act 1988.

First published in 2021 by
HEADLINE PUBLISHING GROUP

1

Cataloguing in Publication Data is available from the British Library

ISBN 978 1 4722 8095 4

Typeset in Adobe Garamond by CC Book Production

Printed and bound in Great Britain by Clays Lrd, Elcograf S.p.A.

Headline's policy is to use papers that are natural, renewable and
recyclable products and made from wood grown in well-managed forests
and other controlled sources. The logging and manufacturing processes
are expected to conform to the environmental regulations
of the country of origin.

HEADLINE PUBLISHING GROUP
An Hachette UK Company
Carmelite House
50 Victoria Embankment
London EC4Y 0DZ

www.headline.co.uk
www.hachette.co.uk

For Christopher
A privilege and a pleasure

Three things cannot long stay hidden: the sun, the moon and the truth.

Buddha

ONE

Ash grey on white, a herring gull drifts against the clear June sky.

Alice lies back in her deckchair, letting the bird bring to mind music long not thought of, not heard for years: the dreamy, chilled melody of Fleetwood Mac's 'Albatross'. The guitar rings in her head, the background score to childhood memories of watching *Top of the Pops* in that cramped, unhappy house, her father oozing disapproval of long hair and loose morals from behind his evening paper, her mother darning his socks, bravely defiant and tapping her foot to the songs she liked.

The gull wheels away, out over the sea, which is, for once, the ultramarine blue of Enid Blyton story-book summers, a once-upon-a-time background for shrimping nets and sandcastles, for jam-sandwich picnics and Thermos flasks of lukewarm tea. A boy runs excitedly up the beach, a plastic bucket full of seawater slopping over his naked legs; a teenage girl throws a ball for an overexcited dog. As his grandkids bury his feet in a hole in the sand, an old man smilingly rolls his trousers up to his knees.

Alice's own picnic is made up of foods she chose as her favourites, but the thought of the prawn sandwich makes her nauseous, and the pink-and-yellow Battenberg cake is claggy in her mouth. The first cocktail, though, is still well chilled in the cooler bag.

She drinks the whole can down.

When she was the same age as the running boy, she used to come here with her grandpa, holding his hand as he taught her how to read the sea, watching the wave patterns alter as the tide began to turn. Those changes are evident now. She glances at her watch: 3.15 p.m. Twenty minutes past high tide.

God knows there's no hurry. For a while longer she sits on, feeling the sun on her forearms, pulling up the hem of her sundress to expose her thighs to the heat. The days when she had legs men would drool over are long gone. Now she can't even imagine how it would feel to be admired, pursued, desired.

The water is retreating, leaving the glistening sand studded with pebbles and pearly shells. As the exposed beach grows wider, Alice watches pools emerge at the base of the groyne. In similar pools she used to paddle after scuttling crabs and – with Grandpa's guidance – hunt for razor clams. She has a mark in mind. When the sea falls back level with the fourth seaweed-covered post, it will be time.

All that remains is the second cocktail. Pulling it from the cooler bag, she pops the cap and raises the can to the sky. A toast: to everything that's been, good and bad; to whatever's to come, to face it with courage; to her blessed, beautiful girls, lights of her life, may they forgive her.

She drinks down the fizzy sweetness, then gets up from

the deckchair to pack away her picnic. When the cooler bag is zipped, she removes the watch from her wrist. It was a wedding-day gift from Rob, always treasured and cared for, and she touches its face to her lips before placing it on the chair's striped fabric. Pulling her black sundress over her head, she folds it and lays it over the watch.

Her new swimsuit is in bright shades of scarlet and fuchsia, an uplifting fabric that causes a pang of regret for her wardrobe full of dark, downbeat clothes. Other paths could have been taken. Different choices might have been made.

But in the long run, different wouldn't necessarily have turned out better.

Down the beach, the water has receded further. Soon it will reach a stretch of mudflats, which must be avoided.

Removing her glasses, she folds them and lies them on top of her sundress. The gold ring on her left hand has grown too tight; before today, she can't remember when she last wore it. The girls might like to have it, and yet she's reluctant to leave it behind. She decides to take it with her, wherever she's going.

Over and over, a voice in her head whispers, *Why not go home?* But home has become a nest of insoluble problems. Home is no haven, but a snare.

The alcohol is going to her head, but bringing melancholy rather than the careless euphoria she intended. As she heads down to the sea, the loose sand is warm under her bare feet, though her legs feel heavy. Weaving between family groups surrounded by their paraphernalia, a lump rises in her throat. Frisbees, racquets and crabbing lines, damp towels, wet dogs and suncream: all were part of her life, once. She remembers Marietta, four years old and skinny, skipping prettily down to the sea, pursued by toddling Lily, plump and naked, always anxious not to be left behind.

Those were good times.

At the waterline, the sand is hard, and the cold water runs up over her feet, turning them blue-white, like Arctic ice.

Alice turns her back on the sea, and sees through the flattering blur of her myopia the familiar view of the town: to the west and east the cliffs, the harbour with its boats between, and the gift shops, pubs and cafés along the quay. On the rising land behind is a spread of traditional Cornish cottages, white-walled and slate-roofed, matted together along the narrow lanes. And somewhere among them, close to where a church tower rises, is Alice's house.

Think of the girls. Just go home.

She turns back to the sea and wades in, pushing through the breakers. A big wave – a seventh wave – rolls towards her, already curved and foaming as it prepares to break, just about where she is. A woman paddling with a small child is watching, and to her, Alice doesn't seem afraid as she summons the guts to dive through the wave, reappearing moments later further out.

She's out of her depth. Treading water, bobbing over rollers that break inshore from her, she runs her hands over her face to wipe the stinging salt water from her eyes. Then she faces another wave, which will certainly break before it reaches her.

The woman watching is concerned now, but Alice takes the dousing and surfaces again, beginning to swim out away from the beach until she reaches the undulating swell beyond the breaking waves. She's in a place where no casual swimmer should be, lonely territory haunted by precocious currents and riptides.

Still she keeps swimming out, making for the line where the sea meets the sky.

The woman watching takes out her phone.

Alice has changed her mind. Too tired to swim further, she spits out another mouthful of salt water and turns onto her back. The water cradles her, but she's afraid of where she finds herself, suspended over an expanse she daren't imagine, disturbed by the thought of what might be swimming in the depths. Turning her head to the left, she sees nothing but the sea's vastness, so for comfort she looks instead to the right, where the world she's abandoned is a dwindling smudge. Carried like driftwood over the curves of the swell, she knows she's at the whim of the ebb tide, riding it with hours left to run.

If she were younger, fitter, stronger, she might attempt the swim back to shore, but that became impossible for her some minutes ago. Though she doesn't know its name, cold shock has set in, rendering her leg muscles weak and useless and her arms too heavy to lift. All her limbs will do for her is eventually drag her down.

Relax, rest and wait for help. Telling herself the sea's benign and that she's safe being flotsam at its whim, she stares up to marvel at the clearness of the sky. Drowsiness is creeping over her. She blames it on alcohol, and seeing no reason to resist, lets her eyelids flicker and close, picturing in her mind a white bird wheeling overhead, hearing the guitars of that long-forgotten song, playing only for her.

Even though the sun's hot on her face, Alice begins to shiver.

*   *   *

5

Part of Selmouth's lifeboat crew were already gathered for a training exercise, so when the coastguard's call comes in, the dinghy launch is fast.

The casualty's been reported as close inshore. Speeding away from the beach, they know they don't have far to go, but single swimmers are hard to spot.

The skipper on this shout has thirty years' service under his belt. He's learned to look for guidance and take whatever help he can get, and when he scans the shoreline he sees a woman with a child, waving to indicate a line directly ahead of her.

'Somewhere here,' shouts the skipper, and the helmsman slows the boat.

One of the men grabs the binoculars and scans the water further out. These outgoing tides run fast, and will carry a body a long way.

The newest crew member is keen, and his young eyes are sharp.

'There!' He points to their eleven o'clock. 'Something red.'

The boat rises, falls, and as she rises again, all four of the crew see a flicker of scarlet in a dip in the swell.

Mercifully, Alice is still afloat.

The music in her head stopped when the shivering took hold, and since then she's heard nothing but the lapping of waves, interspersed with the dense silence of underwater. Now, she hears a new sound.

Somewhere in her failing consciousness, she understands that it's an engine. Forcing open her eyes, she sees the hull of a boat, brilliant orange, and a crew all in yellow.

A man is shouting, 'Get her inboard, get her inboard, fast as you can!'

Someone's bending down to the water, grabbing her hand. 'Keep hold of her! Don't let her go!'

But the boat rises, and her hand pulls free. Alice's face slips under, and unthinking, she swallows the salt water flooding her mouth. When she surfaces again, she's drifting away from the boat, barely floating now as her legs sink lower.

'Come on, boys, Chrisssakes, get alongside! Grab hold, one of you, grab hold!'

Her hand is gripped again, then her arm, and she's being hauled out of the water.

'Keep hold of her this time! Bring her in, bring her in.'

She's tumbled into the boat, falling heavily on the boards. Maybe she'll have bruises.

Alice doesn't care. She only wants to sleep, and closes her eyes.

The skipper radios back to the station to report one casualty on board. He's told an ambulance is already on its way.

One of the men puts two fingers to Alice's neck, and finds a faint pulse.

The newest crew member is cheerful as he hands across a survival blanket, but the other men are sombre. This isn't over yet.

As they motor back to shore, the blue lights of the ambulance flash alongside the lifeboat station. Drawn by the drama, a crowd is gathering.

They wrap Alice in the blanket, and check again for vital signs.

The pulse has stopped.

'CPR!'

The skipper claps a crew member on the shoulder, letting him know he's the man. Kneeling down beside her, the crewman begins to pump, counting as he's been trained, determined to do his part until the paramedics take charge.

But when they reach the beach, there's still been no response.

For Alice, their help came too late.

The PCSO is in only her second week on the job, and she's been given this straightforward task as being suitable for a probationer. She's to be a visible presence for anyone who's lost a relative or friend; failing any approach, her instructions are to try and locate the deceased's personal effects to help make an identification.

As the afternoon wears on, she watches from the top of the beach. Families pack their bags and dry and dress their children before leading them across the soft sand, up the steps onto the promenade.

As the stragglers return their deckchairs, the attendant's chaining up his stock. The afternoon's growing cooler as the breeze picks up, and the breakers begin to look tempting to the surfers, who run down to the water in their wetsuits, keen for action.

The PCSO's legs begin to ache, but by 6 p.m. she's got a target: a lone deckchair, unvisited since she arrived two hours before.

Overdressed in her boots and black trousers, she crosses the sand. When she reaches the deckchair, she finds everything left tidy, and picking up the black sundress, she knows she's in the right place. She gathers up Alice's spectacles and her wedding-day watch. There is, the PCSO notices, no form of ID.

As she carries away Alice's belongings, she pauses to have a quick word with the deckchair attendant.

'There's one of yours still down there,' she says, pointing with her thumb. 'I think you're going to be keeping the deposit.'

TWO

There are those who will never forget.

Across the Devon border and forty-seven miles from Selmouth, the church of St Just's squats dour among the tombstones of its own graveyard, the only building of note in the backwater hamlet bearing its name.

On Mondays, the underemployed women of the locality gather there as caretakers. Breaking the church's sullen silence with their chatter, they sweep the cold stone floors, rub beeswax into the oak pews and polish the candlesticks and brasses, mixing the stink of Brasso with the breath of mildew rising from the crypt. They beat the dust from the hassocks and arrange fresh flowers, before retiring to the vestry to enjoy coffee and home-made shortbread, and finish off their conversations about their children and their grandchildren.

By their tradition, Miss Hopper always has charge of the key, along with the responsibility for returning it to the vicar. She says her goodbyes in the porch as the women disperse, then locks the studded door, turning the iron handle to check it's secure.

Sometimes she brings a posy of wild flowers, leaving them

on the porch bench until everyone's gone, when she carries them between the tombs to the farthest wall of the churchyard.

There, sinking year by year into the turf, is a small headstone, simply engraved *Baby Michael, 17th June 1993*. In front of the headstone, a jam jar holds the remains of Miss Hopper's last offering. She disposes of the dead stems on the compost heap where the groundsman dumps the grass clippings, and rinses the jar at an outside tap, refilling it with clean water.

She likes to take her time arranging the flowers she brings, placing pink willowherb behind white meadow daisies, with cornflowers or borage – if she can find them – always to the front, since they are two of her favourites, and blue for a boy. In seasons where there are no flowers, she cuts evergreens and red-berried hawthorn.

At Christmas, she brings a teddy bear and a chocolate Santa Claus, and at Easter she leaves an egg, though when the season is past, the disposal of these more permanent objects is difficult. Even though she wraps them in polythene against the weather, and the chocolate and toys are in perfect condition, it seems inappropriate to pass on what are grave goods to other, living, children. She can't help feeling they might carry the taint of Baby Michael's fate, and so the teddies and the eggs and the Santa Clauses all end up – with deep regret – in the dustbin.

But he should know he's not forgotten, and Miss Hopper remembers all too well.

On this Monday, the other women have already walked away down the path towards the lychgate, and she's locked the door and slipped the key into the pocket of her skirt. But as she turns the corner at the side of the church, someone is already there at Baby Michael's grave.

Miss Hopper is so surprised, she stops. Very rarely has she seen anyone else here, though of course others have a perfect right to pay their respects, and she considers going to wait in her car, or returning to the porch until this other visitor is gone. Curiosity gets the better of her, and she continues forward. As she crosses the buttercup-strewn grass, she notices the nettles are becoming unruly around the oldest tombs, and ivy is choking the stone cherub who weeps over little Marcus Wright, a victim of influenza aged only three. In the tragic brevity of his life, Baby Michael is not alone.

The visitor has his back to her. Tall and broad-shouldered, he has his hands in the trouser pockets of a navy suit that's a shade too big, as if he might have lost weight since he bought it, and his haircut's vaguely dated, what her father would have called a short back and sides. Not wanting to startle him, she gives a light cough as she draws close.

He turns round, and she sees he's older than she thought, but his face is lean, with none of the sagging jowls mature women are prone to. She finds herself wishing she'd run a comb through her hair and put on lipstick.

'Good morning,' he says.

'You've come to see our poor orphan.' She holds up her flowers. 'I like to let him know he's not forgotten.'

'Never that.'

She holds out her hand. 'Jayne Hopper.'

His eyebrows rise, and he shakes her hand. His own is warm, almost overheated, although the day is mild. Cold hands, warm heart, she thinks. So what's the opposite?

'Russell Fox,' he says. 'Hopper . . .' He scrutinises her again. His eyes, she notices, are blue. 'Any relation to . . .' Trailing off, he points to the small, forlorn headstone.

'It was my brother Daniel who found him,' says Miss Hopper.

Fox nods. 'That must have been a terrible thing for him.'

'They've never got anybody for it, have they?' She's not asking a question but making a statement, a criticism of lax and inefficient authorities. 'I don't suppose they ever will. Not after all this time.'

'Never say never,' says Fox. 'You and your brother still live locally, then?'

'My brother passed away. Two years ago now.'

'I'm sorry to hear that.'

'I'm still up at the old place, though it's a farm in name only these days. You remind me a little of Daniel. He was a big chap too. Are you ex-army, by any chance?'

'Long, long ago, in a galaxy far, far away,' smiles Fox. 'It's the way they make you stand. It never leaves you.'

'I expect that's it.'

'I'm surprised to find anyone here. I come here occasionally if I'm in the neighbourhood, but I've never seen anyone else.'

Miss Hopper gives him a wry smile. 'You must have your reasons. We're three miles from the nearest shop and ten miles from the nearest town, down lanes not wide enough for two cars to pass without one of them tipping into a ditch. No one's ever in this neighbourhood except with very deliberate intent.'

Fox laughs. 'My definition of neighbourhood is quite broad.'

'Well, I'm pleased,' she says. 'He deserves to know people still care.'

'And it's good to know someone's keeping an eye on him,' says Fox. 'I expect I'll be seeing you again. If you're still in the same place, we'll no doubt have your details on file.'

'Oh,' says Miss Hopper. 'So you're . . .'

'Like I said,' says Fox, beginning to walk away, 'Michael is far from forgotten.'

THREE

Lily's had one hell of a morning at the nursery; the kids have all been hyper after the weekend, unable to settle, misbehaving and tantrumming, and Violet even threw up. Happily, Monday's a half-day for Lily, so as the tables are cleared for lunch, she grabs her bag, saying her goodbyes to her frazzled colleagues as she leaves.

She has fifteen minutes left on her parking ticket. The pharmacy isn't far, and she can make it if she's quick.

Knowing the shop's layout, she goes straight to the shelf and finds the product she wants, the 6 Days Sooner test. The price has gone up again, to almost ten pounds. Their budget's tight, and this isn't in it, so she'll be going without lunch for a couple of days. She'll still have to be careful; if Connor finds out she's bought it, he'll sulk for days.

The queue to pay is short, but there's only one girl serving, and she's helping a young mum find cough medicine for a feverish-looking toddler grizzling in a buggy. This isn't going to be quick. Lily thinks about the parking ticket and wonders if she should wait until tomorrow, but the nagging need to know compels her to stay.

As she joins the checkout queue, her phone rings, embarrassingly loud. People turn to look at her, disapproving. She pulls the phone from her bag, intending to turn it off and return the call later, but she glances at the screen and sees a number she doesn't know.

A Selmouth number. That makes her uneasy.

Leaving the blue box behind her on a shelf, she walks out onto the street and swipes right to answer. 'Hello?'

'Is that Lily?' A woman's voice, but older and far less in-your-face than any cold caller.

'Who is this?'

'It's Ivy, Ivy Dunmore, your mum's friend.'

The uneasiness ratchets up a notch. 'Oh, hi, Ivy. Is Mum OK?'

In the moment's silence following her question, Lily realises she should know. She called her mother a couple of times yesterday, but Mum didn't answer. Lily thought nothing of it, assuming she'd be down at the beach, or shopping somewhere, or doing an extra shift at work. In the end, she left a message, but Mum hasn't called back. That's out of character – usually she's only too keen to chat – and Lily feels a stab of guilt, knowing she should have followed up. As her mother's closed in on her sixties, the unwelcome spectre of health emergencies has crept into clearer focus.

'I was going to ask you. I thought you would know,' says Ivy.

'Know what?'

'Where she's gone. I said I would look after Josie – I don't mind sometimes, she's a good dog and no trouble – but she never said it would be for this long, not overnight. It's after lunch now, and still no sign of her. I thought she must be staying with you.'

16

Lily's unease is becoming full-on worry. 'She hasn't been here, no. Where did she say she was going?'

'Running errands, she said. But that was yesterday morning. I've been to the house, and knocked, but I didn't get any answer.' There's a silence while she considers. 'Her car's there, though. Maybe she took a taxi somewhere.'

'Why would she take a taxi?'

'It's not my business to ask questions like that. And I didn't like to go inside the house either, not without her permission. I do have a key so I can water the plants when she's away for longer, but then she has a place where she sends Josie. They have a bit of land and outside kennels. My little cottage isn't suited to dogs, not longer term, so I can't be keeping her. I thought you'd know where your mum is and when she'll be back.'

'I'm sorry, I don't,' says Lily. She glances at her watch, and begins to walk towards the car park. 'I hope she hasn't had some kind of accident.'

'Could be her heart,' says Ivy. 'She's been having palpitations.'

'Has she? How long has she been having those?'

'On and off, two or three months.'

'She never said anything to me.'

'She doesn't like to worry you.'

'She's worrying me now. Could she be at work?'

'I went there to get dog food, but she wasn't there. They said she wasn't on the rota for this weekend.'

It'll be nothing, Lily tells herself. She'll be back home by now.

'Did you try her mobile?'

'I did. It just rang and rang.'

'I'm sorry to ask, Ivy, but would you mind checking again at the house? I'll look a real fool if I start a missing persons search and she's at home in bed nursing a cold or something.'

'She could answer the phone with a cold, couldn't she?'

'I'm just reluctant to do anything without being sure she isn't there. You know how she sometimes is, she gets lost in a world of her own.'

Lily hears the lightest of sighs before Ivy says, 'It's a fair walk. But I don't suppose Josie will mind going out again. I don't like leaving her at my house by herself in case she barks.'

'Will you ring me and let me know what you find? If she's actually there, please tell her to ring me immediately.'

'And if she isn't there?'

'One bridge at a time,' says Lily.

'I'll ring you back, then,' says Ivy, and hangs up.

Back inside the pharmacy, the blue box is still where Lily left it and the queue's diminished. She pays cash, and hurries out. When she reaches the car, there are two minutes left on the ticket. She gets in, but doesn't immediately start the engine. Instead, she finds her phone again and dials her mother's landline, which rings a while and goes to answerphone. As Ivy's said, the mobile does the same.

This time, she leaves no message. Setting the phone up for hands-free, she sets off for home.

She's only a mile from their estate when Ivy calls back.

'I'm at the house,' she says. 'No sign of your mum here. There was post on the mat. I didn't go upstairs, mind. It's not my business to go poking round up there. I shouted plenty loud enough, though. If she was up there, she'd have heard.'

'I think I'd better come down there,' says Lily.

'I'll leave Josie here, then, shall I? If you're not going to be too long. Save me the walk back up the hill when you arrive.'

At home, Lily hastily eats a sandwich and downs a mug of tea. The blue box from the pharmacy is still in her handbag. Carrying it upstairs, she takes it into the bathroom, and even though there's no one there to see, locks herself in. Extracting the plastic stick, she stares at it for long moments before sitting down to pee on it.

The wait is a long five minutes.

Negative. No pregnancy.

The hour-and-a-half drive to Selmouth is made stressful by hold-ups and the persistent strange knocking sound the car's been making recently, which Connor hasn't yet found time to investigate. Ten minutes from her destination, an orange light appears below the speedometer, and Lily prays it's nothing serious, promising herself she'll look it up in the handbook before she heads back home. The last couple of miles especially are grindingly slow, the narrow access roads clogged with tourists, the park-and-ride car park already full. Before she makes the turn into the back streets, she catches a view of glittering sea, and the air con draws in seaweed and salt water, candyfloss and doughnuts. To Lily, it's the smell of home.

She parks in a residents-only space behind her mother's old Renault, not caring as she gets out that her rear bumper is only borderline passable on the lane. Glancing through the Renault's driver's window as she passes, all appears normal: the leather loafers Mum wears to drive are in the footwell, the ridiculous fake flower in a vase she bought on a trip to London is stuck to the dashboard.

At the end of the path the gate stands open, lopsided on its one good hinge. Connor's often offered to fix it, but for some reason Mum likes it the way it is. The lavender bushes along the path are in purple bloom, spreading so wide they almost cover the front terrace, where there's a bistro table Mum never uses, and a bird feeder the birds rarely find.

Trelonie House is no more than a grandly named terraced cottage, with a frontage – two sash windows on the ground floor but only one upstairs – as quirkily asymmetric as the lopsided gate. Lily knows there should be a key on a window ledge round the back. Despite the brightness of the day, the passage leading there is dank and gloomy, and she shivers in her summery top and skirt. The key's in its usual place, not very well hidden under a pebble. Inside, Josie's barking, running from room to room to get to the potential intruder, pausing when Lily calls to her to calm down, starting up again when she hears Lily's footsteps returning to the front of the house.

As Lily steps into the entryway, Josie – a pretty, white Westie who always seems to smile – jumps up and rests her paws on Lily's knees, her tail madly wagging. Lily bends down to stroke the dog's head and tickle her ears. Josie runs to her basket in the kitchen, and returns with a red ball in her mouth, wanting to play.

Lily picks her up and squeezes her, moving her face as Josie tries to lick her mouth.

'Not now, princess. We have to find Mum. Silly old Mum. Where's she got to?'

Still holding the dog, she glances round the small entryway. Everything appears as it should, comfortingly familiar. The shabby rag rug Mum won't get rid of because Grandma made it covers part of the stone floor, which has its perpetual smattering of Josie's pawprints; the landline handset stands on the junk-shop wicker table, along with a couple of unopened bills Ivy must have picked up. On the wall above the phone, the three watercolours of seabirds hang in their usual places. The air smells faintly of candle smoke, and already of settling dust, that same staleness of coming back to a house after a holiday or absence. From that alone, Lily believes Ivy was right and that her mother isn't here.

Even so, she calls up the stairs. 'Mum! Mum, are you there?'

Unsurprisingly, there's no answer. Lily puts Josie down, and the dog follows her into the kitchen, giving up on the idea of a game and settling in her basket under the table.

It's a while since she was here. Last time she visited was Easter; there were daffodils on the roadside banks as she and Connor drove down, and the wind was still cold off the sea, making the cottage as chilly as she remembers it growing up. Only the living room, with its wood burner, was ever truly warm in three seasons out of four. The bedroom she shared with Marietta was made bearable not by the hopeless, clanging heating (why was there never money for a plumber?) but by the heat from the chimney flue running behind the wall. Today it isn't that cold, thank God, but she wishes she'd brought her cardigan in from the car.

The kitchen is a surprise. Her mother's never been the best of housekeepers – as she says, when she comes home from work, she's better things to do than tidy and clean – but everything's been put away, the surfaces are wiped, the floor's mopped, and the sugar, tea and coffee jars all have their lids on and are arranged with their labels face out. Ironed tea towels hang by the sink, and the fruit bowl – usually full – is empty. The whiteboard where Mum writes notes to herself in multicoloured pen – shopping lists, appointments, phone numbers, birthdays – has been wiped clean, but for a red heart drawn in one corner. All that's left to show someone actually lives here is the unruly collection of souvenir magnets on the fridge door, and a teardrop-shaped dreamcatcher, hanging where it's always done at the centre of the window.

This kind of cleanliness is usually reserved for visitors; but if visitors are expected, why wouldn't Mum have said?

Lily's sense of disquiet is growing stronger. In the living room, she finds the carpet vacuumed, with none of the magazines her mum enjoys – *Woman's Own*, *Bella*, *Look* – lying around. The hearth under the wood burner has been swept, the sofa cushions are plumped, and the framed photographs on the windowsill – Mum and Dad elated on their wedding day, a very young Lily posed with Marietta in front of a Christmas tree – have been dusted.

Several of the white candles Mum likes to light in the evenings are on the mantelpiece, but the carriage clock which stands among them has stopped.

'Mum?' In the silence, Lily's voice sounds loud.

With an unaccustomed feeling of intruding, she goes upstairs, noting that the stair carpet is also clean. The door to the bedroom she and Marietta shared is ajar, and when she looks in, it appears the same as always, the space-saving bunk beds replaced some years ago with a not-quite-double bed, small enough to fit in the room and guarantee a poor night's sleep when she and Connor visit.

The bathroom is spotless, smelling faintly of bleach.

The door to Mum's room is closed. Lily knocks before she goes inside, praying her mother will be there, undeniably afraid that she might find her unconscious, or even worse.

But the room's empty. The bed's been made, and Mum's clothes have all been put away, her shoes lined up in pairs under the polished dressing table.

To any outsider, the house would look completely ordinary. But Lily lived for years with her mother's untidy habits, and she knows this isn't normal. The house has been prepared, but is it for an arrival, or a departure?

She doesn't know what to do. Is it appropriate to ring the hospitals, even the police?

If she asks Connor's advice, he'll tell her she's being melodramatic, that her mother's a free person who'll be home when she's ready. Probably he'd be right.

She'll ring the mobile one more time, and try and keep the relief and anger out of her voice when Mum answers. Some would say this is tit-for-tat, payback for how Mum must have felt all those teenage nights when Lily came home late, or not at all.

Her phone's only showing one bar of signal, but that should be enough. She clicks on her mother's number, impatient as *Dialling* shows on her screen for too long a time. When it switches to a ringtone, she breathes a sigh of relief, but that relief is cut short by what she hears next.

Mum's phone is ringing right next to her, in the bedside cabinet drawer.

FOUR

The number calling Marietta's phone appears there only rarely.

Marietta puts her coffee down on the bar, signals to the barman to keep an eye on her stuff and wanders out into the morning sunshine. She's in no rush to answer. If the call goes to answerphone, so be it.

Standing among the outdoor tables, she feels through the soles of her sandals the day's heat building in the concrete pavement. Along the boulevard, the leaves of the palm trees stir in the whisper of a breeze. Down on the beach, the white sands are empty, except for a barefoot man at the waterline guiding a painted fishing boat out to sea.

'Hi.' Marietta's a long-distance pro, and knows not to fill the empty space after she's spoken with more words. Instead, she imagines her voice travelling up to the star-borne satellites, then beamed down to a faraway place she used to know very well.

'Mari?' Lily's voice is unmistakable, even though its quality is distorted. 'Are you there?'

Marietta waits to be sure there are no more words coming that her reply might bump into before saying, 'I'm here. What's up?'

But Lily hasn't waited the requisite time; instead, her reply barges garbled and scrambled into Marietta's ear. 'You have to come home.'

Marietta frowns. A trio of stray dogs – ugly, brutish mutts – are sniffing in the gutter. One stops to cock its leg against a palm tree. 'What do you mean, come home? What's going on?' She waits for Lily's answer, but hears only a rustling sound, as if Lily's stuffed her phone into her handbag. 'Are you OK?'

'No.' The word is drawn out, filled with anguish.

'Lily, tell me. What's going on?'

Now there's static on the line, and Marietta only hears the word *police*.

Not worrying about echoes or talking over her sister, she says, 'I didn't hear any of that. It's a terrible line. Say it all again, slowly.'

The silence that follows is prolonged, and Marietta looks at her phone to check they're still connected. 'Lily?'

Lily's voice returns mid-sentence.

'. . . to say Mum wasn't at home, so I drove down to see what was going on. I couldn't find her, I didn't know what to do, so I called the police. There's a body they found in the water off the beach here, and they want me to go and look at it and see if it's her, but I don't want to go by myself.'

Marietta feels a trembling in her knees. She sits down.

'You mean a drowned body? How could that be Mum? Just calm down, Lily. You're being overdramatic.'

Once again, Lily's reply begins some way in. '. . . tell me I'm being overdramatic! Mum's missing, she's been missing for two days, so of course I called the hospitals and the police, the same as anyone would have done. And they have a body which fits her description.'

'Have you tried her mobile?' Such a ridiculous question, which Marietta immediately regrets.

'Have you?' Lily snaps back.

The rebuke is well justified. Marietta can't remember exactly when she last called her mother, though they must surely have spoken since Christmas. In truth, she can't even be confident of that.

'Because why don't you try right now,' continues Lily, 'and I'll be able to hear it ringing upstairs.'

There's a silence which might mean disconnection.

'Lily? Can you hear me? Do you mean she hasn't got her phone with her?'

'What else would I mean? It's in her bedside cabinet.'

On the sea, the fisherman raises his sail, and all seems right with the world.

'Ah, come on, Lily, she'll turn up, surely.'

'When?'

'I don't know. Have you tried all her friends?'

Marietta hears the rustling sound again before Lily says, 'Why are you always so fucking patronising? Of course I've tried her friends, work, everyone I can think of. I'm not a complete moron, Mari. Something's wrong here, and don't you dare leave me to handle it all by myself. Just come and do your share for once, all right? Because if you think I'm going looking at dead bodies on my own, you can think again. I won't go until you get here.'

'I can't just come at the drop of a hat, Lily. I have a job, remember? I'd have to find someone to run the bar, book a flight—'

'Well do it, then. You can text me your flight details and

I'll send you the train times. I'll come and pick you up from the station.'

'It's not as simple as—'

But suddenly Lily's gone, and Marietta's left staring at a screen asking her to rate the quality of her call.

For a full five minutes, she stays sitting where she is. At the horizon, clouds are gathering, turning the blue sky mauve. Looks like they're in for a storm.

As she walks back inside, the barman gives her a sly up-and-down. Marietta isn't youthful anymore, but she still looks good, slender in a short cotton shift dress, her long legs lightly tanned. To the locals, her red hair – the bane of her life back home – is exotic, the mark of a fiery and passionate nature. In the past, she's dyed it every other possible colour – black, brunette, ash blonde – before realising that here, it's her biggest natural asset.

The ice in her coffee has melted. Leaning over the bar, she tips the dark liquid into the sink.

'Where's Bernardo?' she asks the barman in Spanish, and he points upstairs. Her foot is on the first step when she turns back. 'Call Emilia and ask her if she can work the next few days. I have business I need to take care of, out of town.'

In the office, Bernardo is looking at something on his laptop. He's hirsute, leonine in the face, ten years older than Marietta. Women find him attractive, though his wife, according to him, does not. The fan on his desk is lazily turning, ruffling a pile of invoices where a fat fly crawls.

The door is open and Marietta doesn't knock, so by the time Bernardo lifts his eyes from whatever is holding his attention on the screen, she's in front of him. He closes the lid of his laptop a little too quickly.

'Hey, *muñeca*,' he says. 'What's up?'

Marietta is feeling upset, but hoping she doesn't cry. Bernardo has very little patience with women who cry.

'My sister called.'

'The sister you don't get along with?'

'I only have one sister.'

'So what did she say?'

'Something's going on with my mother. She's gone missing.'

Bernardo leans back in his chair, eyebrows raised. 'What do you mean, missing?'

'As in, can't be found. My sister thinks she might be dead.'

Now Bernardo frowns. 'Surely it's not so bad as that?'

Marietta shrugs. 'I don't think so either, but my sister's prone to hysterics. She wants me to go back to the UK, help her out.'

Bernardo studies her face. 'And are you going to go?'

'Yes.'

'How long will you be gone?'

Marietta shakes her head. 'I don't know. A while.'

'So God has intervened, taken the decision out of our hands. I will miss you.'

'I don't think so. You'll have Emilia to keep you company. I told Freddy to ask her to take my shifts.'

'Let us at least have a farewell dinner, then. We'll go somewhere special.' He puts his hand out to his phone. 'I could get us a table at El Camino.'

'I don't think so. I have to pack, sort some things out.'

'If there's anything I can do . . .'

'Thanks.' Downstairs in the bar, Freddy cranks up the music, up-tempo salsa. 'I'd better go.'

When she reaches the door, he says, 'You'll call me when you get there, let me know you're safe?'

She gives him a sad smile. 'Of course. If you're lucky, I might even send you a postcard.'

FIVE

Sometimes, you don't get what you deserve.

Back in the day, DI Russell Fox was a hotshot headed for a top job – DCI, superintendent, maybe even higher. But politics and policing aren't always compatible skills, and Fox's abilities in the latter arena didn't compensate for failings in the former. A reputation for being a safe pair of hands kept him his desk in CID, until younger men who knew the right buzzwords and embraced the new best practices came through to take the reins. First he was sidelined and shunted down the hall, then moved outside to the annexe, an afterthought of a Portakabin across the car park from the main headquarters building, a last-chance saloon appropriate to two old-timers like him and Lianne Budd.

There's a red circle around his November birthday on the coastal scenes calendar Shauna bought him last Christmas; the circle was there when she gave it to him. *Keep your mind on the things you'll be able to do when you're retired, Dad*, she said. When he objected that fifty-five was too young to retire and that he had every intention of keeping going until he was sixty, she fired back her constant mantra: *life is short*.

She's too damn right about that. For some, it barely even starts.

He daren't tell Shauna, but the truth is, he won't easily step down until one particular case is solved.

The St Just's case. Baby Michael. An infant only days old, whose burned remains were found on a remote hilltop a couple of miles as the crow flies from the church. A jerrycan still containing unleaded petrol was recovered by a search team two fields away. Beyond that, in over twenty years, there's been nothing: no identity established on the mother or the father, no clue as to whether it was one or both of them, or some other person unknown, who decided to dispose of an unwanted child in that disturbing way.

When the pitiful, blanket-wrapped body was first discovered, Fox's career trajectory was – in hindsight – already on the wane. But the case rapidly grew to be one of the biggest of the decade. Child murder is always emotive and never fails to make an impact, but this one had an extra fillip to rouse public outrage, and for weeks, the investigation was never out of the headlines. Every possible resource was made available – tracker dogs, roadblocks, even a world-renowned psychic – and when no quick results were forthcoming, every member of the nation's CID who could possibly be spared from current duties was drafted in to help.

Fox's name was on that list.

Those were hectic, gruelling days. Every spare inch of office space was crammed with investigators and their support teams, all confident that the breakthrough was coming any day. A permanent camp of news reporters set up outside the main entrance to police HQ, and it seemed the building was in the constant glare of TV lights as one media update after another was presented. For some of the team – those who were parents and grandparents especially – sometimes it got too much. Fox recalls one of the hard-bitten senior ranks being so overcome, he abandoned a press conference mid-sentence.

For everyone, it was a tough case to work. Fox's first reaction to the crime scene pictures – his revulsion, his distress – has never left him, and they roused in him – alongside a quiet rage – a cold, immutable determination to see the perpetrator locked permanently in a cell, with the key buried under three metres of concrete.

Yet in spite of everything – the manpower, the publicity, the offer of a very generous, privately funded reward – no progress of any real value was made. Silted up in its own paperwork and lacking any solid leads, the investigation ran aground, while public interest slowly stagnated, stifled by the regurgitated pap served up by news outlets with nothing new to say.

Baby Michael was laid to rest, and the world moved on.

Except for Fox.

When offered the last transfer of his career, he accepted on one non-negotiable condition: that Devon and Cornwall's highest-profile cold case would fall under his remit.

Officially, he has two files under his review at any time, but Baby Michael is always his third. Whatever else he's working on, it's never off his radar.

And he senses a break coming in that inquiry. He can feel it in his bones.

That kind of premonition has been with him since his earliest days in CID, and though he feels it rarely, it's never steered him wrong. Give something your attention, and things start to move. A place with some connection gets a casual mention on TV. He finds himself stuck in traffic behind an old car the exact make and model as one mentioned in a witness statement. He bumps into an old mate who's been out of the job for years, who just happens to remember a long-forgotten detail.

It's all about focus.

And, of course, taking the finest of fine tooth combs to go back over old ground.

DS Lianne Budd is at her desk finishing her sandwich lunch, though it's nearly 2 p.m. Here in the outer stratosphere of the car park, she and Fox come and go pretty much as they please, so a late lunch or an early one goes unremarked. No one's keeping tabs. Both of them always put in the time.

Budd smiles at him as he heads for his desk. She's put on a little too much weight this past few months – maybe she's hit the post-menopausal phase, though Fox isn't the kind to ask – but she's well dressed in dark trousers and a jacket, her hair coloured chestnut brown. Even when there's only him and her – which is four days out of five – she makes an effort. The woman has standards, same as Fox himself.

She drops her sandwich wrapper in the bin and holds up an empty mug with a force coat of arms on the side. Budd's proud of the job she does, and celebrates it.

'Tea?'

Fox is removing his jacket, hanging it on the back of his chair. 'You read my mind.'

Budd crosses to the corner of the office, where there's a small sink and a countertop fridge. Not a vending machine in sight, for which Fox is grateful. No chance of a Chunky Kit Kat to ruin his diet when the afternoon slump sets in. 'Been anywhere of interest?'

Fox sits down, and hits the enter key on his keyboard to wake his monitor. 'As a matter of fact, yes. I wasn't far from St Just's, so I thought I'd go over there, pay my respects.'

Budd is holding the kettle under the tap, but turns to face him. 'You've been up there again, have you?'

Fox nods. 'Doesn't hurt to keep an eye on things. And I won't be sitting at this desk forever.'

Budd laughs, and turns off the tap. 'They'll need a crowbar to get you out of here. Anything to report?'

Fox smiles. 'There was.'

'Oh.' Budd throws the switch on the kettle, and leans back, arms folded, against the countertop. 'Tell me.'

'There was a woman there, bringing flowers. I think she was surprised to see me. We got chatting . . .'

'As you usually do.'

'I can't help having the gift of the gab. Anyway, she turned out to be Jayne Hopper.'

Budd's eyebrows lift. 'Hopper? Wasn't it a Hopper who found the body?'

'Daniel Hopper, her brother. She's still living in the same place, apparently, though her brother died a couple of years ago. Anyway, I told her I might be paying her a formal visit at some point in the near future, to which she didn't seem averse.'

The kettle's boiling. As she's pouring hot water on tea bags, Budd says, 'Still taking flowers after all this time, and her brother made the discovery? Shouldn't she be on the list as a suspect? Suspected of being the mother, at least? Remote country area, lonely farm. Is incest out of the question?'

Fox shrugs. 'Daniel was a suspect at the beginning as the person who made the discovery, but there was nothing solid to connect him to the crime.'

Budd removes the tea bags from the mugs, and adds milk to both, one sugar to Fox's.

'Yet she's still taking flowers. There has to be a connection, surely?'

'I don't know. Could just be an act of kindness. Those things still happen.'

'Maybe.' Budd carries Fox's tea to his desk. 'Keep at it. Here you go.'

'I will. Any news from your end?'

'I'm going to re-interview one of the original witnesses in the Jocelyn Sands rape this afternoon, though she insists she's got nothing new to add to what she said at the time.'

'That's what they all say,' says Fox. 'Keep at it yourself.'

SIX

On the bus journey along the coast to the city, Marietta found herself feeling no heartache at the growing distance between herself and Bernardo, but rather the sense of a weight being lifted from her shoulders, and relief, actually, that it was over and done.

Reluctant to leave anything behind in a place where she's unlikely ever to return, she's travelling with the maximum baggage allowance. That made everything difficult, hauling her heavy cases around unassisted, until she finally waved them goodbye for a while at Cartagena airport. Then every part of the journey seemed to be hindered by delays: the flight late into Heathrow, a cancelled train between Paddington and Plymouth leading to a just-missed connection, so by the time she reaches St Austell, she's ready to weep with fatigue.

Dragging her cases outside the station, she looks round hopefully for her sister, only now realising she's no idea what car she drives these days. After ten minutes, there's still no sign of Lily, until Marietta's phone buzzes with a message: *Sorry can't get to the station. Taxi OK? See you at Mum's.*

'You're kidding me,' Marietta says aloud.

She presses the phone icon by Lily's name. Lily takes her time picking up.

'Hi! Where are you?'

'St Austell station, waiting for you.'

'Oh, look, I'm sorry. There's something wrong with the car, so Connor dropped me in Selmouth before he took it to the garage. I didn't think you'd mind. You can get a taxi, can't you?'

Stress and dehydration are giving Marietta a headache and a short temper.

'Are you mad? I've been travelling for over twenty-four hours at your request. A taxi to Selmouth will cost me the best part of fifty quid, which, having paid for my air ticket, at the moment I don't have.'

'Oh. Right. Sorry. I didn't think.'

Silence.

'I could get Connor to come and get you,' says Lily eventually, 'but he's not collecting the car from the garage until four.'

'What time is it now?'

'Just after one.' A pause. 'That's a long wait, isn't it?'

'Yes, it's a long wait on no sleep and with two huge suitcases.'

'I suppose I could pay for the taxi when you get here.'

Out of pride, it's an offer Marietta is reluctant to accept, but there seems little choice.

'Let's do that then, shall we?' she says, crossly. 'You will be there to let me in?'

'I'm already here,' says Lily, as if the question's unreasonable.

'Well, don't go anywhere. Any sign of Mum?'

'No, still nothing.'

'I'll be there in an hour or so, hopefully,' says Marietta. 'We'll get to the bottom of it then.'

Everything's familiar, yet nothing's the same.

Marietta directs the taxi through the lanes and back streets of Selmouth, feeling like a modern-day Rip Van Winkle who's slept time away while this part of the world moved on. What used to be a florist's is an arty ceramics studio, and the butcher's shop now sells Italian gelato. The renamed and rebranded Golden Lion – a once-sleazy place where she had her first ever illegal drink – offers boutique accommodation and craft beers, while the newsagent's has become a very contemporary Spar.

The backdrop to all this change, though, is unscathed; the beach, the sea and the sky are untouched and uplifting. She's glad too to see boats she remembers by name still moored at their customary berths in the picturesque harbour, as if in all the time she's been gone, they've never even put to sea.

At the front gate, she asks the taxi driver to wait, and he leaves his engine running. Heading up the path, she's annoyed that Lily hasn't registered there's a vehicle outside and come to deal with the finances as she said she would.

Trelonie House is subtly aged, as she knows she must be herself. The moss on the roof has spread and thickened; the honeysuckle has overrun the rusty guttering; the paint on the window frames is lifting like old scabs. *Why doesn't Mum get someone to sort this stuff?* she thinks, but of course the answer is simple: lack of money. Money was always in short supply. It's a family tradition that Marietta just can't kick.

In the old days, she had a key to the Yale lock, kept in her purse along with a lipstick and a black-and-white photo of her teenage self posing with Rickie Whiteman, taken in a photo booth at Bodmin bus station. Where is Rickie Whiteman now? She used to think the sun shone out of his big brown eyes, until she discovered it most definitely did not.

The lock's different now, so it doesn't matter that her key is long lost. The knocker's the same, though, in the shape of a rope-entwined anchor, the brass still unpolished and ingrained with verdigris. She lifts it and raps on the door.

Lily, it seems, is in no hurry to answer. Marietta hears her feet on the stairs and smiles in anticipation of the door being thrown open, but instead Lily calls out, 'Just a minute!'

Marietta hears her sister heading away down the hall, and scowls. *Thanks a lot. I've come thousand of miles but it's no big deal. Just take your time.*

The taxi driver kills his engine.

Marietta is lifting her hand to knock again when the door opens and there's dishevelled, disorganised Lily. She's grown plump, her below-the-knee dress making her dumpy, and she looks really tired. This business must be worrying her even more than Marietta thought. She's smiling the too-bright smile she's always had when she's stressed or nervous; when Marietta sees it falter for a second, she knows she was right about looking different – older, probably – herself. Well, life hasn't been easy. That takes its toll.

Lily opens her arms, and she and Marietta embrace, awkwardly, reluctantly, like the strangers they've become.

They pull apart, and Lily begins to babble. 'I'm so glad you're here. It's been a nightmare, I didn't know what to do. I mean, I just have no idea where she is. I've asked everyone—'

'Do you have money for the taxi?' interrupts Marietta.

'Oh. Yes.' Lily holds up three twenty-pound notes. 'I left it in the kitchen. I hope that'll be enough. We're on a budget, so I couldn't really take out any more.'

In his hurry to be gone, the taxi driver is decanting Marietta's luggage onto the pavement.

'Is the kettle on?' asks Marietta. 'I'd love a proper cup of tea.'

Once dragged inside, the suitcases seem to fill the whole entryway, leaving little room to get round them to the staircase. Dubiously, Marietta eyes the steep, narrow stairs. Carrying them up there isn't going to be easy. The dog sniffs round the cases, more interested in them than she is in Marietta. As long as she doesn't pee on them, Marietta doesn't care.

The kettle boils, and Lily's found mugs and the familiar teapot like someone who's in this kitchen every day. Marietta looks around, noticing that the woodwork's been painted a pale yellow and the tiles behind the sink have been replaced. A different calendar hangs on the back of the door and there are more souvenir magnets on the fridge. Apart from that, it's still the place she left, a long time ago.

'I assume that's Josie,' she says, inclining her head towards the dog.

Lily turns from making the tea. 'Haven't you met?'

'Pixie was still around when I was last here. I don't think Josie likes me.'

'She just takes a while to get used to strangers.' Lily turns back to the tea-making, looking for a teaspoon to hide her embarrassment at what she's just said. 'I don't mean you're a stranger or anything. Just that you haven't been introduced.'

'Stranger's the right word, then, isn't it? Don't worry about it.'

'You know,' says Lily, 'I can't remember how you take your tea.'

'Milk and none. A proper strong brew for preference. I'm done with horse-piss tea. They're all coffee drinkers over there. Tea is only for old ladies.'

'Thought you'd like your favourite mug.' Lily hands Marietta a mug decorated like a carton of Pot Noodles. Marietta's drunk from it many times before, but the design has faded from frequent washings.

'Thanks,' she says. 'Though I can't remember when I last had a Pot Noodle. Are people still eating those things?'

'All the time. They've got loads of new flavours. Thai, Italian, Japanese. Let's sit in the lounge.'

Lily leads the way. Marietta finds that the living room, too, has changed very little, except for the lack of clutter.

'Wow, why so tidy? Did you do this?'

Lily shakes her head, and sits down on the rocking chair that was once their grandmother's. Always her sister's favourite place, remembers Marietta as she takes the end of the sofa nearest the wood burner, which long ago was hers. Even now in summer, when it's likely weeks since it's been lit, she catches the smokiness of ash and carbonised wood, and that familiar smell invokes a memory of being blanket-wrapped and cosy in this same seat, sipping Mum's special hot chocolate as she and Lily watched something on TV. This sofa used to be her sanctuary.

The tea, when she tastes it, is ambrosial, refreshing and restorative. One good reason, at least, to come home.

'The house was tidy like this when I got here,' says Lily. 'Mum must have done it before she . . . well, before whatever she's done.'

'Tell me the whole story,' says Marietta, and Lily does, recounting the phone call from Ivy, the dead end to making contact once she found Mum's mobile phone, the shock of the police's suggestion that she might view the body at the hospital morgue. As she tells this last part, she becomes tearful.

'That's when I phoned you. I knew you'd say I was being pathetic, but I don't want to go on my own.'

A wave of sisterly concern comes over Marietta. 'Lily! Sweetie, please don't cry.'

Lily tries to brush away the tears. 'I'm sorry, I'm just not as tough as you. And anyway, I know it isn't her. How could it be? But I don't want the trauma of going peering at a dead stranger. Lots of people would feel the same, wouldn't they? I've never seen a dead body before.'

'It's not as bad as you think,' says Marietta. 'They're like empty shells. It's obvious there's no one home.'

'What, you mean you've seen one? Who?'

'Long story. Best saved for another time.'

'Anyway,' says Lily, 'don't you think it would be different with someone you know? What if it is Mum, by some horrible chance? How would I cope if I were there by myself and it was her?'

'Couldn't Connor have gone with you?'

'He couldn't face it, not so soon after his dad's death. And he doesn't think it can possibly be her. He thinks she's gone on some jaunt and just forgotten her phone.'

'For what it's worth, I think so too.'

'But she's been gone for days, Mari. If she knew she was going to be away so long, wouldn't she have made proper arrangements for Josie?'

That, thinks Marietta, is the unwelcome fly in the ointment of her theory. Mum has always been mad about her dogs. If she were planning a few days away, no question at all she'd have made sure Josie was being looked after.

Lily is looking at her for what Marietta realises is guidance.

'Before we do anything, I need a couple of hours' sleep,' she says. 'Can I go in our old room?'

Lily looks doubtful. 'I've been sleeping in there myself. I've had to stay to look after Josie. You could use Mum's room. I don't think she'd mind, under the circumstances.'

'I don't suppose she would. In the meantime, why don't you ring the hospital and tell them we'll be there late this afternoon?'

'To see that body, you mean? Today?'

'I think we have to,' says Marietta. 'We have to know whether or not it's her.'

'What if it is?'

'If it is, we'll deal with it. But we just have to pray that it's not.'

SEVEN

Lily drives them to the hospital in their mother's Renault. In Outpatients, Marietta stands in the information queue to ask for directions to the morgue, and when she hears that word, the woman behind her takes a step back, as if Marietta is somehow tainted, a carrier of bad outcomes. The morgue, she's told, is in the basement. She beckons to Lily, and they head towards the lifts.

They're the only passengers going down from the busy ground floor. When the lift clangs to a stop, there's a long delay before the doors open, and the sisters look at each other, eyebrows raised, suppressing laughter.

'It's like a horror film,' says Marietta. 'What if we're stuck down here with all the dead bodies, and Pennywise is waiting on the other side of this door?'

'Who?' asks Lily, but the doors finally open, and there's no need for Marietta to explain.

Superficially, the basement's like any other floor in the hospital: austere decor and hard lighting. What's unnerving is the near silence, the lack of beeping alarms and monitors, the absence of staff to administer care. They are the only visitors in an other-worldly place, and as they follow the signs to reception, their footsteps sound disturbingly loud. Away down the corridor, there's a clatter of metal, as though someone has dropped a box of knives.

The reception area is small. Sitting behind the desk, a woman in blue scrubs gives them a sympathetic smile of welcome, but before she can speak, a second woman stands up from a chair and approaches. She's wearing a black skirt suit and white blouse, and Marietta wonders if she's an undertaker.

The woman asks, 'Is one of you Lily?'

'I'm Lily.'

'I'm Tina Makepeace, family liaison for Devon and Cornwall Police. I think you spoke to my colleague on the phone.'

'Yes,' says Lily, and Marietta notices she's gone pale.

'I'm Marietta, Lily's sister. Lily, are you OK?'

'I'll just sit down a moment,' says Lily.

Tina looks sympathetic. 'I'm sorry to have to ask you to do this. I know it's distressing. But you might help us put a name to someone who doesn't have one at the moment. Take your time, though, Lily. There's no hurry.'

Lily shakes her head. 'I'm OK. I'm ready.'

'Are you sure?' asks Tina.

'Do we both have to do it?' asks Marietta, and Tina shakes her head.

'No. We only need one of you to make an identification, or tell us it isn't your mum.'

'It isn't,' says Lily, firmly, from her seat. 'But I don't think it's fair for only one of us to do it. Neither of us wants to be looking at dead people. I'll be fine.'

'Let me do it, Lily,' says Marietta. 'Just stay where you are and try to relax.'

'Can I get you a cup of tea?' the woman in scrubs asks Lily. 'Or some water?'

Lily looks grateful. 'Some water would be great, thanks.'

'Back in a few, then,' says Marietta, and she lets Tina lead her away.

Afterwards, this walk comes back to Marietta in dreams where she's alone and doesn't know where she's going, where everything's stark white, shrouded in overwhelming dread.

Here in real life, the floor and ceiling tiles are grey, and only the walls are white. In her black suit and shoes, Tina gives away through her nonchalance the fact that she's been here many times before, in this situation Marietta hopes will be for her an ordeal she'll never have to repeat. A sickly chemical smell hangs in the air, making her feel queasy, or maybe the nausea stems from nervous apprehension. Like Lily, she can't believe she's about to see her mother, but that doesn't make the situation less stressful. The thought crosses her mind that Bernardo would find all this grimly fascinating.

They reach a door with no signage. Tina opens it and walks through, but Marietta's reluctant to follow, afraid this is it, straight in, no preamble. She remains in the corridor until Tina peers round the door to see where she is.

'Come in, Marietta.'

Marietta steps across the threshold, into a small room lit only by a lamp so the light is little better than twilight, shining on soft chairs and a low table.

Nothing at all to be afraid of.

Except for a second door.

Tina closes the first door behind them. 'Are you OK?'

Marietta isn't certain, but says yes anyway.

'You can take all the time you need to be sure whether or not it's her,' says Tina. 'Is there anything you want to ask me?'

The chemical smell is stronger in this room. Marietta's nausea is growing.

'Is it . . . Are there any injuries?'

Tina shakes her head. 'The body's intact. There's nothing to worry about in that regard. Whenever you're ready, we'll go in.'

'Are you coming with me?' The question makes Marietta feel childish, but when Tina says she'll be there the whole time, it's a comfort.

'I'm ready,' says Marietta, and Tina opens the second door.

A room of tiles and steel, and a gurney; and on the gurney, plainly dead, a woman, covered to her neck with a sheet, only a naked arm exposed. A hand to hold.

Whatever Marietta was expecting, it wasn't this: her mother lying alone in this cold place, waiting to be given a name.

She doesn't need to go close to know it's her. She looks almost the same as she does – did – in life, except for the waxy, yellowed skin, and the lack of a smile.

Something is happening in Marietta's head, a loss of focus, the ominous vertigo which precedes passing out. She thinks she might need to sit down.

'Mum?' Irrationally, she thinks her mother's head will turn and her eyes will open.

She's starting to shiver. Crossing to the gurney, she touches her mother's hand. Why is it so cold, why so hard?

Behind her, Tina asks, 'Do you know her?'

Marietta finds she is crying. 'I didn't think it would be her. I thought Lily was just being hysterical.'

'Can you tell me her name?' Tina coaxes.

'She's my mum, Alice Ansley. Can I stay with her a while?'

'As long as you need. There's no rush.'

'Can I have a chair?'

'Of course.' Tina fetches one, and Marietta sinks down onto it. 'Shall I go and get your sister?'

Dazed, Marietta shakes her head. 'What will she say? I don't know how to tell her.'

She strokes her mother's hair; that, at least, is the same. One of her tears falls on Alice's arm, and she apologises as she wipes it away with her thumb. When Tina leaves the room, Marietta doesn't notice.

A little time goes by, and she's content to sit at her mother's side, holding her hand, touching her cheek. In life, many years have passed since they shared such intimate contact.

She hears Lily's voice outside, strident and filled with panic. 'It isn't her. Why is she taking so long? Mari? It isn't her, is it?'

Marietta knows she should go to Lily, but stupefied by shock, she stays seated, straightening the sheet over Alice's chest. A lullaby from earliest childhood comes back to her, and in her head she begins to sing.

The door opens, and Lily's wail of despair jars Marietta into realisation that the time for reconciliation and building bridges has run out.

All those missed opportunities; all those things she could have said. Now it's too late.

I'm so sorry, Mum, she thinks. *Please forgive me. How in God's name was I to know?*

EIGHT

The midsummer sunrise comes early, provoking the cries of seagulls. Marietta has been wakeful much of the night, dozing only intermittently, feeling afresh each time she wakes the heaviness of loss.

Once the birds are clamouring, there's no question of trying to sleep more. Dawn seeps through the floral curtains, bringing all Alice's most personal things back into the light – her hairbrush on the dressing table, a pair of slippers worn to the shape of her feet, her dressing gown on the hook behind the door, all abandoned now. On the long journey home, Marietta was rehearsing a conversation with her mother, planning how to explain her point of view. There were questions that needed answers, and things that badly needed to be said. None of that will ever happen now.

At 6 a.m., she finds one of Alice's cardigans and puts it on over the T-shirt and leggings she slept in. The cardigan's baggy and an unflattering shade of grey, and she wonders why her mother never bought nice clothes, never made anything of herself. Lily seems to be following in those footsteps. Closing her eyes, she sniffs the sleeve, hoping to find some scent she recognises caught in the fibres, some trace of the living woman, but there's nothing there.

Downstairs, she lets Josie out into the back yard, where the pots of geraniums have seen better days and the wheelie bin's overflowing with rubbish. Josie trots past her, and after a cursory sniff at an ailing runner bean plant, squats gratefully for a pee, then continues sniffing as if the whole place is new to her.

Marietta makes herself black coffee and sits down at the kitchen table, listlessly leafing through the pages of a local newspaper that somehow survived Alice's last cleaning and was left on top of the microwave. The news reported is all depressing: a respected GP one week into his retirement has been killed in a cycling accident; enquiries into the murder of an infant twenty-five years ago are to be reopened; a protest has been held against the closure of a library and arts centre. The obituaries are on page two; Marietta recognises a teacher from her schooldays, dead at only fifty-nine. Probably she and Lily should think about putting in an entry for Alice. There are so many things to do, things she's never had to do before – things she might have asked Mum's advice on. In that thought is a reluctant acknowledgement that despite everything, her mother was still the first person she'd turn to in a crisis; how come she never realised that before?

Josie comes trotting back in, and sits down at Marietta's side. Marietta strokes her ears, then decides to spoil her by giving her a pre-breakfast snack, and drops a handful of dry food in her bowl. Overhead, she hears Lily's phone ring and the murmur of her voice.

Marietta's coffee has gone cold. She pours it down the sink, and makes another.

When Lily appears, she's already wearing the dress she wore yesterday, though her feet are bare. She's deathly pale, and purple below her eyes. From her basket, Josie looks up at her, wags her tail and settles back down to sleep.

Lily refills the kettle and gets out the tea bags. They're low on milk; someone will have to shop, but the thought of facing the normal world is more than she can bear. She asks Marietta if she wants tea, and Marietta shakes her head, refolds the newspaper and tosses it onto the counter behind her.

'How did you sleep?'

'I don't think I did,' says Marietta. 'You?'

'Not really.' The kettle boils and switches itself off. Lily makes her tea, stirring it for too long, forgetting what she's supposed to be doing. Placing her cup on the table, she sits down.

'I still can't believe it,' she says.'

Marietta reaches across and squeezes her hand. 'We'll get through this.'

'I just don't know what to do, where to start.'

'There isn't much we can do,' says Marietta. 'Not until after the post-mortem.'

Lily hides her face in her hands. 'I can't bear it. The thought of them cutting her . . .'

'Don't. Just don't let's think about it.'

Lily sips her tea. 'Connor sends his love.'

'Thanks.'

Marietta senses hesitation before Lily says, 'He says we should find her will.'

Marietta looks at her. 'Do you think she made one?'

'I think she did. It was a while back. I don't even know if it would still be valid.'

51

'What did it say?'

Lily shrugs and says nothing. In the silence that follows, Josie twitches in her basket, fast asleep and chasing phantom rabbits.

'What we should do first is let people know,' says Marietta at last. 'We could make a start on that. Friends and family, work.'

Lily nods agreement. 'But it's too early now.'

'Then I'll go and grab a shower,' says Marietta. 'Let's start at nine o'clock.'

When she comes back downstairs, the kitchen smells of toast. Lily's made a lacklustre effort at laying the table with preserves she's found in the cupboard, a carton of olive oil spread and a couple of knives. On her own plate, a piece of toast remains half eaten. Marietta sees she's been crying; there's a box of tissues by her hand, two damp ones balled up by her plate.

Lily gives her a wan smile. 'Do you want breakfast? I've tried to eat but I just feel sick.'

Marietta feels a burst of compassion. Lily looks young and very lost, the way she sometimes used to as a child, when the older children they played with picked on her for being slow or clumsy with a ball. She always had an air of passivity about her, which unscrupulous playmates sometimes read as vulnerability, and on many occasions Marietta stood as her defender. She's powerless now to spare Lily the misery of her grief, but she can at least be grateful for her sister's efforts to feed her.

'I'll make it.'

Crossing to the toaster, she drops in two slices of Hovis. Seeing the almost empty jar of Golden Shred, a lump forms in her throat. Mum's last jar. Is this how it's going to be, tears over everything, even a jar of marmalade?

She sits down, and for Lily's sake keeps it together while she spreads both slices.

'This reminds me of teenage schooldays,' she says, and takes a bittersweet bite, oranges and nostalgia. 'A slice of toast and a run for the bus. Poor Mum, every morning trying to get us out of bed. She used to yell herself hoarse, and I still wouldn't move. I missed the bus one day and she made me walk. By the time I got there, it was time to come home.'

Lily sits silently beside her, gazing into space, squeezing the crumpled tissue in her hand.

The little carriage clock on the lounge mantelpiece strikes eight.

'I wound it up,' says Lily. 'She likes to keep it going. Liked.'

Marietta finishes her toast and clears away the cups and plates. Lily excuses herself and goes upstairs; a few minutes later, Marietta hears the shower running. When the water goes off, Lily is silent and absent a long time.

When she reappears, she sits down in the same chair she left. Moments later, the clock strikes nine.

Marietta pats her on the shoulder. 'Come on, sister mine. There are things that must be done. We have to make some calls.'

Forlornly, Lily looks up at her. 'But how do we know who to ring? Where do we start?'

'The best place I can think of,' says Marietta, 'is upstairs.'

Their beginning must be with an intrusion they don't want to make. Even though Marietta slept last night in this bedroom and her bags are open on the floor, this is a different level of intrusion into their mother's life. Understanding is beginning to dawn that the first casualty of her death will be her privacy.

All their lives, this has been their mother's room, and it still feels irrevocably her territory, as if her essence has permeated even the fabric of the walls. Now she has no claim on anything here, and that sense of her possession must be unravelled. Everything she owned they must sort through and deal with.

The room faces north, and no matter how bright the day outside, in here it's always gloomy and very rarely warm. In winter, when overnight temperatures drop below zero, frost paints the windows with swirls and ferns where the sisters used to scratch out their names with their fingernails. Marietta left open a window while she slept, but the air feels unnaturally still, as if with Alice's death the room has ceased to breathe. In a corner of the ceiling a brown stain shows where water's been oozing through – another essential repair that never got fixed.

Lily stands behind Marietta in the doorway, looking in on the bed covered in dove-grey sheets, at the folded tartan blanket and hot-water bottle on Grandma's old washstand, at the water glass inverted on a crocheted doily on the bedside table.

'We need to find her address book,' says Marietta.

Lily looks doubtful. 'Do you think she still has one? Won't all her contacts be on her phone?'

But Marietta's remembering a small book bound in blue fabric which appeared every December when the time to write Christmas cards came. She was indulging in magical thinking, that all their answers would lie in its pages – a list of everyone Alice ever knew and had cared for, with all those deceased or disowned crossed out. But Lily's right. Their mother was no more likely than anyone else to keep a hand-written record up to date these days.

Lily crosses to the bedside cabinet, moving carefully as if she's afraid to give offence. Before she opens the drawer, she touches the crocheted doily, clumsily made in peach yarn.

'I made this,' she says, wistfully. 'Granny helped me make it for Mum's birthday when I was about ten.'

'Looks like she really treasured it.'

'I wish I'd made her more things. It was always easier to get chocolates or wine.'

'She appreciated those things too, though, didn't she? Especially the chocolates.'

Lily smiles as her eyes fill again with tears. 'I hope she did.'

She opens the drawer in the bedside cabinet. Alice's phone lies in a random scatter of the casualties of her tidying, betraying her hurried efforts to leave the place looking clean. What was on the surface has just been swept in here.

Lily reads the dispensing label on a bottle of pills. 'Cipramil. What's that for?'

Marietta shrugs and shakes her head. 'No idea. Did she have blood pressure issues?'

'Not as far as I'm aware.' Lily picks up the phone. 'Do you think it's OK to do this? I'd be fuming if anyone touched mine.'

'Under the circumstances, what choice do we have?'

'Hey, guess what?' From under painkillers, hand cream and lip salves, Lily pulls out the address book bound in blue fabric. 'Can't hurt to have this, can it?'

She hands the book to Marietta. The binding is coming unstitched, and some of the pages are loose. With care,

Marietta flips through the entries, all written in Alice's large, looping hand. Not one of them has been crossed out.

'I suppose she knew who's dead and who's not,' she says.

Lily has powered up the phone. 'Are you ready for this?'

'Password?' asks Marietta, but Lily shakes her head.

'No password needed.'

'Almost like she left it ready for us.'

'Don't say that,' snaps Lily. 'She just didn't think she needed one. Lots of people don't password their phones.'

Marietta raises her hands in a gesture of apology. 'OK, OK. Just open the contacts file. No need to go probing into anything else. We can leave her some dignity.'

'I'm in,' says Lily, scrolling through the entries. 'Bad news. Mum knew a lot more people than I thought.'

With the phone and the address book, they head downstairs.

'I'll make us a cup of tea,' says Lily, heading for the kitchen.

While she's gone, a thought strikes Marietta. She takes out her phone and googles Cipramil.

The overcast sky is denying warmth to the lounge, and it's cool in that way Marietta recalls, needing a cardigan or jumper to be comfortable even in summer.

Lily picks up a box of matches from the hearth and lights the candles on the mantelpiece, pausing for a moment after each one is alight so Marietta wonders if she's saying prayers.

When all the candles are burning, their mellow light catches Lily's face, melting away her pallor but deepening the shadows under her eyes.

'She liked the candles lit,' she says, watching them burn. 'She said they help the spirits find their way home.'

'There are no spirits,' says Marietta, though the flickering light seems to have made the room darker, and for a brief moment she wonders if that's true. As Lily takes the rocking chair, she settles into the sofa. 'We could light a candle for Mum at the church, if you like. I'll go with you if it's something you want to do.'

But Lily shakes her head. 'We have candles here at home. I don't see any point in doing it anywhere else.'

Home, notices Marietta. Is that still how Lily regards this house?

'One thing we have to decide. People are going to ask us what she died of, and I was wondering what we should say. After what the family liaison officer said.'

Lily frowns. 'What d'you mean?'

'Well, I know she was trying to break it to us gently, but don't you think it might have been . . . You know. Deliberate.'

'How could it have been deliberate?'

Marietta sighs. 'Come on, Lily. Don't make me spell it out.'

Lily's frown deepens. 'You'll have to spell it out, because I've really no idea what you mean.'

Still the same old Lily then, thinks Marietta. Still pushing away anything that doesn't fit her picture-perfect view of life.

'You know what she was suggesting, Lily. Those tablets we found upstairs, they're antidepressants. She was saying Mum might have killed herself.'

Like an upset child, Lily shakes her head. 'Don't you dare say that. Mum would never leave me like that. She wouldn't do it.'

Me. Not *us*.

Marietta wants no battles, so she backs down. 'I suppose

we'll have to wait for the inquest, but she said that could be months.'

'I don't see why we need an inquest in the first place.'

'So we'll just say it was an accident, shall we?'

'It *was* an accident,' insists Lily.

They begin to make a list, comparing numbers in the phone's contacts with entries in the address book to avert duplications. Some of the names are known to them – Mum's workmate Harriet, her old school friend Barbara, neighbours they remember from years ago, long moved away but still in contact.

Those labelled by profession – doctor, hairdresser, plumber – Marietta puts on a separate list to be notified in due course.

'Humbert Eaves,' says Lily. 'They're the solicitors.'

Marietta looks up from the note she's writing. 'How do you know?'

Lily doesn't answer, but continues scrolling through the contacts.

'Lily?'

'It just rings a bell. Anyway, I think we should get in touch with them. Connor says without their help we'll run into problems with bank accounts and access to funds to pay bills.'

'Is Connor legally qualified, then?'

'Don't be so snide. His dad died last year, so he's only just been through it all.'

Marietta recalls Connor's father from Lily's wedding, a sour-faced man who spent most of his time at the bar. 'I'm sorry to hear that. Did he leave Connor any money?'

'Mari! You're so blunt.'

'I just thought you might have had a bit of a windfall.'

58

'We did. A bit.'

'So what did you spend it on? I hope you went to Monte Carlo and put it all on number six.'

Lily smiles. 'We put it on eleven and lost the lot.' The smile fades. 'Actually, it wasn't as much fun as that. I'll tell you some other time. Here's a number for the vicar, Reverend Northcott. I suppose he's the local man now.'

'A vicar?' Marietta's surprised. 'Has she been going to church?'

'Not that I'm aware of. But if she knows him, maybe she'd like him to do the service.'

'Are we having that kind of funeral? A church service? Do you really think so?'

'Why not?'

'It'll be expensive, Lily. How would we pay for it? Anyway, I didn't think she was religious. Don't you think she'd have preferred something less fussy? A humanist funeral maybe?'

'She's got the vicar's number in here. We could at least ask him.'

'I don't mind asking, but the question of money stands. I think it'll have to be a fairly modest affair. She wouldn't mind that. She was a modest kind of woman.'

Lily's face is crumpling. 'I'm not burying her in a cardboard coffin. She was our mother.'

'I didn't mean that. I only thought . . . Please, Lily, don't get upset. We'll do our best for her, of course we will.'

Lily sniffs, and rubs at her nose. 'I don't want to scrimp. That would be too awful.'

Marietta considers. 'Maybe others might contribute. You know whose name we haven't found? Uncle Simon's. I haven't seen him for decades, not since we were kids.'

'Oh.' Lily sounds doubtful. 'Of course we ought to let him know, but how will we get in touch? I don't think they've spoken for years, not since he moved to America.'

'America? I'm sure Mum said he was in Australia.'

'He went to Denver, didn't he? Or was it Dallas? Wherever it was, as far as I know it's a long time since they were in contact. That happens a lot these days, doesn't it? Look at us. We've barely spoken since you moved to Colombia.'

Marietta looks sceptical. 'We've spoken pretty regularly. Haven't we?'

'We haven't, Mari. We've messaged each other occasionally. Rarely, actually.'

'The time difference makes it difficult.'

Lily shrugs. 'I suppose that was true for Mum and Uncle Simon. Give it a couple of years and we'd probably have lost touch too.'

Lily's right, Marietta realises. But would they really have drifted so far apart? In her heart of hearts, she can't deny the possibility was there, not because of a specific intent to cut ties, but rather via the slow-death route of careless omission. Close as they were to estrangement, their mother's death has brought them one blessing at least, in the opportunity to be together.

'The question remains,' says Marietta, 'how will we track Uncle Simon down if we can't even agree which country he's in? I didn't see anything in here.' She flicks through the blue book to check, looking under *S* for Simon and *Y* for Youlden. 'Nothing.'

'Google him,' suggests Lily. 'Men don't change their surnames like women do. And it's not like it's a common name, is it?'

Marietta picks up her phone and opens the browser. When she puts the search term into Google, very few results pop up, and none of the related photos look anything like how she remembers Uncle Simon, even allowing for two decades of ageing.

'What if he's died?' she asks.

'Wouldn't Mum have gone to the funeral? Probably he had a wife or children who would have got in touch, the same as we're trying to do now. And I'm sure if Mum knew he'd died, she would have told us. That's a big thing, isn't it, your brother dying?'

'We could write to his last-known address,' suggests Marietta. 'Someone where he used to live might have stayed in touch with him. Didn't we used to visit him sometimes, somewhere out in the country?'

'He had a cottage that was really untidy, with a donkey in a field we used to give peppermints. Uncle Simon made us scampi and chips once, and I didn't like mine.' Lily pulls a face. 'I still don't like scampi.'

'We could advertise for him, like Sherlock Holmes. Don't lawyers sometimes do that, advertise for people who may learn something to their advantage? I expect she's left him something if she had a will.'

'That's another reason why we need the will,' says Lily. 'His address might be in there. If he's still alive.'

'If she hasn't left him anything, probably we should take it as proof positive that he's not around any more. But I want to find out what happened to him anyway. He's our flesh and blood. Who else do we have?'

There's a knock at the front door.

Josie jumps out of her basket, her claws clicking on the stone flags as she heads down the hallway and sniffs at the base of the door. Marietta follows. Josie isn't barking, suggesting the visitor is someone she knows.

But the woman's a stranger to Marietta – a little older than her mother, wearing the kind of cotton dress you'd only buy on holiday in the Med, and ugly Velcro-fastened sandals that show her bent and bunioned toes. Her long, grey hair is plaited and pulled forward over her shoulder. Marietta sees a shade of guile in her smile, which puts her on her guard.

But Josie has no such reservations. Tail wagging, she jumps up to rest her paws on the woman's knees. The woman bends down to stroke her head.

'Can I help you?' asks Marietta.

The woman prefers to reply to the dog, in an accent that's pure Cornish, slow and beguiling.

'You know me, don't you, missy?' Still petting the dog, she looks up at Marietta. 'I'm your mum's friend, Ivy Dunmore. You must be Lily. I spoke to you on the phone.'

'I'm Lily's sister, Marietta.'

Ivy stops petting Josie, who having performed her greeting duties slips past Marietta and pads away down the hall. Ivy gives that smile again, and subtly casts her eyes over the length of Marietta's body. 'I can see that now. Look at your lovely tan. Where is it you've been, Cambodia?'

'Colombia.'

'Colombia, that's right. All those thousands of miles away. Your mum misses you, you know. I've just come to see if you've managed to track her down.'

'I think you'd better come in,' says Marietta.

NINE

Ivy's shock and upset at the news is plainly heartfelt. She sits white-faced in an armchair, while Marietta hands her tissues. Lily brings her a cup of sweet tea laced with a splash of brandy, and Ivy blows her nose before taking a sip.

'You've put a little bracer in there, haven't you? I'll tell you, I think I need one. This news has knocked me for six, it really has. You can't properly take it in, can you? I keep expecting her to walk in at any moment.'

Lily realises she's been feeling the same, that Alice will appear, pleased to see them but bemused at their intrusion. That's wishful thinking. If only it could be so.

'I knew something was wrong,' Ivy goes on. 'She wouldn't just have left me in the lurch with Josie, considerate as she was. She was never one to take advantage. Was it her heart?'

'We don't know yet,' says Marietta. 'There's going to be a post-mortem.'

Ivy shakes her head. 'Why is that necessary? They should just leave her be, let her rest.'

'There'll be an inquest too,' says Lily. 'There are so many questions.'

'Something must have gone wrong,' insists Ivy. 'She was a good swimmer, your mum was, a good strong swimmer. I've seen her in the water myself. Maybe it was a cramp she got. Or could have been a stroke.'

'There's no point in our speculating,' says Marietta. 'They'll tell us soon enough.'

Ivy drinks more tea, and placing the cup back in the saucer says, 'Well, she's thrown you girls a real spanner in the works. You've plenty to sort out, haven't you? Always the same with a death. All the things they expect you to do, this office, that form, just when you don't want to do anything. I could help with the funeral refreshments, if that would be useful.'

'Thanks,' says Lily. 'I think we're a way off that yet. There is something you could help with, though. There're some people in her contacts we don't know. Could you have a look and see whether they were close friends, if you think we should get in touch with them?'

'Of course.' Ivy dabs again at her eyes. 'I'm sorry to be so upset, but it's the shock, isn't it? I never thought she would be . . . I thought she must have got carried away with one of her boyfriends.'

Marietta frowns. 'Boyfriends? What boyfriends?'

Ivy looks from one sister to the other, and Marietta sees again a hint of something unlikeable, Ivy's pleasure in holding knowledge they don't have, her lack of tact in bringing up what must obviously be a sensitive piece of information in such a thoughtless way.

'My stupid mouth,' she says. 'Forget I said that.'

'No, please, Ivy, tell us,' says Lily, and Marietta can see that her sister is troubled. 'We need to know.'

'Oh, there was nothing serious. Any chance of a drop more tea?'

Lily picks up the empty cup, thinking she'll put more brandy in this one and loosen Ivy's tongue a further notch.

'She dabbled a bit on the internet, that's all,' says Ivy. 'I warned her against it, to be fair. Meeting strange men always seemed to me an odd thing to want to do, but your mum seemed . . . Well, I suppose with you girls gone, she found herself lonely sometimes, and an old woman like me, I'm no substitute for a male friend, am I? No criticism of you two intended. You have to live your lives, of course. That's what she said herself.'

Lily slips out to the kitchen.

'It doesn't look as if Mum was lonely,' says Marietta, somewhat defensively. 'She's got loads of contacts.'

'Maybe she was looking for love,' says Ivy, with a touch of poorly faked wistfulness. 'However old you get, you never quite let go of the idea that there might be someone out there for you, someone special.'

'Mum had Dad,' says Marietta.

Ivy tuts. 'And how long has he been gone? You can't expect a red-blooded woman to live her life without looking for another man.'

No, you can't, thinks Marietta. She recalls an incident that troubled her greatly at the time: an early return from school, and finding her mother crying at the kitchen table, her eyes red and swollen so she knew it wasn't just a few tears about Grandma, as Alice insisted. Sometimes in the night, she would hear sounds she tried to pretend weren't stifled sobbing. She was too young then – and too unwilling – to face up to the truth, that Alice was horribly lonely, a woman who needed an adult relationship and the emotional and physical connection that would bring. As a child and into adolescence, Marietta fondly believed that their little threesome – her and Mum and Lily – was enough for them all, that Alice needed nothing outside this home. Only now, with her own lived experience, can she begin to appreciate that she and Lily were – in total innocence – burdens who held their mother back from living her own life. Was it likely her mother trod the path of unsupported single parenthood voluntarily? And why did Marietta never thank her for the sacrifices she made, which Alice, to her credit, never mentioned? At least, not until . . .

Lily brings in more tea. Ivy immediately takes a drink, her mouth puckering at the strength of the alcohol.

'Can we go through some of these names then, Ivy?' suggests Marietta.

Ivy takes the phone and scrolls through the contacts list, identifying a work colleague who will want to know the news, and a supervisor Alice intensely disliked, adding that this woman is probably who they need to notify officially. Three more names are local acquaintances, who Ivy agrees to let know.

The vicar is unknown to her.

'If your mum had an interest in the church,' she says, 'it's news to me. But you never know people the way you believe you do. You go thinking you know someone inside out, and they'll still surprise you.'

'What about Barbara Constant?' asks Marietta, referring to the address book. 'Isn't she one of Mum's old school friends?'

Ivy hesitates. 'Barbara, Barbara. I believe so. I think she may have come to stay once or twice. Not recently, though.'

'What about our Uncle Simon?' asks Lily. 'Do you know if Mum was still in touch with him?'

Ivy shakes her head. 'Never heard her mention a Simon. But you shouldn't rely on an old memory like mine. Do you think I might have that little clock as a memento? She always knew I liked that clock.'

Lily also has a fondness for the clock. 'We'll have to see,' she says. 'It's early days.'

Ivy stands up. Despite the brandy and the fact that it's still well before lunch, she seems remarkably steady on her feet.

'I know how it is. You'll have to get everything valued anyway, for probate. I doubt she's left anything for me specifically, but you never know. I believe I was the closest friend she had.' When she reaches the front door, she says, 'You'll stay in touch then, won't you? Like I say, I'll put the word out where I can. You ought to put a notice in the paper. You've got my number, haven't you?'

'It's in my phone,' says Lily. 'I was wondering, if you were thinking of something to remember her by, whether you might consider . . . Well, Josie's very attached to you, and—'

Ivy shakes her head. 'I don't have the room in my poky little place, not full-time. I mean, I love the dog to bits, but I don't think I could take her on as a long-term thing. Of course if you're struggling, I could ask around.'

'That might be helpful,' says Marietta.

'Your mum would want her to go to a good home.'

'We'll make sure of it, definitely.'

As Marietta opens the door, Ivy points to the three watercolours on the entryway wall. 'Make sure you get proper value for those when you come to sell. They're by that local artist, aren't they, whatsisname? Alice always said they were her life assurance policy.'

'Oh,' says Marietta. 'Thanks for the tip.'

'I'll be seeing you, then,' says Ivy. 'Let me know as soon as you've any news.'

The morning feels long, the hours lengthened by struggling through fatigue, the fatigue increased by the strain of holding back tears. Together Lily and Marietta work through their list, retelling the bad news time after time, repeating Alice's address for cards, leaving messages where they get no answer. Some of the calls are needless, turning out to be acquaintances so casual they barely know Alice's name, and apologies are needed for troubling people. But more than once emotion breaks through, as someone they're talking to themselves is upset, or recalls a fond memory of their mother.

Marietta receives condolences from unexpected sources: staff at the dog rescue where Alice sometimes volunteered; a colleague from a farm shop where she worked a few Christmas shifts; a counsellor at a bereavement charity, who Marietta assumes her mother contacted after Grandma's death.

When that call is over, she takes a few minutes to think. When Grandma died, Alice seemed to be coping, but appearances can deceive. The truth is, Marietta has no idea whether Alice was or wasn't, because she never asked.

In latter years, she's been too wrapped up in her own life, and shut her mother out.

And nothing can be done now to make amends.

Though it feels frivolous and a betrayal of their grief, they grow hungry. Marietta searches the kitchen cabinets, finding among the more current conveniences a few childhood favourites –

rice pudding, Bird's custard, tinned peaches – which have the power to fill her eyes again with tears. Blinking them away, she settles on a can of chicken soup, which she heats for them to eat with more toast. The food's bland, no longer Marietta's taste. One of them is going to have to do some shopping.

Lily puts down her spoon and gets up to pour them both a glass of last night's wine. Marietta wants to refuse, but Lily fills her a glass anyway and brings it to the table. Marietta thinks, *What the hell,* and decides to drink it.

When they've eaten, they sit for a while at the table, stupefied by emotional exhaustion and tiredness. Marietta has a pain in her chest, one she's never felt before. Lily's complexion is ashen, as if she's been drained of blood. The little clock ticks on the mantelpiece, and Lily's eyelids flutter.

'You should go and rest,' says Marietta. 'Go and lie down for a while.'

Lily shakes her head. 'There's too much to do.'

'An hour will make no difference.'

'What about you?'

Marietta doesn't want to admit her reluctance to return alone to their mother's bedroom. Her fears are totally irrational, but she can't help dreading some visitation, afraid that Alice might not yet quite have left. 'I'll stretch out on the sofa.'

Lily agrees, and climbs listlessly up the stairs. Hearing her footfall, Josie trots into the hallway, following Lily with her eyes as if she might be beginning to wonder where Alice is. She wanders into the lounge, wagging her tail when she sees Marietta stretched out on the sofa, and seeing a space in the curve of Marietta's stomach, jumps up and settles down. Her fur's soft, and her warmth is a comfort.

Marietta finds herself glad of the company.

TEN

Fox follows the A39 across the border into Devon, making a turn not long after into the minor roads which lead towards St Just's. Of necessity he drives slowly – on these winding lanes, a hazard may hide around any corner – catching glimpses of the sea through the field gateways that break up the high banks and hedges. As the road begins to climb, the church tower appears between the trees, but his directions steer him away from there and upwards, towards where the meadows become purple-heathered moorland.

At a junction overshadowed by a venerable oak tree, he stops. A rusting pre-war signpost indicates the villages of St Just's behind him, or Beamsford if he carries on. In that direction the lane dips, suggesting this is the high spot of habitation, and as if to confirm a change in contours, the hawthorn hedges have been replaced by dry-stone walls. Ahead of him stands a farmhouse, the gate leading into its yard standing open. Nailed to the gate's top bar is a sign, hand-stencilled on a piece of wood: *Bleak Tor*.

Fox drives through the gate, parks alongside a Volvo estate and switches off the engine. Tightening the knot of the tie he loosened while he was driving, he retrieves the jacket of his navy suit from the back seat and gets out of the car.

As he puts on his jacket, he looks around. The house is attractive in today's sunshine, but it's squat and solid, clearly built to withstand the batterings of winter storms. Working all his career in the West Country, Fox has visited plenty of farms, and what strikes him most about this one are both its silence and its cleanliness – no machinery running, no stinking manure, no bleating sheep or barking dogs. The concrete yard in front of the house has been hosed down to an almost new-laid white; the doors to the old cow-byre are closed and padlocked; the barn – which should be stacked high with straw bales – is empty and swept. The yard reminds him of a racing stables he visited once in Newmarket, taken there by his ex-father-in-law, who had contacts in that game. The horses in the Newmarket yard lived in more luxury than some people Fox has run across. But Bleak Tor is different. It's clean because the business of farming here has stopped.

He remembers meeting Jayne Hopper in the churchyard, and wonders why she still lives here with her brother gone, with the land all leased and the animals sold; surely she must be lonely in this isolated old house as the icy winter winds blow in across the moors? Maybe she has her reasons, but neither the beauty of the place nor family tradition would keep him here.

The front door looks original, a traditional stable type painted gloss white. The paint is a touch of gentrification that sits badly with the place, which seems to be crying out for the tractors to return and bring in mud from the fields, breathe life and soul back in.

Fox lifts the horseshoe-shaped knocker and raps on the door. A breeze rattles a loose corrugated panel on the barn roof, and he wonders how bad that gets when the wind blows hard, knowing it would rack his nerves to lie awake in the blasts of a gale, worrying whether the panel would stay *in situ* or come flying in the direction of the house.

When she opens the door, Jayne Hopper is smiling. Fox had put her in her fifties, but he's thinking now it might be closer to forty-five; she's more attractive than he remembers, but that's likely to be the lipstick and the nicely done hair. She carries her maturity well, wearing a dress and flat shoes, far too chic for farm life, but the farm life, of course, is all gone.

'Miss Hopper. Russell Fox. Nice to see you again.'

'Jayne, please.' She stands back and allows him to pass into the house, closing the door behind him. 'Come through to the kitchen,' she says, and he follows her down a low-ceilinged passage. 'Mind your head. Daniel was forever grousing about the height of the ceilings in this place. He was about the same height as you, give or take. This house was built in another era, when people didn't grow as tall as they do now.'

The kitchen's a light, bright room, with stone mullioned windows looking out onto an orchard of wind-crippled trees, holding on tight to thin crops of apples and ripening plums. Fox is expecting an Aga, with terracotta floor tiles and whole hams hanging from hooks in the beams, but the style is cautiously contemporary – cabinets in a buttery cream, the floor laminated in a light wood he thinks might be ash, and a large American-style fridge – though some elements of traditional character show through in sisal rugs and chintzy curtains. He's a believer in judging people by their surroundings. When they met in the churchyard, he took Jayne Hopper to be a woman of conservative tastes. Now he sees she may be somewhat more complex.

'Tea? Coffee?' she asks. 'Or something cold?'

'Coffee, please.'

'I'm afraid it's instant. I'm a tea drinker myself.'

'Instant's my brew of choice. Milk and one, please.'

'Can I offer you something to go with it? I have some home-made shortbread.'

'Not for me, thanks.' Fox pats his stomach. 'I'm mostly desk-bound these days, so I have to watch the ever-expanding waistline. I used to rely on nicotine to keep my weight down, but now I just have to say no.'

'A fellow ex-smoker,' says Miss Hopper. 'I know exactly what you mean. Why don't you have a seat over there?'

She points him to an alcove, which Fox surmises was once a pantry. Didn't all these old farmhouses have a pantry, for storing those preserves which would carry you through winter? Now two oak armchairs stand there with hand-sewn cushions on their seats, placed under a small window with a view of upland moors but facing into the room. Fox wonders again what that says about Miss Hopper's character, whether it suggests too much introspection. There's a small table between the chairs; a pair of glasses and a book of cryptic crosswords have been tidied away to a shelf below the tabletop.

As Miss Hopper is spooning coffee, Fox says, 'Thank you for seeing me.'

'Oh, not at all.' She's adding sugar to the coffee from a splendidly ornate sugar bowl, which looks like part of an antique tea service – Fox would say Minton or Wedgwood –

though the rest of the service is nowhere to be seen, and his coffee is to be served in a pale-blue mug. 'I was so pleased to hear you're looking into this business again. I think it's long overdue, though I know you people can't do everything. But I feel I'd like some closure – is that what they call it? – for Daniel's sake. For mine too, to be honest. It affected us both very deeply, even though it was nothing to do with us really. Not beyond Daniel's unhappy discovery.'

She hands him the mug, which is very hot. As he moves to put it down, she slips a coaster with an image of a hare beneath it.

Sitting down with her tea, she says, 'I would like to know, though, why now. You've come too late to speak to Daniel.'

'Good question. Let me start by telling you about what I do. I'm in charge of the cold case unit. We're a very small team, just me and a colleague. If I'm honest, the unit's a last stop before retirement, but that has its advantages. We're both experienced investigators, and we've been around the block a few times. We're not the quickest out of the traps, but cold cases don't need speed. They need method and perseverance, and we have those in spades.'

'You look too young to be thinking of retirement.'

'I've done nearly thirty years.'

'That's a long time.'

'As to why now, cold cases – by which we mean any serious crime that remains unsolved – come up for regular review. Things change, our methods change, we get new tools through scientific advances. I'm going to be honest, and tell you our clean-up rate is not high, and certainly not as high as we'd like. Cold cases are notoriously difficult to solve. Memories fade, people pass away or move out of the area and we lose track of them. What can't be solved at the time, often can't be solved twenty years after the fact either. But just sometimes, people who thought they had good reason to keep quiet at the time, come forward with new evidence. Loyalties change, or fear of reprisals isn't there any more. Sometimes people want to get things off their chests, especially if they're approaching the end of their life. We could get lucky in Michael's case. I very much hope we will, but there are certainly no guarantees.'

'I understand.'

He reaches into his jacket pocket and produces a small electronic device. 'Do you mind if I record our conversation? My memory's like a sieve these days, and I've never been much for handwriting. My mother always tried to tell me I'm dyslexic, but I put my lack of ability down to good old-fashioned cack-handedness. May I?'

He holds up the device, and she shrugs agreement.

'A short preamble, and we'll forget it's there.' He places the recorder on the table between them, presses the red button and states the date and his name. At his request, Miss Hopper gives her name and address.

'So.' He looks at her. She folds her hands in her lap, a protective gesture, as if the machine has made her nervous. 'What do you remember of that day, Thursday 17th June 1993?'

Miss Hopper shakes her head. 'It was a day like any other. We were always busy then. We had the sheep, and all the other business of the farm. We were waiting for the shearer to get to us, and I remember Daniel was fretting because he was having to wait another two days for him to come. The weather was getting warmer, and he worried about the sheep being too hot. That's where he was going, to check on them.'

'What time was that?'

With no hesitation, Miss Hopper says, 'After lunch. We always had a proper lunch. Daniel started his days early – five a.m., winter and summer – so by midday he was ready for something substantial. After our mother died, kitchen duties were down to me. As soon as we'd eaten, he said he was going up to the top fields.' She pauses.

'Please, go on,' prompts Fox.

'He was gone for over an hour.'

'And how long is the walk up there?'

'Ten, fifteen minutes. But I doubt he went straight there. Often after lunch he made phone calls while he let his food settle. I don't remember for certain, to be honest, but I don't think he had a mobile phone at that time. Even if he did, he'd have been more likely to use the office phone. Signal up here isn't always reliable even now. But I couldn't say for absolute certain if he made any calls that day, or not.'

But we can, thinks Fox. Phone records were checked, and two calls were made, to a feed store and a vet's practice. The recipients of those calls were spoken to at the time, but they're on his list to speak to again. If they're still alive.

'Anyway,' continues Miss Hopper, 'he came back to the house much quicker than I would have expected. Normally he'd be off working and I wouldn't see him till teatime. I was making scones for the church fete, and he appeared in the doorway there white as a sheet, and told me to call the police. Of course I asked him why, and he said he'd found a body in the spinney. He didn't say at the time it was a baby's body. I suppose he didn't want to upset me.'

She's becoming upset now, and Fox knows he must tread carefully. Even with so much time gone by, traumatic events affect lives, as she said, blighting them. Some things, once seen, cannot be unseen.

But she continues without any further prompting. 'I asked him if I should request an ambulance too, and he said there was no need for that, and when I asked if he was sure – I meant sure there were no signs of life – he shouted at me, actually shouted, "Just call the bloody police." Which was totally out of character. He was such a calm sort of person usually, sunny-natured. He was doing what he was born to do, run this farm the way our father taught him, the way our grandfather and great-grandfather had done before that. But after what happened to Michael, I think it was spoiled for him – this place, I mean. He never said so, but I suspect he felt the land he'd loved had spawned something evil, and he couldn't forgive it for that. I often wonder, why there in our spinney? With all the thousands of acres to choose from, what made someone pick there?'

'That's a very good question,' says Fox. 'Do you have a theory?'

Miss Hopper shakes her head. 'I think we were just unlucky. Sometimes in life that's the way it goes.'

'So you made the 999 call as he asked?'

'I did. I'd never done it before. When the police operator answered, I didn't really know what to say, so I just said my brother had found a body on our land.'

Fox has listened to the call and read the transcript, so he

already knows the answer when he asks her, 'What time would that have been?'

'I think about two thirty.'

Actually it was 14:27. She's pretty close. Not for the first time, Fox is amazed how well people remember traumatic events, even decades later.

'What did you do then?'

'I made Daniel sit down, and I gave him a shot of brandy. Which isn't something I'd ever normally do, but there was a bottle in the cupboard for making the Christmas puddings. He drank it straight down, and it brought the colour back to his cheeks. I asked him to tell me what was going on, and he said that as he walked up the fields he could smell burning. He thought maybe someone had set up camp somewhere and he'd better go and move them on. We do get people from time to time and it isn't usually a problem. But sometimes they leave litter, and sometimes they have dogs, and town dogs and sheep are rarely a good mix. So he followed his nose up to the spinney, glad he'd got his gun in case there were undesirables.'

'He took a gun with him?' Fox isn't sure he's seen this in the files.

'He took his gun most places. He was always on the lookout for foxes. Do-gooders bring city foxes up here occasionally thinking they're doing them a favour, rescuing them from a life of scavenging in bins, whereas it would be kinder just to put them down if they're a nuisance. They've no idea how to hunt. When the poor things begin to starve, they get bold and go after the sheep, especially the lambs. Daniel always protected his flock like they were his own children.'

'But he didn't have any actual children?'

'None that I'm aware of.'

'You?'

Miss Hopper blushes. 'I suppose neither he nor I were the marrying kind. It was something we both regretted, I think. And it made it much harder to come to terms with what happened to Michael. There are people who would have taken in a baby like him gladly, given him a home. We would have done that. He could have taken over the farm. There's no one, now.'

Her grief – Fox assumes over lost opportunities, as well as the loss of her brother – shows briefly in her face, a shadow there and gone.

'You must miss him.'

'I do.' She nods emphatically. 'I really do. We were always close, and to lose him so suddenly was a terrible shock. I mean, he wasn't in perfect health – which of us are, when we reach our middle years? – but he took the medicines the doctor gave him, and his blood tests always came back fine. I think in retrospect the business with Michael took its toll more than I realised. He was a gentle soul, and I don't think he could come to terms with such heartlessness.'

'I'm sorry.'

Fox leaves a few moments' silence in case she's going to go on, but she looks at him, waiting for the next question, so he provides it.

'What happened to the gun that day? Was he carrying it when he came in here?'

'I really don't remember. Probably. But he was meticulous about putting it away, so it would have been back in the gun safe before the police arrived. They don't need much excuse to revoke a licence.'

Quite right too, thinks Fox. 'What did he tell you about what he'd found at the spinney?'

'Someone had made a fire. I'm sorry.' She gets up from her chair, and crosses to the counter to pull a couple of tissues from a box and dab at her eyes, before sitting back down. 'I get upset every time I think of it, the cruelty of it. It's as if it happened yesterday.'

'Take your time.'

'He said there was something on the fire, something wrapped in a blanket, but most of the blanket was burned away. He said he could smell petrol, but then you'd need a lot to light damp wood, wouldn't you? He didn't tell me at the time, only afterwards when I knew it was a baby who'd been found, that when he first saw what was inside the blanket, he thought it was a doll.' She dries her eyes again. 'That poor child. Who would do that to an infant? Who could be so wicked?'

Fox would like to reassure her that the child was dead before the fire was lit, but in fact the forensics were inconclusive. Better not to dwell on that.

'I'm sorry to make you go through all this again. But the more we go over it, the more likely we are to uncover something new.'

Miss Hopper falls then into a different kind of silence, a silence he knows well from interviewees. She's considering telling him more, wondering whether or not to speak.

He leaves her space, before saying, 'Is there anything else?'

Silence.

'Jayne?'

'It's not helpful, really. A few days before Daniel died, he became very broody, and I kept asking him what was on his mind, but he never said. But when I was emptying his closets . . .' She stops, and gives him a smile of heart-rending sorrow. 'Can there be an unhappier occupation than to dispose of your loved one's possessions? I did it for Mother and Father, and I've done it for Daniel. Everything you throw or give away feels like a betrayal, like gathering up their lives and dumping them in a skip.'

Fox has been there, knows how it feels. 'I understand. It's hard.'

'Anyway, that aside. In one of his overall pockets, I found a phone number scribbled on a piece of paper, and I thought before I threw it away that I should ring it. I thought it was likely to be something to do with farm business. But it went through to a police station, someone called Chandler, Chancery, something like that. When I realised who it was, I didn't know what to say so I just hung up.'

Fox frowns. 'Do you know where this guy Chancery was based?'

'I remember it was an Exeter number. I think that's why I didn't just toss it in the bin. He had no business with anyone in Exeter, as far as I'm aware.'

At Fox's request, Miss Hopper agrees to show him the way to the spinney, though she insists she won't go with him the whole way.

'I've no need to go there ever again,' she says. 'The land is rented, and it's up to the tenants to take care of it.'

'I'll be trespassing, then, if I go on there without permission,' Fox points out.

'I'll ring Angela. I'm sure she won't mind if she knows who you are.'

She takes a few minutes to make the call. Before they head out, she changes into well-worn outdoor shoes and offers him a pair of her brother's wellingtons, but Fox declines. The ground is dry underfoot, but if it weren't, he has his own boots in the car. Wherever he goes, bad-weather footwear goes with him: wisdom born of long experience.

She leads the way through the orchard, where the grass is long and alive with insects. Crickets leap ahead of Fox's feet, and bees buzz in patches of clover. A clear line of less lush grass show this is a well-worn path, where the packed earth makes it difficult for the grass to flourish. The path leads to a gap in the orchard wall bounded by two upright stones, small monoliths to form a way through; but just as the farmhouse ceilings were low, this passage from the orchard to the sloping meadow beyond was made for more slender men than Fox, and while Miss Hopper easily slips through, for him it's a squeeze.

'In his younger days, Daniel just used to vault the wall,' she says.

Never in a million years, thinks Fox.

He follows her uphill, until she stops by a galvanised trough where water trickles in from a pipe. The ground is muddy, trampled by sheep. At the top of the meadow, beyond its far wall, is a stand of trees. A magpie flies down and settles on the wall, as though waiting for him.

One for sorrow.

'This is as far as I want to go,' says Miss Hopper, and Fox nods his understanding. 'Shall I wait for you?'

'I can find my own way back,' he says. 'I'll let you know when I'm done.'

She's turning away when he asks, 'The petrol can, where was that?'

'In a straight line from here, more or less. Against the wall between the spinney and the field beyond, on its far side.'

Fox continues up the field alone. As he grows closer, the magpie flies away.

At the time of the original investigation, his role was office-based, and it's gratifying to understand at last the place's geography.

The spinney is an anomaly in the landscape, grown up on the crown of a hill little more than a mound. Arriving here by chance, you'd think it charmingly secluded, a place to pick bluebells in spring, or in summer spread a picnic rug on the turf, lie back and watch the clouds pass overhead.

But Fox knows the place's history, and sees the shadows that spoil the sunlight.

The trees form a rough circle, mainly of beech and oak interspersed with a few slender silver birch. They're not as old as he expected – mature, but not ancient – which makes him wonder why they're here at all. Are they remnants of some forest, or were they planted here because this is a place of special meaning? The spinney's the kind of high-country location druids might have made a place of worship, even of sacrifice. Paganism will sound fanciful if he mentions it back at the office, but the killer chose this place for a reason. Maybe it was simply for its remoteness and concealment; maybe there was something more. At this point, he's ruling nothing out.

Hands in pockets, he stands at the spinney's centre. Judging from the crime-scene pictures, this is where Daniel Hopper found Baby Michael's little body on its makeshift pyre. Glancing round, he can see there's plenty of dead wood to make a fire, but in the shade of all these trees, it's always going to be damp. Not the best fuel to start a blaze. Whoever came here knew that, and came equipped. More evidence for his theory that the person who lit that fire didn't just wander up here. Fox believes strongly they'd been here before.

He walks round the perimeter trees. Looking back the way he's come, nothing of the farm buildings is visible, not even a chimneypot. On the opposite side, he finds a crude stile of protruding flat stones, suggesting the public footpath (if that's what it is) must continue from here. But where does it go? Does it meet a road or a lane anywhere nearby? An Ordnance Survey map would tell him. The original investigation drew no conclusions on which route the killer had taken to this spot, but it appears there are only two practical options for someone carrying a baby and a petrol can: either up this hillside, or through the farmyard. Surely the farmyard option was too big a risk – unless they had prior knowledge no one was home?

The petrol can left behind the wall bore no prints. Whoever handled it wore gloves, and that would have looked odd in the warmth of June. And the killer was confident enough to leave the can behind.

Or was he? Was his intention craftier, to leave it as a decoy, a strong suggestion that was the route he'd used?

He. Mentally, Fox is favouring the male pronoun. But Baby

Michael was only a few days old, and weighed no more than eight pounds; the fuel can was small, with a capacity of only a couple of litres.

There's no logical reason at all why the person he's after couldn't be a woman.

Back down at the house, Miss Hopper answers the door before he knocks. 'All done?'

'For now. But I may want to come back. Sometimes it helps to really get the feel of the place.'

'Whenever you like. I'm usually around, but if I'm not, help yourself.'

'That stile on the far side of the trees, where does it lead to?'

Miss Hopper shrugs. 'Eventually to Fordingley, about two miles away.'

'Nowhere else?'

'Not officially. But there's nothing to stop someone cutting across country, is there? No one's there policing trespassers, usually.'

She's right. From what he's seen, you'd be unlucky to bump into anyone in that empty terrain. He needs to find where the nearest road is regardless of established rights of way, start thinking as the crow flies.

'I'll get out of your hair, then. Thanks for your time.'

'I'm more than glad to help. I'm so pleased you're taking an interest. Though you're not alone in that.'

Fox looks at her quizzically. 'Meaning?'

'I've seen a couple of women at the churchyard over the years. I couldn't help wondering what their interest was, but I suppose cases like Michael's attract all sorts.'

'You have no idea, believe me. What kind of women were they? Old, young?'

Miss Hopper seems unsure. 'I only saw them from a distance. Middle-aged. Late middle-aged, if I'm being ungenerous. They might have been anyone, of course. Journalists, writers. I know there's been at least one book written about the case. I was quite interested to read it, but Daniel said he wouldn't have it in the house. Someone rang up and asked if we'd be interviewed for it, but he firmly declined. It won't surprise me if we see it on TV at some point, in one of those cheap shocking-murder series people seem to love.'

As if he hasn't heard her, Fox asks, 'How do you know they were different women? Couldn't it have been the same woman more than once?'

Miss Hopper hesitates.

'Their hair was different. I remember one with blonde hair, and another who was dark.'

'Women change hair colour all the time.'

'When you put it like that, I see your point.'

'Did you ever see a vehicle?'

'A red car, once. Or maybe it was blue. I'm sorry, I'm not much help.'

'Can you remember when you saw these women?'

Miss Hopper shakes her head. 'Not really.'

It's all too vague to be useful.

'If you remember anything else, will you let me know?' asks Fox.

'Of course.'

She's closing the door when he turns back. 'As a matter of fact, there is one more thing. We've made huge advances in

DNA processing techniques, which might make a difference in our investigation. Ideally, we'd have liked a sample from Daniel, but in his absence, would you be prepared to give one?'

'What use would that be?'

Fox has his untruth ready. 'If we recover DNA from the body coverings, we'd need to rule Daniel out. Your DNA won't be identical to his, but it would be similar enough for us to see what was his and what wasn't.'

'You mean the blanket?'

'Yes.'

'But I don't think he touched it. I don't think he touched anything.'

'It's for completeness, mainly. If we ever get to court, we wouldn't want the defence barrister to cast doubt on our findings. Without Daniel's DNA, the defence might easily get any new evidence we find thrown out. We have to cover all the bases, belt and braces. If you don't want to do it, I completely understand, but I wouldn't want you to have to go through the stress of your brother's exhumation.'

'Exhumation?'

'It's always a difficult process for the family, but of course we'd offer you appropriate support.'

Miss Hopper's hand goes to her throat. 'Oh my Lord. I wouldn't want that. I couldn't bear for him to be disturbed.'

'Then please, consider it. It's a really simple process and only takes a few minutes. I can even send someone out to take the sample. Any time that suits you.' He notices the slightest of hesitations. 'For Baby Michael's sake.'

'How can I say no?' she says, but Fox sees something in her eyes that suggests she'd prefer to decline.

ELEVEN

Marietta thinks she won't sleep, but when her phone rings, it wakes her. Josie wakes too, jumping off the sofa to return to her basket, where she won't be disturbed. The hands of the clock have moved on; it's past 3.30. The phone has fallen on the floor, and blurred and confused by sudden waking, Marietta fumbles answering the call.

'Hello?'

'Hello?' A woman's voice. 'Is this Marietta?'

'Yes.'

'This is Reverend Kate Northcott here. I had a message to call you.'

Marietta sits up, annoyed at herself for being surprised Reverend Northcott is female. 'Oh, right. Yes. Thanks for calling back.'

'What can I do for you?'

'It's about my mother, Alice Ansley.' She waits, expecting an acknowledgement, an expression of recognition at the name, but none comes. 'I think she may have been a member of your church.'

A short silence.

'I'm sorry, the name's not familiar. I do know an Alice, but not with that surname.'

'Her surname was Youlden before she was married. Maybe you knew her as Alice Youlden.'

'I'm sorry, I don't think so.'

'My sister and I found your number in her phone.'

'Well, my memory's not what it was. Why don't you tell me why you're calling and something may come to mind.'

'She's died.' The words come out as a blurt, ungracious and clumsy.

'I'm very sorry to hear that.'

'So we were wondering if you might take her funeral. Preside over it or whatever the word is.' Marietta feels tears coming back. 'I'm sorry, I have no clue what I'm doing or saying. It's been such a shock.'

'Of course I'll be pleased to help. Which parish was your mother resident in? I look after more than one these days.'

'She lived in Selmouth.'

Another silence. 'I'm afraid I may not be able to help you after all. Isn't Selmouth in Cornwall?'

Marietta frowns. 'Yes.'

'I think there's been some kind of mix-up. Selmouth would fall under the diocese of Truro, whereas all my parishes are under the Exeter diocese, being in Devon.'

Marietta's frown deepens. 'You're in Devon?'

'Yes.'

'So why are you in Mum's phone?'

'I'm sorry, I really don't know. If it would help you, I can give you a number to call to help you get in touch with your local pastoral team.'

'That's OK,' says Marietta. 'I can find it. I'm sorry to have bothered you.'

'Not at all,' says Reverend Northcott. 'Once again, my condolences for your loss.'

Marietta remembers teenage Lily's partiality to carbonated drinks, but she's learning grown-up Lily has a preference for tea. Just like Mum. If she'd stuck around, would Marietta have become an addict, too?

Yawning, she boils the kettle, dunks a tea bag in a large mug and pours in the last of the milk from the fridge.

Upstairs, the door to the bedroom they used to share is closed, and she feels as much an interloper as she does in Alice's room. Plainly, she doesn't belong here; but that being the case, where does she belong?

She taps at the door. 'Lily?'

'Come in.' Lily's answer is immediate, and Marietta's glad she didn't have to wake her. Opening the door, she finds her sister propped up on three pillows, texting.

'I brought you a cup of tea.'

Lily presses send, drops her phone on the bed beside her and shows Marietta a face full of grateful thanks.

Marietta hands her the mug, and Lily takes a sip, not caring the tea's too hot.

'Don't burn your mouth,' says Marietta.

Lily gives her a look. 'Thanks for the tip.'

'Sorry. Old big-sister habits. Last time we spent time together, you were drinking nothing but Coke.'

'I remember that. One day I drank so much I threw up. Never touched it again after that.' She pats the bed. 'Sit.'

Marietta does so, and from that vantage point looks round the room she used to know so well. Everything's changed: from untidy teen den to respectable spare room, new wallpaper and curtains, fresh paint. The pink rug she spilt silver nail varnish on at fifteen is gone too, replaced by carpet in a tedious shade of oatmeal. Why is everything in this country so muted, so beige and grey? She feels a pang of regret for the place she's recently left, where even the outsides of the houses are painted eye-zapping oranges, yellows and blues. When all this is over, she'll be moving on.

But where to?

Lily's phone pings. She snatches it up, reads the screen and puts it down again.

'How are you feeling?' asks Marietta. 'Did you sleep?'

'Not really. You?'

'I must have. My phone woke me up. Reverend Northcott rang back. She turned out to be a woman, but she didn't remember Mum.'

'Oh.'

'I know. So much for the easy guide to the funeral.'

Lily's head drops. 'I don't want to think about that.'

Marietta points at Lily's phone. 'Is Connor coming down tonight?'

Lily hesitates. 'He wants me to go home. He thinks I'll sleep better in my own bed.'

'Have you told him you can't go?'

'Actually he's coming to pick me up after he's finished work.'

Marietta feels a rush of a familiar shared emotion: anger. 'You're kidding, right? You can't leave me here by myself.'

And Lily's face takes on an expression Marietta's seen there

91

all too often: petulance. 'You mean the way you left me and Mum? Why not? I'll come back tomorrow. You could sleep in here instead of, you know. In Mum's bed.'

'For Christ's sake, Lily. How would you feel if I left you here by yourself?' Marietta's eyes fill with tears, and she curses her neediness. 'This is our thing, Lily, together. Connor will still be there in a few days. He can manage without you for a bit, can't he? This is about us, about family. About Mum.'

'I don't have any of my stuff, any clean clothes,' says Lily, weakly.

'Wear some of mine. Wash yours. Wear Mum's.'

'Neither of you are really my size.'

'Fine. Well fuck off then,' says Marietta, slamming the bedroom door behind her as she leaves.

Fuming, Marietta grabs Josie's lead from its peg behind the kitchen door. Josie is immediately on her feet, tail wagging and keen to go. Marietta clips the lead to the dog's collar and marches down the hall, slamming the front door too as she leaves.

Outside, the world appears normal, no crises or griefs on show. The lane is quiet and calming, underlining how claustrophobic the day has been. She's used to outdoor living, and it's good to stretch her legs, feel the breeze on her face. More than that, years have gone by since she and Lily have spent time together, and it's hardly a surprise they've fallen out; arguing was the running theme of their childhood. Poor Mum spent half her time yelling at them to stop fighting, the other half mediating in the latest disagreement. Maybe it's better if Lily leaves for a while. Marietta will be fine by herself. If she gets lonely, she still has Josie.

Josie seems impervious to what's going on, with not enough time yet elapsed for her to realise Alice isn't coming home. Sniffing her way along a route she plainly knows well, she pulls Marietta eagerly along, and Marietta finds the dog's jauntiness therapeutic, a lift to her mood. The afternoon's reaching its end, and the day visitors are beginning to leave, though when she reaches the seafront, the water is still dotted with surfers riding the breaking waves. The outgoing tide has washed the sands clean, leaving behind shallow pools reflecting the blue of the sky. Where the bay curves, seabirds bob in the water as shallow waves run up the beach. She sees it's beautiful, though it's beauty of a softer, more modest kind than the brash colours and hard, hot light of Colombia, and she's surprised to find that – for the time being at least – she might prefer this cooler, more muted coast.

Then a cloud crosses the sun, and the water turns dark. Marietta shudders, unable to resist thoughts of her mother alone out there in those vast depths, of how cold it must have been, and how awful the fear, sensing she wasn't going to be reached in time. Help came, but too late. Lily won't countenance the thought, she knows, but Marietta is a realist. Did help come too late because their mother deliberately put herself out of reach?

Josie is tugging at the lead, keen to go down onto the beach. Not ready yet to return to the house and her sister, Marietta follows her down the cobbled ramp, giving her the full length of her extendable lead, slipping off her shoes when she reaches the sand. Normally, her choice would always be to walk close to the waterline, but thinking of her mother's end has left her unsettled by the sea. Instead, she chooses a path near the road, giving a wide berth to anyone else there, feeling isolated, cocooned inside her loss.

Up ahead, the lifeboat station's utilitarian ugliness blights the quaint seafront, yet as usual it's attracting a crowd of visitors. An idea, a compulsion, takes hold of her, and shortening Josie's lead, she heads up the next steps from the beach to the road.

The gift shop is as it always was, a confusion of cards and calendars, aprons and pencils. Alice volunteered here for a while, Marietta remembers. She and Lily would sometimes come to visit while she was working, making themselves useful tidying the displays, more often nagging her for money for ice cream.

That was years ago. Now an elderly woman sits where Alice used to, her eye on Josie and about to ask Marietta to take the dog outside.

Marietta musters a smile. 'Hello.'

'Can I help you?'

'I wonder if I could speak to one of the crew? About my mum. They rescued her a few days ago. Well, they tried at least.'

Recognising the distress in Marietta's face, the woman says, 'I'll see if I can find someone to help you,' and disappears through a Staff Only door. She isn't gone long; when she reappears, she beckons Marietta to join her behind the counter. 'Adam's here. He'll speak to you. In the office, straight ahead.' She steps aside to allow Marietta to pass, and closes the door behind her as she returns to her post.

For the first time, Marietta's in the cavernous concrete boatshed that has been a landmark she's known all her life.

From outside, the shed seems huge, and yet the boat inside – splendid in its navy and orange livery – dwarfs it. Admiring it, for a moment she forgets why she's there, but a voice says, 'She's a gorgeous girl, isn't she?'

A young man is watching her, smiling. She walks towards him, passing a side room where hooks on the walls are hung with yellow waterproofs and orange life jackets, and ranks of yellow wellingtons – like the ones on the souvenir pencils in the gift shop – are lined up in racks.

He's tall, broad-shouldered, wearing a washed-out T-shirt and tracksuit bottoms. His face is as tanned as Marietta's own, and his scalp is shaved almost bald. Josie reaches him first, and he crouches down to welcome her, rubbing her ears and grinning like a true dog-lover.

When Josie has finished her greeting, he stands, and holds out his hand.

'I'm Adam. Welcome to Selmouth lifeboat station,' he says, and Marietta begins to cry.

Adam makes strong tea, which is far too sweet for Marietta, but she's glad to have it. With a mugful for himself, he sits down opposite her. In the background, a VHF radio crackles into life, and he tenses, listening. When a voice responds, he relaxes.

'Not for us.'

'I'm so sorry,' says Marietta. 'I was out walking, and I just thought I'd come and say thank you. I didn't mean to turn into a blubbering wreck.'

'Blubbering wrecks are a speciality here. We see several in a day sometimes.'

'It was my mum,' says Marietta. 'You saved her a few days ago. Well, not saved exactly. The police said she was still alive when you got to her.'

Adam's face becomes sombre. He stands and goes to the desk, turning the page of a ledger. 'When was this?'

'Last Sunday afternoon.'

He picks up a business card from a stack near the radio and returns to the table. 'I remember. I was there. The lady in red.'

'Red?'

'She did us all a favour by wearing a red swimsuit. Made her easy to spot. People wearing black – wetsuits especially – make life more difficult for us. Listen, we appreciate your thanks, and I'm really sorry for your loss.' He pushes the business card towards her. 'You might want to give these folks a call. You can ring them any time, day or night. They're good. I've spent a few hours on the phone to them myself, in my time.'

Marietta glances at the card and sees a logo and the words *Bereavement Counselling*.

'Did she . . . Do you think she suffered?'

Adam shakes his head. 'I'm not the person to deal with those kinds of questions. Really, ring those guys. It'll help.'

'Thanks,' she says. 'I'd better go. We'll make a donation, of course, my sister and I.'

'Finish your tea,' says Adam. 'It's all quiet at the moment. Where are you from?'

'Here,' says Marietta. 'Born and bred. My dad was a fisherman.'

Adam frowns. 'Really? Not many of them left now. I don't think I've seen you around.'

'I've been away a few years. Travelling. Shaking the sand of Selmouth off my shoes.'

'And I'm an incomer, all the way from the Midlands. You can't get much more landlocked than that, but I always had a yearning to be by the sea. I came for a holiday and never really left.'

'You'll get bored soon enough. Trust me.'

But Adam indicates the view through the window, where the calm sea is lapping up the beach. 'How can you get tired of a view like that? Never the same two days running. Winter and summer, I love it.'

A silence. The VHF crackles again.

'I'd better go,' says Marietta. 'Please pass on our grateful thanks to all the crew.'

'I will.'

As she stands up from the table, he says, 'Selmouth's a small place. I expect we'll be bumping into each other.'

She notices that his eyes are kind.

Returning home, Josie seems to have lost her spark, tired perhaps after what was a long walk with her short legs. At the same time, Marietta's anger has calmed. Passing the candyfloss stands and souvenir shops, the thought is niggling that she may have been unfair to her sister. Lily and Connor have been together almost since primary school; they're rock solid and joined at the hip, soulmates for life, like swans. Now here she is, the prodigal sister who almost didn't take Lily's call when she rang, demanding that Lily stick around to hold her hand because she's bewildered and grieving. But Marietta's realising she's earned no hand-holding privileges. Lily needs comfort, and she wants it to come from the man she loves, from her husband. It's an uncomfortable feeling, but Marietta has no right to make demands of Lily as she did. They're blood relatives that time and distance have made almost strangers. An apology may be required.

Realising she'll need to eat, Marietta forces herself to go into a mini-market, fastening Josie to a railing, where she settles as though accustomed to it. The other customers seem mostly to be holidaymakers, and their cheerfulness underlines her grief and her growing loneliness. She shops for dinner for one, finding little to tempt her on the shelves filled with baked beans and pasta. After finding milk, in the end she chooses an avocado and tomatoes, bananas, sweet potatoes and goat's cheese, red wine and coconut water, while realising that to make a meal from such an odd combination of ingredients will require creativity she doesn't believe she can summon. At the last minute, ducking briefly out of the queue, she drops a large bar of Dairy Milk in her basket. Chocolate is the most dependable of comforters.

Apprehensive of being there alone, she takes it slowly on the uphill walk to the house, praying that if Lily's already gone she's left a key. The echo of her arrival yesterday provokes a sense of déjà vu, though this time, everything seems drenched in poignancy: the gate crooked on the hinge which never got fixed, the unruly honeysuckle overrunning the frontage, the dried, cracked paint. And the stark truth finally hits her: that her mother wasn't neglectful, or laid-back, or lazy. Simply, she couldn't cope, and was in need she never voiced, lacking physical help and struggling for money.

Marietta could have helped. She should have helped.

Too late now.

As she knocks again to be let in, she's expecting a wait before Lily gets her act together and opens the door, but she's there quickly. Josie wags her tail and trots past her, in anticipation of her dinner.

That Lily's been crying again is obvious from the redness of her eyes. She pulls a rueful face and says, 'Sorry.'

Tears well in Marietta's own eyes. 'I'm sorry too. I'm such a cow.'

Lily stands back to let Marietta past her. From the kitchen comes the smell of frying onions.

'I'm making dinner,' says Lily. 'I found some frozen mince and pasta.'

Marietta reaches into her carrier bag and holds up the bottle of wine. 'Good job I brought this, then. But you don't need to stay. I'm a big girl. I'll be fine. You go and be with Connor.'

But Lily shakes her head. 'I told him I'm staying with you.'

Marietta feels ashamed of her temper before. 'You didn't have to do that. Go and ring him. Tell him you're coming home.'

'I'm staying,' says Lily. 'No more arguments, please.'

While Lily chops and stirs, Marietta feeds Josie and pours wine. The little clock on the mantelpiece strikes six.

'So why the change of heart?' she asks, handing Lily a glass.

'After you left, the house was so quiet, and I realised how alone it made me feel. And you don't have anyone to call if it gets too much.' She goes pink. 'Sorry. I didn't mean you're a Billy no-mates or anything. You know, just that you've been away, lost your local connections. Anyway, you were right, we have to get through this together. That's what I told Connor.

99

This is about you and me, not me and him. He said he'll drop me off some stuff tomorrow. Besides, someone phoned while you were out. The post-mortem's been done. They're releasing Mum's body, so we've a funeral to organise.'

But after dinner, they push away thoughts of the funeral. Marietta goes digging in a cupboard, and finds a biscuit tin full of old photographs. She and Lily spend a while going through them, laughing at pictures of themselves in childish poses, becoming wistful over photos of their grandmother smiling in her apron, helping Lily make fairy cakes. They find Alice in a nightdress looking down on a newborn baby, and wonder which of them she's holding in her arms. The photograph looks well handled; the corners are a little bent, and there's a mark on the baby's face, which Marietta tries to rub away, but it seems to be a permanent stain.

'It must be you,' she says. 'Just look at all that hair.'

'Too blonde for me.'

'Doesn't it darken as babies grow? Same way as their eyes change colour. Aren't all of them born with blue eyes?'

'I wouldn't know,' says Lily. She seems suddenly bored with the photographs. 'You know, I'm really tired. If you don't mind, I'm going to take myself to bed.'

'Are you OK?' asks Marietta, but Lily doesn't answer, and moments later Marietta hears her footfall on the stairs.

TWELVE

Lily says they shouldn't drive to the solicitor's because there'll be nowhere to park. Marietta's happy to agree; walking's always fine with her, and anyway she's keen not to upset Lily, whose grief lapses into tearfulness at the slightest provocation. The extent of her weepiness feels like a reprimand to Marietta, who – though bereft, without appetite and suffering debilitating insomnia – knows she's coping so much better than Lily with the practicalities which must be handled that she's beginning to wonder if she's grieving less than Lily, feeling their loss less deeply, loved their mother less. At least, that was how she felt in the beginning. Now she can't help wondering – with Lily's constant texting, and the low-voiced calls she hears between her and persons unknown – whether her sister's almost excessive response may have a second root cause, though if it has, Lily's keeping it to herself.

The walk from the house to the offices takes them to the far side of town, to a disused quayside warehouse converted to a business centre. With its stone shell plugged with reflective glass and a chrome and glass atrium added to the front, the building's barely recognisable as the alluring ruin where

Marietta used to hang out with her teenage friends, smoking illicit cigarettes and passing round cans of strong cider.

What happened to those friends? How did they lose touch? Reflecting that it might be nice to see some of them again while she's here, she's uncomfortably aware that losing touch was down to her, that it was she who stopped replying to messages or sharing photos of her travels, in the days when she believed she'd never be coming home, that she didn't need them. She ghosted them all. A penitent friend could take the trouble to find out how they're doing, maybe make amends.

At the entrance, a brass plate tells them Humbert Eaves is on the second floor. In the same way she was right about there being no available parking, Lily seems somehow already to know, and heads straight for the lift without needing to refer to the building plan. Marietta follows, awed by the building's transformation into voguish industrial chic. Between the red-painted exposed girders and steel-railinged walkways, she can find no trace of the cobwebbed beams and rotting floorboards she remembers.

As Lily presses the call button, Marietta asks, 'Have you been here before?'

Lily looks up at the descending lift. 'Once.'

Marietta doesn't push it, assuming it's none of her business. In a similar situation, she'd reserve the right to silence the same way.

Humbert Eaves' suite is fronted by plate glass, etched with waves and trading vessels in full sail with seabirds flying overhead. The mural's attractive, but Marietta can't help feeling it's a sorry end to the warehouse's historic past.

Lily pushes open the heavy door, and a receptionist at a polished desk looks up from her keyboard and wishes them good morning with a practised smile.

'We're here to see Mr Regis,' says Lily, 'about our mother's will.' She's relieved to have said the words; she was afraid she wouldn't be able to get them out, or that thinking about their implication would start her crying again, and she's oh so tired of crying. She doesn't feel well – too much alcohol again last night, and too little food – and she hasn't slept in several days. Even when she drifts off for a few minutes, her head fills with dark dread she's grateful to wake up from. If she doesn't sleep tonight, she'll call the doctor and ask for medication.

The receptionist switches off the smile.

'Is it about Mrs Ansley?' Standing up from behind her desk, she asks them to follow her, leading the way in her high heels and fitted dress down a corridor to a dim conference room. She offers drinks, and Lily asks for tea, Marietta for water. The receptionist teeters away, noiseless on the sisal carpet.

The room's been cleverly styled – a glass table, chrome chairs, and antique portraits on the walls – suggesting modern thinking combined with traditional values.

The sisters take seats next to each other. The odd, unflattering clothes Lily's wearing – a baggy dress that hangs to her knees, and red canvas sneakers – don't hide the fact that she's losing weight, and she's so pale, Marietta wonders if she'll survive this meeting. Where Marietta's been living, the women make the best of themselves, dressing for the macho culture. Maybe it's liberating not to have to do the same, but she can't help wondering how Connor feels about his wife dressing almost like a child. Doesn't any young woman want to look good for her partner? Maybe, it occurs to her, things aren't good with their marriage.

'Listen,' she says. 'If you want to go home later and spend some time with Connor, I don't mind. Maybe I could come with you. I still haven't seen your new house.'

But Lily's listlessly indifferent. 'I don't mind. We've so much to do, and Connor says he might come down here in the next couple of days.' She's vague, distracted, which Marietta wholly understands. She herself is finding it difficult to focus, difficult to care about much at all.

The receptionist brings their drinks, Lily's tea in a vending machine paper cup, Marietta's water in clear plastic. Somehow Marietta expected something more sophisticated, a carafe and a glass, a proper cup for Lily. Maybe the upmarket rent means – for a small-town outfit – that costs have to be cut elsewhere.

'Mr Regis is on a call, but I've let him know you're here,' says the receptionist, and leaves them again.

'I think we were a few minutes early,' says Lily, as if it's her fault they have to wait. She's been biting her nails – a childhood vice Marietta thought she'd conquered long ago – and has snagged one at the edge, making it bleed.

'This place is pretty flash,' says Marietta. 'I thought Mum would have gone somewhere more traditional.'

'There's not much choice in Selmouth. Besides, she wasn't totally decrepit. You make her sound like some Victorian throwback, as if she'd no business in the twenty-first century.'

'I only meant . . .' begins Marietta, but they hear a door close and the tail end of a phone conversation as someone approaches down the corridor: *I'll talk to you later, cheers now, bye.*

The door to the conference room opens.

Mr Regis breaks all lawyer stereotypes. Marietta is taken aback by his clothes – a tight blue suit, pink shirt, tan shoes. Aren't lawyers supposed to dress conservatively? This man looks as if he belongs in advertising or media. His blonde hair is styled with gel, and his designer glasses sit incongruously on his thin face, which is so youthful, Marietta's tempted to ask how long he's been qualified.

He drops the hefty manila file he's carrying on the desk. 'Edward Regis. I'm very sorry for your loss.' When he's shaken both their hands, he points at Lily. 'I think we've met before.'

Lily blushes. 'It was a while ago.'

Mr Regis smiles. 'Indeed.' He pulls out a chair and sits opposite them, leaning forward on his elbows. Marietta catches a whiff of aftershave, citrusy and sweet. 'So. I know you may be feeling apprehensive. There's a lot of myths around the reading of wills, but actually it's a very straight-forward process, no big drama, nothing to worry about. Your mother did you a big favour by actually making a will. It means there'll be no doubt about her wishes, and no arguments between yourselves and other members of your family. It's all laid out here in black and white.'

He opens the manila file, and produces several pages of creamy paper, archaically bound with burgundy ribbon. He lays it on top of the folder, and Marietta reads the upside-down cover sheet: *The Last Will and Testament of Alice Mary Ansley.* The words are Dickensian and fantastical, and at the same time horribly upsetting. She feels a little faint. Reaching across to squeeze Lily's hand, she finds it cold.

Mr Regis turns to the first page of the will, running his finger down it as he reads.

'When I heard you were coming in, I took time to review the contents so we don't have to close-read the whole thing now. I'm able to summarise it for you, if you agree that would be a good place to start? Then we can go into the small print, as it were. There are one or two personal bequests we need to deal with.'

Peering over the top of his glasses, he looks at them for agreement. His manners are those of a much older man, and Marietta wonders if he's followed a parent into this profession.

'Well.' He glances down at the document. 'Essentially, your mother left pretty much her whole estate to the two of you, her daughters Marietta and Lily, to be shared between you equally.'

'Oh!' Lily seems overcome. 'Oh.' She squeezes Marietta's hand.

'What is the estate?' asks Marietta.

'Essentially,' says Mr Regis, 'there's the property – Trelonie House. The contents of bank accounts, savings, minus any debts. Aside from that, there are what we still call goods and chattels, which is everything she owned – clothes, furniture, I assume there was a car, jewellery. All of those items are subject to the process known as probate, whereby they need to be valued, and submitted to the executors to be tallied up and divided as your mother wished.'

'Who are the executors?' asks Lily.

'I should have said. She named you, Lily – as you probably already know – and myself.' Marietta pulls her hand from Lily's. 'Of course there will be a charge for my services, but we usually deduct our fees when the probate certificate is finally issued, so you've no need to worry about that at the moment. Off the record, obviously that means the more you can handle by yourself, the less you'll be paying us.'

'Marietta will help me, won't you?' asks Lily. She looks at her beseechingly.

Marietta gives a brave smile. 'Of course.'

'If I may advise you, it will be down to you as joint beneficiaries to decide when you should sell the house. You do not have to do so immediately, of course, if market conditions are not favourable.'

'Sell Trelonie House?' says Lily. 'Do we have to do that?'

'Not if you can come to an amicable arrangement on how to share it.'

'You mentioned other bequests,' says Marietta. 'Can you tell us about those?'

'Of course.' Mr Regis turns the pages of Alice's will. 'There are a dozen or so listed here, mostly personal or sentimental items at a glance. Perhaps it would be best if you read through them yourselves and come back to me if you have questions or issues contacting any beneficiaries. I am quite happy to write to anyone you don't know. Your mother has, by the way, made financial provision for care of any dog she owned at the time of her death. Does she have a dog?'

'Yes,' says Marietta. 'Josie.'

'When you decide who will have care of her, if you let me have their contact details I will speak to them directly about the provisions made. Do you have anyone already in mind?'

'Not really, no,' says Lily.

'You might then wish to advertise for a new home, or contact the RSPCA. Often they will take animals where the owner is deceased.'

Lily and Marietta both look at him.

'You mean she'd be a rescue dog?' asks Lily.

'I suppose that's what you'd call it, yes,' says Mr Regis.

Outside, the sisters stand unsure of what to do next.

Lily clutches a copy of the will. 'We've so much to sort out. Everything has to be valued. We have to find all her bank accounts. How are we supposed to get into them?'

'Lily,' says Marietta evenly, 'why didn't you tell me you came here with Mum?'

Lily looks at her feet and shakes her head. 'It would have been too awful. I would have made it right. I already promised myself that.'

'Made what right?'

She shakes her head again. 'Don't push me, OK? She changed her mind and saw sense, that's all that matters. Let's walk.' She leads the way, not in the direction of home but towards the seafront. 'We'll get coffee somewhere, and something to eat. There's not much in the house.'

'I'm not really hungry,' says Marietta. 'Tell me what's been going on.'

They reach a side street, not much more than an alley, between the backs of two houses, and grabbing her arm Lily pulls Marietta down it, out of the way of other pedestrians. The alleyway is dank and sunless. Marietta shivers.

'Listen,' says Lily. 'It was years ago, not long after you took off.'

'Took off? Is that what I did?'

'Call it what you like. You weren't home any more. I suppose she thought you wouldn't be here. She probably thought you'd spend the rest of your life thousands of miles away.'

'And I wouldn't ever come back and visit? Did she really think she'd never see me again?'

'She said to me one day that now it was just her and me, she needed to make sure I was looked after. She took me there, to those offices, and said she was going to make her will, leaving everything to me.'

Marietta's eyebrows lift. 'Really?'

'I didn't understand the implications at the time. I was only just eighteen, and I only knew vaguely what a will even was. The prospect of Mum not being here seemed light years away. Ever since we knew it was her in the morgue – before that, even – I've been dreading it, because I thought you'd never forgive me. I thought you'd be thinking I'd influenced her against you, that I'd been devious and greedy. When he said the money was split, I nearly threw up with relief. Please don't blame me, Mari. I never wanted it to be anything but fair, a fifty-fifty share. You believe me, don't you? I don't even know whether she ever signed that version. I think she was just upset. You hurt her by leaving.'

'It was a two-way street.'

'Don't let's fall out, please. Whatever she was thinking then, she had second thoughts. She loved us both the same, I know she did.'

'You were always her favourite. You always did as you were told.'

'You make me sound like some kind of goody two-shoes.'

'Come on. You were.'

'I just never saw any reason to be a rebel. I'm one of those boring people who likes to stay close to home, and I never had your guts. But if you'd asked me to go with you, I would have. You didn't just leave Mum behind, Mari, you left me, without a backward glance. I was lonely when you'd gone.'

'I missed you too.'

Lily's expression is sceptical. 'Yeah, well, that was obvious. Some years you didn't even send a proper Christmas card. Nothing says you can't be arsed louder than an e-card.'

'The foreign mail's totally unreliable,' objects Marietta, but even she can hear how hollow that excuse sounds.

'Not only the mail, though, is it?' says Lily, and she leaves Marietta behind, walking fast in the direction of home.

Marietta calls after her. 'Lily! What about lunch?'

'It would choke me,' Lily calls over her shoulder, as she keeps walking.

THIRTEEN

Marietta takes the long way home, to give herself time to think. Their world's a mess, and she's played a part in making it so. Being careless of what she left behind, she never really understood the hurt she inflicted. Too late to fix things with Mum, but the time to make amends with Lily is long overdue.

She calls in at the supermarket and buys supplies for a couple of days, including more wine. Carrying the two bags of shopping, she's thoughtful as she heads up the hill, planning what she'll say.

But as she turns the corner to Trelonie House, Lily is unlocking Alice's car. Marietta calls out to her, but Lily's face is stony.

Marietta hurries towards her. 'Where are you going?'

'Home. I want to be with Connor.'

Marietta feels her eyes fill with tears. 'Come on, Lily, don't go. Look, I'm sorry. For everything. Give me a chance to explain, please.' She holds up the bags. 'My turn to cook. I'll make you Colombian food, Cornish style. I couldn't get everything I needed, but I'll give it a go. And there's wine.'

Through the open driver's door, Lily throws her handbag

onto the passenger seat. 'I'll come back tomorrow. We can talk about things then. I have some things to sort out with Connor.'

'What things? OK, not my business, but please, Lily, don't leave me here by myself. What would Mum say if she knew we were falling out?'

Lily looks at her for a long moment; then, to Marietta's surprise, she smiles. 'That she'd knock our heads together?'

'Sounds about right.'

'I do need to spend time with Connor.'

'I know you do. When you go, I'll come with you. Or not.'

'What's on the menu?'

'Red beans and rice. I got some chorizo, and the avocados look pretty good. I won't make it spicy. I know you don't like hot stuff.'

'Actually, I don't mind it so much now.'

'So you'll stay?'

'Red or white wine?'

'Both.'

'You have to cook and do the washing-up.'

'Deal,' says Marietta.

After several days of picking at their food, both of them are hungry. The body's demands are proof that, no matter what happens, life goes on.

Marietta finds herself anxious that Lily enjoys the meal, and relieved that after the first tentative mouthful, her sister begins to eat like a born-and-bred *paisa*, glad to be fed something her grief-tight, churning stomach will tolerate. When Marietta offers seconds, Lily refills her plate.

'Where did you learn to cook?' she asks. 'I know it wasn't from Mum.'

'She wasn't the best in the kitchen, was she?' Marietta says, tentatively. 'Though she was pretty good when it came to fish fingers.'

Lily smiles. 'Do you remember the year after Grandma died, when Mum tried to do Christmas dinner? Raw sprouts and undercooked turkey. It's a miracle we didn't all get food poisoning.'

Marietta laughs. 'The day was saved by chicken tikka masala from the Saffron Lounge. Mum had some talents, but she was no domestic goddess.'

The first bottle of wine doesn't last long. Marietta clears away the plates, and holds up a second bottle.

'Shall we?'

Lily shrugs. 'Why not?'

'Let's go in the lounge and light the fire.'

'In June?'

'In memoriam.'

Lily needs no more persuading. She enjoys lighting the fire; she made it her job from being a teenager and is good at it, taking time as she always used to, making kindling out of rolled-up newspaper, picking the smallest logs from the basket so they'll catch easily, sniffing the heady paraffin smell of the firelighters before she strikes a match to light them. Then, there's the fascination of watching the fire grow, from a fragile orange flicker to a satisfying blaze, feeling the heat on her face and sensing the warmth spreading to the ever-damp corners of the room.

Marietta's content to sit, sipping her wine, watching the firelight shadows flicker on the walls.

When the fire's going strong, Lily sprawls on the rug in front of it, half her face in light, half in shadow. 'Can I ask you something?'

She isn't looking at Marietta but into the fire, and Marietta has the feeling she may not like what's coming. Still.

'Ask away.'

'Why did you and Mum fall out?'

This isn't what Marietta is expecting; she was expecting questions on her current lifestyle, boyfriends, plans and intentions, but it turns out to be about ancient history. History she'd prefer to forget. History that never leaves her.

'I've wondered ever since, and Mum would never say,' continues Lily. 'If I tried to ask her about it, she just pretended she hadn't heard. All I know is that one day we were all together, the next day you were gone. I was desperate to know what had happened, because how could I fix it if I didn't know what was wrong? You didn't even say a proper goodbye. I really missed you, Mari. For a while I was afraid you might be dead.'

Marietta sees she's telling the truth. Her departure affected Lily in ways she never guessed.

'Didn't Mum tell you anything?'

Lily sighs, and takes a long sip of her wine. 'She only ever said you'd decided to make your own way in the world. She missed you too, you know. I'd come home from school sometimes and she'd been crying. I know it was about you. Weren't you ever homesick? Didn't you ever miss us?'

'Of course I did.'

'So why? What happened?'

There's no reason for any more secrets.

'I got pregnant.'

Teenage pregnancy: predictable, almost clichéd. But Lily appears shocked, and stares at Marietta wide-eyed, her fingers touching her throat in a gesture Marietta finds almost comically Victorian. 'You were pregnant?'

'By the time I told Mum, eight weeks.'

'Who was the daddy?'

'Does it matter?'

'Do you know?'

'Lily! Of course I know. Rickie Whiteman. He asked me to marry him. For a few hours I thought I might.'

'But you didn't keep it?'

'No.'

'Oh Mari. Why not? Mum was always quite liberal and progressive. I know she'd have supported you.'

Marietta gives a bitter laugh. 'I thought that too. That's why I told her. I thought she'd let me choose what to do, make up my own mind. Which I pretty much had. I wanted to keep the baby.'

'I would have been an auntie.'

'And I'd have been a fifteen-year-old mother. I was confident she'd help me cope, but when I told her, she went mental, completely mad. She started shouting at me, telling me that I'd ruin my life, like a row out of *EastEnders*.'

Lily shakes her head, incredulous. 'I don't know what to say. That just doesn't sound like her.'

'She said if I insisted on keeping it – it! – I could pack a suitcase and get out. She didn't leave me with a choice. But where on earth could I have gone? She took me to some clinic where they gave me tablets, and sent you off to a friend's house while I aborted. It was really, truly horrible. I felt like all the love I thought she had for me just vanished. I don't know what shocked me more, her making me go through that awful process, or thinking she didn't actually love me. Things between us festered after that, until I knew I had to go. To this day I haven't really forgiven her. I always hoped she'd say she was sorry, but she never did.'

'Mari, that's awful! Why didn't you tell me?'

Marietta shakes her head. 'When, Lily? When could I have told you?'

'I'm glad you've told me now.'

'Are you? Now you'll see Mum in a bad light. It was my issue with her, not yours.'

'She did really love you, you know.'

'Do you think so?'

'I know so. She loved us both.'

Marietta pulls an expression of disdain. 'Not enough to stick around.'

Lily stiffens. 'What do you mean by that?'

'Nothing. I didn't mean anything. I'm tired and emotional and I've had too much red wine.'

Lily goes quiet, and Marietta is reflective for a few minutes, remembering that difficult time. When she looks again at Lily, the firelight is highlighting wetness on her cheeks, and Marietta realises her sister is crying.

'I'm sorry. I didn't mean to make you think badly of Mum.'

'It isn't that.'

'What, then?'

Lily's trying to smile away whatever her trouble is, but her eyes tell their own story: disappointment and pain. 'Connor and I have been trying for a baby.'

'Lily! That's marvellous!'

Lily shakes her head. 'We aren't very good at it. I've had three miscarriages.' She holds up her right hand, showing Marietta three delicate silver rings on her middle finger. 'One for each lost soul.'

Marietta feels huge sympathy for her sister, yet hurt at her own exclusion. 'I'm so sorry for you. But how could you not have told me?'

'You weren't here to tell. Anyway, the first one was early, and we weren't going to tell anyone anyway until twelve weeks.'

'Not even Mum?'

'Well, I did tell her. You always tell your mum, don't you? Then I lost another, and I was devastated. I'd done everything right: vitamins, plenty of rest, my weight was good. What could possibly go wrong? But we were out shopping one day and I knew it was happening. Connor rushed me home and I went and sat on the loo and said goodbye as he passed. That's when Connor bought me the first two rings. He thought we should remember our lost children. He felt it too, though he hid it better than I did.

'The third time we did better, and got to ten weeks. That was hard, because I was feeling really, properly pregnant and I was sure we were going to be fine. Mum was nearly as excited as we were. We went shopping together, starting to buy little outfits and furry bunnies. I know you're not supposed to, but I couldn't resist. I already loved her so much, and I was so sure it was going to be OK.'

'Her?'

'I just knew she was a girl. In my head, I'd chosen her name. Sasha. When we lost her, I was really depressed. I tried to pull myself together again, put all the clothes and toys away until the next time, except there wasn't a next time, even when we did all that passion-killing business with taking temperatures and counting off days. We tried everything, and still nothing. So when Connor got his inheritance from his dad, we decided to go for IVF, which seemed like a good way to spend it – on an heir for Grandpa. But it was massively stressful, the process itself and the waiting and the expense. We spent everything we had, and we were still unlucky. And do you know the worst thing? I feel such a failure. I'm a barren woman, Mari, and it makes me feel like some kind of freak. Everyone I know is having babies or even trying not to have more babies, and all my friends' lives have reached that stage where they revolve around their children, and I'm an outsider. I know there's things they don't invite us to any more. They think they're being sensitive and kind, and I know they mean well, and in some ways they're right. Every baby shower and baptism I feel like I'm crying inside, and actually I am, crying for my lost babies, and though I hate to say it, eaten up with jealousy. Why shouldn't it be us? What did we do wrong? You meet people who say it's God's will or nature's way, and we should think ourselves lucky we just have ourselves to look after, that we're free to enjoy life. But I don't enjoy my life. There's a huge hole at the heart of it, and now Mum's gone, that hole's twice the size. I ache and ache to have a child. Every month I do test after test, hoping against hope and always being disappointed, and then I hear from you how easy it was, and how you let it be taken away.'

'It wasn't my choice, Lily. I told you that.'

'I don't understand why Mum would do that, though.

She seemed so into my pregnancies, so fired up about being a grandma.'

'Probably she thought I was too young, or not married enough. Probably she was right. About the age thing, at least.'

Lily looks thoughtful. 'Does it ever worry you to think you might not have children?'

Marietta shrugs. 'To be totally frank, I never think about it. I might, if I met the right man. If I despair of anything in life, it's that I'll be forever by myself.'

'I thought you had a boyfriend?'

It's Marietta's turn now to look despondent. 'I had a lover, who I kissed goodbye before I got on the plane to come here. I've had plenty of those. I suppose we both envy each other for different reasons. You and Connor found each other so early in life. You're like soulmates, and I'm still searching for someone even vaguely suitable, never mind someone I'd stay with forever.'

'But you've had such an exciting life, all that globetrotting. You're a traveller, a free spirit. I've spent all my adult life looking after other people's kids, desperate for one of my own.'

'You've spent all your adult life with a man who thinks the world of you, who'd walk barefoot on broken glass to save you from trouble. Nearly all of my men have been married, and most of them were not far off being old enough to be my father. Maybe I've got a serious daddy complex, always looking for the first love of my life.'

Lily gets up from the rug and begins to light the mantel-piece candles.

'I think the candles are for Dad,' she says. 'I think Mum never got over him. Do you remember him? I've no memory of him at all.'

'Bits,' says Marietta. She looks into the fire, as if more memories might be glowing there. 'I remember him carrying me on his shoulders, like I was at the top of the world. At least I think that was him. Maybe it was Uncle Simon.'

Lily picks up the poker, and uses it to turn a smouldering piece of wood. When its bark hits the red-hot embers, it throws up a crackle of sparks and intensifies the flames.

'I remember Uncle Simon. He used to bring us things, do you remember? He made us those beautiful boats out of driftwood we used to sail at the beach.'

Marietta nods. 'And mermaid outfits for our dolls, all glittery and shiny.'

'I remember those. I wanted to be a mermaid for years afterwards.'

'Sometimes I still do,' Marietta says, wistfully. 'Mermaids can just swim away, leave everything behind.' She glances at Lily. 'Do you think that's what Mum was trying to do? Just swim away?'

Lily stiffens. 'Why do you keep saying things like that? Mum got caught in a riptide. It was an accident.'

'We don't know that for certain. Don't you think we should prepare ourselves?'

'For what?'

Marietta gets up to share the last of the wine between their glasses. 'I keep thinking about those antidepressants we found in her bedroom. She must have had them for a reason.'

'She wasn't depressed,' insists Lily. 'I would one hundred per cent have noticed. Anyway, why would she have been?'

'Loneliness. Money worries. An illness we didn't know

about. Maybe all of the above. And maybe she hid it from you, Sis. For sure she wouldn't have wanted you to know.'

'I just don't think so,' says Lily. 'They were probably left over from years ago.'

Marietta keeps silent, remembering the issue date on the bottle label was only six weeks before.

Lily throws another log on the fire. 'I'm glad you didn't marry Rickie Whiteman, by the way. He's such a knob. He owns a DIY shop in town.'

Marietta laughs. 'I could have been a DIY queen.'

Lily gets up off the rug and joins her sister on the sofa. 'Fancy watching a bit of nostalgia? Something for old times' sake?'

'What did you have in mind? No weepies.'

'Why not *The Little Mermaid*? We could make popcorn.'

'And drink more wine?'

'We definitely should drink more wine.'

FOURTEEN

Sunday afternoon, and the estate is lively with kids, splashing with hosepipes in back gardens, playing tennis in the road.

Connor hears his wife pull up in the drive and downs the final mouthful of his sandwich, dropping his plate and the knife he used to spread chilli pickle into the sink. She's caught him on the hop; he was thinking she'd be here later, and with no work the last two days and Lily not around, he hasn't shaved. That will bother her, and she won't be happy to see him in his old tracksuit bottoms and a jokey T-shirt either. Under the circumstances, the T-shirt has to go.

He takes the stairs two at a time, finds a plain navy T-shirt she'll much prefer and swaps it in double-quick time, tucking the jokey one in the bottom of the laundry basket. From the bedroom window, he looks down on her as she climbs from the car, listless, pale, thinner than she was before she left. She looks unwell and heartbreakingly unhappy, even more unhappy than she usually does, these days. If only he could do something to help her. If only he could be more of a man.

By the time he's back downstairs, she's got her bag out of the boot. In next door's back garden, children are shouting, and he sees her lower her head. Opening the door, he spreads his arms to welcome her. But she doesn't get that far. Locking the car, she drops her bag and buries her face in her hands.

Lily's grateful to be led inside, to be comforted and held, to feel – after these harrowing days – properly cared for. Connor dries her tears, and makes them mugs of tea and, for Lily, toast the way she likes it, thinly buttered, thickly spread with honey.

She's glad to be home, even though it's untidy and Connor's wearing his oldest clothes, which make him appear even tubbier than he is, and he hasn't shaved for days. But he's looking at her with real concern, like she's the most important person in the world. He'll never be a film star, but he's balm to her very soul.

He pulls his chair round so they can sit knees touching, and takes her hands, kissing them each in turn.

'You've been eating that chilli pickle,' she says, and when he smiles, she finds herself smiling back.

'When the cat's away,' he says, and touches her nose. 'Tell me everything.'

When Lily's eaten and the tears have almost stopped, they go to lie down on the bed so Connor can wrap her in his arms. She rests her head on his shoulder. He smells of fabric softener and muskiness and him.

'Mari didn't want me to leave her,' she says, 'or I'd have come home before.'

'I can understand that,' says Connor. 'Who'd want to be all by themselves at a time like this? You could have brought her here.'

'What about Josie?'

'The more the merrier.'

'We're not very merry, though, are we? Anyway, I said I wouldn't stay away long. I just wanted to spend some time with you.' She closes her eyes, and he strokes her arm, knowing from her silence she's building up to say something, even knowing what it is she'll say, and eventually she does. 'I did another test.'

He breathes in deeply and lets the breath go, bracing himself for the disappointment.

'I suppose if it was positive you'd have told me.'

'I suppose I would.'

He kisses the top of her head. 'It wouldn't have been a good time anyway, would it, eh? With all this going on. We'll have plenty of time to try again when things have settled down.'

'Do things settle down?' asks Lily. 'I feel I've got a great big hole inside me where Mum should be.'

'The hole gets smaller. Kind of scabs over.'

'Oh, I hope so.' She's quiet for a few moments, and he wonders what's coming next. 'Can I tell you something? Mari's got this idea . . . I don't even want to say it. She thinks Mum may have killed herself.'

'What? That's ridiculous.'

'I don't think she did. She wouldn't have done that, I know she wouldn't have left me.' Her face creases into doubt. 'Would she?'

Connor kisses the top of her head. 'Not in a million years.'

They lie silent for a while, listening to the children outside, while Connor wonders whether Marietta could possibly be right. There was something about Alice that was always hidden away, a part of her you never got to know. When she was cheerful, not all of her was laughing; when she relaxed, her eyes showed a sadness at her core. You could say that, though, for millions of people. But suicidal? That's the province of the seriously depressed, surely, and Alice was never that.

Or if she was, it never showed.

Lily's eyes close, and he thinks she might be starting to doze when she says, 'Has anyone been in touch?'

'Rhianne.' He feels her stiffen.

'What did she say?'

'She dropped something off.'

'What?'

'An invitation to her baby shower. I told her you might not be able to go, what with your mum and everything. I thought it would be a good excuse.'

Lily stays silent.

'You're not going to go, are you?' asks Connor. 'You'll only get upset.'

'If I don't go to hers, she might not come to ours,' says Lily. 'And one day we'll be having one ourselves.' She squeezes his hand. 'You promised me we will.'

FIFTEEN

When Fox arrives at the office, there's good news and bad news. The good news is, Lianne Budd has called into Waitrose and picked up butterscotch pecan doughnuts to have as a treat with their morning brew. The bad news is, it's one of those mornings when he's had time to eat a decent breakfast, and the thought of deep-fried sugariness has limited appeal.

What the hell. Live dangerously.

Budd's already made coffee, and as they eat, she gives him a précis of her rape case, how traumatised the victim still is after all these years.

'She was completely agoraphobic for a while,' she says. 'Didn't go out of the house for two years. She's doing better now, thank God, but the only thing that's really going to help her is knowing her attacker's well and truly banged up.'

'Did you get anything new?'

She shakes her head. 'Not really. I'll just keep plugging away.'

Fox eats the last bite of his doughnut. 'These things are nothing but a rocket ride to diabetes. Why do they make them so good?'

'Addicted to sugar, that's me,' says Budd. 'I have no idea how I'm getting away with it, but the last blood tests I had showed no sign of diabetes at all.'

'Lucky you. It's a nasty disease. My uncle lost his leg to it.'

'It gets people in the end, even if you don't have the type that needs daily injections. That can't be much fun. Anyway, how did you get on? Did you go to St Just's?'

Fox takes his time to recount his interview with Jayne Hopper and his walk up to the spinney.

'It's a lonely spot,' he says, 'bleak but beautiful in its own way. But so out of the way that I can't help thinking a stranger hanging about would have been noticed by the local residents, by which I mean the farmers.'

'Interesting.'

'Also, I keep thinking about Jayne Hopper's ongoing attachment to Baby Michael, whether it suggests some level of guilt. And it turns out neither she nor her brother ever married. Living together in the back of beyond, who knows what was going on?'

Budd gives him a hard stare. 'So you're still thinking incest?'

Fox looks doubtful. 'I have to say she really doesn't strike me as the type for that. But we both know it's a myth that it's something that only happens in the dark depths of England's backwaters.'

'Except that's actually where they were living. Makes a stronger case, wouldn't you say?'

'Good point. Anyway, everything's on the table, including the outside possibility – which I can't find discussed in the files – that the baby was Jayne Hopper's by her brother.'

'Backwoods incest would be quite the scandal, wouldn't it?

The tabloids would love it. Do you really think that could be the answer?'

'They lived alone together for years, no serious girlfriend for him that she knew about. So yes, I think it's enough of a possibility that it needs looking into. I've asked her for a DNA sample, so we can see if there's any tangible connection to Baby Michael.'

'Where's the brother?'

'Deceased, two years ago.'

'What did he die of?'

Fox frowns. 'You know, I didn't ask. I'll put that on my list. There was one other thing. Jayne Hopper found a phone number in one of Daniel's pockets. Long story short, it was a direct line to one of ours. She remembers the name as Chancery or Chandler, something like that. Based at Exeter. Any ideas?'

'Could be Griff Chancellor, he's up there now. I'm sure you must have bumped into him at some point in your long career. Big bloke, sharp dresser. He was with the Met in Organised Crime for a while, came down here for a quieter life.'

'Don't think I know him. I need to get in touch with him and see if Daniel ever got round to making the call.'

'He'll have a record of it, if he did,' says Budd. 'Griff's old-school, everything in its place, filed and indexed.'

'But why would Daniel Hopper have Chancellor's number in his pocket?'

'You're the detective, Russ. It's your job to figure that out. Anyway, I can't sit here chatting to you all morning. Places to go, people to see. Are you in tomorrow?'

'Not me,' says Fox. 'I've a plane to catch. Two glorious weeks in sunny Spain.'

'You'll have a great time. Is your brother meeting you at the airport?'

'That's the plan.'

Budd picks up her copious handbag. 'Just stay away from those bar crawls. I don't want to see you on *Holidays from Hell*. And have a glass of sangria for me.'

'I'll have two,' says Fox, with a smile.

When Budd's left, Fox puts in a call to Forensics and asks a technician to arrange to get a DNA sample from Jayne Hopper. At first, the technician makes noises about workloads and three-week lead times, but when Fox mentions what case he's working on, she becomes interested, and promises to bump his request up the list. Even so, he knows not to hold his breath.

If there's an advantage to budget cuts and staff lay-offs, it's that there's usually room to spread out, and in the cold case Portakabin with only himself and Budd in residence, there are two desks spare. One, though, has already been appropriated by both of them equally as storage for the paraphernalia of work-in-progress. Their cases were pre-digitalisation, and most of what they need is on actual paper ordered in physical files.

But the other desk is easily cleared. He moves the monitor and keyboard to one side, heaping the remaining detritus under the desk.

Then he goes to his bookshelves, which he dared to put up himself, without reference to Building Services or Health & Safety protocols. They hold some standard volumes – the PACE manual, Blackstone's *Effective Prosecution* and *The Senior Investigating Officer's Handbook* (a fourth edition and slightly out of date, so not to be one hundred per cent relied on) – and on the bottom shelf, a selection of paperbacks he sometimes reads while eating lunch: Clive Barker's vividly imagined fantasies, anything by Stephen King, the first two volumes of Conn Iggulden's *Wars of the Roses* trilogy, with a bookmark part way through book one.

Most of the shelves, though, are filled with his personal reference section, assembled through the mediums of second-hand bookshops, junk shops, garage sales and eBay. He has an impressive collection of old phone directories – indispensable for finding witness and suspect addresses in the time before Google – alongside street atlases and road maps for Devon and Cornwall, also covering the previous several decades, and editions of Ordnance Survey maps for the areas he polices dated from the 1950s through to the present day.

Fox is no Luddite – he sees the benefits of digitalisation as well as anyone on the force, and any reduction in physical paperwork, which must be curated and stored, can only be a good thing – but he regards his collection as invaluable additions to conventional databases and search engines. Sometimes, when you need to study, and think, and mull over, there's no substitute for an of-its-time hard copy.

It's his Ordnance Survey maps he consults now, finding a 1999 edition 1:50,000 scale of the area covering Bleak Tor. The map is well used; back in those days, it saw active service as a current map, though he's had no cause to open it recently. As he unfolds it and spreads it out on the cleared desk, he finds the stain of a carelessly placed tea mug marking the age-discoloured paper, happily some way out to sea.

Tracing the route with his finger, he finds where the red line of the A-road meets the brown of the B-road leading to St Just's. The village is shown as a small assemblage of rectangles, with the church marked as a black square topped with a cross, and close by is the symbol for a telephone box, which Fox doesn't remember seeing on his visit there. Beyond the church is the winding lane he followed to Bleak Tor, which is marked by name, as are the neighbouring farms.

He fires up the office's temperamental copier, places this area of the map on the glass and makes an A3 colour copy. Pulling a chair up to the desk, he pushes the map to one side and begins work on the copy, using a ruler and a red pen to draw out to scale the area within three miles of Bleak Tor. Three miles is an arbitrary figure, but he's thinking someone walking with a baby and a petrol can is not going to want to go too far on foot, though if poor Baby Michael was already dead by then, he'd be easy enough to carry in a backpack.

Fox doesn't want to dwell on that.

He begins to study the land features in the area he's drawn. The route he took to the spinney with Jayne Hopper is indeed marked as a public footpath. As she told him, the path continues over the hill and down to the small village of Fordingley, which is well within his drawn boundary. Looking at this, he'd come to the same conclusion as his predecessors: that the killer's most likely route up to the crime scene was from there. Even so, Fordingley's the kind of place where someone going for a country walk with a can of petrol would likely attract attention, and so would the vehicle they arrived in, assuming it would have to be parked for at least two hours to allow time to walk to the spinney and back, and make the fire. That minimum two hours could be as long as three or four. All the more time for a car or van to be noticed.

A thought strikes him. It must have been considered at the time, but what if the killer came by bicycle or motorbike? He makes a note on the pad beside him. A bicycle, even a motorbike, could be tucked away behind a hedge, and no one would be any the wiser. But that would make local knowledge all the more likely. Increasingly, Fox is inclined to believe that whoever brought Baby Michael to Bleak Tor had been there before.

What, though, was the attraction of that spinney? The map shows a largely empty landscape of pasture and bog-ridden moorland, with villages and scattered farms the only human habitations. Almost anywhere, the corner of any field, would have provided enough cover to bury a tiny body. Fox can see nothing special or unique about the stand of trees. Though it's marked, it bears no name, nor is there any symbol of an ancient monument, no indication that it might have been a site of worship or ritual, designated sacred by Druids or even their ancestors. That's disappointing; the theory that the choice of location was influenced by pagan beliefs or practices was high on his list. He sees no marker of more recent use either, no beacon for the Battle of Trafalgar or to warn of the Spanish Armada, or even the Queen's 1977 Silver Jubilee, which Fox vaguely remembers. His grandfather presented him with a commemorative coin, which is probably still in the attic somewhere, tucked away.

So what made that place desirable, worth the hike? Open fields and empty moorland . . . When it hits him, it seems obvious. In this area, the spinney's the only thing close to a woodland, the only place you'd find fuel for building a fire.

Buried bodies leave cornucopias of evidence.

Someone was smart enough to know that burning leaves far less for investigators to work with.

Thoughtful, he spends a few minutes studying the lie of the land before him. Two reasonable ways in, and two ways out.

Why did no one see anyone arrive or leave?

What if he – or she – was already there, and never left?

If Fox had to name his prime suspects at this moment, Daniel Hopper and his sister would be high on his list.

He makes a cup of tea, resisting a second doughnut to go with it. Before he goes away, there's one more piece of the puzzle he wants to pursue. It's an easy matter to find a phone number for DI Griff Chancellor, and as he copies it into his notebook, Fox wonders if he can be sure this is the same number Daniel Hopper had in his pocket. A positive response from Chancellor could mean a step forward in the case; a negative will be frustratingly inconclusive.

The phone's answered on the third ring.

'Chancellor.'

Fox introduces himself and the case he's working on. 'Thing is, there's a possibility this number we're speaking on now was written down on a piece of paper found in the pocket of a key witness, now deceased.'

'Right,' says Chancellor. He sounds big and bluff; his voice matches exactly Budd's description. 'Name of witness?'

'Hopper. Daniel Hopper. This would have been a while ago. It's two years since he died, and I'd suggest from what his sister said about his mood in the last days or weeks of his life something was eating at him. I'm surmising he might have been considering making some kind of statement, and if he did get in touch, he'd probably have mentioned the Baby Michael case. Do you recall any phone calls relating to that?'

'Off the top of my head, I'd have to say no,' says Chancellor. 'Give me half an hour and I'll get back to you.'

But Fox's phone rings before that. Chancellor opens with his rank, full name and the location of his office, as if Fox might have forgotten who he was talking to only twenty minutes before.

'When I was in the Met, I took a lot of calls,' says Chancellor, 'so I developed a personal system, a little database I can access by date, name or number.'

Fox's eyebrows lift in admiration. Maybe he could find someone to build something similar for him.

'So I searched by surname, and separately by first name, for the whole of the year 2016,' Chancellor goes on. 'I checked 2015 and 2017 too, for completeness.'

'He was already dead by 2017.'

'Anyway, I got no matches, nothing even close, so I'd assume he didn't get around to calling me.'

'Or he bottled it,' says Fox.

'Could have been that.'

'What I'm wondering, though,' continues Fox, 'is why you?'

'I have a bit of a reputation,' says Chancellor. 'People have heard of me.'

Mentally, Fox dismisses that possibility as being unlikely. 'Do you have any connection to that area of Devon, around St Just's?'

He can picture Chancellor shaking his head. 'Not me, mate. Never heard of it.'

Fox thinks back to the Ordnance Survey map, and wishes it were still laid out on the desk.

'Bleak Tor, ever been there?'

'Don't think so.'

Fox thinks of villages he drove through. 'Summersford?'

'No.'

'Fordingley?'

Chancellor hesitates. 'Fordingley, Fordingley. Yeah, I know that place. That's where my mum's sister has her pub.'

That evening, Fox leaves the office on time – his flight's an early departure, and he hasn't even started to pack – but it's only as he turns onto the dual carriageway, with Sainsbury's in his rear-view mirror, that he remembers he'd meant to pick up something for dinner. Too late now. Looks like it'll be another takeaway.

There are only a couple of cars outside the Jewel of Bombay, and he hopes that means the wait won't be too long. In the reception area, the manager's on the phone behind the counter, keying in a long order as he receives it. Giving Fox a smile of welcome, he signals him to take a seat.

The manager hangs up the phone. 'Good evening, Mr Fox. I hope you are well?'

'I'm good, thanks, Sajjan. How's business?'

'The phone keeps ringing, so I don't complain. Are you having your usual?'

Fox hates being someone who has a usual, but actually, it's what he wants.

As if reading his mind, Sajjan says, 'Chicken bhuna, chana chat, pilau rice. You want any poppadums today?'

'No poppadums,' says Fox, patting his stomach. 'I'm going on holiday tomorrow. I need to look after my beach body.'

'Hey, you don't need to worry about that,' smiles Sajjan. 'You look really good for your age.'

Fox's eyebrows lift in acknowledgement of the intended compliment. The phone rings, and Sajjan answers it.

Fox picks up a dog-eared local paper from the low table in front of him: last week's news. The headline's about a case currently going through trial, the vicious murder of a schoolgirl by one of her drug-addicted brother's friends. Fox isn't up on the details, as he tends not to be these days. The Portakabin's isolation sometimes leaves him out of the loop.

He's turning to the sports section when the door opens and a tall man enters, slipping his phone into the pocket of his slick suit as he swaggers up to the counter. Even over the spicy scents coming from the kitchen, Fox can smell his aftershave. The man speaks – 'All right, mate, got an order for Garrett?' – and Fox's heart sinks.

Liam Garrett, lead detective in the case Fox was just reading about. What are the chances? Why didn't he turn round and go to Sainsbury's?

Sajjan tells Garrett his order will be out in a moment, and suggests he takes a seat. Fox keeps his head in the newspaper as if he hasn't seen the man, but it's too late. He can sense the grin spreading over Garrett's big mouth, and the sweetness of the aftershave draws closer.

Garrett's a master of subtle intimidation. He doesn't sit, but stands over Fox, looking down.

'Hello, Russ. Fancy seeing you here. Big night in, is it?'

Fox folds the paper, drops it back on the table and looks up. 'Liam.'

Garrett appears gleeful at his opportunity. He points to the newspaper headline. 'Big day for my team, as it turns out. Jury came back in this afternoon, unanimous on the guilty verdict. Great result for us. We'll be in the nationals tomorrow.'

'When you say us, I assume you mean Devon and Cornwall Police?'

Garrett shrugs. 'You have to be honest, don't you? Some deserve more credit than others. You still working cold cases, are you? No-hopers they are, mate, no chance at all. Didn't you pick up that infant unsolved from decades back? My dad worked that case when it happened, and I'll tell you what, if he couldn't crack it then, you can't crack it now. You want to take a leaf out of his book, cash in your chips, free up space on the payroll for somebody younger, someone with a bit more va-va-voom. My dad's got himself a place out in Marbella, spending his old age drinking sangria and lying in the sun.'

Fox remembers Garrett's father: a cold, unscrupulous advocate of dubious methods of policing with a reputation for hard drinking and bullying his team. If what Fox remembers of Paul Garrett is right, unless he can organise himself a liver transplant, his retirement will be short.

Sajjan comes out of the kitchen with two carrier bags heavy with food, and a much smaller third with three containers.

He holds up the two big carriers. 'Mr Garrett?'

Garrett gives Fox a wink. 'I'm treating the team, curry and a few beers. I'd ask you to join us, but it looks like you're all set.'

He takes his two bags, and as he heads out the door, calls back, 'Hurry home, Russ, don't let your chips get cold.'

'Here you are, Mr Fox,' says Sajjan. 'Enjoy your meal.'

Getting into his car, Fox finds that somehow his appetite is all but gone. Sliding the key into the ignition, he's grateful that Spain is a vast country, where his chances of bumping into Paul Garrett are – please God – infinitesimally small.

SIXTEEN

Life, in its new incarnation, goes on.

Lily has gone back to her home and her work, coming down to Selmouth on her days off to help Marietta with the unending tasks created by death: online forms and paperwork, phone calls, the melancholy task of throwing most of Mum's life away.

Marietta's getting used to being alone, trying to find solace in solitude, taking long walks along the seashore, still sleeping poorly, eating way too much of the wrong kind of food. At first when she was in the house by herself, she had the radio on constantly, trying to blot out the creaks of old wood which made her heart pound, always afraid there was someone in the bedroom, in the attic, on the stairs. Sometimes, she thought she glimpsed Alice looking in at her through a window – or, more accurately, on entering a room she'd sense some movement outside, as if a face had quickly pulled back from the glass – and became obsessed with the worry that her mother wasn't at peace, that there was some message she needed to convey, or that she was lost in a world beyond and desperate to find her way back home.

Those feelings, those fears, are passing at last. She's relearned the old house's ways, recalled that the creaking floorboards are nothing new, and it's been days since she's felt any presence but her own and Josie's. As time slips by, Alice seems slowly to be departing, as Marietta reluctantly settles in her place.

But Josie's not herself. Abandoning her bed under the kitchen table, she's taken to lying by the front door, head on her paws, ears pricked, softly whining any time she hears anyone outside. If Marietta persuades her into the lounge, Josie hurries straight to the window, standing on her rear legs to peer out into the empty lane, and when she's fetched away from there to be with Marietta on the sofa, the dog's sighs are long and frequent. Beyond a desultory mouthful or two, her appetite is gone, and Marietta's attempts to tempt her with morsels of chicken and sausages are all rejected. Josie's eyes have lost their sparkle, and she's no enthusiasm even for her walks, trotting listlessly at Marietta's heels instead of pulling her along.

Under different circumstances, Marietta would have taken her to the vet. But instinct tells her there's no drug for Josie's malaise, and no treatment to help her deal with her realisation of the painful truth. Even dogs, it seems, must grieve, and poor Josie must deal – alongside Marietta – with the fact that the person she loved most in the world is never again coming home.

The small bequests in Alice's will are being sought out and made ready. For each recipient, Lily writes a gift label in her artistic hand, before Marietta wraps the keepsakes in pink tissue and packs them ready for posting. The items Alice valued enough to make presents of feel intimate, reflecting common pasts and tastes with the chosen legatees, but most are objects the sisters weren't even aware their mother owned. A cameo ring, a vintage Hermès scarf, a selection of vinyl LPs by artists they've never heard of: this is the memorabilia of a woman the sisters didn't know as well as they believed.

From the back of the wardrobe, Marietta hauls out a round leather box. The interior, when it's opened, smells musty. She lifts out a broad-brimmed hat, flamboyantly decorated in once-white feathers now dirty and discoloured.

'Remember this? Where on earth did she get it from?' She puts it on, and the broad brim falls over her face.

'I think it was Great-Grandma's,' says Lily. 'I wore it once in a school play, *Lady Windermere's Fan*. I think I only got the part because I had the hat.'

'I remember playing dressing-up with it,' says Marietta. 'Mum used to let us wear her nightdresses and shoes, and be princesses. She had those dangly diamond earrings, and that necklace I thought was rubies. When I put those on, I felt like Cinderella ready for the ball.'

Lily smiles. 'Do you remember when she helped us build a castle in the back yard, all draped with duvets? We hung up torches with bits of string to be chandeliers. Then we invited her to tea, and she brought chocolate cake and Maltesers. What a feast.'

Marietta removes the hat and studies it, wondering how this family handled a woman with the boldness to wear something so extravagant. Whoever Great-Grandma was, no one remembers her now. Perhaps she was the genetic source of what Marietta likes to consider her own adventurous spirit,

140

even though that spirit is failing her now. The hat itself is faded and marked with spores of mould. On close inspection, she finds moth holes in the felt.

'What do you think she was like,' she asks, 'the woman who owned this hat? Nothing like Mum or Grandma, that's for sure.'

'I don't suppose she was,' says Lily. 'It's sad that there's so much about our family we don't know. To own a hat like that, she must have had the dresses to go with it. Maybe she was rich, or married well.'

'Grandma and Mum weren't that clever,' says Marietta. 'They chose men who were never going to make a million.'

'They married for love. That's the best reason of all.'

'Not if you want to wear hats like this. What shall we do with it? I'd like to keep it, really.'

'You're kidding, aren't you? How would a nomad like you carry that around the world?'

Regretfully, Marietta removes the hat, puts it back in its box and closes the lid. Lily turns back to the wardrobe.

'What's in here?' She pulls out a shoebox, and removes the elastic band holding on its battered lid. Inside, it's crammed with greetings cards. Tipping them onto the floor, she begins to sift through them. 'Look at this.' She holds up a Christmas card, a clumsily painted Santa with glitter on his red suit and a cotton-wool beard. 'I made this in my first year at school. And look. I gave her this on Mother's Day last year. She must have kept nearly every card we ever sent her.'

Marietta sent no card last Mother's Day, nor in any of the preceding several years. Reaching into the pile, she studies her own adolescent handwriting on a generic birthday card, a photograph of swans on a river she's never seen. The message, such as it is – *Have a great day, from Marietta x* – is carelessly written in blue ballpoint ink. How old was she when she sent this? Thirteen, fourteen? Lily's cards, she notices, are very different to her own – floral tributes *To a wonderful mother*, the sentimental kind of card Marietta would never pick. Was she too careless – or too emotionally guarded – in her choices? Do the roots of recent estrangement go deeper than she thought? And had she known they were destined for preservation, would her choices have been different?

From the heart of the pile, Lily extracts a brown envelope, bent-cornered and tatty with handling. There's no letter inside; the cellophane window through which the address would have shown is blank, but the flap's sealed and the envelope's back has been written on, a few lines in green ink.

Lily shows it to Marietta. 'I think that's Dad's handwriting.'

'What does it say?'

Lily begins to read. *My beautiful Alice – I didn't want to wake you and the tide won't wait. You'll have to forgive me – I forgot the day again – blame my sieve of a brain. But no card and no flowers don't mean you aren't everything to me, sun, moon and stars. Wherever I am, you're the light that guides me home, my heart and very soul. In haste, all my love, Rob. Valentine's Day 1987.*

For a minute they are silent, Lily staring at the words she's just read out.

'That's before I was born,' says Marietta. 'She must have been pregnant with me at the time.'

'He really loved her, didn't he?' whispers Lily. 'They were so in love, and then one day he was just gone. I can't imagine how that must have been. If I lost Connor like that, I'd just want to be with him.'

'She had us to take care of, though, didn't she? But now she's gone the same way. Do you think that's coincidence?'

Lily's starting to put the greetings cards back in their box, the envelope among them. 'Yes, I do. That was aeons ago. People do get over things, eventually.'

'I suppose you're right,' says Marietta, but her expression suggests she really isn't sure.

SEVENTEEN

As far as Lily and Marietta remember, the trio of watercolours have always been there at Trelonie House, hanging in the shadows of the entryway. Their subjects are seabirds – a red-legged kittiwake in flight, an oystercatcher stepping through shallows, a guillemot standing alert on a limpet-covered rock – and all are masterful little paintings, capturing the birds' essence in the spread of a wing or the angle of a neck, bringing them to life against seashore settings of soft blues, ochres and greys, so cleverly done that when the sisters were young, they believed the paper they were painted on could be wet.

When Lily lifts them down, the marks of them stay on the walls, clean rectangles against the grubbier emulsion. She runs a yellow duster over the varnished oak frames.

Marietta peers through the covering glass, trying to figure out the artist's pencil signature. 'It's just a squiggle. Even with a magnifying glass, we'd never read it.'

'If Ivy's right, they'll know who it is,' says Lily. 'She seemed to think these were going to make our fortune.'

Lily drives. Truro is summer-busy, but she knows where she's going and finds a parking space in the Lemon Quay multistorey. From there, it's a short walk to the gallery, which they find down a cobbled side street of recently renovated Georgian terraces. The gallery's frontage is unobtrusive and pretentiously downplayed, the fascia board plain white with the single word *Windrush* written in barely-there cursive lettering in one corner. But the windows speak loudly, arranged with attention-grabbing works in ceramics, paint and glass, though not all of them, in Lily's and Marietta's eyes, are of obvious artistic merit.

The gallery's apparent austerity is forbidding, a barrier to entry for those of less than serious intent. No casual browser would be tempted inside, and Lily feels she wants to walk away, find somewhere less intimidating.

But Marietta appears not to share her misgivings. In well-cut jeans, a linen shirt and ballet flats, her red hair up in a modishly messy bun, she might have recently stepped off one of the harbour-moored yachts. Giving Lily a wink, she pushes open the door, with Lily trailing uncertainly behind.

White walls and brilliance: the gallery's skilful lighting creates a mood of Mediterranean mornings, of southern summer landscapes and sunlight's glare on sand; and the art transforms the room into a palace of exuberant colour, adding bold splashes of blues, oranges and reds.

Marietta gazes round at experiments in tone and texture, perspective and form, and is amazed.

A young woman stands to one side of the room, wearing an expensive dress the colour of froth on cappuccino, and pretty shoes in an exactly matching shade. Lily notices her first, and smiles an acknowledgement, thinking how much she looks like a hostess from the early days of commercial flight.

To Marietta, the young woman's face is familiar – a little older, certainly, the warmth she used to see there somewhat cooled, the openness she recalls become more guarded.

'Tigi?'

The young woman responds with a professional smile; but as she looks at Marietta more closely, the smile broadens, and she opens her arms to welcome her in a hug.

'Oh my God, I don't believe it! Mari, is that you?'

Tigi leads them to a plushly carpeted side room containing nothing but a trio of chairs and a huge table covered in grey oilcloth. On the table is a wicker basket filled with white cotton gloves.

'I'm really sorry about your mum,' says Tigi. 'She was so lovely. Do you remember when I used to come to yours after school? Sometimes she used to make us cheese on toast and it was amazing. What was that sauce she put on it?'

Marietta's face is pink, both with delight at the reunion and embarrassment at her long-term neglect of a friend who deserved much better.

'Worcester sauce,' she says. 'I'm so sorry we lost touch. I'm just hopeless—'

But Tigi – always generous, always ready to see the best in anyone, even the undeserving – interrupts. 'Oh, I know you must have been so busy! Where on earth – I mean literally where – have you been? The last I knew you were in France.'

Some years have gone by since Marietta lived in Europe. Why didn't she try harder to stay in touch? What made her prioritise spending time with careless strangers over the people

146

who cared about her? Tigi isn't the only good friend she's neglected. And then, there was her mother.

'I went from France to Portugal,' she says, and this is news to Lily. 'I met a guy from South America there, and I went with him to Brazil. When he and I split up, I travelled round a bit, wherever I could find work, basically. But I fell in love with Colombia, and ended up staying there.'

Tigi's pulling white gloves onto her long-fingered hands. 'God, Mari, that's amazing!'

'What about you? What have you been up to?' asks Marietta.

'Oh, nothing really.' Tigi's smile diminishes, hinting at disappointment in where life has led her. 'Married to the job, that's me.'

'No man in tow?'

Tigi pulls a face. 'No one worthy of mention. I wish you'd let me know where you were. I'd have come out to visit. South America, wow! We'd have had such a blast.'

Marietta realises she's right; it would have been uplifting to see Tigi's smile in a crowd of airport arrivals, fun to have a confidante, a drinking buddy, a good companion for a while. Maybe she should have invited Lily too, though Lily's really not the type for the challenges of intercontinental travel. But she didn't have to be always so alone. How come it's taken a tragedy to make her see that?

'These are the paintings we need valued.' Lily's laying the watercolours side by side on the oilcloth, afraid as she does so that they've made an embarrassing mistake, that Tigi will think them idiots. The gallery is filled with the cutting-edge and contemporary, and there seems no place for their unfashionable seabirds.

But Tigi looks at them and says, 'Oh.' She bends down to study the oystercatcher. 'Can I just pop them out of the frames? Then we can see what we've got.'

'Be our guest,' says Lily. 'They're probably not worth anything, though Mum always seemed to think they were valuable. Old people get ideas, don't they? I have to say I've always liked them, though I know they're not exactly what you'd call on-trend.'

'Is the *Mona Lisa* on trend?' asks Tigi, turning over the oystercatcher. 'We deal in pretty much anything, as long as it has merit. Oh. Looks like this frame's properly fastened down with these little nails. No matter.' She turns the painting face up again. 'It's so lovely, really nice. And a trio, all from the same period. Has he signed them?' She peers at the squiggle at the bottom corner. 'That's him, all right. He'll be delighted to know these are still around. Unless he already knows you've got them?'

'Who?' asks Lily.

'The artist, Simon Orchard,' says Tigi. 'Sorry, I thought you'd know. He's a bit of a celebrity in these parts.'

'Simon *Orchard*?' asks Marietta. 'Is that his real name?'

'As far as I'm aware,' shrugs Tigi.

'Do you know him?' asks Lily.

'Absolutely. He comes in here from time to time.'

'Do you have a picture of him, by any chance?' asks Marietta.

'I'm sure we do. We did an exhibition of his work not so long ago. He'll have submitted a portrait photo for that. Just give me a minute.'

As she leaves them, Lily looks at Marietta and says, 'Simon.'

'Has to be Uncle Simon,' says Marietta. 'Doesn't it? That would be fantastic, wouldn't it? But why is he calling himself Orchard and not Youlden?'

'I suppose Orchard is catchier. She seems to rate the pictures, anyway. Maybe Ivy was right.'

Tigi returns with an exhibition catalogue, whose cover shows a painted wetland at dusk, red-tinted sky and water filled with the dark shadows of birds. The pastel shades of the watercolours have become denser, vivid acrylics, and the careful detail's been lost to a form of impressionism, but although Simon Orchard's style has evolved over the years, his favoured subjects apparently remain the same.

Tigi flips to an inside page, and shows them a black-and-white photo of a man in his sixties, his face turned in moody profile from the photographer's lens.

'I think that's him,' says Lily, uncertainly. 'I think that's Uncle Simon. Does that mean our pictures might be worth something?'

Tigi raises her hands. 'Please don't ask me to guesstimate. It's not my province, and I'd hate you to be disappointed. Marc's our senior valuer, and he'll be here in the next couple of days. I'll get him to take a look and give you a figure.'

'Thanks, Tig,' says Marietta. 'Is there any chance you can ask Uncle Simon to get in touch with us? I'm sure he'll want to come to the funeral, and he probably hasn't even heard that Mum's died.'

'Course.' Tigi hands her a pen and a sheet of notepaper, and as Marietta writes down her mobile number and email address, says, 'Look, I know now's a bad time, but when the dust has settled, why don't we get together for a drink? For old times' sake. We've so much to catch up on.'

Marietta smiles, and says, 'I'd love to.'

*   *   *

That night, an hour before midnight, a storm breaks. Lying in Alice's bed, Marietta stares at the ceiling, hearing rain batter the windows and the rumble of thunder, blinking as lightning breaks the darkness. Downstairs, the kitchen is silent, so maybe Josie hasn't woken; or maybe she's decided, since whining earns her no relief from her grief, that she has no choice but to be stoical in her fear.

In that recently lost life she thought would always be hers, Marietta was a queen of the night, thriving in the heady hours after dark, and better yet, after midnight, where sex was the subtext of every encounter. The pulsing music, eyes across a crowded room, a few drinks or a couple of lines: all of it was exhilarating, seductive, intense. Wherever she travelled in the world, she'd find work in some club or bar, easily slipping into the rhythm of the place, soon adopted by the beau monde of wherever she was trying to make home.

But time cast a hard light on those beautiful people, who flitted away whenever she was down, ill or broke. Life's lesson was a hard one: rely on nobody. When Lily's call came through, in her heart of hearts she was already ready to leave it all behind.

Now, the night hours are for sleeping, and she hates it when sleep won't come.

As the storm passes and the thunder moves away, Marietta turns her pillow and closes her eyes. The rain is gentle on the roof, and the drip of water from a leaky gutter to the path below is rhythmic and soothing. In the kitchen, Josie turns round in her basket, and settles with a sigh.

Beyond the curtains, the sky turns from black to ruby red so bright, Marietta sees it behind her eyelids. Climbing from the bed, she crosses to the window and looks out on a hellfire glow.

A distress flare has gone up.

As children, whenever they saw a flare, their mother made them say a prayer for those in trouble to be brought safely to dry land.

Rescue for their father came too late.

The eerie redness begins to fade. The lifeboat must surely be on its way.

Marietta puts little faith in the power of prayer, but the kindness in Adam's eyes has stayed with her.

And the words she whispers are truly meant. *Please God, keep them all out of harm's way.*

EIGHTEEN

Alice's funeral is in two days. Thinking she needs new shoes, Marietta checks her bank balance and sees she's uncomfortably overdrawn.

She needs to find a job.

Josie comes reluctantly from her bed, and trots listlessly behind as Marietta heads for the promenade. The morning's grey, the dankness of a sea fret muffling even the cries of the gulls following an incoming fishing boat.

The smell of bacon wafts through a café door. Marietta fastens Josie to a railing, and fixing on a bright smile, goes inside.

The owner's pleasant but apologetic: no vacancies.

At the surf shop five doors down, the lank-haired girl behind the counter yawns. The sound system is blasting out Agent Orange so loud the girl can't hear what Marietta says even when she raises her voice,

Surf punk all day long, she thinks as she leaves. They couldn't pay me enough.

She tries a gift shop overburdened with tat: china cats and dolphin wind chimes, scented candles and clotted cream fudge. The decor is overwhelmingly pink, and the woman who greets her is dressed to match.

'Can I help you?'

Marietta finds that smile again. 'I'm wondering if you might have any vacancies. Part-time for preference, but I can be flexible.'

The woman looks her up and down. 'Do you have retail experience?'

'Customer services.'

'I'll put your CV on file,' says the woman, and Marietta hands her a copy, knowing it's unlikely to be read.

The sea fret has made the morning cold, and outside the gift shop, Josie is shivering. Her lack of appetite has caused her to lose weight, and she seems to suffer in all but the sunniest weather. Marietta picks her up, tucking her under her jacket and stroking her under her chin.

'You might be skinny these days, but you're still a heavy girl, so don't be thinking I'm carrying you home. Let's go and get you warmed up.'

Down on the beach, she unclips Josie's lead. For once these days, Josie seems glad to be here, and begins to run around like her old self.

Marietta wanders down to the water's edge, where the outgoing tide has left a broad scatter of debris on the wet sand. While Josie sniffs at parts of dead crabs and empty shells, Marietta picks up a mermaid's purse, a copper-brown pouch with tendrils at its corners. Time was she and Lily believed these leathery objects really were mermaids' lost property, opening them up in hopes of finding caches of marine money or pearls, until Lily watched a children's TV presenter explain that the purses were nothing more than the egg sacs of sharks.

Marietta drops the purse and walks on along the waterline. A flash of blue catches her eye, and she bends to pick up a fragment of sapphire sea glass, opaque from the salt water's tumble. In her schooldays she had a collection of these gems, and wonders where it went. Dropping the glass in her pocket, she calls to Josie.

'Come on, young lady. Let's take the long way home.'

The long way home. Is that the road she's been on all this time?

Scouring the sand for more glass, she leads Josie off the beach and turns towards the harbour. Sunshine is evaporating the damp dullness of the fret, and blue sky's breaking through.

Where the tourist boats moor, the first customers of the day are buying tickets to go mackerel fishing, and Marietta recalls how a friend's dad included her and Lily on a similar trip once. Lily was frightened of the flapping fish as well as being seasick, but Marietta remembers the exhilaration she felt when a fish tugged on the line, and the thrill of actually landing a real live mackerel. If she'd been a boy, she might have followed her father's trade, though no question Mum would have tried to dissuade her from such a capricious career. She must have inherited something of him, though, in her DNA; as the amateur fishermen board the boat, she feels the tug of the sea, and for a fleeting moment wishes she were going with them.

In no hurry to return to the empty house, she dawdles past the shops lining the harbour road – places built mainly as drinking dens for fishermen and the women who gutted and packed the fish into barrels. A vintage vinyl record place takes her eye, and she wonders why she didn't take more interest in Alice's collection. Next door, a window is filled with silver jewellery set with sea glass, each piece a eulogy to some underwater creature or flowing plant.

It seems the right thing to do to donate the pieces she's just found.

Inside, Marietta has the impression of being below decks in the last century: aged oak draped with gauzy nets, lights behind faux portholes. Traditional shanty songs play quietly in the background, a touching echo of those who used to spend time in this place. In one corner, a woman bends over a bench welding silver, a clear mask covering her eyes. When she sees Marietta, she lifts the mask.

'I wondered if you can use these.' Marietta holds out the glass. 'There's not much, but it's no use to me.'

'If it's beautiful, surely it's of use,' smiles the woman. 'But I'll gladly have it if you don't want it.'

'I don't have anywhere to keep it,' says Marietta. 'I'm just travelling through.'

The woman stands. She's older than Marietta, dressed in casual clothes that look expensive but well worn, with the tanned hands and face of someone often outdoors.

'Really?' she says. 'I can hear something local in that accent.'

Marietta's surprised, believing that any trace of her Cornish origins is long lost.

'Maybe Selmouth's getting back under my skin more than I thought. I'm from here originally, but I haven't lived here in years. I'm only here now because my mum died.'

She says the last three words casually, caught off-guard

when their truth hits her all over again, and a lump rises in her throat.

'I'm sorry to hear that,' says the woman. 'I know how tough it is. But if you're a Selmouth native, you're a rarity these days. I'm all the way from Lancashire.'

'I'm ashamed to admit I've never been that far north.'

'It's cold and wet, like they say.'

Marietta smiles. 'You've found a home from home in Selmouth, then.' She drops the pieces of glass into the woman's hand. 'If I find any more, I'll bring it in. Your work's really beautiful.'

'Sells well, too. I could sell far more if I had the time to make it. I'm a victim of my own success, and while God knows I appreciate every customer, I find selling and creating a very poor mix.'

'Maybe you need someone front of house. I'm good at selling.'

The woman looks at her. 'Maybe I do. I'm Nancy, by the way.'

'Marietta.'

'Well, I'm very pleased to meet you, Marietta.'

Late afternoon sees the sea fret return, and the house is cold.

Marietta decides to light the fire. She lacks Lily's expertise, but eventually manages to coax it into flame, and for her mother's sake lights every candle in the room. With Josie snuggled close to her in the fire's warmth, the feeling of being adrift she's had since Alice's death is somewhat eased. For the time being, at least, she belongs here.

For a while, she stares at the flames, until an alert on her phone interrupts her.

An email, from an address she doesn't know.

The message is short.

Dear Marietta, I had your contact details from the gallery and of course I'd be delighted to see you. I'm in Selmouth on Tuesday this week – might that day suit you to meet for lunch? Kind regards, Simon (Orchard)

If his brother were pale-skinned from living under Britain's watered-down light, Fox might be more certain whether or not he was unwell. Never overweight, David's become almost gaunt, and his sun-bleached T-shirt and shorts are loose on his bony frame. But a deep tan puts a healthy veneer on anyone, and David insists his weight loss is no cause for concern.

The evening is warm, and they've walked down to take a table on Almeria's beachfront, where rainbow lights glimmer on the water and a guitarist is playing softly by the bar. David's ordered beers and tapas, and the food's good, though Fox notices his brother isn't eating.

He points to a plate of croquettes. 'These are great. You should try them.'

David waves a hand. 'Too early for me. I've got used to eating Spanish style. No appetite before midnight.'

Except for the beer, thinks Fox. Then even ten in the morning isn't too early.

'Maybe we could go for a tour round tomorrow,' he says. 'There's a restaurant up in the mountains I'd like to try.'

David picks up his beer. 'Which one?'

'Jabalí.'

'Hugely overrated and ruinously expensive. You're better off relaxing, little brother. Find yourself a place by the pool, recharge your batteries.'

Fox helps himself to a slice of Serrano ham. 'Don't you ever get bored, lying in the sun all day?'

'I don't lie in the sun all day,' smiles David. 'Sometimes I lie in the shade.'

The smartass answer makes Fox think of Paul Garrett, retired somewhere on this coast, possibly close by. Just in case, he glances round, checking faces at the nearby tables.

'What happened to that woman you were seeing?' he asks.

'Melanie?' David's eyes flicker. 'She didn't approve of my laid-back habits either. She wanted me to get into yoga and clean eating. Not really my thing.'

'Come on, mate,' says Fox. 'You're only sixty-two. It's a bit young to be taking to your bed, isn't it? There must be something you want to do with the rest of your life.'

'I'm doing it,' says David. 'And if I have time to get bored of it, I'll do something else. What are your plans, anyway? What will you do when you hang up your boots?'

That looming question. Fox shrugs. 'Travel, maybe. I'd like to see Japan.'

David studies him. 'Will that be solo travelling, or are you taking someone along for the ride? And by the way, this is where you tell me all about that special new someone in your life, because if there isn't anyone, I might be tempted to say pot, kettle, black.'

Fox forks another croquette onto his plate. 'The job makes it difficult. Always has done.'

David laughs. 'That old chestnut. Come on, Russ. It's been years, too many years. Hasn't there been anyone who's lit a fire in your loins? It's a sad picture, you on your solo trip to Japan. And what happens when you get back?'

'To be honest, I'm not sure.'

'So come and spend some time out here while you decide. We haven't seen enough of each other these past few years.'

'I don't speak Spanish.'

'Neither do I, but so what? Everyone speaks English.'

'So does everyone in Cornwall. Why don't you come back and spend some time with me there? We could go fishing, maybe buy a boat.'

David's expression is dismissive. 'Who do I know in Cornwall any more?'

'You know me. And Shauna. Who do you know here?'

'I know plenty of people. And I can enjoy three hundred and twenty days a year of sunshine. What do they have in Cornwall? Three hundred and twenty days of bloody rain.'

'Actually the sun's a bit much every day, coming straight from the perishing north,' says Fox. 'I could do with a break, to be honest. Why don't we go and find this restaurant? I'm buying. I'll even do the driving, if you like.'

But David shakes his head. 'Long, drawn-out lunches just aren't my thing, these days. Why don't you go? I know a rental car place where they'll give you a good rate. And when you get back, we'll have a drink and you can tell me all about it.'

Later that night, Fox lies awake, wondering what happened to the man his brother used to be. At twenty-two, David backpacked across India. At thirty-one, he made a small fortune, and lost it all before he turned forty. Two marriages, a thousand women, no kids to get in the way. And now, apparently, totally out of ideas.

Or could it be he's out of time?

That's not happening to me, thinks Fox. What's it all been for if that's what happens to me?

NINETEEN

Marietta is bewildered by Uncle Simon's choice of venue. According to Tigi, he's a highly successful man, and Marietta expected to meet him in one of the places on the seafront, Grainger's Crab Shack or one of the foodie pubs, maybe even Mayberry's chintzy tearooms.

But he's suggested the Dolphin café. Marietta doesn't know the place, but finds it – after wandering lost in the back streets for longer than she'd like – at the rear of a charity shop, with one entrance through the piled-high, picked-over junk, and a second leading out into a council car park. The café's empty. A youth with a curtain hairstyle and a stained white apron over his jeans is sitting on a stool behind the counter, playing on his phone. When Marietta arrives, he puts the phone down and stands ready to serve her, giving her an awkward smile when he notices she's pretty.

A short menu is pinned to the wall. The food on offer seems to be bland sandwiches, and baked potatoes with beans, cheese, both or neither. A pair of plain scones and several pieces of cellophane-wrapped fruit cake are covered by a Perspex dome.

She looks behind the youth to the fridge and sees nothing there but cans of Pepsi.

'I'll have a tea,' she says.

The youth doesn't offer to bring it over, so Marietta waits while he pours hot water onto a tea bag already in a single-serving teapot and puts a white mug, milk and sugar on a tray.

'One eighty-five.'

She gives him two pound coins, and lets him keep the change. Carrying her tray to the only one of the four tables not covered with crumbs or dribbles, she sits down on a hard chair where she has a view of both doors.

Uncle Simon is already ten minutes late.

She's finishing her tea when someone arrives – a man she'd swear she's never seen before, in his sixties, a heavy beard. He's wearing almost desert camouflage, pale utility trousers and beige walking boots, a military-type vest with multiple pockets over a short-sleeved white shirt, and his belly marks him out as a man who enjoys a pint.

He seems harassed, and runs a hand through his thinning blond hair to push it off his face. Seeing there's no one else in the room, he looks directly at her and says, 'Marietta?'

She nods and tries to smile, but her heart is sinking. She's been a fool, building Uncle Simon up into some kind of saviour, landfall to her and Lily while they're so lost without their mother. In reality, he's nothing but a stranger to them, and no more certain of her than she is of him. If they'd passed each other on the street, she wouldn't have known him.

He seems prepared, though, to make the best of where they find themselves, approaching her table and pulling out a chair, standing the paper carrier bag he's brought with him on the floor. The bag's from Ingham's, a renowned delicatessen selling French cheeses, Italian salamis and wonderful patisserie. They also do great coffee, so it seems ironic he's been shopping there before coming to meet her in this place.

As he sits, he says, 'I'm so sorry I'm late. I see you got yourself something. That's good. Can I get you a refill? Something to eat?'

Marietta recalls the dismal-sounding sandwiches and baked potatoes. 'I'll have another tea.'

He signals to the youth and points to her teapot. 'Another tea, please. And a coffee for me.' He turns back to Marietta. 'Well, you look fantastic, I must say. How many years has it been? Twenty? More, I should say.'

'I don't really know. I was hoping you might tell me.'

'I was very sad to hear about your mother, really very sad indeed. We were great friends back in the day, very great friends.'

'Friends?' Marietta frowns. 'I don't understand. Why don't you have the same surname?'

The youth brings over their drinks, and Marietta and Simon sit in silence while he removes the empty pot and milk jug and replaces them with fresh ones. The coffee he puts in front of Simon looks watery and tasteless. Simon rips the tops off two packets of sugar and stirs them in.

He clears his throat. 'I wonder if you've been labouring under a misapprehension. That's why I thought we might meet here, so we could talk privately. Your mother and I were not related by blood.'

'What do you mean? Aren't you her brother? How can you be our uncle if you're not?'

Simon appears embarrassed. 'Children get the wrong end of the stick, don't they? Our fault, probably, mine and your mother's. I suppose we thought it would be nice for you girls to have an uncle, especially after your father passed away.'

'Are you telling me we're not actually related?'

'We're not, no.'

'Oh.' Marietta feels the sting of another loss. 'I don't know what to say. Lily and I, we thought we at least had you.'

Simon shakes his head. 'I should explain. I'm sorry if this comes as a shock. Your dad and I were great pals, and I met your mother through him. My interest is in wildlife – I've made quite a success of it, as a matter of fact – and I used to hire your dad to take me out to the crags to photograph the birds there.'

'We have some of your paintings,' says Marietta.

'Perhaps we might talk about that.'

Marietta pours herself more tea she doesn't want, wondering how Lily will take the news that he's no more than a once-was old friend of their parents.

'We thought you'd moved abroad. Mum mentioned Australia or America.'

He shakes his head. 'I've never lived abroad, no. I've travelled a lot, in my time. Perhaps she was referring to that.'

'So why did you and she lose touch, if you were both still living in the same area?'

Simon spreads his hands in a gesture of bafflement. 'To be honest, I couldn't say. Though I admit we artists are at the whim of our muses, and dedicate too much of ourselves to the work. Your mother had you girls to look after, and interests of her own. I suppose that's how life goes.'

He takes a sip from his cup, grimacing at the quality of the coffee.

'She was lonely, at the end,' says Marietta, feeling tearful at this truth. 'Did she try to get in contact with you at all?'

'Not that I recall.' Simon looks across the room as he says this, and Marietta has the uncomfortable feeling he may not be telling the truth. His answer seems oddly vague, but what reason could he have to lie?

He tears open another envelope of sugar and stirs it into his cup.

'Was she ill?' he asks. 'You wonder, don't you, what people have died of, but it seems indelicate to ask.'

'She drowned.'

Simon nods, as if it's nothing unexpected. 'The cruel, cruel sea. How are you girls coping?'

Marietta shrugs. 'It's early days, but it's hard.' She hesitates. 'There's something I've been wondering about. Lily doesn't like to talk about it and it's hard for me to say, but I can't help wondering if she took her own life.'

He looks at her directly, his face set with the same rigid resistance to the suggestion she sees in Lily.

'Why would you think that?'

How can she explain a conviction born of intuition? Best to begin with the rational deductions.

'When we went to the morgue . . .' She's interrupted by a flashback: white walls, a turned-back sheet, a stiffened hand. 'The police family liaison officer was trying to tell us it might be that, planting the idea they were thinking it was suicide. And things do point that way. She left her phone at home.'

'Nothing odd about that,' interrupts Simon. 'Who wants one of those bally things pinging at them all the time?'

'But if the police thought so . . . I suppose they see enough to know the signs. And I wondered if you might shed any light on why, whether she was prone to anything that might have predisposed her . . . We found antidepressants in her room.'

He shakes his head. 'I really wouldn't read too much into that. Doctors prescribe them to everyone these days, they're common as Smarties.'

'So she wasn't unhappy when you were seeing a lot of her? I've been so far away all this time, and I'm worried I missed something. It's hard to think if I'd been closer, I might have helped.'

Pushing his unwanted coffee out of the way, Simon reaches across and squeezes her hand.

'Of course it's hard, my dear, of course it is. And it's natural to ask yourself if you might have behaved differently. Everyone does. If it's any comfort, I remember your mother as a very happy person – after she got over your father's death, of course – and I think the police will conclude it was just an unfortunate accident. You mustn't blame yourself for something you couldn't have prevented. And if you'll take advice from an old man, it does get easier. Everyone will tell you time's a great healer, but the good news is that it's true.'

Marietta nods. 'Thank you.'

'Your mother wouldn't have wanted you to be unhappy, Marietta. That much I do know.' He glances at an expensive-looking watch. 'Forgive me, won't you, but I'm going to have to cut this short. But I'm so glad we've had the chance to talk.'

'We'll see you at the funeral, though, won't we?'

'Yes, of course you will. When did you say it is?'

'Tomorrow.'

'I remember, you mentioned it in your email. Of course I'll be there.' He begins fumbling in his trouser pocket for change. 'I'll get this, my treat. Just that other thing, about my paintings, the ones your mother kept. They were a loan only, to be honest. I'm prepared to pay fair market price for them, but I would rather like to have them back. I'll get the gallery to make a formal offer for them, keep everything above board. I understand how necessary that is when you're going through probate.'

'I'm not sure we want to sell them. Mum really treasured them. They're like heirlooms to us.'

'I'm hugely flattered that she valued them so highly, but I'd hate you to be disappointed when you find out they're not worth much after all. I know you have a lot on your plates, and all I'm saying is, I'd be more than happy to take them off your hands, save you the hassle of finding a buyer.' Simon puts a five-pound note down on the table. Behind him, an elderly couple shuffles in. 'I can let you have signed prints to replace them, framed and at my expense. Indulge my vanity, won't you? I have this notion that as I approach the end of life, I want to gather all my children together. That's how I think of my paintings, as my offspring, which is ridiculous, I know. But I feel the need to have them near me, to warm my old age. I'll be generous in my offer. The gallery will be in touch.' He glances again at his watch, stands and picks up his Ingham's carrier bag. 'I'm so sorry to rush away. It's been a real pleasure to see you. You'll give my regards to your sister, won't you?'

'You can give them to her yourself tomorrow.'

'Tomorrow?'

'The funeral.'

'Of course, of course. I'll see you there,' he says, and he leaves her alone at the table, without either a handshake or a kiss.

TWENTY

Lilies are the scent of life's end.

The last time Marietta was in this place was for her grandmother's funeral. She was much younger then, twelve or thirteen, still young enough to be more bewildered than upset, still inexperienced enough in life to not truly understand what it means for someone to leave and never come back, how the months stretch into years but the dregs of loss never disperse. Except for her father, of course. With him, she still has the sense of something intangible missing, though more a facet of her than the man himself, who in truth is no more to her than a hazy memory.

Three weeks have gone by since Alice's death, and the initial shock has passed, the grief's intensity diminished. Even so, none of this seems real: not the black dress and hat she's wearing, not Lily quietly crying beside her, not the minister's ponderous speech about their mother, whom clearly he had never met. And emphatically not the wooden box on trestles where Alice's body lies.

They stand, sing, sit. A poem she and Lily chose is read, a

piece of music Alice loved is played and provokes tears. The minister says a prayer, and the purple curtains close.

Marietta and Lily's mother slides away.

Black cars, rain and bright umbrellas, the sickly scent of lilies: those are the things Marietta will take from this day. Those, and the depths of her desolation.

The wake is in an unremarkable pub function room, where the buffet, though generous, is bland. But glancing round, Lily thinks her mother would have been gratified to see how many people have walked over from the crematorium to be here. Thinking no one cared enough to join them would have broken Lily's heart.

One of her hands is clutching Connor's; in the other is her second glass of red, because what better excuse can there be for lunchtime drinking than having laid your mother to rest? If that's what they've done. Everyone has their phobias, and Lily's terrified of fire. Cremation would be her worst nightmare, but money mattered, so for Alice, that's what they chose.

She and Marietta acquitted themselves well: no breaches of etiquette, no stumbles or embarrassment. Preparations for the funeral have been pressing on her mind for days, waking her in the small hours with worries over the order of service, the choice of music and whether the florist would deliver on time. Now at last it's behind her, she finds herself almost ready to smile.

Over by the buffet, Marietta's chatting to Ivy, who's holding a loaded plate and a half-pint of cider. In Lily's eyes, Ivy's more welcome here than anyone; she was a good friend to Mum, and a godsend with Josie. Maybe with the help of Mum's bequest for the dog's care, she might still be persuaded to adopt Josie full-time.

Because it was a reason to reminisce, she and Marietta sorted through the family photos and stuck them in an album as a review of Alice's life. The album's on a side table now, and a woman is leafing through it.

The choice of what to include was hard; what they learned about their mother in the process was that there were facets of her they'd never seen, aspects of her life and character of which they had no knowledge. Which, after all, was more her: a very young Alice, grinning in the back row of the school hockey team Alice with Dad before they were married, picnicking during a Lake District hike; Alice nursing one of them as a baby; Alice drinking champagne on a ladies' trip to Paris?

What made Lily sad was what she didn't want to say to her sister – that as the years went by in the photos, as lines developed in their mother's face and she lost her slenderness and looks, the sparkle in her eyes also faded. Undeniably, there was unhappiness there, by the end. How deep it went, she doesn't want to contemplate.

The woman looking at the album catches Lily's eye, and gives her a small wave before heading in her direction. Grandma would have called her a bottle blonde, but Lily thinks the woman's platinum hair – tied in a loose ponytail with a black velvet ribbon – is classy. A black A-line skirt and flat black boots, and a black jacket that nips in her waist make her head-to-foot in Alice's favourite colour, but beyond that there's little comparison to be drawn between them. With almost aristocratic features, this woman's still a beauty, whereas Mum had long ago slid into late-life invisibility.

'You're Lily, aren't you?' She holds out her hand, and Lily drops Connor's to take it, noticing the diamond rings on two of her fingers. The woman's scent is vintage French, Chanel or Guerlain, blended with the tang of foreign cigarettes, and her voice is a smoker's husky burble, actually quite sexy. 'You don't remember me, I'm sure. I'm your mum's old friend Barbara, Barbara Constant. Last time I saw you, you were so big.' Letting go of Lily's hand, she holds her palm about a metre from the floor, signifying the height of a child of about eight years old. 'I'm so very sorry about your mum. You'll miss her desperately, I'm sure. We all will. It was too long since I'd seen her, far too long. Life gets in the way, doesn't it?' She smiles at Connor. 'Is this your intended?'

'My husband, Connor.'

'Aren't you the dashing one?' Barbara gives Connor a roguish wink. 'Could I persuade you to be a gentleman and fetch me a drink? I hate to be a lone woman leaning on a bar. Here.' She opens up a black patent clutch bag, and presses a twenty-pound note into his hand. 'Do you recommend the red, Lily?'

'Not really.'

'A glass of rosé for me, then,' says Barbara. 'And whatever you and Lily are having.'

'Another red, please, sweetheart,' Lily says to Connor.

He heads for the bar, and Barbara gazes round the room, as if looking for people she'd know. 'Is your sister here?'

'That's Marietta, over there,' says Lily, pointing her out.

Barbara gives a smile which would have dazzled any man forty years ago, when her teeth were her own and not obvious dentures.

'I see her now. You won't recall, I'm sure, but when you were little, you came to stay with me for a few days. You were both completely adorable, though I'm not sure I was much of a babysitter. I fed you nothing but chocolate and beans on toast and quite a lot of sausages. When your grandmother came to fetch you, we were playing dressing-up, and you were wearing my cherry-red lipstick and most of the contents of my jewellery box. Your grandmother told me I'd got you done up like cheap French whores, and was terribly offended when I laughed. I've never forgotten it.' She puts her hand on Lily's arm. 'I don't want to be indelicate, but I confess I'd like to know what your mother died of. She used to tease me about my insatiable curiosity, you know, but she was never rude enough to call it by its proper name of nosiness. If there's something to know, I want to know it. I've found her passing sobering, I must confess. I'm only a few months older than her.'

'We don't know the cause of death,' says Lily. 'There's going to be an inquest.'

Barbara's pencilled eyebrows lift. 'An inquest. Dear me, I didn't realise. Is there some doubt, then?'

'Not to me,' says Lily. 'She . . .' The words seem difficult to say, and she takes a drink. 'There was an accident while she was swimming.'

'What, in the sea?'

'Yes.'

'She drowned?'

Lily's eyes fill with tears. She looks round for Connor, who's in a crowd at the bar.

'Oh Lily, I'm so sorry.' Barbara appears mortified at Lily's distress. 'I didn't mean to upset you. Why am I always so blunt? My ex-husband used to say it was my worst fault, wading in where angels fear to tread. I only meant to suggest how unlikely that seems. But she was a good swimmer, wasn't she? I wonder, did she have heart problems?'

'I don't think so.'

'She had a strong heart, and a good heart. From the first days I knew her at school, your mother was always so thoughtful, always putting everyone else first.' Barbara places a hand on Lily's arm. 'I know you don't remember your grandfather. Your mum was only fifteen or so when he died, and I don't need to say she was totally devastated. She'd always been such a daddy's girl, and he was a lovely man, always cheerful, always carrying her off on some adventure. He was fanatical about trains, and once a month or so, he and she used to set off from Truro station with a packet of sandwiches and a flask of tea to see how far they could get. Off they went, wherever the railway took them, whether it was Penzance or Plymouth, and when they arrived they'd eat their sandwiches, have a cup of tea and catch a train back home. I suppose you'd call him an eccentric, but I think he was just a man who had a zest for life, and was interested in everything.'

Lily thinks of her grandmother – a morose woman in later life, martyred to the pains of arthritis – and wonders why she was never included in the railway jaunts. Glancing over towards the bar, she sees Connor is at last handing over Barbara's twenty-pound note.

Barbara is continuing with her reminiscences. 'I'm sure you know your grandfather was a musician.' Lily doesn't know, and is surprised to hear it; she was only ever told he worked in the council planning department. 'He played the clarinet, I think, or was it the trumpet? Anyway, his great passion was for jazz music. I remember seeing his record collection whenever I went to your mum's, and he'd always play us something, though I must be honest and say it was never really my taste. He had a room he'd made his study, and in there were shelves and shelves of records all across one wall, and always music playing, and a list pinned with a drawing pin to one of the shelves with what he called his Holy Grails, records he'd been searching for forever but had yet to find. There was no internet or eBay or whatever in those days, of course, though I think collectors had a lot more fun, digging round in junk shops and second-hand places, seeing what treasures they could find.'

Relieved to see Connor's making his way back to them, Lily drains her glass. Over Barbara's shoulder, she sees a blond, bearded man in his sixties walk up to the bar and lean forward on it, impatient for service. Uncle Simon. Without Marietta's description, she'd never have known him, but for Mum's sake, she's glad that he's here.

'When your grandfather was taken ill,' Barbara goes on, 'there was only one record left on his Holy Grail list. *Round About Midnight at the Café Bohemia*, by Kenny Dorham. It sounded so exotically romantic, I've never forgotten it. The irony was, by that time he'd tracked down a copy at a specialist place in London, but it was expensive and there was no money to pay for it. So your mother sold her hair to buy it.'

Lily thinks she's misheard. 'What?'

Barbara's eyes are distant, drifting back into the past. 'She had the most beautiful hair, something like your sister's but not that striking red. That's not on your mother's side. Marietta gets that from your father. Alice's hair was a glorious chestnut brown, and she'd been growing it for years, right down to the middle of her back. I helped her cut it off. She tied it in a ponytail and gave me a pair of dressmaker's shears and told me to make the cut. I couldn't do it at first – it seemed such a terrible shame – but she was insistent, and so I did. And she packed it in an envelope, and she and your grandma – who by the way wept when she saw what Alice had done – went up to London and sold her hair to a wigmaker in Clapham, and came back with that record. They played it to him as he was dying.' She touches her eye, where a tear is forming. 'Your grandfather took his last breaths at the Café Bohemia.'

By the buffet, Ivy has moved away from Marietta, who's being talked at now by someone else, a man.

'Here we are.' Connor hands the women their drinks and gives Barbara her change, which she drops into her clutch bag without checking it. 'I'll just go and fetch my pint.'

'I like a man who enjoys his beer,' says Barbara. 'There's something very masculine about a man with a pint.'

'It's shandy,' says Connor. 'Not very masculine at all.'

Barbara laughs. 'In the old days, my husband used to drink and drive without a second thought. All well and good until he put us in a ditch. It was a huge relief to me when they tightened up the rules.'

As Connor heads back to the bar, Lily says, 'Have you had anything to eat yet, Barbara?'

Barbara's eyes are on Connor. 'Do you know, I haven't, and I am actually quite peckish. I think I might . . .'

She stops speaking, her mouth open so Lily can see her tongue poised to say what were to be her next words. Lily's alarmed. Is this what happens with a stroke?

But Barbara recovers herself. Offering Lily an unconvincing smile, she puts her almost full wine glass down on a nearby table, and says, 'I'm so sorry, would you excuse me?'

Lily watches her walk away, apologising as she pushes her way through the people crowding the bar. Connor has disappeared, she assumes looking for the gents. Left by herself, her reason for being at this gathering comes back to her, and she feels lost all over again, newly bereft.

She wants no more chat with strangers, and looks round for Marietta, who's still talking to the man she doesn't recognise. Poor Marietta: she's probably finding this as much of a trial as Lily is.

But as she makes up her mind to go to her sister's rescue, someone touches her arm.

'I think you must be Lily. I'm Simon, Simon Orchard.'

'Uncle Simon.' Lily blushes. 'Only Mari told me you're not.'

No hug, no kiss. Simon switches his glass – a dark brew of real ale, already half empty – to his left hand, and gives Lily his right.

'I must say it's lovely to see you girls,' he says. 'If only the circumstances were happier. I'm very sorry about your mother. You'll miss her, I know.'

'We do.' He looks at her, and behind the changes of passing decades, in the intensity of his eyes, she glimpses the man she remembers, recalling vaguely a memory from years ago of something he used to say, about seeing with the eyes of angels. 'Thank you for coming today.'

'Oh, I was glad to make the time. Busy as we all are, these rituals are important.'

Ritual? Without quite knowing why, Lily bristles.

'What are you doing with yourself these days?' asks Simon, and the cocktail party question throws Lily off balance.

'Doing?'

'Job-wise, I mean. Are you gainfully employed?'

'I work with children. At a kindergarten. Only part-time at the moment, but—'

'Time,' says Simon. 'You remind me.' He glances at his expensive watch. 'Lily, you must forgive me, there's somewhere I have to be, and I'm already late. Give my regards to your sister, won't you? Maybe we could all have lunch?' He drains his glass, and places it on a table behind him. 'Such a pleasure to see you. I'll be in touch.' And he's gone.

Lily places Simon's empty glass on the table by Barbara's almost full one, and makes her way to where Marietta's listening to the man she doesn't know, interrupting him to say, 'Hello, I'm Alice's other daughter, Lily. Thank you for coming.'

'Oh, I wouldn't have missed it,' says the man. He's wearing drab – grey suit, grey shoes, mauve tie – and now the room's becoming hot, his comb-over is slipping off the moistness of his scalp. 'I'm Laurence, Laurence Byfall. I was just saying to your sister, I'm feeling horribly guilty. I'm hoping your mother's death was nothing to do with me.'

His prominent eyes are over-eager, and there's an obsequiousness about him, born perhaps of being an unlikeable person too keen to be liked. When he stops speaking, his dry lips purse open and closed like a fairground goldfish.

'How did you know our mother?' asks Lily.

'Mr Byfall's already explained,' says Marietta.

But Laurence disregards her implied suggestion that he not repeat himself.

'Laurence, please. Your mother and I were – well, I hesitate to say romantically involved, so let me say we were friends. We took a few outings together, trips to the theatre, things of that nature. But our friendship ended badly. It came to a rather sudden end, actually, after a silly argument. Since then we hadn't been in touch in a while, and I wonder if my absence might have left her rather lonely. Too lonely, if you get my drift. I can't help wondering, if I'd stayed in touch, picked up the phone and apologised, whether it might have prevented—'

'What?' asks Lily, bluntly.

'Well, we all have our low moments, don't we?' suggests Laurence. 'I know I certainly do. I wonder if I was being insensitive, whether she was more attached to me than I thought. Whether the loss of our friendship might have affected her more deeply than I gave credit for. I'd been thinking about getting back in touch before I read the obituary in the paper. And as I was saying to your sister, if there's anything I can do to make amends, please ask.'

'Truly, I'm one hundred per cent certain no amends are required,' says Marietta.

'It brings it home to you, though, doesn't it?' Laurence shakes his head. 'How disordered everything is these days.'

'What do you mean?' asks Lily.

As he answers, Laurence wags a long-nailed finger to emphasise his points. 'Let's start with how many of us are lucky enough to have a send-off anywhere near our homes. Your mother didn't live in this town, did she? She lived twenty miles away, but here we are at the nearest convenient council facility, which isn't really convenient at all. In the old days, you were buried among your friends and neighbours, in the place you lived all your life.' He leans forward towards Marietta. 'Be honest, how many of the people here do you actually know? I assume a good portion of them are Alice's work colleagues, but if she'd changed her job recently, they'd be a whole different set of faces. People move about so much these days. They have new neighbours, rub along with them for a few years, then it's all change again. Everything's temporary, and nobody's got anybody they can one hundred per cent rely on, not even family. Your kids grow up and scatter to the four winds. Look at me. I've got two sons. One's in Canada and the other's in Inverness, and the only time I see them is Christmas, and even then likely as not on some computer screen. What happened to lifelong relationships, living your whole life among people you know and who know you inside out? It's no surprise to me, the suicide statistics. People are adrift, all at sea.'

Behind his ingratiating, pasted-on smile, Marietta sees pain she recognises, the outcome of being a stranger in too many towns, of substituting technology for touch and true connection, of always searching for that mythical place called home. But don't they say you can't go home again? Sadly, Laurence is right: most of these people are strangers to her and Lily. They knew so little of their mother's present life.

'I tried to make friends with her,' says Laurence, gloomily. 'But I don't think she wanted new friends. I think she wanted her family.'

He has no suspicion of the brutality of his words. He isn't to blame for Alice's death, but whatever the reasons behind it, Marietta must bear some guilt. Wouldn't Alice have adored grandchildren to bring her joy and purpose in later life? But instead, there were only poor Lily's tragedies, and Marietta herself drinking rum in a distant country, thinking she was doing enough by calling home once in a blue moon.

She feels a hot flush of shame. Terrible mistakes have been made, tragic errors that can never be rectified, and here is her reward. She herself was unreliable, and who does she have to rely on? Only Lily, who she's treated shabbily too. Everyone else is gone.

Laurence has finished his drink, and Marietta can see he's debating with himself whether to leave, or have another. She knows too well how that goes. His loneliness will persuade him to stay.

Right on cue, he says, 'Can I buy you ladies a drink? For your mother's sake.'

Marietta musters a smile, for their mother's sake. 'Thank you, Laurence. Why not? By the way, have you ever thought about getting a dog?'

Connor drives them back to Trelonie House. On the way, Lily recounts Barbara's story of the Café Bohemia.

When she finishes, all three of them are silent, until Lily says, 'I wonder why she never told me?'

In the back seat, Marietta is feeling sleepy from the wine she's drunk.

'She had so much sadness in her life,' she says. 'First her father, then Dad. Maybe it just got too much to bear.'

'She was a strong woman,' objects Lily. 'And all that was decades ago.'

Marietta closes her eyes, and lets it go.

180

TWENTY-ONE

The aftermath of Alice's death is almost past.

In the stillness of the house, the carriage clock ticks. Alongside the evening lighting of candles, its winding has become one of Marietta's daily homages to her mother, though how long these small ceremonies can continue she doesn't know. Usually, she finds the clock's brisk rhythm homely and comforting, but sometimes – like now – it's unsettling, sixty prod-in-the-back beats a minute marking how life is slipping by.

Too much solitude drives her to her phone, trapping her in a compulsive cycle of firing it up, finding that catnip number and powering it off before she presses the green icon which would dial the call.

What help would Bernardo be to her anyway? He'd stroke her ego, tell her he wants her back, and that would be true, but only because she's reliable labour and a compliant mistress. A return to that life would be a Pavlovian response to the difficult discomforts of anxiety and restlessness, whose roots – if she dares acknowledge them – lie in her faltering self-reliance and confidence. With no path or plan or even inkling of what to do next, she's floundering, lost in apathy. When the house is sold, where in the world will she make her home?

The clock strikes 4 p.m. Two hours to high tide.

She fetches Josie's lead from the kitchen. As she grabs a jacket from hooks behind the front door, the watercolours catch her eye. Even though she told Simon they wouldn't part with them, should sentiment be sacrificed to practicality? The proceeds from their sale might soften Lily's insistence on selling the house. And that would buy Marietta time to come up with a plan for the rest of her life.

At the airport, Fox succumbs to an urge to give David a hug. Taken by surprise, David stiffens, submitting rather than reciprocating, and after an awkward moment, Fox lets him go.

'Well,' says David. 'Safe travels. I'll see you soon.'

Fox wants to say, *Come back with me, regrow your roots where people know you, where you belong,* but he knows there's no point. If David ever comes home, it'll be in his own time.

So instead he says, 'You take care of yourself, you hear? I'll ring you when I get back.'

Walking away to join the crowd queuing in Departures, his mood is blue. Life is rarely kind. Why can't there be more happy endings?

He shows his boarding pass, and turns to wave a final goodbye.

But David is already gone.

In recent days, Josie is more her old self, and when Marietta – out of a need for variety – heads in a different direction to their usual route, she pulls keenly ahead.

Marietta's following a nostalgic impulse, down a path leading from the clifftop to a place from childhood memory. Since she was last here, the path's been improved from the steep scramble it used to be by the installation of concrete steps. As she and Josie descend, they pass several people coming up, and as she waits to let them by, glimpses of rolling sea tell her the tide is almost at its height.

At the bottom of the path is a cove, a beach of silvery sand divided by a granite outcrop, and a cave hollowed out in the cliff base. Waves are running high up the beach, but a broad strip of sand is still exposed, enough to walk round the end of the outcrop to the beach on its far side.

Marietta wanders into the cave, where the dank air stinks of seaweed and rotting molluscs. Standing under the chilly refuge of its black roof takes her back to summer days spent here with Mum and Lily, when this place seemed filled with magic. Was what Mum told them true, that this was once a smugglers' cove, notorious for rum-runners and wreckers? To her and Lily, the truth didn't matter; they were pirates anyway, hiding treasure in the cave's barnacled crannies, climbing the rocks to keep lookout for vessels to pillage. When they were tired, they lay in the sun on sandy towels, eating sausage rolls and salt and vinegar crisps, reading *Captain Underpants* and *Goosebumps* while Mum dozed in her fold-up chair, and on the way home, as often as not, she'd buy them ice cream.

They were happy in those days. Weren't they? Mum took good care of them. Or at least, she did her best.

Marietta wanders down to the waterline, aware that the tide comes in fast here, that she doesn't have much time.

On the next stretch of beach, a soft-looking grey lump left

by the last tide has caught Josie's attention. Marietta assumes it's clothing or a towel, but whatever it is, Josie's sniffing round it in excitement, tail wagging.

Marietta glances back. The waterline is creeping closer to the end of the outcrop which she has now passed. Josie's find is a bloated herring gull, dead for some days and stinking, and she looks around for something to pick it up and throw it back in the sea, out of the dog's reach.

But Josie senses Marietta's intention. Catching the tail feathers between her teeth, she drags the bird across the sand towards the cliffs, its wings spread as if trying to catch the wind and be airborne.

'Josie! Come here!'

Josie isn't listening, but her prize is heavy. Before she reaches the cliff, she drops the bird and panting, lies down.

An incoming wave covers the sand between the outcrop and the sea. The way back to the cliff path is closing.

Marietta calls to Josie again, and sure that the dog will follow her, heads back the way she's come. At the outcrop, she waits for another wave to retreat before she can run across the newly wet sand. Beyond that, the beach in front of the cave is still dry.

Safety. Except Josie isn't with her.

'Shit.' From her side of the outcrop, she watches two more waves roll in. The second leaves a film of water over the sand. 'Josie!' Her voice is swallowed by the sound of the sea. Even with a dog's hearing, she doubts she'd be heard. 'Shit.'

She tells herself to have faith in herself, that she's quick on her feet. Treat it like a game. There's still plenty of time.

But the next wave that rolls in is faster and deeper, throwing up spray as it hits the rocks, leaving behind not a glassy veneer of water, but a pool. The part of the beach where Josie is will soon be cut off. Whatever happens now, Marietta's likely to get wet feet.

Because if Josie – wretched dog – won't come to her, then she must go to Josie.

Pulling off her trainers, she tosses them onto a rock well out of the water's reach, and rolls up her jeans to her knees, then paddles across the stretch of shallow water.

Josie's still up by the cliffs, chewing on the dead bird. Marietta grimaces, hoping there's nothing smelly on the dog's fur.

'Josie!'

Josie looks at her, stands up and begins to drag her trophy back down the beach.

'Good girl! Come on, we have to go.'

Confident that Josie's on her way, Marietta paddles back to the far side of the rocks. The water's deeper now, over her ankles. If Josie doesn't hurry she'll have to swim, and she really doesn't like cold water.

Marietta climbs the rocks to retrieve her shoes, but when she jumps back down onto the sand, there's still no sign of the dog. The water she paddled through is already much deeper, turbulent and swirling.

On the far side of the rocks, Josie barks. A wave has caught the dead seagull and is carrying it back out to sea. Happily, Josie's decided to let it go.

'Josie!' To Marietta's relief, the dog appears. 'Silly girl. Come on, we really have to go.'

Josie trots into the water, which straight away is up to her belly. A wave rushes in and she runs back.

The best way out of this predicament would be if Josie

would run back up the beach and make her way across the base of the cliff and over the outcrop, but how can she be persuaded to do that? If Marietta heads that way, will Josie get the message? Prepared to try, she begins to walk away, praying the dog will be brave enough to swim.

Instead, she hears a plaintive bark and whining, and knows walking away won't work. Josie's become too devoted to Marietta to think for herself, and if Marietta leaves her, chances are Josie will simply wait until she returns. Even if that puts her own life at risk.

And the truth is, Marietta's too attached in return to think of leaving Josie behind.

Marietta fastens up her trainers and scrambles up the rocks. On the far side, the descent is treacherous – the lower rocks are greasy with seaweed and the barnacles are sharp on her hands – but Josie is waiting for her at the bottom, running up and down with excitement, oblivious to the danger Marietta can see. When she reaches the shrinking strip of sand, Marietta picks the dog up, tucking her under her jacket. Josie is trembling; Marietta's hands are shaking.

Despite her small size, Josie's a significant weight. The route back over the outcrop is doubly hazardous with only one hand, but they're on their way out, and that gives Marietta courage.

But as she reaches the highest rocks and can see what's beyond, her heart stops. The beach is all but gone, submerged under roiling water whose depth – knee deep, thigh deep or up to her shoulders? – she can only guess.

Intimidating and grey the water rises and falls, and Marietta is afraid. Josie is very still under her jacket, her head pushed under her arm, as if she knows something is wrong. Inevitably,

Marietta thinks of her mother, of how it must have been for her, the fear and the cold. If her death was deliberate, does that make Alice brave, or stupidly naïve?

And if Mum were here now, what would she say? *Get out of there, Mari, get out of there now. Get help, and don't leave it too late, the way I did.*

Her phone shows no signal, but even so, she tries 999, praying what she's heard about miracle networks for emergency calls is true.

Thank God, over the breaking waves she hears a phone ringing, and when an efficient voice asks which service she needs, hugging Josie to her chest she says, 'Coastguard.'

Jubilation and relief.

At first there's only a distant buzz she's not even sure she's hearing, but the buzz soon becomes the roar of an engine.

Josie pulls her head from under Marietta's arm and pricks up her ears, listening.

Marietta bends down and kisses the top of the dog's head. 'They're coming. We'll be home in time for tea.'

An orange dinghy with a four-man crew: Marietta's so pleased to see them, she wants to cry.

One of them jumps from the boat onto the rocks, and her heart pounds. How will she dare to do that when it's her turn?

He's wiry and fit, but not young. 'Give me the dog, my love,' he says, and holds out his arms.

'Don't worry, sweetie, I'm coming too.' Marietta strokes Josie's head before strong hands lift her away, and pass her to a crewman in the boat.

'Give me your hand now, sweetheart.' Her rescuer patiently

guides her down the slippery rocks. 'Watch how you go,' he says, 'or we'll both be taking a bath,' and somehow Marietta laughs.

Where the sea hits the rocks, the water's choppy, throwing up frothing spray. Her feet are wet and cold, her jeans soaked through. From the sloping rock where she's balanced, he wants her to jump onto the boat.

'I can't.' She shakes her head. 'I can't.'

'Hold my hand tight,' says the lifeboatman, 'and when you're ready, you'll give your other to young Melvin there, and he's going to haul you in.'

Marietta can't help thinking of her mother, of how it could end. 'I can't do it. It's too far.'

'Take Melvin's hand.'

Stretching her arm as far as she can, she touches Melvin's fingers, and before she knows what's happening, he's gripped her wrist and pulled her across. Melvin and a crewmate break her fall, lowering her competently into the cold water swilling over the dinghy floor.

With no hesitation, the crewman left ashore leaps into the bows. The helmsman opens the throttle and they motor away.

Josie's placed in her lap, and a silver blanket's wrapped around them both. The men are exuberant, as delighted to have her in the boat as she is to be there.

As they round the headland and Selmouth lifeboat station comes into view, the helmsman turns round and smiles.

'Hello again, Josie,' says Adam.

After her heartfelt thank yous have been said, and Josie's been fed too many biscuits, Marietta is heading home when she hears someone jogging to catch her up.

Adam.

'You look shattered,' he says. 'Can I give you a lift?'

His car's a battered old Jeep. As he clears the passenger seat of CDs and chocolate wrappers, Josie jumps in the back as if she belongs there. Marietta directs him towards home, but at the final turn he stops and says, 'Do you by any chance fancy a drink? Because I could definitely do with one, and I'm betting you could too.'

Marietta shakes her head. 'Thanks, but look at the state of me. I'm absolutely wet through.'

Adam laughs. 'Welcome to my world. I spend at least fifty per cent of my life soaked to the skin. Happily I know a little place where they don't mind if you're a bit damp.'

She hesitates. At home there's a warm bath, dry clothes – and four walls to talk to.

'Yes, OK. But I've got no money.'

'My treat.'

She laughs when she sees the place he has in mind: a vintage caravan converted to a tea bar, decorated with hippy flowers and overhung with a candy-striped awning, parked under trees at the far end of a car park, where many of the vehicles have surfboards fastened to their roofs.

He fetches hot chocolate and walnut-studded brownies, handing Marietta hers before he climbs back behind the wheel. 'Glucose fix, just what the doctor ordered. And chocolate, of course, can never be wrong.'

'Unless you're diabetic. I noticed the wrappers. Sign of a true chocoholic.'

'Can I make an embarrassing confession?' asks Adam, as

they eat. 'I can remember Josie's name, but I can't remember yours. Only that it's something long and pretty.'

'Marietta. Friends call me Mari.'

'Easier for an idiot like me. You're shivering.'

She is, and in the after-effects of shock, she finds herself overcome with tiredness.

He starts the engine. 'Maybe we can continue this at a later date, but Mari, Marietta, I really think it's time I took you home.'

TWENTY-TWO

Fox returned from Spain late last night, driving home from the airport in the small hours to a pile of junk mail on the doormat and an empty fridge. Driving to work, he's looking forward to a cup of tea, and more than half hoping Budd might have brought in welcome-home doughnuts for breakfast.

But the office is deserted. His desk – cleared before he left except for stationery essentials – appears untouched, though the mess of paperwork on Budd's desk has spread to one of the spares, suggesting she might be making progress in one of her cases.

Fox turns on the power on the desktop, and as it fires up, checks the fridge to find enough of last week's milk to make a single mug of tea. Logging in, he opens up the online staff calendar and finds Budd's taken a long weekend and won't be in today.

Maybe after the holiday's excesses, doughnuts were a bad idea anyway.

Juggling ever-changing priorities has honed Fox's ability to pick up where he left off, though it seems a long time since he was immersed in the Baby Michael case. With any luck,

Jayne Hopper will have given a DNA sample by now. If there's a match to Baby Michael, that will be a massive step forward. If not, he could be heading back to square one.

A quick flick through his notebook reminds him of the case highlights so far: the key witness is deceased, but died with a CID phone number in his pocket.

As he drinks his tea, the fact that no call to that number was ever made is foremost in his thinking. When someone writes down a number, generally it's with serious intent, so what – or who – derailed Daniel Hopper's intention?

The question strikes him as pertinent, and possibly important.

Important enough, actually, to interest him in the circumstances of Hopper's death.

Fox's preference is to do business in person whenever he can; face-to-face lets whoever he's talking to know they're worth his time, and builds solid connections. Besides, the route to the coroner's office takes him past a supermarket, so he can pick up a few essentials on his way back. Budd would be impressed at how close that is to multitasking.

County Hall's a red-brick faux-Georgian building constructed on three sides of a quadrangle. No doubt on the architect's drawing board the design was attractive, but not even the smoothed lawns and curated flower beds stretching out front disguise the fact that – lacking any embellishments or flourishes – the utilitarian facade as it came to be built resembles a low-security prison. At the main entrance, the impression of a custodial facility is strengthened by the security circus, putting everyone who walks in the door through scanners and bag searches, even the local government employees the security staff know well enough to wish good morning every working day.

Fox accepts that he's an unknown, and that carrying a warrant card doesn't absolve him from the pat-down treatment. Either the county council's paranoid, or it knows it has enemies.

The coroner's office is at the end of a lengthy corridor on the second floor, well enough hidden that few people would be aware this place of sad purpose is here. Before his first ever visit, Fox remembers expecting Dickensian dark wood and black-suited clerks scribbling in leather-bound ledgers, but the office's reception area is airy and light, enjoying views of the lawns and furnished with low, contemporary furniture. In one corner, a water-cooler bubbles. The lavender-painted walls are bare, but for a notice announcing that violence against staff will not be tolerated.

The woman behind the desk looks up when she hears the door open, and takes off her reading glasses to assume a polite but interested expression. When she sees her visitor is Fox, she breaks into a broad smile.

'Well, hello, stranger!'

'Hello, Julie. How's tricks?'

'Look at you, don't you look well with your tan? Been anywhere nice?'

'Spain, Almeria. My brother's got a place there.'

'Shame you didn't ask me, I'd have gone with you like a shot. We haven't seen you in a while. I was thinking you must have retired.'

'No such luck,' says Fox, 'though I'm treading the standard route. I'm working cold cases, which is usually a prelude to being ushered quietly out the back door.'

'Anything I might have heard of?'

'Remember Baby Michael?'

'Oh.' Julie's expression shows her discomfort, a reaction Fox sees often when people are reminded of matters too evil to comprehend. 'Well. I hope you get somewhere with it.'

'It's about that matter I'm here,' he says. 'It doesn't help that a key witness passed away. I'm wanting to have a look at the coroner's report into his death.'

'I can find that for you. I'm afraid the fees have gone up.'

'I don't think there's ever been an occasion when I've come in here and the fees haven't gone up.'

Julie laughs. 'That's modern life, isn't it?' She hands him a clipboard with a form already attached. 'Can you fill this out? The paperwork doesn't seem to get any less.'

Fox finds a pen in his pocket and begins to write. 'I haven't got as much detail as you'd like. Name and address, approximate date of death, that's about it.'

'You'll never change, Russ,' says Julie, pulling her keyboard towards her. 'Let's get started, then. Give us a name.'

'Last name Hopper. First name Daniel, of Bleak Tor Farm, St Just's.'

'And when might we have seen him? I can search between two dates.'

'Try the whole of 2016,' suggests Fox. 'See if that brings anything up.'

Julie's fingers move fast on the keyboard, and her brow furrows in a way Fox has always found attractive. He keeps silent, letting her focus, until she says, 'Got him. October 21st.'

'You're a marvel.'

'And it's going to be right up your alley,' continues Julie. 'They recorded an open verdict.'

Lily has sacrificed her lunch to browse the baby clothes at M&S, even though knowing all these delightful things aren't for her – not now, anyway – brings on the familiar sadness.

Connor would tell her she's being masochistic, that she should buy something online, but Lily's persuaded herself this visit is an affirmation of future success rather than wallowing, and that the ache under her ribs is anticipation of future happiness rather than prodded grief.

She stares at the display for three-to-six-month-olds, hardly daring to touch. Rhianne's already overstocked with newborn clothes; she's shown them to Lily a dozen times, periodically interrupting her own excited chatter as she goes through the inventory to ask if Lily's OK with it, telling her she'll take good care of everything so she can pass it on to her when her turn comes round.

Ashamed of the deep-green depths of her envy, Lily insists she's fine, because she and Rhianne have been best friends since the beginning of time. But the truth is, she can't begin to understand the unfairness, why Rhianne's glowing through her weight gain and third-trimester discomforts, while Lily hides the losses she can't talk about, afraid the smile fixed on her face will curdle from jealousy and malice.

She lifts a pair of dungarees covered in foxes from the rack, replaces it and picks up a fleecy all-in-one with bear cub ears on the hood. There's a pink dress with polka dots and ruffles which is an absolute delight, but Rhianne's baby is a boy, whose name – Aaron – is already picked out. Then her eye's caught by a yellow jumper with red-uniformed toy soldiers round the yoke. It's perfect. Rhianne will love it.

She's short of time, but on her way to pay – even though she knows she shouldn't – she permits herself a detour through the newborn section. Just a tiny peep won't hurt.

In only moments, she's fallen in love with a pink onesie sprigged with daisies and the cutest mice. Sasha would have looked a dream in it. She holds it up to admire it, then presses it to her face to feel the softness of the cotton. Such a pretty thing, so tempting. What harm can it do?

She takes the onesie to the checkout along with Rhianne's jumper, knowing it will be easy enough to hide.

Because she's told Connor she's stopped doing this, and he believes her.

Haven't they always promised each other they'll have no secrets?

TWENTY-THREE

Sometimes, you're just unlucky.

Actually, Fox was counting his blessings, having slid straight into a generous parking space between an older-model BMW and a Kia Sportage.

But as he's collecting his bag from the back seat, someone's heading for the BMW, and Fox's heart sinks.

Liam Garrett's looking sharp as ever, in the kind of suit he probably admired in *GQ* and bought at TK Maxx. He's scrolling through his phone, and Fox thinks there's an outside chance he might not be spotted, until his car gives him away by beeping as he locks it.

Garrett looks up, grins, and slips his phone into his pocket.

'Hello, Russ. Are you early for the late shift or late for the early shift? Hey, look at you with your tan. Been anywhere nice? I'd like to say we missed you, but we never noticed you were gone.'

'That your Beamer?' asks Fox. 'Nice motor. I always say buy quality if you can't afford new.'

He's walking away when Garrett calls after him, 'How's that cold case coming, Russ? Let me guess, no breakthrough.'

All in good time, thinks Fox as he opens the Portakabin door. *All in good time.*

First things first. Fox is hungry, and settles into his chair with a ham and English mustard sandwich, a bag of Walker's cheese and onion crisps, a cherry flapjack and a fresh mug of tea.

The report Julie's printed out for him is on the desk, and he's keen to read what it says. As she pointed out, an open verdict – where the coroner couldn't rule for certain on how Daniel Hopper died – brings the possibility of another twist in the case.

As he eats, he does a quick scan of this morning's incoming emails, pleased there's nothing that won't wait. When he's finished his meal, he clears his rubbish away, and washes and dries his crockery at the sink.

Now he's ready to focus. Opening his notebook at a fresh page, he writes the date, location and case reference number, and draws a line with a ruler under this as a heading.

Skipping a line for clarity, he writes, *Inquest report into death of witness Daniel Hopper*, with the exhibit number he's assigned to it, and underlines that too.

The post-mortem report is necessarily technical, but Fox knows enough to work out that Daniel Hopper suffered from type 1 diabetes and what killed him was an apparent overdose of insulin. That's unfortunate, but Fox has some understanding of the increased risks of mortality among diabetes sufferers. He's also aware of more than one case where insulin was used as a fast-acting poison.

Daniel was wearing one of the newer-type insulin pumps,

which should have automatically provided the exact amount he needed. However, the pathologist reported finding a single puncture wound in Daniel's left upper arm, suggesting what would have been an unnecessary injection. The pathologist has supplied a diagram of the puncture wound site, and Fox touches the matching spot on his own arm.

Interesting.

He makes a note summarising the post-mortem findings, and moves to the report of the inquest itself.

The circumstances of Daniel's death are spelled out: he seems to have died alone, his body found by his sister, who had been away overnight.

Fox makes a note: *Where was Jayne Hopper?*

She gave an answer to that question herself at the time, telling the coroner she spent the night at a friend's home in Bristol. In answer to further questions, she found her brother cold on the kitchen floor on her return to Bleak Tor, and called an ambulance immediately, even though it was obviously too late.

A police officer from a local station reported attending and finding nothing suspicious about the death, and a GP was called to certify that Daniel was definitely deceased. No death certificate was issued at that time, it being the purpose of the inquest to establish the cause.

The endocrinologist called as an expert witness explained that rapidly dropping blood-sugar levels could cause severe hypoglycaemia – diabetic shock – which would undoubtedly have clouded Daniel's judgement. Was it possible he might have injected himself thinking he'd feel better? asked the coroner, and the endocrinologist confirmed that in a state of confusion, it definitely was, though the correct action would have been to eat a high-carbohydrate snack.

She was dubious, though, that the pump had failed. Lives depend on those devices, she said. They're tested and tested until they're completely safe.

So the inquest succeeded in establishing the cause of death, but the question remained whether Daniel had taken his own life. Miss Hopper testified that her brother had seemed distracted and anxious but not depressed, though she conceded the management of his illness sometimes troubled him. His new insulin pump was supposed to make things easier, but three weeks in he was still suffering highs and lows, which might, she agreed, have been the source of his anxiety. She blamed herself for not being there to help. As a diabetic, Daniel really shouldn't have been left alone.

As to the source of the insulin overdose – the expert witness confirmed it was not possible to overdose through the pump – Miss Hopper explained that Daniel had kept some of his old insulin pens in the fridge, not yet feeling one hundred per cent able to trust his new dispenser.

Asked outright if she thought he had committed suicide, Miss Hopper said emphatically not.

The coroner seemed less convinced.

In his summing-up, he laid out two possible scenarios: that Daniel had injected himself accidentally after feeling unwell, or that he had deliberately intended to take his own life.

Unable to rule for certain in the case, he recorded an open verdict.

But when Fox finishes reading, he can't help wondering about another possibility, which wasn't even considered.

Maybe Daniel was injected by someone else.

And if that someone understood the likely consequences of their action, Daniel Hopper's death should have been classified as murder.

TWENTY-FOUR

The essence of the English village, thinks Fox as he drives down Fordingley's main street, *with every cliché a foreign tourist could wish for.*

Undeniably, it's all here: ducks waddling round a pond on the village green; a mullion-windowed manor house with roses round the door; a garage with petrol pumps so retro they must date back to the days when driving was still called motoring. A red phone box, a tea shop and a quaint second-hand bookshop – as far as he can see, nothing's been missed, which makes it all the more surprising there's nobody about.

With its thatched roof and window boxes in full summer bloom, the Plume of Feathers is Fordingley's crowning glory, and yet on a Friday lunchtime the front door is shut. Round the back, there's no car park to speak of, only a yard over-strung by a washing line filled with bar towels. Fox seems to be the only one here, and it's a long way to have driven for nothing. Parking close to the kerb, he walks to the entrance and presses the latch, relieved when the door opens.

Inside, it's as he expects it, and as it should be: stone flags and a beamed ceiling, horse brasses and sepia photographs, an open hearth for winter fires below a smoke-blackened chimney breast. Deep-set windows make the room dim and yet not gloomy; it's a place with good vibes, as if it's waiting for the party to start. The bar itself is well lit, with an impressive row of ales on tap, and on a chalkboard a short lunch menu which may well tempt him to stay and eat. Top of today's list is a home-baked, traditional Cornish pasty.

As he waits to be served, the pub scores another point in Fox's book: no music. From the next room he hears the rattle of bottles, and knowing someone is close by, he pings an old-fashioned service bell with the palm of his hand. The ring it gives out is satisfying, and he wonders if the bell might be a risky thing to keep on a bar. If he'd had a couple of pints, he'd be tempted to ping it a couple more times, just because it's fun.

But the woman who enters from the next room doesn't look as if she'd tolerate that kind of nonsense. Her hair is bleached white and clipped to no more than three centimetres all over, showing off the large gold hoops dangling from her ears. She's stocky and broad-shouldered, in denim jeggings that feed into black and white Converse trainers and a T-shirt tight enough to show formidable upper arms, which though bulked with fat rather than muscle still look as if they'd power a punch that'd knock you flat if needed.

Fox moves his hand away from the bell.

'Now then, my lovely.' Something about her says big city, but her accent's pure West Country yap, rich and slow, and she gives him a smile unexpectedly warm with welcome. 'What can I get you?'

Fox knows he shouldn't, but who'll know? Such opportunities don't come along every day. 'Pint of Ferryman, please.'

She puts a glass under the tap, and as the brown ale flows, says, 'Don't think I know you, do I?'

'First-timer.'

'Thought so. I have a good memory for faces, I do, and I don't reckon I've seen yours before.'

'It's a nice place,' says Fox.

'Was my dad's, and my grandad's before that, and now it's come to me. We've all pulled pints behind this bar. They thought a girl couldn't handle it, but here I am.'

She places his pint on the bar, and Fox points to the chalkboard menu. 'I might try a pasty.'

'You're a man of good taste, I can see that. Made them myself this morning. You find yourself a seat and I'll bring it out to you.'

Fox chooses a table near the window and settles himself in. He tastes the Ferryman, finding it smooth with the right hint of sweetness. Somewhere, a clock ticks. Away behind the bar, he hears the rattle of crockery and cutlery.

The landlady isn't long in bringing out his food. The plate is large, the pasty a magnificence of golden pastry, carrying savoury scents of beef and gravy.

'There you go. Enjoy it.'

As she's turning away, Fox says, 'Can I ask you a question?'

'Fire away.'

'Do you know someone called Chancellor, Griff Chancellor?'

'Who's asking?' She dips her head, and peers at him closely. 'You're the law, aren't you? I wondered whether you might be. We don't get many as well dressed as you in here.'

Fox finds his wallet and hands her a card.

'CID, is it?'

'I spoke to Griff. You're not his aunt, by any chance?'

'As a matter of fact, I do have that honour.'

Fox holds out his hand. 'Like it says on the card, DI Russ Fox.'

Her grip is firm. 'Like it says over the door, Frankie Keast.'

'I'd really like to talk to you for a few minutes, if you don't mind.'

'Regarding what, exactly?'

Fox hesitates. 'Indirectly, the Baby Michael case.'

An expression comes over her face he can't quite read. 'You raking over those old coals, are you? I don't know anything 'bout that.'

'It'll just take a few minutes.'

'Well, I don't mind, but I'm fairly certain I got nothing to tell you. Your pasty's getting cold. Why don't you eat your lunch, and I won't be far away when you're done.'

The pasty's as good as it promised to be, though when he's finished, Fox regrets both it and the beer. Back in the day, he'd have taken the carbohydrates in his stride, but as he's got older, a heavy lunch tends to be a mistake, and he knows he'll be feeling a longing to doze before the afternoon's done.

More customers arrive as he's eating – a young couple who order non-alcoholic drinks and the light salad lunch Fox should have had, and a rural-looking youth in work clothes with black oil under his fingernails, who takes what looks like an accustomed seat at the bar and is served a pint of cider.

Fox waits to be reasonably sure the landlady isn't busy, and rings the bell again. She appears from the back drying her hands, and smiles. 'All done?'

'Yes, thanks. That was a great pasty.'

The youth finishes his pint and climbs down from his stool. 'See you later, Frankie.'

'See you, Georgie. You go careful.'

Frankie raises the bar flap for Fox to pass through. 'We'll not be disturbed out the back.'

She leads him through the kitchen, where a second youth who bears a remarkable similarity to the one who was drinking cider in the bar is refilling ketchup bottles from a catering-sized jar.

'Keep an eye on the bar for a few minutes, will you, Kev?'

Frankie leads Fox on through a store room, and out through an already open fire exit into a yard, a cobbled quadrant formed of outbuildings with tiled roofs dipping into curves, where ring doves coo on the ridges. Most of the buildings must once have been stables or cowsheds; the half-height rest were probably pigsties. Frankie heads for a covered area where it's easy to picture hay wagons and carts, though there's nothing there now but stacks of tables and dining chairs, a set of which have been laid out under the shelter of the overhanging roof. Fox glances up, wondering about the stability of the woodwormed, rotted beams.

An ashtray and a packet of cigarettes wait on the table.

'Have a seat.' Frankie herself sits, and picks up the cigarettes. 'Do you mind if I . . .'

'Your house, your rules.'

She lights up and inhales. 'Old habits die hard. Still, you have to die of something, don't you? Anyway, what can I do for you?'

'Daniel Hopper.'

Fox watches for her reaction, and sees her eyebrows lift.

'It's Danny, is it? What about him, then? He's been gone a while now, has Danny.'

'I've been wondering why he had your nephew's phone number in one of his pockets.'

Frankie shrugs, and flicks ash off the end of her cigarette. 'That's an easy one. I gave it to him.'

'May I ask why?'

'Because he asked me for it. He knew Griff was one of your lot. He might even have met him in here. Griff's been here once or twice, and I knew he wouldn't mind.'

'Did Daniel tell you why he wanted to speak to the police?'

'He didn't say, but I drew my own conclusions, same as you've probably done. I assumed it was something to do with Baby Michael. And here you are, so I reckon I was right.'

'Did Daniel ever say whether he'd spoken to DI Chancellor?'

'Never said another thing about it to me. Mind you, he didn't get much chance, did he? It wasn't long after that he died. That came as a shock to folk round here, I'll tell you. One minute he was here in this bar, large as life, the next we're all at his funeral. I knew he wasn't well, but I wasn't expecting that.'

'How long before he died did you last see him?'

'Well, I don't know exactly, not to the minute. All I can say is, he was fine when he left here.'

'He was here the night he died?'

'Yep. Till about nine o'clock.'

'Did he have a lot to drink?'

'He never had a lot to drink. He couldn't with his illness,

could he? So he never stayed late. I think when people started to get their drinking heads on and things got a bit loud, he felt left out, you know? It's no fun being the only sober one at a party, is it? He always used to have two halves and drink them slow. That was it for him.'

'Did he come in every night?'

'Not every night, no, but he was pretty regular, Tuesdays and Fridays mostly. I think it got him out the house. Living together there, the two of them – I don't think it was always easy. Brothers and sisters, they get to bickering, don't they?'

'Was he talking to anyone that night, anyone in particular?'

'I don't remember anyone. Just the usual chat around the bar.' She stops, frowns, draws on her cigarette, exhales. 'There was that guy come in asking for him, but Danny was gone by then.'

Fox feels a prickle at the back of his neck.

'What guy?'

Frankie shakes her head. 'I don't know him, but I remember him vaguely. Like I say, I have a memory for faces. My dad taught me a little trick to remember people. It's good for business, but it's a nice thing too. Gives folk a boost if you give them a bit of a welcome-back.'

'So what did he look like?'

She pulls a face. 'Bad news if you're wanting to find him. Totally average-looking guy, medium height, medium weight, hair quite long for his age.'

'How old?'

Frankie considers. 'Late fifties, maybe early sixties. He came to the bar and said he was looking for Dan Hopper. That sounded odd to me, because Danny always went by Danny, or his sister called him Daniel. So I had the impression that he didn't know him well. I told him Danny had just left.'

'What did he do then?'

'What you did. Ordered a pint and a pasty, sat down and ate it. When he finished, he paid for what he'd had and left.'

'He didn't ask you where Daniel lived?'

Frankie shakes her head. 'Not that I recall.'

'You've never told anyone this before?'

'Why should I have done? What's it got to do with anything? Danny's death was accidental, wasn't it? I don't believe them as said he killed himself. Like I say, he was right as rain when he left here. If he was planning on killing himself, I reckon he'd have gone about it with a skinful, not just a couple of halves.'

'No one asked you to state that at the inquest?'

'Inquest, me? No.' She exhales more smoke, and peers at him through it. 'What are you thinking? Not foul play, surely?'

'Probably not,' says Fox, 'but it pays to be thorough. If you think of anything else, will you ring me? You've got my card.'

'Yeah, course. What's this got to do with Baby Michael, though?'

'At the moment, I have absolutely no idea,' says Fox honestly, and he leaves her to finish her cigarette in peace.

TWENTY-FIVE

Partly because he's so close by, and partly because it's always good to remind himself why he's doing what he's doing, Fox drives the short distance to the hamlet of St Just's.

As he walks up the path towards the church, he sees the porch door is wide open and someone's inside, pinning paper on the parish noticeboard. He's about to step off the path and make his way among the graves to find Baby Michael when that figure – a slender woman wearing black trousers and a black shirt under a tweed jacket – appears in the doorway, studies him for a moment and waves.

Fox never needs more than that kind of acknowledgement to start a conversation, and he changes his direction to continue walking up the path, noticing as he draws closer the white dog collar round the woman's neck.

Fortuitous indeed.

'Good afternoon.' He holds out his hand, and she takes it. Her handshake's surprisingly limp, her hand cold. Her haircut's severe, and her face is covered in unfortunately unattractive raised warts, but when she smiles, the lines in her face suggest she's someone of unusually good humour. 'DI Russell Fox.'

'St Just's is honoured. Kate Northcott, vicar of this parish, for my sins. May I be of any assistance? Please do say yes. A visit from the constabulary is a rare glimmer of excitement in what's been a rather dull day thus far.'

Fox returns her smile. 'Good to meet you, Reverend. I've been here before, so I know where I'm going. I'm paying my respects to Baby Michael.'

'Ah. Our small unfortunate. Please, call me Kate. We don't stand on ceremony here. If you know your way, I'll leave you to it. I have neglected tasks inside calling my name. Dare I say I'm afraid I don't think you'll find any clues over there.'

'Never say never,' says Fox.

She's turning away when he says, 'Can I ask you about one of your parishioners?'

Reverend Northcott turns back to him, interest on her face. 'Of course.'

'Jayne Hopper. She takes a great interest in Baby Michael's case.'

'We all do. Such tragedies very rarely fall on one's doorstep.'

'She leaves flowers for him.'

'I think she feels a level of responsibility for his death, that she was nearby. Not quite survivor guilt, but something like it. It blighted their lives ever after, hers and Daniel's.'

'She must miss him very much.'

It's a slight movement, but Fox picks up on it: a glance away from him before she answers.

'I'm sure she does. They were very close. Practically joined at the hip all their lives.'

'If I were joined at my brother's hip, I'd have killed him years ago.'

She looks at him directly now, and there's wisdom in her eyes. 'Happily, my relationship with my own siblings is usually very cordial.'

Deftly avoiding further reference to the Hoppers, thinks Fox. 'Is Daniel buried here?'

The vicar nods. 'He's in the cemetery extension, beyond the far wall, where the newer graves are. Alongside his mum and dad.'

'Baby Michael's is a new grave.'

'But he needed only a tiny plot, and was a very special case. We put him where we could keep a close eye on him. He brings us a level of notoriety, and notoriety draws some strange visitors.'

'Does he have many visitors, then?' asks Fox.

'Some.'

'Any I should know about?'

Again, a hesitation. 'As a police officer,' says Reverend Northcott, 'you're bound by a code of confidentiality, as am I.'

'And you'll say no more?'

'Not unless I'm persuaded that it's pertinent and wholly necessary.'

'I understand.'

She leaves him, disappearing into the shadows beyond the church porch.

At Baby Michael's grave, he finds in the jam jar flowers a few days old, their blue petals still intact.

From idle curiosity as much as anything, he follows the vicar's directions to where he might find Daniel's grave, an area where the memorials are polished granite rather than mossy Gothic stone. St Just's is a small place, and the graves

212

are few. Daniel's is easily found, and he reads the engraved script describing him as a beloved son and brother.

In that order, thinks Fox.

No need for jam jars here; Daniel's memorial has a built-in vase for flowers – but the vase, he notices, is empty.

There's always a risk in turning up without calling first, but Fox has his reasons for wanting to catch Jayne Hopper unawares. And since he was in the district anyway, if she's not home, nothing's been lost.

As it turns out, when he pulls into the gateway of Bleak Tor Farm, the Volvo estate is there, and by the time he's out of his car, Jayne Hopper's in the open doorway.

She looks less pulled-together than when he was last here, more as she was when he first met her in the cemetery. Something tells him she's not too pleased about that, but he's not here to make her feel comfortable.

Anyway, her smile looks genuine.

'I wasn't expecting you,' she says, without preamble. 'You look very tanned. Been anywhere nice?'

'Spain. And the tan's fading rapidly. It seems to wash off in the rain.'

'It's not raining today. In fact I was sitting in the garden. Will you join me?'

'Gladly.'

'Can I get you some tea? Coffee?'

'Coffee, please.'

'Milk and one, isn't it?'

'Well remembered.'

She shows him round the side of the house, where a

cast-iron table and chairs stand on a small terrace with grass growing up between the flagstones. Fox sees no evidence that she's been sitting out here – no book, or newspaper, or empty cup – but he accepts as a fact of life that when you call unannounced, the downside is you're not always welcomed inside to view the day-to-day messiness of the unprepared visitee. The garden's a pleasant spot, and he'll be happy to sit there.

She doesn't keep him waiting long. She brings coffee for him and tea for herself, both in the same plain blue mugs as before.

'So,' she says, sitting down, 'to what do I owe the pleasure?'

'Just keeping tabs, really,' replies Fox, non-committally. 'I gather you gave a DNA sample?'

'Must be two weeks ago now, I think. Don't you have the results?'

'The wheels of modern-day policing grind exceeding slow, these days.' Fox tries his coffee, which is a little sweeter than he normally has it, but all the better for that. 'They'll take another week or so at least, I imagine.'

'What happens if something's urgent?'

'You get the right form signed in triplicate, and try and jump the queue.'

'Not too easy with cold cases, I imagine.'

'Next to impossible would be closer to it. There was something else, actually, if you don't mind. I'd like to talk to you about your brother's death.'

'Oh.' Her face is hard to read, somewhere between dismay and confusion. 'Why do you want to talk about that?'

'Just covering all the bases,' says Fox. 'When you have very little to go on, you tend to clutch at straws. Daniel's death was quite sudden, and the coroner returned an open verdict, as you'll know.'

'Only because he thought it might have been suicide.'

'As opposed to an accident, you mean?'

'Yes. What else would he mean?'

'Do you have a picture of Daniel?'

A barely noticeable hesitation. 'Yes, of course. Do you mean you need one to keep?'

Fox shakes his head. 'Not at the moment, but I like to have a mental picture of who we're talking about, put a face to the name. It's just the way I work. Call it a personal foible.'

'You want to humanise him.'

'In my job, you see a lot of names on pieces of paper. I like to be more visual.'

'I understand completely. Let me see what I can find.'

She leaves him briefly, returning with a photograph in a silver frame. Both the frame and its covering glass are free of dust, which to Fox means one of two things: either it's cared for and regularly dusted, or it's kept away from daylight in a cupboard or a drawer.

The mood of the photograph is cheerful. A tall man – Daniel, Fox assumes – stands between an elderly couple. All of them are smiling, raising a glass, the woman of wine, the men pints of dark ale. The old man's checked jacket and cap mark him out unmistakably as a countryman, and Daniel's plainly an outdoorsman too, ruddy-cheeked in a green quilted waistcoat over twill trousers, and a cap similar to the old man's. While he's not exactly handsome, he appears the kind of man women would feel comfortable around, warm-hearted and open. All the more curious, then, that there were no serious relationships, no marriage in his life.

Fox studies the building in the background. That pub could be the Plume of Feathers.

'How recent is this photo?'

'Not terribly, to be honest,' says Miss Hopper. 'That's our mother and father he's with. I remember taking the picture, not long before Dad had his stroke. Things seemed to fall apart after that. Baby Michael. Daniel's diagnosis.'

'I'm sorry, Jayne. Tell me about Daniel's illness.'

Miss Hopper takes a sip of her tea. A grey cat is stepping confidently along the top of the garden wall.

'Looking back, it seemed to come from nowhere. He was in his late twenties, and he'd always been in excellent health – nothing more than the occasional cold, and even that wouldn't keep him indoors. But he started to go downhill. He was always hungry – which wasn't that unusual – but thirsty too, and losing weight. When he began to feel tired, we started to panic. To be honest, we thought it was some kind of cancer. He went to see the GP, who suspected diabetes and sent him for urgent tests. After that, everything changed. His life became a non-stop cycle of blood tests and injections, don't eat that, eat this. He coped OK – Daniel was that kind of a man – but it got him down.'

'What happened that night?'

For a long moment, she seems to be watching the cat, which finds a spot on the wall it likes, and, stretching out a leg, begins to wash.

'Do we have to go through this?'

'I'm sorry. But for completeness, I think we do.'

He sees realisation in her eyes. 'You think that phone

number he had – you think it has something to do with his death? How could it?'

Fox takes time to choose his words. 'The thing is, Jayne, Daniel didn't obtain the contact number of a CID officer for no reason. If he was worried about sheep rustling or antisocial behaviour or vandalism, he'd have dialled 999 or 101, same as anyone else, and he'd have been put in touch with the neighbourhood policing team. But apparently he wanted to speak to a detective, which suggests to me he'd got something to say, and if he had something to say, there's a chance it was related to Baby Michael. Only he never made that call. Maybe he changed his mind and decided it was nothing, and his death was an accident, as you suggest.'

He doesn't go on, but watches to see if Miss Hopper is joining the dots.

And she is.

'You think there's a possibility someone didn't want him to talk to you, don't you?'

'I do think that, yes. But I need to stress, I have no evidence to support that idea. To be frank, I'm trying to rule it out, not rule it in. But I do think it needs consideration.'

'But who on earth . . .'

'With respect, you're jumping the gun. It's an outside chance, that's all. What we need to do is go over the circumstances of his death – and I'm sorry if that's difficult for you – and try and work out if there's anything there at all that suggests another person was involved.'

Miss Hopper shakes her head. 'I should have been here. He shouldn't have been left alone. But he told me to go. He said he would be fine. And he wasn't.'

'Where did you go, Jayne?'

'I have a friend in Bristol I see sometimes, for a change of scene. Nothing special. We do a bit of shopping, usually eat somewhere nice.'

'Did you contact Daniel while you were gone?'

'To be honest, I can't remember, but probably not. I've never been someone who's glued to a phone. I have one for emergencies, and that's about it, really.'

'But Daniel owned a mobile?'

'Yes, of course. Doesn't everyone, these days?'

'And what happened to it after he died?'

Miss Hopper watches the cat stand up, stretch its back into an elegant arch and jump down on the far side of the wall. She frowns.

'I never thought about that. It was only a cheap thing – he wasn't one to spend thousands on technology, no iPhones or anything – so I didn't worry about it.'

'You didn't worry about what?'

'That I couldn't find it. In fact, I've never found it. The coroner asked why he didn't call for help, and I told them he didn't have his phone close by. But actually it wasn't anywhere in the house. I hated to think it, but I wondered if it being missing added weight to the suicide theory. I thought maybe there was something on there he didn't want me to see, something he wanted kept private.'

'But you didn't say this at the inquest.'

Miss Hopper bows her head. 'No.'

'May I ask why not?'

'I didn't want his death recorded as suicide. Not irrevocably. What would Mother and Father have said? It would have broken their hearts, and in their eyes been a stain on the family name. To be honest, I kept thinking it would turn up, that I'd find it on a shelf in the workshop or in a pocket or a drawer. But I never have.'

Fox is silent.

'You're thinking someone could have taken it, aren't you?' asks Miss Hopper. 'But why?'

'Do you still have a record of the number he was using?'

'It's still in my contacts, yes. I couldn't bear to delete it.'

'Could you forward it to me? And the contact details of the friend you were staying with?'

Miss Hopper bristles. 'You make me feel like a suspect.'

'Not a suspect, only a box to be ticked. According to the post-mortem report, Daniel died from an overdose of insulin, even though he was wearing a pump which should have prevented that kind of event.'

'He hadn't had the pump very long. He was still getting used to it. There was a possibility he might have accidentally switched it off, or that it malfunctioned and he went into a crisis. We'd had incidents like that before, several times over the years, always very frightening with him pretty much out of it and not knowing what was going on. If that happened, I think in his confusion he probably headed for the fridge and grabbed one of his old insulin pens, which were still in there.'

'They were readily to hand, then?'

'Yes. We always kept them where they were easy to grab. Just in case.'

'He went to the pub at Fordingley that night, did you know?'

'Did he?' She seems surprised. 'No, I didn't know that. Well, he did go there quite often. Maybe he was feeling lonely. I do hope it wasn't that.'

'Any chance he went to meet a girlfriend?'

Miss Hopper shakes her head. 'If he did, he didn't tell me.'

'Is there any possibility at all that Daniel might have been gay?'

'Why on earth would you think that?'

Fox indicates the photograph. 'He was an attractive man, yet you say there were very few women in his life.'

'That was nothing to do with his sexuality, and everything to do with farming life. There's so little free time, and scant opportunities to meet new people, not to mention the fact it wouldn't be every woman's taste, living out here in the wilds. Such a shame for him, though. I know he'd have been a good husband, and he'd have made a wonderful father. Can I offer you more coffee?'

The hint's subtle, but Fox knows it's time to leave.

'No, really, thank you. I've taken up enough of your time. I'll keep you updated, of course. And if you wouldn't mind sending me your brother's mobile number and your friend's details . . .'

She follows him as he heads back to his car, arms folded across her chest. Either she's feeling cold, or she's pushing him away.

As he presses the key fob to unlock the car, he says, 'I went to the cemetery, by the way. I see you've been keeping up the good work with Michael.'

'I'm glad to do it,' says Miss Hopper. 'He should be remembered.'

But no flowers for your brother, thinks Fox. That's a conversation for another time.

Once, a long time ago, home to Fox was a house with a garden, where over the course of the summer Shauna turned three, he built a bench under an arbour. That arbour became a portal between work and blessed normality, a place where he could sit and watch things grow, hold the hand of the woman beside him, breathe deep and let it all go.

He doesn't have a garden now, only a trio of cacti on the second-floor kitchen windowsill, all of them indifferent as to whether he waters them or not. In this home, he makes himself a meal of oven chips and sausages, eats without relish and clears everything away. His plan then is to do his ironing.

Instead, he sits a while on the sofa, gazing out on a view of rooftops. Shauna was right about this one. He should have found a nicer place.

Picking up his phone, he dials her number.

When she answers, there's music in the background, loud voices and laughter.

'Hi, Dad! How's it going?'

'Hi, sweetheart. I'm fine, back from Spain. Is now a good time to chat?'

'You know what, Dad, I'm out with some people, so to be honest, not really.' At least she sounds regretful. 'Can I call you tomorrow? Oh no, wait, not tomorrow. Sunday? Are you around then?'

'Yes, of course, whenever you're free. I'll speak to you Sunday. Have a good evening.'

'Thanks, Dad. Love you.'

He says, 'I love you too, sweetheart,' but she's already gone.

TWENTY-SIX

Marietta has settled into work at the jewellery business. The job's pace is undemanding, for which – fragile as she still is – she feels grateful, and she's comfortable around Nancy, who's grounded and creative and keen for Marietta to learn her craft.

Josie seems to enjoy spending time there too; the attention she gets from customers is lifting the last of her depression, and when she's not being made a fuss of, she's content to curl up and doze under the display cases.

In a quiet moment, Marietta calls Tigi at the gallery.

Tigi answers in a low voice, and asks Marietta to wait while she heads for the staff room. Down the line Marietta hears a door close and the chilled music fade, replaced by the rattling of china and the running of a tap.

'Perfect excuse to grab a coffee,' says Tigi. 'We've been so busy today, getting ready for the exhibition opening tonight. You should come, Mari. All the great and the good of Cornwall will be here. And your uncle's coming. Warm wine and hummus, what's not to like?'

Tigi laughs the way Marietta remembers, and she smiles. 'Sorry, but not really my thing.'

'So why don't we meet up after?' asks Tigi. 'I'll be finished by eight, back in Selmouth within the hour. You and me and two pints of Sandford, just like old times.'

Now Marietta laughs. 'I couldn't stand the hangover. And I can't remember the last time I drank cider.'

'Then it's time you got back to your roots, girl. Come on, your choice, the Blacksmith's or the Red Cow. The Cow's probably got a band on.'

'Blacksmith's, then,' says Marietta.

'Fab. See you later. Let's say nine-ish. We've so much to catch up on.'

'Just before you go, can I ask you something?'

'Of course.'

'I had a call from someone at the gallery – was it Matt or Mark?'

'Marc with a C. He's the valuer.'

'He passed on an offer from Simon Orchard for our watercolours – you remember the seabirds?'

'Of course I remember. They're gorgeous.'

'He offered two thousand each, six grand in total. What do you think? Should we take it?' A lengthy silence makes Marietta thinks Tigi has lost signal. 'Hello?'

'I'm still here,' says Tigi. 'Wow, is that really what he's offered his own niece?'

'Apparently there's been a mistake about that. A story for later on.'

'Well, if you're not related, I should have no hesitation in telling Mr Orchard to shove his offer up his arse.' Marietta smiles again. Tigi hasn't changed. 'I can tell Marc for you, if you like.'

'So what should we be asking? Assuming we're going to sell them, of course.'

'I'd be starting around ten thousand apiece.'

Marietta feels herself flush. 'Ten grand? You mean thirty thousand for the three?'

'Three early works by a collected-by-everybody artist like him? You betcha, sweetheart. We've got a local artists sale coming up in October. It's massive, buyers come from London and everywhere. Put them in for that and you'll get thirty grand all day long.'

When she ends the call to Tigi, Marietta dials Lily straight away, and Lily annoys her by answering with a questioning 'Hello?', as if she's no idea who's ringing.

'It's me.' Marietta recounts the conversation she's had with Tigi, and waits for Lily's response.

'He's trying to rip us off,' says Lily. 'What a bastard. But I still think we should sell them.'

'Whoa, just a minute. Not at the price he's offered, we shouldn't. And don't you want to think about it? Would Mum want us to let them go?'

'I think she'd want us to use the money to do what would make us happy.'

Marietta sighs. 'Are you thinking about more IVF? You know, Lily, sometimes you have to know when to stop.'

'I have to go,' says Lily, abruptly. 'Maybe we can talk more over the weekend.'

TWENTY-SEVEN

Fox is on his way to work when his phone pings twice with incoming texts. For a mile or two he ignores them, but he decides to open them while stuck – again – at the temporary traffic lights on Birdlow Road, which appeared over two weeks ago and seem in danger of taking root.

Both messages are from Jayne Hopper's mobile, and they come with no preamble or sign-off, no *hi* or *hello* or *speak soon*. The first is a share of contact details for the friend she was staying with the night Daniel died. The second is Daniel's mobile number, which his own phone has highlighted for him to dial, as if it has some miraculous way to contact the dead.

And Fox thinks how much easier his job would be if only that were possible.

He's filling the Portakabin kettle when the door opens, and before he turns round, he finds another mug to make tea for Budd.

'Hello, Russ.'

It isn't Budd, but an admin assistant, a woman Fox knows

well from his pre-Portakabin days, who recently married, if he remembers rightly, some bloke from Traffic.

'Hey, Hayley!' He's pleased to see her. Mostly he appreciates the calm quiet of isolation, but he misses the sociability of the main building, being included in the banter and the chat.

'So this is where you've been hiding. I thought you'd left us long ago.'

'Reports of my retirement are greatly exaggerated,' says Fox. 'What's new and exciting in proper CID?'

Hayley spends a few minutes updating him on the gossip: friction between team leaders, a senior officer who should know better having an affair with a very junior colleague, a whisper of redundancies among civilian staff.

'And how's married life?'

Hayley's face goes a pretty pink. 'It's good. We're expecting a baby in November.'

Fox's congratulations are heartfelt. When he tells her she'll make a wonderful mother, he means it.

'Yeah, well, thanks. It'll be a change from this place, that's for sure. Anyway, I'd better get on. DCI Bradwell asked me to drop these off.'

She lays two manila files on his desk, both labelled with names he doesn't know, victims of unsolved cases waiting their turn for review. He owes it to their families to give them his attention, but he'll be severely grieved to pack Baby Michael's files back in their box without adding anything new. Once he's retired, the case's next review could be decades away, and he has a feeling he's on the cusp of some discovery, about to find a lost piece of the jigsaw and drop it into place.

But gut instincts don't justify delays in picking up other cases. The only thing that would do that would be a solid new lead.

'He's asking if he can have a report on the current case by the thirtieth.'

'No problem,' says Fox, inwardly wincing. 'See you around.'

When Hayley's gone, he sits down with his tea to consider the position. Before he has to move on, it's reasonable to have a period of transition, and there are still things he can do. He makes a handwritten copy of Jayne Hopper's messages in his notebook, then fires up the desktop and submits for approval a request for all data relating to Daniel's phone for one month prior to the date of his death, and two weeks after. If Jayne Hopper can't find her brother's phone, chances are its battery's gone flat in some corner of a barn, but it would be remiss not to check that. The records will show whether the battery died *in situ*, or if the phone was switched off, either at Bleak Tor or elsewhere.

Taking a sip of his tea, he dials the other number Jayne Hopper provided.

A woman answers with her full name, Rosemary Mears. Her voice is genteel, almost old-fashioned, and she sounds somewhat older than Jayne, but that could be the effect of her unfashionable speech.

Fox explains who he is. Rosemary expresses no bewilderment at hearing from him, nor does she question his identity. In Fox's experience, that suggests she's been tipped off to expect the call.

Which tips him off to wonder why.

'Really, this is an exercise in box-ticking,' he says. 'I'm

'simply looking for confirmation that Jayne Hopper visited you in Bristol on the nineteenth of October 2016.'

'Yes, she did,' says Rosemary.

'You sound very certain,' says Fox. 'Most people would have to go and check a diary, or at least have a think about it.'

'I have a good memory, generally,' says Rosemary. 'But it's etched in my mind because it was the day Jayne's brother died.'

'Actually, it wasn't. Daniel Hopper died on the twenty-first. I asked about the nineteenth.'

'Oh.' Fox can sense confusion and embarrassment coming down the line, and feels a heel for his subterfuge. 'In that case, I was wrong. She told me you wanted to know about the day Daniel died, so I assumed that was the day you mentioned.'

'When did she tell you that?' asks Fox. Silence. 'Rosemary?'

'I'm still here. I don't want to get anyone into trouble, least of all Jayne. She's had trouble enough in her life already. She only rang so I wouldn't be taken off guard when you called. Not off guard, I don't mean that. She didn't want me to get all flustered. It's not every day I speak to the police.'

'I understand,' says Fox. 'So Jayne rang you to let you know I'd be in touch and remind you exactly when you saw each other, in case you'd forgotten.'

'Yes. She was only being kind. She is a kind person, always.'

'And she reminded you that – what?'

'That she came to visit on the twenty-first. On the day Daniel died.'

'And you're happy to confirm that?'

'Yes.'

'You'd swear to it on a Bible, in a court of law?'

'Oh dear.' Another silence. 'I don't want to let her down,

but if it came to swearing, I'm not absolutely sure I could. But if she says that's when it was, then I absolutely believe her. Why on earth would she be untruthful?'

Why indeed? thinks Fox.

'Why don't you tell me about the time you spent together?' he says. 'What time did she arrive in Bristol?'

'It's hard to be exact after so long, isn't it? But it's usually late morning. We like to have lunch before we go shopping. That's what we do, go and have a good rummage round the shops. I don't remember that occasion being any different.'

'Do you see each other often?'

'Not often, but regularly. Usually we meet up two or three times a year.'

'And this visit was planned well in advance?'

There's a short pause. 'To be honest, I'm not sure it was. I think we had another date planned and she rang to say something had come up and could we swap? She suggested a day that week and I agreed.'

'So actually quite spontaneous?'

'About as spontaneous as we ever are.'

'And what time did she leave your house the next morning?'

'We would have had breakfast as we always do. Usually she catches a train somewhere around mid-morning.'

'And when did you hear about Daniel's death? Did she call to tell you as soon as she arrived home?'

Another pause. 'That's not how I remember it, no. I think when she called he'd already been dead for several days. She gave me details of the funeral in case I wanted to go, but in the end I didn't. I would have gone for her sake, but I barely knew Daniel at all, and she said there'd be plenty of local people there. She was terribly upset, as you can imagine. To find him dead on the floor and realise he'd died alone must have been truly awful.'

'I wonder if you have any way at all of checking the exact date Jayne visited you, whether you might have an old diary or calendar somewhere?'

Rosemary sighs, and Fox knows he's going to be disappointed. 'I'm afraid not, no. I buy a National Trust calendar every year – I'm a member and I like to do all I can to support them – and I write all my engagements on that. But I never keep them past the end of December. Look, I've known Jayne for years – decades, actually – and I've never known her to be anything but totally straightforward and honest. I really do think you can trust what she says to be the truth.'

But Fox has been in the job way too long to even think of doing that.

After he ends the call, he considers what Rosemary Mears has said. Jayne Hopper was in Bristol sometime around Daniel's death, but without definite confirmation from Rosemary, she has no alibi for the evening he died.

If an alibi is needed.

Everything might have happened exactly as she said.

But with so much time elapsed, how will he find out?

The joys of cold cases.

A quick scan of his emails reveals Jayne Hopper's DNA has finally been processed, so he submits another request, for comparison of her sample with the one held for Baby Michael. A hit there would be justification to continue with his enquiries. Anything else, and he might have to move on.

Glancing at the time showing at the bottom of his screen,

he sees there's a while to go before lunch. Maybe he'll work straight through and leave a little early, give himself plenty of time to get to his veterans' five-a-side match, which kicks off at six.

He moves the case files Hayley's brought to the centre of his desk. Placing them side by side, he lays a hand flat on each one, trying to sense through his palms which one talks to him loudest.

Definitely the one on the left.

He opens it up and begins to read.

At Rhianne's baby shower, everything's an excess of blue: blue and gold helium balloons tied to the gatepost, blue banners across the windows and over the doors. Even the kitchen's been painted pale blue for the occasion, with *Heaven Sent* in inflated gold letters strung across one wall.

When Lily arrives, Rhianne's mum is presiding over a buffet of dainty sandwiches and pastries, with a tower of blue-iced cupcakes as its centrepiece. She pours a splash of Prosecco into a paper cup, popping in a blue-and-white straw tagged with an *It's a Boy* flag as she gives it to Lily.

'I was sorry to hear your sad news,' she says. 'At least you can have a drink, eh? I couldn't even face a glass of wine while I was pregnant with Rhianne. Funny how it changes you, isn't it? Go on through, love, go through. The girls are all in the lounge.'

She's right: the girls – all Lily's friends, and several of Rhianne's relatives and nail clients – are already gathered, chattering while Rhianne delightedly opens parcel after parcel of gifts for her soon-to-be-born son.

Lily says hi and waves at everyone, and Rhianne – too big to easily leave her armchair – beckons her over for a hug. Lily hands over her parcel, painstakingly wrapped and tied with ribbon, and Rhianne gives her a grateful smile. As she opens it, Lily stares down at the presents around Rhianne's feet – a fluffy rabbit, a duckling mobile, matching tiny socks and shoes – and with a sick feeling in her stomach, fiercely covets them all.

Rhianne holds up the jumper Lily's given her and says how much she loves it, and Lily's heartbroken she's had to give it away.

Connor was right. She shouldn't have come.

She doesn't know the woman cradling her newborn in the corner, but wanders over to stand close to her, marvelling at the movements in the sleeping baby's face.

'Girl or boy?' she asks.

The woman smiles up at her. 'Girl.'

'She's beautiful.' The longing Lily feels is overwhelming. 'Could I hold her for a moment?'

The woman suppresses her misgivings, and generously says, 'Of course.'

Lily takes the bundle, cradling it as the mother did, finding the weight of it in her arms an instant anaesthetic for her pain, salve to ease the misery in her soul. Breathing in the heady sweetness of Johnson's and the faint sourness of milk, she's desperate to nuzzle the baby's face.

But she knows better than to do that.

Reluctantly, she hands the baby back, and Rhianne calls out across the room, 'Your turn next, Lily.'

If only that could be true, thinks Lily. Please, God, if only that could be true.

TWENTY-EIGHT

Summer's at its end; the lengthening nights and the changing weather say so. The wind has blown since early evening, rattling a loose tile on the roof, tapping the topmost strands of the honeysuckle on the window, seeding the delusion in Marietta's head that someone's out there trying to get in.

On these wakeful nights, Alice preys on her mind – or in truth, not Alice but her death. Unable to sleep, Marietta broods. Is it possible her mother felt she had reasons compelling enough to take her own life? What might have pushed her to that brink? Nothing Marietta's aware of would be adequate explanation, but her ignorance is irrelevant. Of course Alice could have been under pressures she never spoke of, though if so, Marietta's not sure she wants to know.

Downstairs, the clock strikes three.

Minutes pass, and she's drifting back to sleep when an alarm beeps close to her ear.

The smoke alarm; it must be. She turns on the light. Next to her in bed, Adam's wide awake, fumbling under his pillow for his pager, reading its message with screwed-up eyes before throwing back his side of the duvet.

He's half dressed in moments. 'Sorry, babe. Gotta go.'

No time for kisses. He carries the rest of his clothes with him, calling *I'll ring you later* as he runs downstairs.

Above the wind, she hears him start the Jeep and roar away along the empty lane.

The warmth of him is still on the sheet, and she moves to his side of the bed. The wind is blowing stronger, rain batters the window, the black sea will be roaring in the dark.

And Marietta is afraid.

The day after the storm, Fox has an appointment.

Crantock Grange is a handsome house without pretensions, screened by hedges from its neighbours and facing a view of a river estuary and wooded banks beyond. A rose garden leads to a sloping lawn, and beyond that, at the water's edge, a boat the perfect size for one man and his fishing gear is waiting at a jetty.

If I ever win the lottery, Fox is thinking as he turns into the gravel drive, *I'll buy a house like this.*

Judging by the number of cars already here, he's not the only visitor. He parks behind an aged but well-polished Mercedes, the only vehicle not obviously worth thousands more than his own.

Under the entryway is a brass bell-pull, a 1930s antique that ought to summon a housekeeper or valet.

But the man who answers the door is dressed for golf; he's grey-haired, short and round, not much taller, Fox imagines, than Danny DeVito. Owning a house like this, it's not impossible he has a private course at the back.

Fox introduces himself, and the man offers his hand.

'Felix Lindner. Please, come inside.'

Lindner leads Fox through an oak-panelled hallway, whose intricate parquet floor glows with a sheen of beeswax polish. A vase of showy blood-red dahlias stands on a mahogany table, reflected in an ormolu mirror almost covering the facing wall.

'This is a beautiful place,' Fox says, in genuine admiration.

'My father-in-law built it,' says Lindner, 'on the proceeds of the sale to an American of a minor stately home he was glad to see the back of, falling as it was into rack and ruin. Sound move on his part. My wife has a title which she almost never uses, though it comes in handy for last-minute dinner reservations. We'll go in the library. We won't be disturbed in there. She's hosting a bridge party this afternoon, and the ladies tend to get a bit rowdy when they start on the gin.'

Fox raises his eyebrows, wondering how many of the ladies are intending to drive home.

He follows Lindner into a room he'd expect to find in a country house hotel: tempting shelves of browsable books, both modern and antiquarian; a pair of leather armchairs at the fireside; and within their reach, a trolley filled with malt whiskies and cut-glass tumblers. Outside the French doors is a terrace, where a stone fish spouts water in a lichened fountain.

'Please, sit,' says Lindner, taking one of the armchairs. 'Can I offer you coffee? Tea?'

Fox suspects if he asks for coffee, Lindner will be using the bell-push in the fire surround rather than making it himself; and tempted though he is to see if there actually is a valet to answer the call, he picked up a Costa on the way here and so declines. Sitting down, he finds the chair supremely comfortable, an after-dinner haven for smoking cigars and sipping port.

'So,' says Lindner, 'how may I help you?'

Fox explains his role in the cold case unit. 'A case you were involved in is currently under my review, a 1993 murder I think you'll probably recall.'

Lindner nods, and makes a steeple of his fingers. 'You're going to say Baby Michael.'

'That's very astute of you.'

'It's easy enough to guess. I was a pathologist for over forty years, and you may believe me when I say I dealt with some very distressing cases. In the end, one becomes inured. One has to, or it's impossible to cope. I tried always to treat my clients – that's a euphemism, of course; the unhappy souls were never on my slab by choice – with the utmost respect, but I'm sorry to say I had to regard them while under my knife almost as specimens, because to think of them as people was damaging to my mental well-being. How could I weep for them all? But that poor infant, oh dear, oh dear.' Lindner shakes his head. 'In all my long career, I saw no clearer example of man's inhumanity to man than that child. Why else would you be here?'

'I'm sorry to ask you to go back over ground you'd no doubt prefer to forget.'

'With some things, there is no forgetting, Inspector. I was newly a grandfather at the time, and I remember thinking that you'd better get the bastard for this one. I'm pleased to be able to help you in your renewed efforts to do exactly that.'

'As you no doubt know, cold cases are notoriously difficult to solve,' says Fox. 'And I'm approaching the end of my review.

Without any new evidence coming to light, I'm afraid the file will most likely return to the archives for another twenty years, or maybe indefinitely.'

'Then I must strap on my thinking cap, and hope to dredge up something useful from my ageing memory banks. Where do you suggest we start?'

'In my experience, we'd do best to consider the kind of detail that doesn't get written down. Can you tell me what your initial impressions were when you first saw the body?'

Lindner's eyes go to the French windows, though Fox has the impression he's not seeing the terrace, but a day long ago.

'He was tiny, of course. Not newborn, but no more than a few days old, a fortnight at the very most. He had been well nourished, I think. They need constant feeding at that age. If he wasn't being fed, he would have been skinnier.'

'Someone had been caring for him, then?'

'I believe so. And I think that would most likely have been a woman, don't you? Almost certainly the mother, I always thought. But then why did she never come forward?'

'That's one of the questions I'm trying to answer,' says Fox. 'I understand you didn't find any fractures.'

'No,' says Lindner. 'That at least was a mercy. But I must be honest and tell you that some of the evidence was destroyed by burning, so whether there was bruising, I couldn't say. I don't think you need me to go into the details. Everything of medical interest is in my original report, which I gather you've read.'

'I have. I'm more interested in your personal thoughts, anything that might have occurred to you over the years, any small detail which might have been gnawing away at you.'

Lindner replies without hesitation. 'His feet. The shoes he was wearing, or should I say shoe. One was charred beyond recovery, I believe.'

'Modern techniques would have allowed us to collect much more data,' says Fox, regretfully. 'Back then, it wasn't the case. What about the shoe?'

'Hand-knitted, I would have said. Just adding to my impression he'd been looked after by someone who cared. That isn't much help to you, I suppose?'

'More help than you might think. I've been wondering if the killer might have been a woman.'

'Is there any chance he might have been snatched?'

Fox shrugs. 'There were no reports at the time of missing infants, though of course that doesn't rule out an unregistered birth, or an unwanted pregnancy – in other words, a mother who felt a measure of relief that her baby was gone.'

'It's an odd case, isn't it?' suggests Lindner. 'Do you have anyone in mind for it at all?'

'I have an outside chance, but to complicate matters further, he was a diabetic who recently died.'

'You're thinking he might have been the father?'

'Possibly, yes.'

'I'm afraid I have to cast doubt on that theory.'

Fox frowns. 'Why so?'

'Was he insulin-dependent?'

'I believe so.'

'Then it's not impossible he could be your man, but there's a strong possibility he suffered from impotence. And without going into detail, back in those days many men found the available solutions difficult to get along with.'

'What about Viagra?' asks Fox. 'I thought impotence was a thing of the past.'

Lindner shakes his head. 'Viagra didn't start working its magic on the male population until 1998. Whoever fathered Baby Michael would have had to do so without the aid of any little blue pills, so if I were you, I'd consider widening the field, Inspector.'

Chicken bhuna, chana chat, pilau rice.

Fox eats, washes and dries his single plate and turns on the football.

Shauna said she might ring, so he keeps his phone nearby.

All evening it stays silent.

TWENTY-NINE

The English autumn brings more drab skies than blue. In the garden, the leaves are changing to bronze and yellow, dropping to the ground in slow spirals.

As kids, this was a season Marietta and Lily loved, when Mum would take them up to Turner's Woods to hunt for conkers, and scour the charity shops on their behalf to make Halloween costumes, Brides of Frankenstein or black-cloaked vampires, red-mouthed and giggling with lipstick blood.

That's all long past, and to Marietta autumn feels dank and mouldering. Everything is sinking into inevitable decay, reminding her of what's lost and its insignificance: a life-changing misfortune for her and Lily, and yet the world carries on, regardless.

Where's the adventurer she used to be? What's holding her back? Why isn't she packing to follow the sun, chasing the migrating swallows to the heat of Africa or boarding a flight to Australia or Borneo?

No reason at all – except she doesn't want to go.

In her basket under the kitchen table, Josie's warm and well fed, untroubled by the blowing leaves.

Lily will be here tomorrow, and Marietta decides to bake brownies for her, taking comfort in the mixing and weighing and the sweet smell of cocoa. Baking is something Mum loved to do – her only culinary talent – and they used often to come home from school to the sugary scents of sponge cake sandwiched with jam, or flapjacks or – Marietta's favourite – sticky millionaire's shortbread. Both of them have inherited Alice's sweet tooth, and using her bowls, pans and wooden spoons is a step on the road to reconciliation.

The batter is made, and she's sprinkling in chocolate chips when her phone rings.

The Windrush gallery. If that's Tigi, great. Maybe she'll come over for a wine and chocolate evening, help Marietta chase away the spectre of an uncertain future.

But the caller is Marc, the valuer.

'Is now a good time?' he asks, and Marietta glances at the mixing bowl, where the baking powder will be losing its potency, and tells him yes, if it's quick.

'I've had another call from Simon Orchard,' says Marc. 'As you're aware, he's immensely keen to acquire your paintings, and he's asked me to pass on his improved offer. He's offering ten thousand for the three together.'

Through the kitchen door, Marietta can see the water-colours. In the weak light filtering into the hallway, they're muted and softened, beautiful. They deserve better than a quick sale.

But she isn't by any means sure Lily would agree. Tempted though she is to say a straight no, she needs to consult her first.

'Please thank Mr Orchard again for his interest,' she says to Marc. 'I'll talk it over with my sister, and we'll let you know.'

*   *   *

On Saturday morning, Lily arrives earlier than expected and lets herself into Trelonie House. Marietta is in her dressing gown, eating yogurt and honey.

Josie runs to meet Lily, who bends down to stroke her.

'She's getting fat,' she says. 'You're spoiling her.'

Overhead, a floorboard creaks, and the bathroom door quietly closes.

Marietta goes red.

'Is someone upstairs?' asks Lily, tartly. 'I didn't realise you were entertaining house guests.'

'It's just a friend,' says Marietta. She eats the last spoonful of yogurt and gets up from the sofa. 'Do you want tea?'

Lily follows her into the kitchen. 'I know I'm early, but Connor was talking about going out this afternoon, maybe over to Bodmin.' Marietta hears the slightest hesitation before Lily adds, 'You're welcome to come with us if you like.'

The bathroom door opens and there are footsteps on the stairs. Lily moves so she can see who's coming down, staring as she sees first a pair of male feet, then the whole of Adam.

As he walks down the entryway towards her, he smiles. 'You must be Lily. I'm Adam. I've heard a lot about you.'

'Well, I've heard absolutely nothing about you,' says Lily, and Marietta notices her lips purse before she gives Adam a half-hearted smile in return. 'Have you known each other long?'

She looks to Marietta for an answer, but Marietta's finding mugs, and holds one up to Adam.

'Tea, please,' he says. 'If it's OK for me to stay a few minutes?'

'Of course it is,' says Marietta. 'Lily, Adam was in the lifeboat crew who pulled Mum out of the water.'

'Oh.' Marietta sees Lily's attitude deflate. 'I didn't realise. Thank you so much for doing that. For trying, anyway.'

Adam looks awkward. 'We did our best. I'm really sorry it didn't work out. Sometimes, you know, things just go against you. Listen, on second thoughts, I'd better skip the tea and get going.' He touches Marietta's arm as he kisses her cheek. 'I'll call you later, yeah?'

When he's gone, Lily says, 'I didn't know you were romantically involved.'

'It's not as serious as that.' Marietta hands her sister tea, and puts brownies on a plate. 'Let's sit in the lounge.'

'I don't know what Mum would say,' says Lily, following her. 'A strange man in the house.'

'He isn't strange, he's perfectly normal. And I think she'd be pleased. A house needs both kinds of energy, Yin and Yang.'

'I don't even know what that means. Anyway, I didn't mean to break up the party.'

'You didn't. He had to leave anyway.'

'A lifeboatman, though. Where did you two meet?'

'I made you brownies,' says Marietta. 'Try one. He's a nice guy, and I appreciate the company, that's all it is. I get lonely here by myself. Josie's all very well, but she's not quite mastered the art of conversation.'

'You're a free agent.' Lily takes a bite of brownie. 'These are great, nearly as good as Mum's. So, what's up?'

'There's some more stuff of Mum's I was going through, and I think you should have a look before I make any decisions. And we need to talk about the inquest. Are you coming with me, or not?'

Lily shakes her head. 'I can't do it, Mari. I told you that. It's rubbing salt into the wound.'

243

'I thought you might have reconsidered. You won't get another chance to offer your evidence.'

'I don't have any evidence, any more than you do. I have what I know about my own mother, in here.' She taps her chest, over her heart. 'She wouldn't have left us voluntarily. That's all you need to say.'

'Oh, Lily.' Marietta sighs. 'I know how much you want to believe that, but how can you know it's true?'

Lily's face sets in an expression Marietta knows very well, stubborn and combative. 'You're talking to me as if I'm saying I believe in fairies, or the Easter Bunny. But I knew her a hell of a lot better than you did, Mari, and I'm telling you, she had no reason to . . . to do what you think she did.'

'I don't want it to be true, any more than you do. But people sometimes hide things even from the people they care most about.'

'Go on then. Give me a reason. One good reason.'

'She was short of money.'

'She was short of money for years.'

And I could have helped, a little at least, thinks Marietta. 'Maybe she was ill. Maybe that'll come out on the day.'

'Maybe she thought she had a shitty life and it was never going to get better,' says Lily, almost angrily. 'But we all feel like that half the time, don't we?'

Do we? thinks Marietta. *I don't think I do, not half the time anyway.* 'A chemical imbalance in the brain, then. She had those tablets for a reason, Lily.'

'She was our mother,' Lily says angrily, 'and your job as her daughter is to fight her corner.'

'Come with me, then. Fight with me.'

But Lily's face crumples. 'I can't, Mari. I just can't face it.'

'I'd better go and get dressed,' says Marietta.

When she returns to the lounge, Lily's on her phone, but she switches it off.

Marietta picks up a brownie and takes a large bite. She doesn't need the calories, but chocolate might help her mood. 'I had another phone call from the gallery yesterday.'

'What did they want?'

'Simon Orchard made another offer on Mum's water-colours. Ten thousand for the three.' Lily seems to be looking for more tea in her empty cup, but Marietta knows she's considering. 'That's about a third of their current value, according to Tigi.'

'We'd still get five thousand each.'

'And much less than they're worth. Do you really think we should let them go cheap? Mum loved them.'

'What would we do with them?' asks Lily.

'Don't you like them?'

'Of course I do.'

'So when the house is sold – assuming we sell it – put them on your wall, or I'll put them on mine, if I ever have one. Let's enjoy them, love them like she did, save them for something special, or a really rainy day.'

Lily's face lapses into that dismal expression which is becoming too familiar, gouging out lines of unhappiness that will soon be permanent in her face.

'Ah, come on, Lily. I know why you want a quick sale. But is that really the right thing to do? You're still young. You both are. Why don't you forget about all that for a while, relax, have a holiday somewhere? You might find that if you do that, nature will take its course.'

'That's such a platitude. I thought you had more sympathy than that.'

'I do have sympathy. That's why I hate to see you torturing yourself all the time. Maybe it isn't your destiny to have babies, and if it isn't, so what? There are other things in life. Kids aren't with you for long, anyway. They do what we did and leave home, and then where are you? You're looking round wondering where your best years went and wondering what to do next. All I'm saying is, why don't you do the next thing first?'

'Such as?'

Marietta shakes her head. 'Such as travelling. Such as seeing something of the world.'

'I don't see that's brought you much happiness.'

Marietta sighs. 'No. Maybe not.'

'Anyway, we are selling the house, aren't we? We agreed.'

Startled, Marietta looks at her sister. 'Yes, but not yet.'

'Why not?'

'Because where will I go?'

'I don't know. Rent somewhere. Buy a flat.'

'But I don't want to live in a flat. And what would happen to Josie? She should be able to stay at home over Christmas at least. I couldn't bear to think of her with strangers on Christmas Day.'

'If you don't want a flat, go travelling again. There's plenty of places you haven't been. Thousands upon thousands of them.'

Marietta lowers her head. 'Can I tell you something? Mum's death has hit me much harder than I thought it would, and coming home has been so strange. Wherever I was in the world, I had this house and this town in the back of my mind as Home with a capital H, but now I'm here, without Mum it's just somewhere I used to live. I don't have a home and I don't feel like me, I'm lost and I don't have anywhere to go and I don't know what to do. I'm right back where I started, and I don't know if I should go south, or north, or nowhere.'

Lily looks round the room, at everything that's so familiar, and understands what Marietta means. Even surrounded by things that were their mother's – the rug she chose, the carriage clock, the rose-patterned plate – the essence of her is gone. Alice made this house the family's sanctuary. Now it's just a building filled with objects she used to own.

'I really need some time to get my head together and find my bearings,' Marietta continues. 'So can we please not sell the house just yet? Let's take a few more weeks to lick our wounds. And I know it isn't fair, because this house is our joint inheritance and I'm living here rent-free. When we do sell, I'll make it up to you financially.'

'Can I have my turn to offer some sisterly advice?' asks Lily. 'I don't think home is a place, Mari. Home is the people who love you. I wouldn't care where in the world I was, as long as Connor was with me.'

'You're so lucky to have him.'

Lily considers. 'I know I am. Sometimes I wonder why I think he isn't enough, why there has to be a third.'

'Biology?'

'Probably. Whatever it is, it's a bitch. I do see that.'

'So what do you say?'

Lily shrugs. 'OK, we won't sell until after Christmas. But

what about the paintings? Why do you think Simon wants them so badly?'

'To complete his collection of his own work, is what he told me. Sounds pretty vain, don't you think? But I suppose that's the way artists are. Didn't Monet once take a knife to a whole exhibition of his pictures?'

'Sounds like madness to me.'

'The artistic temperament. And if he makes the right offer, we'll consider it seriously. Do you agree?'

'I'm not getting any younger, Mari,' says Lily, sadly. 'Don't think badly of me.'

Marietta moves to put her arm round her sister's shoulder. 'I don't think badly of you, silly,' she says. 'Everything will work out fine, I promise.'

THIRTY

Two days after speaking to Felix Lindner, Fox finally gets the result of the comparison test between Jayne Hopper's DNA and Baby Michael's.

Negative. They're in no way related.

Which makes a massive hole in his theory of the Hoppers' involvement in the killing.

Outside the Portakabin window, the leaves on the sycamore trees edging the car park are all but gone, many of them lying flaccid on the wet grass. The season's turned, in more ways than one, and it's time to move on to his other assigned cases.

And yet . . .

Somehow he can't quite let this one go. Something is there, a hint of a connection, glinting like a pearl dropped in the muddy waters of information and misinformation.

All is not yet lost. An open mind and time may yet bring a result.

THIRTY-ONE

Four months almost to the day after Alice's funeral, Marietta's dazed from lack of sleep.

At 1 a.m. she went downstairs for a glass of milk, poked the embers of the fire back into life, and sat a while with Josie on the sofa, watching the flames and thinking of not much at all. Back in bed, she tossed and turned for an hour or more, before turning on the light to read a few more pages of *The Phone Box at the Edge of the World*, wondering why her hyperactive brain couldn't process words on a page.

At 4.20 a.m. she fell asleep, and at 6.30 she was woken by the alarm.

Now here she is all ready to go, pale and woolly-headed with fatigue, nervous enough to throw up, uncomfortable in the demure dress and modest shoes Lily persuaded her to buy.

In her usual reliable way, Ivy arrives ten minutes before she's due, dazzling in one of her gaudy frocks and a shawl she crocheted herself.

Josie's delighted to see her. Ivy bends to stroke her head, but Josie soon breaks away to return to Marietta.

'You two getting on all right, are you?' Ivy asks. 'Looks

like you're fair stuck on each other. Is that a new collar she's wearing? And look at that, a lead to match. Your mum would never have bought that pink, though I think it's pretty enough myself. She always wanted everything dark colours, your mum did, grey this and black that. Me, I like a bit of colour. Cheers you up and lifts the spirits. You going to be keeping her now, are you?'

Marietta glances down at Josie, sitting at her feet. 'Nothing's decided yet.'

'You better tell that to Josie,' says Ivy, as Marietta hands her the lead. 'I'll bring her back about teatime, but you just ring me if you're going to be late.'

At County Hall, a family liaison officer greets Marietta with a sad smile, and leads the way upstairs to where the inquest is to be held. Marietta's expecting a courtroom, but is ushered into a conference room laid out as if for a middle-management seminar, tables at the front for the coroner and her entourage, rows of plastic chairs for everyone else. There are no flowers, nothing at all to say the matter to be dealt with is death. The FLO says they must stand when the coroner enters. If there's anything Marietta wants to know, she has only to ask.

The coroner is a middle-aged woman in a charcoal-grey skirt suit. She opens the proceedings by outlining the general circumstances of Alice Ansley's death on 17th June this year.

The first witness is Alice's doctor, who explains that he prescribed antidepressants because Alice came to him in a tearful state. She gave no specific reason for feeling depressed, only that things were getting on top of her.

An RNLI representative is called to give an account of

their response to an emergency call made by a member of the public. Referring to his notes, he says Alice was alive when taken from the water, and recounts how – despite the crew's efforts at resuscitation – she passed away in the boat. Asked if he has anything to add, he does. His understanding is that the lady was from the town, in which case he believes she would have understood the risks of being carried away by dangerous riptides. Once you're out there, anyone at all would struggle to swim back, let alone a lady of her years.

Marietta knows he's right, and closes her eyes. Everyone who lives in Selmouth knows those tides.

The coroner thanks him, and makes a note.

The pathologist who performed the autopsy explains the cause of Alice's death, talking not of drowning but of cold shock and incapacitation, atrial fibrillation and eventual failure of the heart. Many drowning victims suffer cardiac arrest following on from hypoxia, he says, which is essentially catastrophic depletion of oxygen in the body tissues. CPR is sometimes but by no means always successful. There was a high enough level of alcohol in her blood that Alice's judgement may have been impaired, though he feels he should add that people intent on suicide commonly drink to give themselves what is colloquially known as Dutch courage. In his opinion, regardless of the alcohol, for a woman of her age in the water for that length of time, death was almost inevitable.

A statement is read out, and Marietta's surprised to hear Laurence Byfall's name, wanting to protest that a man like him couldn't have played any meaningful part in her mother's life. Laurence's testimony is that Alice could have been lonely and distressed after their break-up.

A PCSO speaks of removing Alice's personal belongings from the beach. In her experience, they reflected a classic pattern in cases of suicide.

Alice's supervisor at work – a woman Ivy says Alice hated – reports dispassionately how her work attendance became erratic in the two weeks before she died. She called in sick three days in ten, and on two other days failed to show up at all. It was becoming a disciplinary matter. In her opinion, Alice had something on her mind, though what it was she couldn't say.

A second statement is read out, from a member of the public who saw Alice go into the sea, asserting that she seemed very determined to swim out beyond where it was safe, and didn't respond when people called to her to come back.

Then the coroner speaks directly to Marietta, asking her to come forward.

On shaking legs, Marietta goes to take a seat at the front of the room.

The coroner offers condolences, which seem sincere.

'We're here, as you know, to ascertain the reason for your mother's death, and some of the questions I must put to you may seem hard,' she says. 'Please try to answer honestly and to the best of your ability. Do you understand?'

Marietta nods that she does.

The questions to begin with are straightforward. What were Alice's circumstances at home? Had there been any setbacks in her life, any bereavements, for example? What were her financial circumstances? Was she worried about her health?

Marietta's dismayed to realise that all her dry-mouthed answers are second-hand, and that all she can do is parrot what Lily has told her over the past weeks. Asked about almost anything from her mother's life, without Lily's input she wouldn't have a clue.

'One final question I must put to you,' says the coroner. 'Can you offer us any explanation for your mother to contemplate taking her own life?'

Marietta shakes her head, and says, 'No. My sister and I aren't aware of anything at all which would make her do such a thing.'

As she returns to her seat, the coroner looks around to confirm there are no more submissions.

A few minutes later, a verdict is given in the death of Alice Ansley.

On the balance of probabilities, it's ruled a suicide.

But Marietta has no better insight into her mother's reasons why.

Archer Lane cemetery is a council-run facility of four suburban acres, where the graves spread up the hill towards the housing estate that has recently appeared at its northern boundary.

At the same time Marietta is leaving County Hall, Fox is turning in through the cemetery's wrought-iron gates, passing the empty gatekeeper's lodge and the notice listing the hours of opening, driving slowly through the grid of narrow tarmac roads, left, right, right, left.

Leaving the car, he picks up the flowers from the passenger seat, and walks across the wet grass to a grave marked by a small slab of polished grey granite, simply engraved: *Oliver Fox, Sleeping with the Angels.*

Fox crouches down, and pats the stone with affection.

'Hello, little man,' he says.

THIRTY-TWO

The fireworks over the bay are spectacular and uplifting, shimmering spangles against the black sky.

When the display's over, Marietta puts her arm through Adam's, and they make their way by the light of his torch back along the clifftop path towards the town, buffeted by a cold wind that makes her press in close to his body. Down in the dark below, they hear the sea breaking on rocks.

'Remember, remember the fifth of November,' she says. 'When we were kids, Mum used to take us up to the Millstone pub. They used to have a bonfire behind the car park –nothing special, toffee apples and sparklers and a few bangers – but we loved it. It was nothing though compared to what we've just seen. Those kind of displays were reserved for royal weddings.'

'I used to love fireworks,' says Adam. 'Now they make me jittery. The red ones make me think my beeper's about to go off.'

His phone rings, and they laugh as he presses the answer key. 'Hello? Hi, Darren, hi.'

The wind drowns out the caller's voice. Adam blocks one ear, and presses the phone hard against the other.

'Sorry, say that again. I'm on the clifftop.' He listens, and a frown spreads across his face. 'That's great news, thanks for letting me know. Listen, Darren, it's hard to talk in this wind. Can I call you tomorrow morning? OK, brilliant. I'll speak to you then.'

He puts the phone away in the pocket of his puffa jacket, and continues walking.

'So?' asks Marietta. 'What's the great news? I have to say, you don't look too thrilled.'

He stops, and turns to face her. 'I applied for a job in Norfolk at a microbrewery. Just on a whim, really. Fair bit more money, more responsibility, and it's near the coast, so I was thinking I could transfer to one of the lifeboat crews there.'

Now Marietta frowns. 'Why didn't you tell me?'

The wind has blown a strand of hair across her mouth, and Adam reaches out to hook it behind her ear. 'I honestly didn't think I'd get it.'

'But you did.'

'But I did.'

'Well.' She begins to walk on ahead, so her words are blown back to him. 'It's been fun while it lasted.'

'Mari, wait. I'm not going to take it.'

She stops. 'Why not?'

'I've developed an aversion to making more money.' He grins, and slips his arm back through hers.

'You should accept,' she says. 'You're mad to turn it down.'

'I don't think so. There's more to life than making money.'

She squeezes his hand. 'You know what, I'm absolutely frozen. Do you fancy a drink somewhere? We could head up to the Millstone, for old times' sake.'

'For your old times' sake,' says Adam. 'Totally new experience for me.'

They tramp the rest of the path in near silence, heads down against the wind, and Marietta thinks about her and Adam. He's going to stay around, for her sake. Does that mean she's also made some kind of commitment to him?

And if she has, is she being fair? When she emerges from the calamity of her mother's death, will Selmouth – and Adam – be enough for her?

The future holds so many unknowns. How can she know if she'll bring him happiness, or heartache?

Winter moves on.

On Christmas morning, Marietta wakes early, while it's still dark. The bed beside her is empty, and even under the warmth of the duvet, she senses the chill in the house before the failing heating system clunks and hisses into life.

This will be her first Christmas as an orphan, but the ghosts of other years gather round. Good memories, happy days: the bed-end heavy with the weight of a stocking; the wonder of a nibbled carrot and a mince pie missing from the hearth; card games with Grandma, coloured sprinkles on trifle, the pantomime at the Corn Exchange.

Wrapped up in a cardigan and Alice's slippers, she goes down to make coffee.

The little clock on the mantelpiece strikes seven. In the silver-framed photo next to it, Alice is laughing.

Marietta picks it up, realising it's the absence of what was normal – no tinselled tree, no turkey, the only gifts those she's bought for Lily and Connor, wrapped in red-striped paper

257

on the hall table – that makes her appreciate the trouble her mother always took to make Christmas special for her and Lily. As for last year . . . Better not to dwell on last year. She'd been drinking when she rang from Cartagena mid-afternoon on Christmas Day, and spoke to her mother for three minutes before she let some man call her away.

On the balance of probabilities, suicide.

In those days, not so long ago, she always thought there'd be next year.

Studying the photo, she sees lines in her mother's face she never saw in real life.

'I'm so sorry, Mum,' she whispers. 'Merry Christmas, wherever you are.'

With Josie on the back seat of Alice's old Renault and her overnight bag in the boot, Marietta's journey is on almost-empty roads. Where it comes into view, the sea is grey and choppy: easy to imagine the bone-chilling cold of it.

An hour later, she turns into a suburban road lined with houses of such similar design, Marietta is always doubtful about which one is Lily's. The UPVC doors are hung with evergreen wreaths; fairy lights brighten the hangover-grey gloom of an overcast day. Marietta parks when she recognises Lily's car in a driveway.

Connor and Lily's home is warm and beige, decorated with gold and red and an artificial Christmas tree, which – as Lily says – you'd never know wasn't real. In the dining alcove, cinnamon-scented candles are burning on a table already set for three with side plates, napkins and crackers. The house feels comfortable, well-ordered, grown-up.

Lily's looking undeniably well, healthier and happier. She makes a fuss of Josie and ushers Marietta into the lounge. Connor offers her a drink and Marietta accepts a glass of the Prosecco he's already drinking. Lily asks for apple juice.

'You, not drinking on Christmas Day?' says Marietta. 'That's a first.'

'Actually, we have some news.' Lily takes Connor's hand. Both of them are smiling. 'I'm pregnant.'

'Lily!' Marietta hugs her sister, and Connor too. 'That's wonderful!'

'It's early days,' says Lily, 'but we're hopeful this time he'll be strong enough to hang in there.'

'I'm so pleased for you. That's the best Christmas present I could have had. Well. Enjoy your apple juice.'

'Actually, I'm not missing alcohol,' says Lily. 'I've been feeling a bit sick, to be honest. And anyway, I'll have a clear head for beating you guys at Monopoly. Lunch will be a while. I'm doing a turkey crown in Mum's honour, but I cheated on the veggies. I got them all pre-done from M&S. Honestly, I don't know how she did it. By the way, look what Connor gave me.'

She touches a pendant at her throat, a silver-set pale stone whose colour alters as she moves, so Marietta can't tell if it's blue or pink.

'It's beautiful.'

'It's a moonstone, to help in pregnancy,' says Lily. 'Did Adam get you anything?'

Marietta laughs. 'Nothing romantic. A bottle of Bailey's. He knows me too well already. What did you get Connor?'

Connor holds up the phone he's playing with.

'Nice,' says Marietta. 'I got you guys something.' She hands over the gift she's brought for Connor, and he opens it, smiling when he finds a black case for his new phone.

'Inside knowledge,' says Marietta.

'For you.' Lily hands her a heavy parcel wrapped in glittery snowflake paper. 'Hope you like it.'

The snowflake wrapping hides a box of books and maps: coastal walking routes, a biography of a Cornish fishing family, a *Beauty of Cornwall* calendar for the coming year, and the *Wild Guide: Devon and Cornwall*, whose cover photo of a girl sitting in a tree-strung hammock might be of Marietta herself.

'It's a gift with a hidden message,' says Lily. 'I thought you could stick around for a while. Maybe explore where you're from before you rush off to see everywhere else. East, west, home's best. Especially since you're going to be an auntie.'

'Oh, Lily.' Marietta pulls her into another hug. 'That's such an amazing present. Thank you so much. Here, open yours.'

She hands Lily a box wrapped in white tissue. Lily takes her time, picking at the Sellotape, trying not to rip the delicate paper.

The box inside is branded *Ancestry.com*.

'It's a heritage gift,' explains Marietta. 'For us, but for the baby too, now. You send off a DNA sample, and they tell you all about your background and your relatives. Long-lost cousins in Canada, stuff like that. You've always said you'd like to do our family tree, so here's a place to start.'

'That's brilliant.' Lily beams. 'What a great idea. I love it, thanks so much.'

*   *   *

On Boxing Day, when Marietta has waved goodbye and Connor's engrossed in the *Top Gear* special, Lily carries Marietta's gift upstairs and makes herself comfortable on the bed.

The instructions are simple: spit into a plastic tube, repack it in the box, send It for analysis.

She spits, seals the tube, and packs it up with her unique barcode.

On the way to Connor's mother's that afternoon, she drops it in a postbox, and thinks of it no more.

THIRTY-THREE

The January squalls are icy, and standing at the window Fox sees what was – until a few minutes ago – merely run-of-the-mill, miserable rain has turned to sleet. The forecast is for heavy snow up on the moors, with road closures expected and the more remote villages cut off. On the weather map on his screen, Fordingley and St Just's are at the heart of it, and he thinks – for the first time in weeks – of Jayne Hopper, wondering how she copes up there at Bleak Tor, all alone.

Budd is running from her car towards the Portakabin, carrying a still-rolled umbrella she's sensibly decided not to pit against the weather. Her black raincoat flaps behind her, and the magazine she's holding over her head is doing nothing to keep her dry. When she throws open the door moments later, an opportunistic blast of wind blows in with her. She kicks the door shut, though not before the wind's carried several carefully arranged pieces of paper from Fox's desk to the floor.

'God's sake.' Crossing to her own desk, she drops the wet magazine onto it. 'It's blowing an absolute hooley. I hear they've given snow, so I shan't be sticking around long. That bloody car of mine is useless in bad weather. As soon as the roads get wet, all the warning lights come on.'

'I told you not to buy French.' Fox is bending to the floor, retrieving his papers.

'Sorry,' says Budd. 'I didn't mean to wreck your mind map. How's it going?'

He picks up the last piece of paper and places it back on his desk. One of his current cold cases is a trio of violent rapes, and a prime suspect with a seemingly unbreakable alibi.

'Not great,' he says. 'Actually, you might have helped me, giving these a good shuffle. How did you get on? Any joy?'

Budd's taken off her coat and is draping it over the back of a chair to dry.

'I'm making tea. You want one?' Fox nods, and she goes to the sink to fill the kettle. 'If I'm honest, I think it's no better than fifty-fifty. The defence put a load of pressure on our star witness, and instead of sticking to his story and just telling it like he remembers it, he went all doubtful. If the jury don't accept his testimony, it's not hopeless but it's not great either. Seems like the defence teams know all they have to do is ask if witnesses can be sure what they saw after so many years, and they'll do a bit of heart-searching and cave in. I've worked on this case for months, and on days like today I don't know why I bother. Have you eaten all those scones?'

Fox's phone pings with an incoming email.

'What do you take me for?' he says. 'I put them in the biscuit tin.'

Budd pours water onto tea bags, and as the tea brews, says, 'Do you ever wonder if it's worthwhile, Russ? Whether we should give it up as a bad job? Maybe I should have a change of career, retrain as an accountant or a librarian. I always fancied being a librarian.'

'You'd be bored stupid,' says Fox. 'Besides, even if we don't get far, we put the wind up a few who deserve it, give them plenty of sleepless nights knowing we're still coming for them. It has to be worth it just for that.'

'Maybe you're right.' She watches the sleet as it becomes lighter, airier, slowly turning to whirling flakes of snow. 'Will you miss it when you're gone?'

Fox unlocks his phone, frowning as he opens up the email.

'Russ?' She turns to see why he isn't answering. 'Russ? Are you OK?'

'Never say never,' he says, and holds up his phone for her to read.

She carries over his tea, and takes the phone. 'Ancestry. com? What do they have to do with anything? What does this mean?'

'That's the profile I set up for Baby Michael,' explains Fox. 'Someone's uploaded their DNA, and it's thrown up a match. Looks like Baby Michael has a half-sister.'

When Lily rings Marietta, she seems vague about what's happening.

'It's something you need to hear in person,' she says.

Marietta's on the beach, scanning the shoreline for sea glass brought in by winter's rough seas. The wind is bitter; Josie's not happy to be there, and follows closely at her heels, nudging her leg every couple of minutes to tell her it's time to head home.

After a slow Christmas, the jewellery shop is closed until

March, but Nancy's got the time now to teach Marietta some of her skills. Marietta's ideas are ambitious, and she's collecting pieces of cobalt-blue glass to make a necklace.

'I can't hear you very well in this wind,' she shouts into the phone. 'Just tell me, good news or bad?'

Lily's reply is distorted by poor signal and the thundering breakers, so all Marietta gets is, '. . . said we'd talk to him.'

'Who?' asks Marietta, but the reply's distorted again. 'Text me,' she says, and Lily is gone.

Moments later, a text comes through:

Agreed Saturday 2 p.m. at Mum's. See you then x

All Marietta thinks at the time is that she'd better remember to buy milk.

On Saturday, there's more rain.

Lily climbs from her car and runs up the path. Marietta's waiting in the doorway, and expects a hug or peck on the cheek, but Lily seems preoccupied. Marietta puts it down to stress from driving in the terrible weather.

Lily shakes the rain from her parka and hangs it over the banister. She's dressed for the cold – a thick jumper over a wool skirt and opaque tights – but despite her heavy clothing, she seems to have lost weight. The healthy glow she had at Christmas is gone.

'Are you OK?' asks Marietta. 'You look very pale.'

'Morning sickness,' says Lily, 'except it lasts all day.'

'Can I get you anything?'

Lily dips into her handbag, and produces a sachet of ginger tea.

'Go and sit down,' says Marietta. 'I'll make you a cup.'

In the lounge, the fire is burning well, and Josie's stretched out on the hearthrug enjoying the warmth. Lily curls up on the sofa, holding a cushion to her stomach. Marietta brings her ginger tea, but Lily shakes her head at the offer of Jaffa Cakes.

'I thought they were your favourite.' Marietta sits in the rocking chair, the plate of biscuits near to hand.

'They are, but just at the moment, chocolate . . .' Lily looks as if she might heave.

'Do you need a bucket?'

'I'll be fine when I've had this. Well, closer to fine.'

'So, what's been going on? What's this thing I have to be told to my face?'

Lily takes a deep breath. 'We have a brother.'

'What?'

'Well, a half-brother. I got my DNA test results from the Ancestry website, and they came with a heads-up that somewhere out there, there's another Ansley sibling. We two are now three.'

Marietta stares at her.

'Aren't you going to say anything?' asks Lily.

'I don't know what to say. I'm in shock. Are you sure?'

Lily shrugs. 'The science doesn't lie, apparently.'

'Wait a minute, though – a half-brother? So which half, Mum or Dad?'

'Mum.'

'How do you know?'

'Because of what I've done so far on our family tree. I've got both sets of grandparents on there, and some of our admittedly fairly distant relatives have uploaded DNA too. The match is definitely on Mum's side, not Dad's.'

'She had another baby.'

'Yes.'

'And she never told us.'

'No.'

'Is he alive?'

Again, Lily shrugs. 'To be honest, I don't know. I didn't find anyone who might obviously be him, but I'm hardly an expert in genealogy, am I? I wondered if maybe she had him adopted. If she did, he'd have a different name, not Ansley.'

'But why didn't she ever say? Why don't we remember him? Is he younger or older than us?'

'I've no idea. But there's more. Almost as soon as that match popped up – and while I was still reeling, to be honest – I had a message about it. From a policeman.'

'A policeman? Why?'

'I don't know. But he was very insistent. I suppose we'll find out when he gets here.'

'For Christ's sake, Lily, how do you know he's a policeman? He could be anyone. You never gave him this address?'

'He's genuine, Mari. He sent me his credentials and I checked them out. Anyway, I want to know what he has to say, don't you?'

'Maybe our brother's a murderer or a bank robber. Then what would we do? Go on prison visits?'

'I can't imagine it'll be as exciting as that,' says Lily, and she sips her ginger tea.

THIRTY-FOUR

Four decades, or five? However many years have passed, it's a long time since Fox was last in Selmouth, brought down for a day trip by his grandparents all the way from Exeter for a treat.

Even in the winter shutdown, he sees things are a great deal changed – the place is smarter, cleaner, wealthier – though it's heartening there's still a fishing fleet in the harbour.

The rain has finally stopped. The harbour car parks are all but empty, and he decides to leave his car there and walk where he's going; Selmouth's a small place, and he could do with stretching his legs. And walking will give him thinking time, let him settle on how to proceed. The kind of trauma he's bringing this family needs a sensitive approach.

He walks slowly up the hill, thinking about what this meeting might mean, for the case, for the people he's about to meet. For him, it could bring the end of the road into sight, and they might come to wish they'd never laid eyes on him. Winners and losers. In this job, it's always the way.

At the end of the lane, he stops and checks his watch, finding he's a few minutes early. Normally he'd wait, but it's raining again.

At Trelonie House, he pushes open a gate in need of some repair.

He lifts the anchor-shaped brass knocker, and raps on the door.

Fox is glad to take a seat near the fire, and accepts the offer of coffee, mainly to ease into the interview.

With a mug and a plate of Jaffa Cakes in front of him, he takes out his notebook and voice recorder and receives their consent to record the conversation.

'You'll be wondering why I'm here, I'm sure,' he says, and explains his role in the cold case unit. 'I've been working on a case for some time, and I must say, Lily, I'm regarding your DNA match as a potential breakthrough. Let's come to why that is in a moment. First of all, can I ask about your mother? I remember you said that according to Ancestry.com, this match with your half-brother is on her side.'

'That's what they said,' confirms Lily. 'And the dots on the site seem to join up with a few distant relatives.'

'Is your mother still alive?' Mentally, Fox has everything crossed for a positive answer. Alive, she'd be a fresh witness, a new suspect, a game-changer.

But Lily's shaking her head. 'She died in June last year.'

'I'm sorry to hear that.'

'Do you know where our brother is?' asks Marietta. 'Is he in some kind of trouble?'

The moment Fox can't avoid has come earlier than he wanted. He takes a breath.

'I'm afraid I have bad news, which will be a blow to you, since you've only just learned of his existence. It's my strong belief he was the victim in a murder case.'

'Murder?' Lily has gone shockingly pale.

'I can't believe it.' Marietta's shaking her head, and her face has also lost colour. 'We've only just found out about him, and it's too late.'

'When did he die?' asks Lily.

'Very soon after his birth, in 1993,' says Fox. 'He was only a few days old.'

Lily's hands go to her cheeks, and Fox is afraid she might cry.

'He was murdered as a baby?' asks Marietta, quietly.

'Yes.'

'We weren't much more than babies ourselves then. How did Mum cope with such a tragedy? She never even told us, she never said a word.'

'I'm afraid I can't hide from you that you'll find the details of the case difficult,' says Fox. 'Your brother's murder was sensational at the time, and the press coverage was extensive. Since he was unidentified, they gave him a name, and called him Baby Michael.'

'Oh my God.' Marietta taps Lily's arm. 'There was a piece about him in one of the local rags Mum left lying around. She must have seen it.'

'That article was down to me,' admits Fox. 'I had them run it to see if it would stir any memories.'

'What if . . .' Marietta glances at Lily. 'You don't think that had anything to do with why Mum . . . you know?'

Lily shakes her head. 'It couldn't be.'

'What are you thinking?' Fox asks.

Marietta looks at Lily for permission to respond, but when Lily shakes her head again, she replies anyway. 'The coroner ruled her death a suicide.'

'It's not true,' insists Lily. 'She would never have left us on purpose.'

'Can you remember exactly when she died?'

'The seventeenth of June,' says Lily, without hesitation.

Twenty-five years to the day after Baby Michael's death. To Fox, that's a very low probability of coincidence.

'You can't think our mother was involved?' asks Marietta. 'In his death, I mean.'

Fox stalls by taking a drink of his coffee.

'The thing is this,' he says, carefully, 'of course we'll be doing our own tests, but from your DNA, Lily, it very much appears that your mother was also Baby Michael's mother. So at the very least, she failed to report her child missing, and at the very worst, she may have been responsible for his death, or she may have known who was. Yet she failed to come forward in what was a very high-profile case. Now you tell me she took her own life on the anniversary of the baby's death. I'm afraid that sounds to me like she knew her part in this tragedy was about to come to light.'

'No,' says Lily. 'I won't listen to this. Our mother was the sweetest, kindest woman . . .'

Marietta recalls her own pregnancy, the shouting, tears and trauma, the disturbing anger in her mother's face. Lily knows this sorry story but won't acknowledge it, and her rose-tinted world view is frustrating. Of course their mother could be kind and sweet, but she was also sometimes difficult, short-tempered and demanding. No one is all good, or all bad.

What more proof of Mum's imperfections could Lily ask for than the news this policeman is telling them?

And yet how can Marietta believe something this bad?

'Maybe Mum gave the baby away,' she suggests. 'Maybe that was the extent of her involvement.'

'There are proper procedures for adoption in this country,' says Fox. 'I hardly need to say giving your child to someone you don't know is reckless in the extreme, and if she took money for him, that's a criminal offence. And supposing she did ill-advisedly or illegally give your brother away, it comes back to why she didn't come forward. I can't sugar-coat this for you. Your mother was a person wanted in connection to a murder inquiry for almost twenty-five years. That's a long time to keep silent if you have nothing to hide.'

'Someone might have threatened her,' insists Marietta. 'What about the father?'

'Do you have any idea who the father might have been?' asks Fox.

Marietta shakes his head. 'Not our dad. He died when I was three.'

'Can you think of anyone else?'

'Not really. Our grandmother might have known, but she died some years ago.'

'Did your mother have any close friends she might have confided in?'

Marietta thinks back to the funeral, to the Christmas card list and the contacts in Alice's phone. 'She didn't have many who stayed friends over her whole life. In fact I can only think of one. She came to the funeral. You talked to her, Lily, the blonde woman – what was her name? Barbara somebody.'

'Barbara Constant. She was just a crazy old bat.'

'If you'll let me have her details, I'll speak to her,' says Fox.

'And there's Uncle Simon,' continues Marietta. 'Not our

real uncle, as it turns out. I think he helped Mum out a bit after Dad died.'

Fox looks at her, and Marietta reads his mind: an uncle not really an uncle, helping out a young mother recently widowed. Suddenly Uncle Simon's a person of interest to the police, and the world is unravelling.

'Can I ask you something?' Lily's expression is hard to read, somewhere between outrage and grief. 'Do you know where he is? You know, our brother's remains? I think I'd like to go and see him.'

'He's in a good place,' says Fox. 'When you've had a chance to digest what I've told you, we'll be happy to arrange for you to pay your respects. I should warn you this breakthrough – because I believe that's what it is – will potentially attract a lot of public interest, though we'll do our best to shield you where we can.'

'You mean people will come here, don't you?' asks Marietta. 'The press.'

'I think it's likely, yes,' admits Fox. 'It's very difficult for us to keep things under wraps longer-term. You may find friends and neighbours surprisingly susceptible to offers of cash for information, and you should be prepared for that. In the meantime, there are a couple of things we'll be needing from you, if you don't mind. Do you have a recent picture of your mother?'

'Lily's got some digital ones,' says Marietta. 'We can forward you one of those.'

'And a DNA sample for us to do our own test. If you've kept a hairbrush or comb, maybe a lipstick or make-up brush—'

'No,' says Lily. 'You're not having any of those things.'

273

'He's only doing his job, Lily,' says Marietta.

'It's fine,' says Fox. 'This is a huge shock, and I know it's a lot to take in. Why don't you take a couple of days to process what we've discussed, then maybe we can talk again. Would that be acceptable?'

'How will you find out who the father was?' asks Lily. 'He has to be your prime suspect, doesn't he?'

'That comes down to detective work,' says Fox. 'As I say, you may be in the best position to help us. If you'll let me have contact details for Mrs Constant and your uncle, it's a place for me to start.'

'I can do that,' says Marietta, 'but I only have an email address for Uncle Simon. We contacted him initially through a gallery where he sells some of his work.'

'An art gallery?'

'Yes. He's an artist, quite well known, apparently.'

'The most important thing is that Mum's name doesn't come out,' insists Lily. 'She deserves to be left in peace.'

'I can't make any promises, I'm afraid, Lily,' says Fox. 'If she's committed a crime, it will be in the public domain. But we're a long way off that. For the time being, no one will know.'

'I want it to stay that way,' says Lily. 'And we'll be taking legal advice, won't we, Mari?'

Marietta sees Fox to the door, and points out the trio of watercolours.

'Those are Uncle Simon's work,' she says. 'I'm sorry, I sound like a child, referring to him that way. Old habits.'

Fox looks at the paintings. The artist's style is distinctive, and for some reason, familiar.

On the way back to his car, his mind runs back over the interview. For him, it went as well as he might expect. For them, it changed their lives.

And the tough road ahead of them is only beginning.

When she's shown Fox out, Marietta returns to the lounge.

The fire is burning low. Crossing to the hearth, she pulls a couple of pieces of wood from the basket and drops them on the embers. In her sleep, Josie's twitching, chasing phantom rabbits again.

Lily is still on the sofa, hugging the cushion tight, staring at the fireplace, where a twirl of smoke is beginning to rise from the scorched bark of a pine log.

Marietta takes the armchair, and for a while sits in silence. Can what they've been told possibly be true? How could Alice have kept such a secret? Such an unpleasant improbability is the fabric of bad dreams.

Yet undeniably, the policeman was here. His empty coffee cup is there to prove it.

'I don't know what to say.' She glances across at Lily, who appears almost catatonic, zoned out from the world. 'What should we do?'

Lily focuses on her slowly, as if waking from her own bad dream. 'Mum would have told us. She would have told me, anyway. She and I were close. And do you know what I'm thinking?' Tears fill her eyes. 'If she did kill herself, then she did the right thing, didn't she? Because if she was still here, that policeman would be coming back to arrest her. And it's all my fault. I shouldn't have done that stupid test.'

Marietta senses the growing heat of blame. 'I didn't know

275

what would happen, Lily. How could I have known? I thought it was a gift you'd love, just some harmless thing.'

'Well it wasn't, was it?' Lily throws the cushion away from herself. 'Our family's totally wrecked. We'll be the talk of the county, the talk of the whole country, probably. How will we stand it? People will be calling her a murderer.'

'Lily, stop it. No one's suggesting that.'

'Aren't they? He's saying she should have come forward, that because she didn't she had something to hide, and he's right. That test has opened a can of worms the size of a planet, and I should never have taken it. What would she say if she knew what I've done?'

'You haven't done anything. This is all down to Mum. I loved her too, but what the hell was she doing keeping secrets like that? We had a brother, and she never told us. That's odd enough in itself, but a brother who was murdered? So it looks like she wasn't quite the saint you always thought.'

Lily jumps up from the sofa, her face tight with anger. 'Why didn't you stay far away? You weren't interested in us anyway, and now you've ruined her reputation for ever.'

Her words hurt; Marietta feels a weight in her chest, and an urge to cry. But the accusation is unjustified, and makes her angry, too.

'Oh no you don't. She did that herself. Obviously she was keeping plenty hidden, and she chose not to trust us. Neither of us, Lily. She didn't trust you or me. Now it's come crashing down on our heads, and we're completely unprepared, and you should be angry with her for that, not me. Fine, they found out through that DNA test, but probably they'd have found out by other means eventually. Would you still be blaming me for everything then? All I did was innocently buy you a Christmas present, in total ignorance of a humongous skeleton Mum had shoved way back in the family closet. Where are you going?'

Lily's heading for the door. 'Home.'

'Fine, go. But you know what? When you've had time to think, you'll realise I'm right. You have to face the fact she wasn't perfect. She did something really bad, and you and I need to stick together to get through this. And for God's sake don't slam the door on your way out.'

THIRTY-FIVE

Marietta sits on alone, barely noticing as the room grows dark around her until Josie – missing her afternoon walk – nudges her legs.

Though walking has always been therapy for Marietta's low moods, she has neither appetite nor energy for it now. Getting up from the armchair, she turns on a lamp and draws the curtains, wondering how the room appears the same when everything is so changed. The policeman's visit has twisted the kaleidoscope of their lives, scattering the pieces into a disturbing new pattern. This house – their childhood home – is no sanctuary, but part of an infamous murder case.

Marietta knows the nation's appetites. Soon – in days, or weeks – the media pressure will begin, and reporters will gather at the front gate, alongside the curious public posing for selfies. The hiatus between her old life and her future is suddenly over. The house must be disposed of – if it can be, with this new infamy – and she must move on.

Shock, sadness, shame: the collision of emotions is distressing. The woman she and Lily called mother betrayed them, abandoning them to notoriety, leaving them unprepared for lives where they'll meet hostility and suffer intrusion. She regrets her argument with Lily. Lily was entitled to her anger, misdirected though it was.

Poor Lily. Just when she thought she had all she wanted, her happiness takes a hammer blow. She and Connor may have to move house too, switch jobs, even change their names.

Marietta lets Josie out into the back garden, finds her bowl and prepares her dinner. She herself has no appetite, not even for wine.

While Josie's eating, she heads back into the lounge and banks up the fire. She leaves Alice's candles unlit. Settling on the sofa, she powers up her laptop, keys *Baby Michael murder* into a Google search page and presses enter.

Her search returns more than four million results, and the policeman, it seems, was kind to them. The details of the case are harrowing.

Part of her wants to stop reading, but she makes herself go on. How can she not? This baby was her brother. Wikipedia entries, newspaper archives, true-crime sites and forums: she browses them all, absorbing alleged facts and theories, more convinced by every word she reads that her mother could not be guilty.

Was she shielding someone?

Her phone rings, a mobile number she doesn't know. Normally, she wouldn't answer, but it could be DI Fox.

'Hello?'

'Marietta? It's me, Connor.'

'Oh, hi, Connor. How's things?'

'Not great. How are you doing?'

'Honestly? I'm in shock. How's Lily?'

'Devastated. Angry.'

'Is she angry at me? Because—'

'Not at you, no. At the police. She thinks they had no right to make accusations against your mum based on a private test. I've done a bit of googling, and it turns out she may be right.'

'What do you mean?'

'Generally, those private DNA tests can't be used as evidence without express permission from the person who took the test. So she says she won't give permission for him to use her data.'

'But he already has a name. She can't make him forget it.'

'True. But if he wants to take it to court, he may have to find other proof your mum was involved.'

'How would he do that?'

'That's the big question, isn't it? Since it's a cold case, seems like they didn't have much luck doing that for the last twenty-odd years.'

'But now he knows where to start digging.'

Connor sighs. 'I agree. But Lily wants to make it as hard for them as she can.'

'And what do you think about that?'

'It's not up to me, Mari. This is about you two.'

Marietta glances across at the photo of her and Lily on the windowsill. How old were they there? Three, four? When that picture was taken, had this awful drama already played out?

'I've been doing some googling too. It was a horrible case, Connor. At best, Mum had to have been shielding somebody, probably the baby's father. However we feel about her, she shouldn't have done that.'

'Then you and Lily are coming from different angles. She

thinks your mum should be protected from any kind of public exposure, that she should be allowed to rest in peace.'

'Regardless of what she did?' For a few moments, Connor goes silent. 'Connor?'

'I think Lily's wishes should be respected. She's my wife, and whatever she decides, I'll stand by her. Maybe you should think about doing the same. We're family.'

'We're a family who just fell into a deep, dark pit.'

'She wants to try and seal it up again. She's going to talk to a solicitor.'

'With a view to what?'

'To telling the police they can't use her data. To preventing them from doing so.'

'Does she really think that will achieve anything, long-term? He'll just come after us via a different route.'

'He has to find that route first. Anyway, she wanted me to let you know.'

'Is she OK?'

'She's lying down.'

'Send her my love, won't you? Tell her we'll talk tomorrow.'

'We're going to see my brother tomorrow. To be honest, I don't think she wants to discuss it. She's going to try and see the solicitor on Monday.'

Marietta sighs. 'You'll ask her to at least let me know how it goes?'

'I'll make sure she rings you,' says Connor.

Lily rings on Monday morning. All the fight is gone from her voice, leaving her sounding defeated and depressed.

'I'm sorry we argued,' says Marietta. 'And I'm sorry for the part I played in getting us into this, even though I still think we'd have ended up in the same place, sooner or later.'

'I'm sorry too,' says Lily. 'I was just lashing out, and you were in the way.'

'Next time I'll move faster.'

Lily sniffs, and Marietta wonders if she's crying.

'Anyway, I spoke to a solicitor this morning,' Lily goes on. 'I know Connor told you I had this idea that I could stop this. Turns out I was wrong. Because Mum's passed on, the police can use anything they want in court. Basically, she has no rights to privacy, and neither do we.'

'So the circus is coming to town.'

''Fraid so. I don't know what to do, Mari. I feel so scared. Will we have to go to court?'

'I don't think so. We can't have been involved. Unless . . . You truly didn't know any of this, did you?'

'Swear to God. Can I say something terrible?'

'Of course.'

'I feel so angry at Mum.' Lily's voice is thick, and Marietta's sure now her sister is in tears. 'For everything. For leaving us. For getting us in this mess and bailing out. That's what she did, isn't it?'

'I think we should be kinder to her than that. Imagine the pressure she was under all these years, keeping a secret like that.'

Lily sniffs again. 'If she'd told us, we could have helped her do the right thing.'

'Even if it meant her going to prison? That would have been so awful. But you know what I've been thinking? We have a chance now to help put things right. For Baby Michael. For our brother.'

'How?'

'We can cooperate. Give the police everything they need, make it easy for them to get to the bottom of it. Information, permission to search if they want it. DNA. Do you agree?'

Lily's voice is small. 'I suppose so. But what will it mean for us, Mari?'

'Some unwelcome changes, probably. But don't you worry about that. You just focus on the baby. I'll give Mr Fox a call, and keep you up to date.'

Upstairs, in what was Alice's bedroom, Marietta sits down in front of the dressing table mirror, and sees her own pale face where her mother's used to be. As a child, she used to stand here chattering as her mother rubbed in face cream or put on make-up, marvelling at the glamour of the cosmetics, longing for the day when she could buy her own.

But she knows now there was little glamour in Alice's pots and jars; they were no more than Boots' staples, cheap moisturisers, bargain-brand eyeshadows and mascara. The allure was in Marietta's eyes, imbued by adoration of her mother.

Out of sentiment, she left some of those very personal things in the dressing table drawer. She opens it, and there they are: a powder compact, half used; a bottle of perfume, almost empty, which she holds to her nose to breathe the poignant scent of mothering; a lipstick in that familiar shade of pink.

And Alice's hairbrush: a cheap, wooden-handled thing from a street-corner chemist. Such a pedestrian article, yet so heavy with meaning.

A few hairs from Alice's head are still entangled in the bristles.

For a while, Marietta holds it in her lap, silently explaining to her mother why she's doing this, why she believes it's the right thing, until she knows if she hesitates any longer, she'll lose her nerve.

The card Fox gave her is in front of her. Unlocking her phone, she adds his details to her contacts, and dials his number.

THIRTY-SIX

Fox is preparing his case. If he's going to justify backtracking and returning his focus to Baby Michael full-time, he'll need some solid reasons for the powers that be.

He fires off an email to Simon Orchard requesting he get in touch at his earliest convenience, and dispatches a detective constable to pick up the sample of Alice Ansley's hair.

A breakthrough isn't a breakthrough unless you make something of it.

Three days later, he's received no reply from the artist. Plainly Mr Orchard's too busy to respond to the Devon and Cornwall Police, in which case, Fox is only too happy to track him down.

The canvases in the window of the Windrush gallery – splashes of primary colour on grey blocks – aren't to Fox's taste. A bronze casting of a greyhound he likes much better, and even thinks he would take it home, until he notices the price tag is in the thousands.

Inside, the gallery's warm and bright, empty of other customers. Briefly distracted from the task at hand by the artworks on display, he's drawn to four small views of Bodmin Moor, studies of changing light from dawn through dusk, strikingly contemporary in bright acrylics.

Maybe when he retires, he should take an art class.

'May I help you?'

He turns to face an attractive young woman, hair up in a practised chignon, slender in a striking blue dress. A lapel label gives her name as Tigi Rowe.

'I hope so,' he says.

'They're beautiful, aren't they?' says Tigi, indicating the four studies. 'Did you have a location in mind for them?'

Fox smiles, and holds out his hand. 'I wish. DI Russell Fox, Devon and Cornwall Police.'

'Oh.' She takes his hand briefly. 'I hate to ask, but could I see some ID?'

'Nothing to worry about,' says Fox, showing his warrant card. 'I'm trying to track down an artist I'm told has a connection with this gallery, Simon Orchard.'

'Simon?' Tigi's eyebrows lift. 'He isn't in any trouble, surely?'

Fox shakes his head. 'Not that I'm aware of. His name's come up as a possible witness in connection with a case I'm investigating, and I'm having trouble contacting him by email. I'm hoping you can give me a phone number for him, and an address.'

She looks doubtful. 'I think that would be OK. I wonder if I ought to check with someone, though? Some of our artists are rather reclusive. They get upset if they're disturbed.'

'Of course. I'm happy to wait.'

Tigi leaves him alone, but isn't gone long. 'I tried ringing the gallery owner, but he's not picking up. If you'll leave me a card, if there's any comeback he can get in touch with you directly. Is that OK?'

'Absolutely,' says Fox.

'Do you know Simon Orchard's work?' asks Tigi She takes a seat at what Fox assumes to be a hand-made desk, pale wood supported by legs sloping at such an angle, it seems impossible it doesn't collapse. The desk has a single drawer, which she opens to find an iPad. 'We've had exhibitions for him in the past. He's hugely popular.' Switching on the iPad, she searches a file. 'I can text these details to you, or email. Whichever's easiest.'

'Email would be great,' says Fox, and spells out his address. Moments later, his phone pings to say it's been received. 'You know, I'd be interested to see some of his work before I speak to him. Better to know whether he's a David Hockney or a Gainsborough.'

'Problem with that,' says Tigi, 'is we don't have anything of his in at the moment. Anything we do get, sells really fast. I'll tell you what, though. Give me a mo.'

She disappears again, and is gone for a while. Untroubled by the delay, Fox spends the time moving round the gallery walls, lingering by the pictures he likes best.

'Found them.' As she returns, Tigi is smiling, holding a large booklet to her chest. 'I knew we still had one or two of these somewhere. It's a couple of years old, but you'll get a really good idea of Simon's style from this.' She holds the booklet out to Fox. 'It's the catalogue from his last exhibition.'

The clock on the wall of the Hare and Moon pub says 12.10. Driven in by his need to find a gents before his drive home,

Fox thinks it would be rude to use the facilities and leave without buying a drink, so he orders a filter coffee and a slice of pork pie. The healthy eating plan's back on tomorrow.

He finds a seat by the fire. The pub is quiet, only a reliable regular starting on the day's first pint, and an Italian couple trying to make sense of a menu featuring specialities such as bubble and squeak and black pudding. The pie's good, home-made, and when he's finished, Fox is inclined to take his time with his coffee.

The brochure from Simon Orchard's last exhibition is on the seat beside him, and idly, he picks it up. The starting date of the exhibition is given as August two years ago. Peak time for wealthy visitors to the area.

The front cover of marsh birds against an evening sky is striking, unique in its way yet still commercial, and Fox wonders if that's part of the secret of Orchard's success, his ability to produce real art that would look good in any home. Inside, the first few pages are filled with what's described as new work – hares in open country, a swan mirrored in still water, a kestrel hovering in its search for prey – all so remarkably lifelike, Fox can almost see the quiver of the kestrel's wings. Remembering the paintings at Trelonie House, he sees how Orchard's style has progressed. All his hallmarks are in those early paintings, but he's developed mastery that in some ways leaves them far behind, though Fox wonders if that early freshness and naïvety is more appealing than this slicker, contemporary style.

He turns the page again, finding examples of older work – wading seabirds, soft-eyed seals, a skein of wild geese –

and sketches, mostly of landscapes. The landscapes are good, capturing riverbanks, coastal cliffs and rolling countryside in only a few strokes of light pencil.

And one of them shows a view Fox has seen before.

THIRTY-SEVEN

The route Fox is following on the satnav involves the same kind of impossibly narrow twists that lead to the Hoppers' farm, but whereas Bleak Tor lies in upcountry moorland, this way leads through idyllic lowlands, lush grazing for cows producing the region's famous clotted cream. Outwardly, the two locations have no connection, but to Fox the common factor's obvious: no near neighbours.

The old bones of Otterburn Cottage still show under the new thatch, and in the random geometry of the black beams criss-crossing the frontage's white render. The outbuildings, though, have undergone expensive alterations; sheds have become seamless extensions to the cottage, and the barn's been transformed into an architectural wonder, stripped back to its medieval framework, the spaces between infilled from ground to roof with glass.

The cottage's front door is glossy primrose yellow, with *trompe l'oeil* red tulips painted along the base. Fox is admiring the tulips when someone shouts from the direction of the barn.

'Can I help you?'

A man is standing in the barn doorway, an expression of annoyance on his face.

Fox raises a hand. 'Good morning.'

He makes his way towards the man, who Fox puts in his sixties – his once-blonde hair and beard are run through with silver – though he's dressed in a younger man's clothes: tracksuit bottoms and desert boots, a hoody with an orange neck-warmer of the type favoured by downhill skiers.

'This is private property,' says the man.

Fox holds up his warrant card and introduces himself. 'Simon Orchard?'

'Yes.'

'I wonder if I might have a quick word?'

He notices Orchard's eyes slide very briefly to the left. Could he be worried?

'In regard to what?' asks Orchard. 'I normally only see visitors by appointment.'

'I tried to make an appointment via email, but you didn't reply,' says Fox. 'Since I was in the district, I thought I'd call in, on the off-chance.'

He sees from Orchard's face that he's not buying the 'in the neighbourhood' story, but he doesn't care. Why would he believe it, after all? His home is too far off the beaten track to be anything but a lengthy detour for anyone.

'I'm not obliged to speak to you, then?' he asks.

'By no means, sir. Though if you don't, since we're here, face to face, I might be inclined to wonder why you'd refuse.'

Orchard sighs to signal his displeasure at being inconvenienced. 'Come inside, then. I really can't give you very long. I'm working on a commission, and I'm already days behind.'

He leads the way inside the barn. Undeniably, it's a beautiful building, light and bright even in the gloomy overcast of a February Tuesday. The vaulted ceiling is high, with many lights hanging down, arranged to illuminate even the furthest corners. All around the interior, a walkway reached by oak steps has been constructed above head height, and from the rail hangs a gallery of Orchard's sketches and paintings, ingeniously displayed so the birds depicted – mostly raptors, Fox notices, kestrels and falcons and a red kite – resemble a lively aviary, swooping and hovering in flight.

At the centre of the barn is a huge, high table, where all the artist's tools – brushes and pens in ceramic pots, paints, paper and canvas – are spread out in an invitation to create, making Fox's hand itch to pick out an implement and draw. Maybe he should think seriously about taking those art classes.

'Very impressive,' he says.

'Please don't touch anything,' says Orchard. 'And I can't offer you any refreshment. I don't allow food or drink in the studio.'

He sits down on a high stool, and signals to Fox to take a seat on a battered leather sofa. Fox declines; the paint stains on the cushions make him nervous for his suit trousers.

'I'll try not to keep you,' he says. 'I just want to ask you about your relationship with Alice Ansley.'

Orchard gives a dismissive snort. 'Alice? What in God's name do I have to do with Alice? I haven't seen her in over twenty years.'

'You're aware that she recently died?'

Fox notes another of those sideways glances, a tell that Orchard may at least be considering not telling the truth.

He counts a full five seconds before Orchard says, 'I did know, yes. I was contacted by her daughter – what's her name, Marianne.'

'Marietta.'

'Marietta, that's it. A flamboyant name, but that was Alice.'

'Can I ask, what was the nature of your relationship with Mrs Ansley?'

'You can ask, of course. My relationship wasn't primarily with her, it was with her husband, Rob. He and I struck up a friendship over a couple of years. He was a fisherman, and I needed someone to take me to remote coastal locations for my work. He knew the coast like no one else, and I trusted him implicitly. Anything I needed, he was happy to oblige. And the best thing about him was his taciturn nature. He had the rare and admirable gift of not speaking unless spoken to. If there were more people like him, the world would be a much better place.'

'You're not someone who enjoys company?'

'I enjoy company when it's appropriate. But noise of any kind is death to the green shoots of creativity. Rob understood that. He was content with the sounds of the sea and the birds, as was I.'

'What happened to him?'

'He died. An accident at sea. Of course, Alice was devastated, and as a family friend – which I was, by that stage – I did my bit to offer succour and comfort.'

'To what degree?'

Orchard regards Fox with narrowed eyes. 'What do you mean?'

'I mean, were you and Alice in an intimate relationship at any time?'

'Define intimate relationship.'

'Did you and Alice Ansley have sexual relations?'

Orchard laughs. 'Spit it out, man. You mean did I fuck her? Well, for the record, yes, I did. Once and once only, after an evening of tears and red wine.'

'And after that?'

'We resumed our platonic footing, to the extent that relations between a man and a woman can ever be truly asexual. I gave her a little money from time to time, until she was back on her feet. That was the least I could do, for Rob's sake. She made a slow recovery from her loss, and as she did, we grew apart. She had no further need of me, and as I said, in the first instance, I was Rob's friend, not hers. I'd heard nothing of her until her daughter contacted me to let me know she'd died.'

'Did you go to the funeral?'

'Yes, I did. I thought it the decent thing to do, though God knows I couldn't spare the time.'

'I wonder if I could ask you to have a look at this?' From his pocket, Fox produces a photocopy of a page from the Windrush gallery catalogue showing a landscape pencil sketch. He holds it out to Orchard. 'Can you tell me where you drew that?'

Orchard glances at the paper, and shrugs. 'I'm afraid not, no. As you can see, it's a fairly generic landscape. I've made thousands of such sketches in my time, and I couldn't begin to give you locations for all of them. Probably I could for one or two that are special to me.'

'And yet in that exhibition there were only two or three other sketches, apart from this one. If you've done thousands, what made you pick this?'

'I didn't pick it. The exhibition was curated by the gallery. They show the works they think will best sell. The idea of art for art's sake is totally outmoded, Inspector. I'm afraid we're all in the business to make what we can. And if I'd been doing the choosing, that sketch wouldn't have been shown. I don't think it's one of my best.'

Fox puts the paper back in his pocket. 'Well, thank you for your time, sir. I'll let you get on.'

'Hold on a moment,' says Orchard. 'You haven't told me why you're asking these questions. I have a right to know, don't I?'

'In law, actually you don't, but I've no reason to be secretive. It's come to our attention that Mrs Ansley had a third child, and it's in my remit to find out who was the father.'

A tiny flicker of the eyelids, and Fox knows for certain Orchard's got something to hide.

He gives a snide grin. 'Surely it's not a crime to have a baby?'

Fox smiles back. 'That very much depends on how the baby's treated. From what you've said to me, it's a possibility the father was you.'

'I doubt it, but even if I was, what of it? That doesn't make me a criminal.'

'Did you know she was pregnant?'

Again a delay before Orchard answers, long enough, this time, for Fox to count to six in his head.

'When it comes to women, I'm not an observant man. I focus my attention on the natural world around me, some would say to my detriment. I've never married, and that's probably why. I think women find me insensitive, whereas what they actually mean is that I'm insensitive to them.'

'So you and she never cohabited?'

'Absolutely not.'

'This is a lovely place you have here.'

'My life's work, or should I say my life's other work. When I first bought it, it was a tumbledown shack, water from a well in the yard and a bucket in a shed for a toilet. I'm proud of what I've done with it.'

'Did Alice ever visit you here?'

Yet again, that hesitation.

'She brought the girls here once or twice, when they were very young. I doubt they'd even remember.'

But they might, thinks Fox. Smart guy, telling the truth on that one.

'Only once or twice?'

'As I remember.'

'And when they came to visit, did the baby come too?'

'Their visits were well before any baby arrived. My friendship with Alice, such as it was, was already on the wane, and having the girls here once or twice was more than enough, from my point of view. Nothing is more guaranteed to disturb my creative equilibrium more than noisy children. Which isn't to say they weren't – aren't – lovely girls. I was very fond of them for a time, as I'm sure they'll confirm. I suppose you've spoken to them, have you?'

'I have, yes. What would really help me in this investigation would be if you'd agree to taking a DNA test. To rule you in, or out.'

'Rule me in or out of what? I've already told you I had sex with the woman. That doesn't make me a criminal. Whatever you're investigating is nothing to do with me.'

'Then you'll have no objection to taking the test.'

Orchard shakes his head. 'I'd have to speak to my lawyer about that. It might be misused. If paternity were established, I could be liable for support.'

'After twenty years? I very much doubt that. Especially as the child is dead.'

Fox can see Orchard making an effort to appear indifferent. 'That's unfortunate, but again, nothing to do with me.'

'To be frank, that's what I'm trying to ascertain.'

'What?' Orchard seems blusteringly outraged. 'Are you accusing me of being involved in the boy's death?'

'Were you?'

Orchard laughs again. 'You have a wicked sense of humour. My involvement with Alice – I had better call it a friendship, so nothing is misconstrued – was terminated more years ago than I care to remember. I shall speak to my lawyer, and if he tells me there will be no come-back on me, you shall have your DNA. Maybe you could leave me your details, and I'll have my lawyer call you when he and I have spoken.'

As he drives away, Fox wonders if he's made any progress at all. With Alice gone, there seems to be only Orchard's word as to how the relationship was, when it began and when it ended, how casual or intense it might have been.

But a DNA test proving Orchard was Baby Michael's father might prove a valuable weapon in Fox's armoury.

Especially since Orchard seems already aware that Alice's baby was a boy.

THIRTY-EIGHT

Rarely do circumstances contrive to make Fox's life easier, but when he learns on Monday morning that Barbara Constant lives within three miles of the police station, he takes it as a win, even more so when she's happy to attend in person.

'A little bit of excitement,' she tells him on the phone. 'When you get to my age, you clutch at any straw.'

Even though he suspects she may have nothing of interest to say, instead of inviting her to the Portakabin, he books an interview room. Mrs Constant will take the matter more seriously in the kind of space that leaves no doubt the business at hand is official.

To that end, he keeps her waiting a few minutes after she's been shown in by a uniformed PC, giving her a chance to settle down from *This is fun* curiosity to the uncertainty of *How long am I going to be here?*

When he finally enters the room – carrying a weighty file – he's putting away his phone, generating the impression he's a busy man who doesn't have time for idle chatter.

First impressions, he puts her in her sixties, expensively dressed in cashmere and a Burberry raincoat. With her blonde hair beautifully styled, she's as well groomed as minor aristocracy. Which, with her accent, she might be.

'I'm sorry to keep you waiting, Mrs Constant.'

She's scented the room with French perfume and cigarettes. When she speaks, the tobacco smell intensifies.

'Barbara, please. And don't apologise. I know how busy you must be. Those of us with limitless time at our disposal don't worry about a little tardiness.'

Is there a reproach hidden under that affability? Her face is hard to read, the mask of civility locked firmly in place.

'Thank you for coming to talk to me, Barbara.'

'Not at all. I'm intrigued.'

'I have some questions relating to a friend of yours, Alice Ansley.'

'Ah. I did wonder if it might be about poor Alice. Is there something untoward about her death? I gather it was ruled a suicide, but I must say I found that very out of character for her. She was always such a cheerful soul.' She hesitates. 'Maybe I should qualify that. She was a cheerful soul when we were at school together, which is – as you may imagine – longer ago than I care to think of. In latter years, she and I were thrust apart by life's vagaries, and didn't see as much of each other as we might have liked. You always think, don't you, that there'll be other opportunities, and then suddenly, just like that, there aren't.'

'How well do you know her children?'

'Oh, not well at all. If you're looking for information about them, I'm afraid I'm not your best source. I knew the girls – at least I met them a few times – when they were very young, but I hadn't seen them for years until Alice's funeral. One of them's a beauty, but I found the other – was it Lily, or Marietta? So easy to get them confused – rather sullen. She'd be pretty too, if she'd smile a little more readily.'

Fox doesn't say he thinks it quite natural to be sullen at one's mother's funeral, but bets all his chips on his next question. Make or break.

'You looked after them for a little while, I gather, when they were small.'

Barbara smiles. 'Yes, I did. I wasn't at all what you'd call a competent childminder. I don't know much about children to this day, never having had any of my own, and by extension, no grandchildren either. But we muddled along all right. I was glad to help out in an emergency.'

'What was the emergency?'

Barbara wafts a hand weighted with rings. 'Some domestic hoo-ha, as I recall. I hadn't seen Alice for ages, and she phoned me out of the blue, asking if I could have the girls until her mother got back from Corfu or wherever it was. I seem to remember Alice claimed to have slipped a disc or some such. I've done it myself, and you really have no choice but to lie still for days and days on end, so I'm not surprised she felt she couldn't look after the children. Probably it was lifting them about that caused it. Anyway, of course I agreed, she dropped them off, and a few days later a very disapproving grandmother came and picked them up again.'

'Was Alice with anyone, do you recall?'

'With anyone?' Barbara pulls a face. 'Are you thinking of a man? Someone was driving the car, yes, but I couldn't see who. It was a bit of a scramble, the girls rather tearful and confused at being left, Alice handing over their luggage and giving me instructions. She didn't come in the house, not even for a cup of tea. I do remember being a bit surprised at that.'

'She handed over the girls' luggage? With a slipped disc?'

'Oh. I never thought of that.'

'Couldn't the driver have helped?'

'Well, he just sat there with the engine running, keen to be on his way. Rather rude, I thought, since I was doing Alice what was by any measure a huge favour. But she said they had a long drive back.'

'To where?'

'To his house. She wasn't living in Selmouth, she was living with him in some ghastly cottage with no running water. I know that because she'd sent me a card with a note over Christmas. She made light of it, but it sounded beyond grim to me.'

'Presumably she gave you her contact details?'

'I'm sure she must have done, yes. Wouldn't any responsible parent? But it was in the days before we all had mobile phones. It was only for a few days, so I suppose she trusted me enough to muddle through and keep the girls alive until her mother could take over.'

'The man driving the car, do you remember his name at all?'

Barbara looks troubled. 'Oh dear. I've never been good with names, and my memory's certainly not improved the past few years. A biblical name, I think. Stephen, maybe?'

'Could it have been Simon?'

'Simon? Yes, I think it could. Do you know, you still haven't told me what this is all about. How is something that happened twenty-five years ago connected to Alice's death?'

An excellent question, Fox is thinking, as he shows her out.

*   *   *

Fox hasn't seen Budd for a few days, so he's pleased to find her in the office, and pleased too that she's helped herself to the raspberry doughnuts that were his treat this morning. The less sugar for him, the better. When he walks in, she's typing on her computer, and holds up a finger for him to stay quiet while she finishes a paragraph.

'Sorry about that,' she says when she's done. 'I just got off the phone with a possible new witness, and I wanted to make a note of her exact wording before I forgot what she said.'

Fox sits down at his desk. 'Will this one get to court?'

Budd shrugs. 'Maybe. Problem is, a witness account won't be enough to convince the CPS to give it a go. They'll want it so solid you could make bricks out of it.'

'Tell me about it.'

'How about you? Are you making progress? Last time I saw you, you were heading off to interview some artist.'

Fox leans back in his chair, hands behind his head. 'Yes, I spoke to him, and it got me pretty much nowhere. So I've got my gut telling me this guy is somehow connected—'

Budd interrupts him. 'What, to the Baby Michael killing? Russ, that's huge.'

'Not necessarily. If I'm honest, I've nothing on him, and he's taken a DNA test, cool as you like, probably advised by his lawyer to play the "nothing to hide" card. As he says, being a father – even the father of a murder victim – isn't a crime, and proves nothing. He says he and the mother had a one-night stand, end of, and all I've got is an elderly witness who saw Alice Ansley at some unspecified date with a man who may or may not have been called Simon. Father or not, he says he never had anything to do with any baby, and I've no one who can convincingly say otherwise.'

'What about the mother? I remember you saying you were thinking a woman could have done it.'

'Same problem. Not a shred of evidence that she did or she didn't. And anyway she's deceased.'

Budd pulls a sympathetic face. 'So we're both stuck.'

'Both officially at the deadest of dead ends. Shall I make us a consoling cup of tea?'

THIRTY-NINE

From the back of Fox's car, Marietta watches the unfamiliar scenery slide by, roads she's never before travelled, places she's never seen. Beside her, Lily seems calmer than she's been in a while, both hands folded over her belly, a little pinkness in her cheeks. This feels like the end of an arduous and punishing journey, which started with a phone call back in Colombia and has led them down long avenues of distress and grief, to a brother they never knew.

'Can I say something?'

Fox glances up to the rear-view mirror, meeting her eyes. 'Of course.'

'Our mum wasn't a perfect person, and we know you have questions about her,' says Marietta. 'But we've talked about it a lot since you told us about Michael, and we're agreed absolutely that she didn't have it in her to kill a child. She couldn't have. Absolutely not. Could she, Lily?'

In the mirror, Fox sees Lily shaking her head.

Nodding to acknowledge the sisters' testimonial, he gives his attention back to the road.

Almost every killer he's ever met has family who'll swear

they're incapable of taking a life. Maybe Marietta and Lily are exceptions to the rule, and maybe their faith in Alice Ansley's innocence is justified.

Except the innocent don't usually keep their secrets so deeply hidden.

On this high ground, the rain is becoming sleet. In the shelter of St Just's porch, Reverend Kate Northcott is waiting, and when she sees Fox's car pull up, she moves forward to meet the visitors, holding up a black umbrella.

Stepping from the car, Lily and Marietta look around, taking in the remoteness of the hamlet, the stolidity of the ancient church. Fox was right. It's a good place for their brother to be at rest.

Lily pulls on a home-knitted hat and gloves, and Marietta zips up her parka and raises the hood. Lily has brought a tied bouquet of white roses. Reverend Northcott greets them, and shakes both their hands.

'Please,' she says, 'call me Kate. I'm delighted to meet you at last, so pleased you've come. We've tried to take good care of him over the years, but you are very special visitors, and very welcome. I'm afraid the weather's against us, but that's not unusual in this part of the world. If you'll follow me, I'll show you where he is.'

Their brother's memorial stone looks small and forlorn. Marietta feels the prick of tears, and Lily takes her hand.

'I'll leave you alone with him,' says Reverend Northcott. 'I'll be waiting with Inspector Fox when you're done.'

*   *   *

Fox is sitting on a stone bench in the church porch, feeling the cold of it seep into his buttocks, wishing he'd brought his overcoat instead of an anorak. As Reverend Northcott approaches, he's pleased to stand up. A few minutes more and he'd be frozen in place.

'How are they?' he asks.

'Emotional. Who wouldn't be? Before they join us, may I ask if you're any nearer to finding his killer?'

'I'd like to say yes,' says Fox, 'but finding a killer and proving his or her guilt are two very different things.'

'If it's any consolation, I know how hard you've tried. You've been a champion for him, and he needed that.'

'I'll keep going as long as I can. As long as they'll let me.'

'Your perseverance is remarkable.'

Fox looks up into the high branches of the winter-bare elms. 'I lost a son, around that time. Cot death. Something like that changes your view of life.'

Reverend Northcott touches his forearm. 'I'm so sorry.'

Fox shakes his head. 'It was a long time ago. You learn to live with it. I found a way of coping and so did my wife, but unfortunately her way involved a bottle and a glass.' He smiles. 'I have a daughter, though. She's beautiful and clever and doing really well.'

'And you've found Michael's family. That's a huge achievement.'

'We've *officially* found his family,' Fox corrects her. 'I think you may have beaten us to it.' Taking out his phone, he scrolls to find the picture of Alice Lily sent him, and shows it to her. 'Do you know this woman?'

'Off the record?' she asks.

306

'If it works both ways.'

'Agreed. Her name's Mary Paine. She comes here very occasionally, shows a lot of interest in Michael. I've talked to her several times. Sometimes she seems to be . . . struggling.'

Fox shakes his head. 'This isn't Mary Paine. Her name's Alice Ansley, Lily and Marietta's mother. She committed suicide last year, on the anniversary of Michael's death.'

'I'm very sorry to hear that. You think she was his mother.'

'I know she was.'

'Do you think she killed him?'

'Honestly, I don't know. It's a definite possibility.'

'That must be hard for them.'

'They've been through a lot. I hope this visit will bring them some kind of closure.'

'I hope so too.'

The sisters, when they join them, are sombre.

'Thank you for taking care of him,' says Marietta to Reverend Northcott. 'Our mother would have thanked you, too.'

Reverend Northcott glances at Fox, enquiring with her expression as to whether she should tell them or not. Fox gives a subtle nod.

'She did thank me. She used to come here, but I've just learned from Inspector Fox that she was using an assumed name.'

'Oh!' says Lily. 'She knew where he was. She came here and she still never told us.'

'I don't know if you remember,' says Marietta to Reverend Northcutt. 'I called you when she died, to ask you to officiate at her funeral, but you said we were way outside your parish.'

'I do remember. I was completely baffled. I'm so sorry.'

'You weren't to know. How could you? But we were wondering, Lily and I, if you'd consider letting us bury her ashes with him. I think it would bring her comfort. It would bring us all comfort.'

'Especially Michael,' says Reverend Northcott. 'I'd have to consult the parochial church council, but assuming they're in agreement, I think reuniting Michael with his mother would be the kindest thing for them both.'

Eleven weeks and four days into her pregnancy, Lily feels the too-familiar tug of cramping in her abdomen. Hurrying home from work, she puts herself to bed, where she lies perfectly still, trying to stay positive and not cry, praying to a God she's never believed in to please be kind.

But that God isn't on her side. By the time Connor reaches home and runs upstairs, their baby's already lost.

Marietta doesn't ask Lily's agreement to do what she believes is the right thing.

Instead, without her sister's knowledge, she takes down the three watercolours and parcels them up in bubble-wrap, leaving the pale shapes of their frames imprinted on the wall, like reverse shadows.

At the Windrush gallery, Tigi is pleased to see her, though her warm welcome soon evolves into concern.

'What's wrong, Mari?' she asks.

Marietta places the paintings on the sloping-legged desk. 'Change of heart. We've decided to accept Simon Orchard's last offer for the three watercolours, provided he can pay quickly. We need to raise some cash.'

Tigi frowns. 'Are you sure? You'd do so much better with them in the right sale. Why don't you wait a few weeks? I can get them in the next one, no problem at all, and you'll get at least double what he's offered, maybe triple. That's my professional advice to you, as well as from me as your friend.'

Marietta shakes her head. 'For Lily's sake, we need to do something now. She's had another miscarriage, and she's in a terrible state, so depressed.'

'Oh Mari. I'm so sorry.'

'So I want to do something to give her hope. The money from these will pay for another round of IVF. She'll have something to look forward to, something to help her pull through.'

'Are you really sure?'

'I'm sure. If Mum were here, I think she'd agree. Lily wanted to sell them ages ago, and I talked her out of it. The time has come, but only if payment's going to be immediate. I don't want to sell cheap and still wait weeks for him to get his chequebook out.'

'I'll pass that message on, and let you know. Will Lily be OK?'

'I hope so. She's taken it so hard. I wish she'd have a break, give her body chance to recover, think about something else for a while instead of rushing into more treatment. I worry it's going to take its toll on her relationship with Connor. But what do I know? I've never been in that position.'

'There are other possibilities,' says Tigi, 'routes she might not have considered. Maybe you could persuade her to at least think about them. Because if she will, my mum knows someone you definitely should talk to.'

FORTY

Sunday morning. Light seeps through the bedroom curtains, and the gulls are crying.

The gulls are always crying. They're one of life's few constants.

Marietta is lying in what used to be Alice's bed, hands behind her head, thinking about how things have changed.

She senses that Adam's awake, and as she turns towards him, he lifts his arm. She moves to rest her head on his shoulder, and he pulls her close. For a while they lie without speaking, her stroking his chest with her fingertips.

His eyes are closed when he says, 'Mari, can I tell you something?'

His tone makes her look at his face. He opens his eyes, and she sees not kindness there, but worry.

'Is it something bad?'

'Yes.'

'Then no.'

He holds her tighter. 'I have to tell you, because it's coming between us. It's on my conscience, and I can't let it go unless you forgive me.'

Marietta's unaware of anything coming between them, but her mind starts running, and suspicions crowd in. Is this going to be about his ex-girlfriend, the one who keeps wanting to pay him a visit? When he said he was going fishing with a friend, was there more he didn't say? Is he about to reveal himself as a complete bastard, like others she's trusted in the past? If it's any of those things, she'll kick him out of bed and it's over right this minute.

But in a voice wholly unlike his usual confident self he says, 'It's about your mum.'

'Mum? What about her?'

Tenderly, he kisses the top of her head. 'I'm so sorry. I did my best, my absolute best.'

Marietta pushes herself up on her elbow to look at him. 'What on earth are you talking about?'

'That day, on the shout to rescue her. It was me who was supposed to pull her out, but when I got hold of her . . . There was a lot of swell. I should have used both hands, but I was holding on with one, so I grabbed her wrist with the other, and she was coming up. I thought I'd got her and I thought I was strong enough, but I wasn't. The boat lifted and somehow I lost my grip. She went down again, and I thought she wasn't going to come back up. Sometimes they don't, sometimes they seem to just give up and sink. But when she was under, she must have taken on more water, she must have thought it was all over, and I can't help thinking that extra minute, when she should have already been on the boat, that extra minute probably killed her. *I* probably killed her. She was alive when she came out, and if I hadn't let her go, she might have lived.' He looks into her eyes, and there are tears in his own. 'I'm so sorry, Mari. I screwed up, and I'm so sorry.'

Marietta places a finger on his lips. 'Don't you dare say that, you hear me? There's only one person at fault for Mum dying, and that's her. Lily still doesn't want to believe it, but now we know about Baby Michael, we're on our way to having a reason for it, guilt or grief or her just being plain tired of keeping something like that hidden. Maybe she knew they were coming for her, and she couldn't face the rest of her life in jail. She was tormented by her demons, honey, and they led her into that water. So how could you be in any way to blame? You and all the lads took risks to go and rescue her, and I know you did your best.'

Adam wipes his eyes. 'I so wish I'd saved her, for your sake.'

Marietta puts her face up close to his, and with the pads of her thumbs wipes away more tears. 'Listen to me, please. You couldn't have saved her, because she didn't want to be saved. But you did save somebody. You saved me. And sometimes that makes me feel guilty, because Lily's been so miserable and nothing in her life's going the way she planned, and it took Mum dying for me to find you, and start to be happy. Somehow that feels all wrong.'

Now Adam shakes his head. 'That isn't wrong. That's the process of healing. Some are fast, and some are slow. What did I save you from, anyhow?'

She smiles. 'A life of nomadic loneliness.'

'I like the idea of a nomadic life. Without the loneliness part, obviously.'

'You can't be nomadic if you're from Stoke-on-Trent. Midlands folks are all stay-at-homes.'

'On the contrary, the most adventurous of nomads all hail from there. So what do you say? Do you fancy a little company next time you go travelling?'

'Who says I'm going?'

'I do. You've got itchy feet, I can tell. In fact the mystery to me is what's stopping you.'

'Oh, a couple of things.'

'If one of them might possibly be me, I thought I might tag along too.'

She grins. 'Really? What about your job?'

'They might have me back, down the line. I didn't say I'm leaving for ever. But what else is on your mind?'

'Lily.'

'She can look after herself.'

'I wish I believed that. And Josie. I keep almost ringing the RSPCA and never quite being able to do it.'

'There's a reason for that.'

'What?'

'You two love each other madly.'

'We do not.'

'Give her away, then. I'll find someone to take her. I'll do it today.'

'Stop it.'

'Face the facts then, young lady. You and that dog have crushes on each other two miles high.'

FORTY-ONE

Fox is doing his best to move on, but the Baby Michael case still haunts him, taunting him at odd moments with the feeling there's more he could have done.

That feeling intensifies the day he gets a call from the lab telling him Simon Orchard's DNA is a match for Baby Michael's.

So Fox has named both parents. How is it possible he has nowhere to go?

In a situation like this, he knows better than to sit down and think. Those lost fragments of memory and intuition work their way up to the light in their own sweet time. Sooner or later, inspiration will strike.

As it happens, it hits him in the canned food aisle at Sainsbury's, deciding whether he wants Branston pickle in his baked beans. Behind him, a woman's mobile rings, and there's the missing link: the realisation he's still never properly examined Daniel Hopper's phone records.

The powers that be would never begrudge him half an hour for that.

Especially when his gut's telling him it's definitely worth a look.

He decides he'll do it first thing Monday morning, before he picks up the threads of his current cases.

The email with the link to the records is buried far back in his inbox, dated three weeks after he returned from Spain. At the time, he had nothing to go on, no names and no idea what he was looking for, and so gave the data only a cursory glance. Now, though, he's two suspects – Alice Ansley and Simon Orchard – further forward in the game.

Pulling up the file on his screen, he scrolls straight to the end. No calls were made from the phone for three days before it went dark, suggesting the battery died rather than that the phone was switched off. The last outbound calls were made on the day of Daniel's death. After that, a number of incoming calls unsurprisingly went unanswered.

Fox googles the location where the phone was last active, and a map appears on screen – a rural area with few distinguishing features – with a blue marker. He scrolls out to see what part of the country he's looking at, and then in to see more detail.

Google's pinpointed Bleak Tor Farm.

So here's a mystery. If Daniel's phone was near at hand when he died, how come it's never been found?

On days like this, Fox is unusually glad to be working cold cases, where the high-pressure time criticality of contemporary policing rarely applies. Going back to this case without explicit permission is undeniably bending the rules, but he can hide a few hours in his time sheets, and if he makes any kind of progress, who will care?

The possibility of spring is in the air, lifting the weight of dreary winter and energising everything: lambs in the fields, new growth in the hedgerows, even Fox himself, who finds himself looking forward to seeing Jayne Hopper.

At Bleak Tor, sunshine makes the farmhouse handsome, and for once Fox understands why Jayne stays.

She opens the door to him smiling, wearing a little make-up, jeans and a sweater. Jeans suit her, he thinks. She looks good.

Closing the door behind him, she tells him to go through to the kitchen, as if the place is familiar to him and he should know the way. Actually, he doesn't remember, but he follows the smell of coffee drifting down the hall.

The kitchen's clean and tidy, as it was before. She asks him to sit down, and points him to the same oak armchairs with their hand-made cushions. As he passes the mullioned windows, he sees the orchard's wind-warped trees are bravely coming into leaf.

He takes the right-hand seat.

Jayne reaches for the pale-blue mugs he remembers. 'I think last time you were here I served you instant coffee. I've invested in a cafetière since then, so I hope you'll taste the difference.'

Fox wonders if the investment was on his account, and finds himself hoping it was, though without much confidence in the possibility. On the little table set between the two chairs, the coasters she used before have been placed ready. He glances at them; then looks again more closely.

Hares in an upland meadow.

He picks up one of the coasters. Jayne is bringing over his coffee, tea for herself.

'These are nice,' he says. 'Who's the artist?'

To his surprise, she blushes, and bends low to try and hide it as she puts down the mugs.

'A friend,' she says. 'Simon Orchard. He's brilliant, isn't he?'

Fox drops his head, and reminds himself that – with her friend Rosemary unable to be certain of the date she and Jayne were together in Bristol – there's a shadow of doubt over her whereabouts on the night of Daniel's death.

Her blush fades, but she's noticed his change in attitude.

'I'm sorry, Jayne,' he says, 'but based on what you've just told me, I'm afraid you shouldn't say anything else to me except under caution.'

Jayne is bewildered. 'What did I say?'

'You have a personal relationship with Simon Orchard, and that impacts on how we have to proceed. I can read you your rights now and we can record this conversation, or you can attend a police station for interview with your solicitor at a later date. If I'm being completely honest, I'd recommend the latter.'

'I don't understand. What does Simon have to do with anything?'

'I'm not at liberty to comment on that.'

'But I haven't done anything. And I don't have a solicitor. Not the right kind, anyway.'

Fox stands. 'I'm sorry, Jayne. We should reschedule.'

'But you only just got here. And what about your coffee?'

The coffee smells good, and Fox is thirsty. He shakes his head with genuine regret.

'Believe me, Jayne, I'm really sorry, but I've no choice but to insist we speak at another time.'

FORTY-TWO

Marietta taps gently at the bedroom door, but receives no answer.

She pushes it open with her foot. Inside, the curtains are drawn against the brightness of the early spring sunshine. The room smells stale and sour, of unwashed bodies and bed sheets, and bad breath.

'Lily?'

The figure in the bed pulls the duvet over her head.

A woman follows Marietta into the room. Marietta goes to the window, elbows a gap between the curtains and puts the mug and plate she's carrying on the windowsill. The chink of daylight shows clothes strewn on the floor, crumpled tissues, chocolate wrappers, an empty pizza box.

With a nurse's efficiency, the woman begins tidying up, using the pizza box to collect the rest of the litter.

Marietta sits down on the bed. 'I brought you some Earl Grey and a raspberry muffin. And there's someone here to see you, a friend of Tigi's mum. She wants to talk to you.'

Lily's voice from under the duvet is muffled. 'I don't want to see anyone.'

The woman puts down the pizza box and signals to Marietta to let her take her place. Marietta stands, and the woman sits.

'Lily,' she says, 'I'm Naomi, and I'm a social worker for the county adoption agency. I just want to have a chat with you, totally off the record. In fact if anyone asks, I was never here. I've been hearing about your miscarriages, and I'm so sorry for your losses. Believe me, I feel your pain. I've been through it myself, so I do understand.'

'Please, Lily,' puts in Marietta. 'Naomi's come a long way. And your tea's getting cold.'

Lily emerges from under the duvet. Marietta draws back one curtain, and opens a window. One of Lily's neighbours is playing a CD as he washes his car, and Marietta can hear a track she loves, Fleet Foxes' *White Winter Hymnal*, beautiful but inappropriate for this uplifting day.

In the half-light, Naomi reminds Marietta of her mother; she has that same smile, tempered by both sadness and resilience, and the same bony hands from which age has whittled away muscle and plumpness. Marietta remembers the leather gloves she's kept, still shaped to Alice's hands.

Petulantly, Lily settles herself upright against a pair of pillows. Since Marietta last saw her, her sister has gained pounds, so her face is fat and flabby and spotted with acne. Her greasy hair's tangled in a scrunchy, and her mouth is beginning to droop from perpetual misery.

'You're very pale,' says Marietta, and it's true: Lily's skin is deathly, tinted the colour of bruises under her eyes.

She hands Lily the mug of tea, and Lily wraps her hands round it as if it's a lifeline she's been thrown.

'I just want to say to you,' says Naomi, 'that other doors

are open to you, and that happy and successful parenthood doesn't have to be the result of you carrying a pregnancy to term. I want to ask you and Connor to consider whether you could provide a loving home to a child who desperately needs one, whether you could open your hearts to a small person who's had a difficult start in life. I'm not going to lie to you, the application process is lengthy and demanding, but you'll understand why it has to be so. From what I've heard, you and Connor would be excellent candidates. What do you say, Lily? Will you at least consider it?'

Lily says nothing.

Naomi smiles. 'Well. I've said my piece. Please, talk to Connor, talk to your sister and anyone else whose opinion you value. I can introduce you to parents who've gone through the process, and we have classes you can join that tell you what to expect and what support is available to you. Obviously it's not something to be rushed, but I have a feeling you'd be a wonderful mother, and there are children who would so appreciate your love and care.' She stands up from the bed. 'I'll leave you two together. I've left my number with Connor, so if you want to talk, just give me a call.'

When Naomi's gone, Lily sips her tea.

'Do you want your muffin?' asks Marietta.

'You could have asked me before putting me through that,' says Lily.

'I asked Connor. I thought if I asked you, you'd say no.'

'But you did it anyway.'

Marietta's expression changes from appeasement to annoyance. 'You know what, yes, I did it anyway. Ten days you've been in this bedroom, Lily. What are we supposed to do, keep feeding you pizza until you're so fat you can't move?'

'So this is an intervention?'

'No, it's not an intervention. It's people who care about you, trying to show you there are ways out, other paths you can take.'

Lily puts down her tea. 'I've been doing a lot of thinking. About Mum, mostly. I lost another pregnancy, and that's bad enough. But she lost a baby she'd held and fed, and that must have been so much worse. How did she cope with that?'

Marietta shakes her head. 'I don't know.'

'Why did she keep it so secret? What was she hiding from the world? She must have been falling apart inside, but nobody ever knew.'

'She didn't fall apart because she couldn't afford to. She had us to take care of. She had to dig deep, really deep, and keep going, for our sake. And you know what? You've got someone you have to keep going for, someone who's shouldering a double load while you're up here grieving, like it only affects you. You're shutting him out, and he needs you. You have to think about Connor, Lily. Don't abandon him to wallow in your misery when he's feeling it too. And what if there is a Baby Michael out there you could rescue? A baby who's been born into the wrong circumstances at the wrong time, who might come to harm if he or she stays there? Just think about it, talk to Connor about it. You don't have to make any commitment.'

Lily tries to smile. 'I know you think I'm some kind of drama queen. But you'll understand one day, when your biological clock kicks in.'

'There's still time, I know.'

'I want to say thank you, by the way. For selling the paintings. I know you didn't agree with accepting Uncle Simon's offer.'

'I just want to see you happy.'

'Same goes for me with you.'

'In some ways, I'm happier than I've been in a while.'

'But not in every way?'

Marietta shrugs. 'Itchy feet, I suppose.'

'And what does Adam say about that?'

'That itches need to be scratched. I think he'd like to come along for the ride.'

'What does that mean?'

'I'm thinking it's time to sell the house.'

Lily bows her head, and Marietta's afraid she might cry.

'Can I think about it a while?'

'Of course. I know it's a big thing. Are you going to eat this muffin, or can I have it?'

'What flavour is it?' asks Lily.

'Raspberry and white chocolate.'

'Are you mad? Of course I'm going to eat it. But you can have the first bite if you like.'

By the time Marietta leaves, Lily's promised to shower and go downstairs, at least for a little while.

Driving back to Selmouth, Marietta goes over their conversation, frustrated that Lily still seems unable to grasp the seriousness of Alice's situation. Pretending that their brother died through some kind of accident or illness – and that their mother deserves sympathy for stoically bearing his loss – is troubling self-delusion.

Sometime soon, Lily must face the hard facts in the case. Michael was a victim of infanticide. Why wouldn't a mother innocent of wrongdoing report her son as missing?

FORTY-THREE

Budd has agreed to come in on the interview as his second, and Fox, if he's honest, is glad of the moral support.

Jayne Hopper is stony-faced and plainly pissed off. Her solicitor's a woman Fox doesn't know, but she's dressed for battle in a black suit and already making notes. He isn't expecting an easy ride.

As he and Budd take their seats, he gives Jayne a smile, but he isn't surprised she doesn't return it. By prior agreement, Budd sets up the recording, goes through the 'thank you for coming in' niceties, makes the introductions and reads Jayne her rights.

Fox switches his brain to professional mode. Jayne Hopper could be a suspect.

But nothing's proven yet, and courtesy costs nothing.

'We just have a few questions today, Jayne,' he begins. 'I want to start by asking about the day your brother Daniel died. You were away from home, I know. Can you tell me where you were?'

He senses Budd tense alongside him, waiting to see if she'll answer. If Jayne goes no comment, they'll know there's something there.

But she says, 'I was in Bristol.'

'Who were you with there?'

A slight hesitation before she says, 'No one.'

So she's changing her story.

'When we spoke before . . .' Fox checks his notes, 'you said you stayed the night with your friend, Rosemary Mears. Are you now saying that's not true?'

'Yes.'

'So where did you spend the night?'

Jayne looks to her solicitor for confirmation she should answer. 'I was at a hotel, the Marriott Royal. I was supposed to be meeting someone there but he didn't show up.'

Fox feels a tingling at the back of his neck, the feeling of being about to score a bullseye.

'Who was it you were supposed to be meeting?'

'Simon Orchard.'

Fox keeps his face deadpan, not wanting to show the extent to which this is of interest.

'Can you explain to us the nature of your relationship with Simon?'

The look Jayne gives him is filled with embarrassment, and Fox feels sorry for her, but he needs to know. He decides to make it easier for her, break it down. 'How long have you known him?'

'Decades,' she says, off-handedly. 'He was a friend of Daniel's. They met when Simon asked permission to come and study the hares on our lower meadows, back in the days when he was struggling to get his name known. He used to come up to paint and photograph them. Daniel loved the hares. He was glad to find someone who shared his interest in them. That was as far as it went, until they bumped into each other some time later at a country fair where Simon was selling his paintings. They got chatting and went for a drink, and discovered a common interest in wildlife conservation. It was only very casual, a pie and a pint in the pub kind of arrangement, but with the amount of work on the farm, Daniel didn't have time for many friends. Probably he appreciated the time away from us. Me and my mother and father, I mean.'

'Did they see each other regularly?'

'Not really, no. Simon was becoming very successful, and had much less time. Though he still kept in touch, always invited us to his shows. He was generous that way.'

'Had you and Daniel been to any of Simon's exhibitions in the weeks before your brother died?'

Jayne considers. 'I'm sorry, I don't remember.'

'Specifically, did you attend this event at the Windrush gallery?' Fox places the catalogue on the table, turning it so it faces her.

When she sees the cover, Fox sees a light blush spread up her neck and into her cheeks.

'Yes,' she says. 'We did go to that.'

'So going by the date, this must have been the last of Simon's exhibitions Daniel went to.'

'It must have been, yes.'

'I'm sorry to be blunt, Jayne, but were you and Simon Orchard romantically involved at that time?'

The phrasing is clumsy, but how else might he put it? Intimate? Lovers? Neither is right.

Unsurprisingly, she's offended, and her reply is sharp. 'We were never "romantically involved", as you put it.'

'And yet – forgive me again – you had arranged a meeting with him in a hotel in Bristol. Can you tell me how that came about?'

Jayne hesitates, and Fox is afraid she'll refuse to go on. But she says, 'Daniel was cheerful enough when we arrived at the exhibition, but as the evening went on he became preoccupied and moody. I think Simon noticed it too – at one point I saw them talking, but whatever Simon said didn't make Daniel feel any better. He came and told me he wanted to leave. I asked if he wasn't feeling well, but he said he was fine, he just needed to get out of there. We hadn't been there very long, and I told him I wanted to have a good look at the paintings and have another drink – it was a rare outing for me, if I'm honest, and I was keen to make the most of it – so he said he'd wait in the car and went off. I was getting myself another glass of wine when Simon came over. I was flattered, actually. There were a lot of people wanting his attention, but he seemed interested in me. After a few minutes, he leaned in close and told me I was looking lovely.'

She stops again, and this time turns to her lawyer. 'Do I have to tell them this?'

'Tell them whatever you're comfortable with,' says the lawyer. 'If you don't want to answer their questions, you may say you have no comment.'

'I don't want them to think I've anything to hide.' Jayne looks back at Fox. 'Basically, he asked if he could ring me. For a date.'

'And did he do that?'

'Yes. We arranged the meeting in Bristol. I was stunned, to be honest. He'd never shown any interest in me before. And while I can't say he was a great catch physically, he's famous, and has money. I thought he'd show me a good time. I don't see many good times, and I'm not getting any younger.'

Budd shifts in her chair, and Fox knows that she, like him, feels embarrassed for Jayne, and admiring of her bravery in laying out her sad appreciation of a man's interest, her keenness to jump at a late – maybe a last – chance at sexual adventure.

'But he didn't arrive.'

'No. And he didn't call, either. He just left me there, and stuck me with the hotel bill to boot.'

'Why do you think he didn't show up?'

'I think Daniel warned him off. When I told him Simon and I were meeting, Daniel was livid. He said Simon was no good for me and I should stay away from him. In fact we had an almighty row about it. I told him he was jealous, that he was worried I might find a man and run off and leave him all alone on his backwater farm, and he told me I had no idea what I was talking about. He was being totally selfish, trying to keep me there with him. He ruined what might have been a great chance for me.'

'Do you still think that?'

'Yes.'

'Is that why you don't put flowers on his grave?'

Jayne regards him, obviously surprised that her omission has been noted. 'Yes. I suppose that seems childish. That's siblings for you.'

'Have you spoken to Simon since then?'

'No. I tried to ring him once or twice, but he never returned my calls.'

'And that night, while you were alone in Bristol, Daniel died.'

'Tragically, yes. And despite our differences, I was heart-broken that I wasn't there.'

'Why didn't you tell me before where you were?'

Jayne shrugs. 'I didn't think it mattered. I was embarrassed about being stood up. It's not so hard to understand, is it?'

Fox draws himself a mental picture: an older woman, new underwear and perfume, angry and hurt, trying to sleep alone in a king-sized hotel bed. No, it isn't hard to understand.

'Have you ever wondered where Simon might have been that evening?' he asks.

'What do you mean?'

'Where's Daniel's phone, Jayne?'

'I told you before, I've no idea.'

'I can tell you it's somewhere at Bleak Tor. We know that from his phone records. Yet you say you've never found it.'

'I haven't.'

'So why wasn't it on Daniel's person, or at least in the house?'

'I really don't know.'

'Maybe someone hid it.'

'Not me.'

'So if not you, who?'

'I don't know.'

'What did Daniel want to tell us in the days before he died, do you think?'

'I don't know that either.'

'But what if someone did know?'

'Who?'

Fox is silent, letting her figure it out for herself.

'Oh my God. You're thinking about Simon, aren't you?'

'Maybe he sent you to Bristol for his own reasons,' says Fox. 'To make sure you were out of the way.'

He turns the pages of the catalogue to find the pencil sketch he showed Orchard, and points to it. 'Do you recognise this place?'

Jayne looks at it, and is ready to say no.

'I think this could have been what your brother saw that night, what upset him and made him want to leave,' says Fox. 'Please look closely.'

Jayne does so.

'It can't be,' she says at last. 'Can it? Isn't that our spinney, where Baby Michael died?'

FORTY-FOUR

The odds are looking shorter on what was a very long shot.

Fox is ready to have a closer look at Simon Orchard's movements around the time of Daniel Hopper's death, and when he gets his five minutes with the powers that be, they're open-minded and receptive, pleased he's managing to build on the work he's done identifying the victim's next of kin. Allowing him to work on the case full-time seems the obvious route to take.

With all the sign-offs in place, Fox submits his requests for Orchard's phone and banking records.

And while he waits for those, there's one more box he might be able to tick.

Even though Fordingley's close by, he won't be visiting Bleak Tor today, though part of him is anxious to apologise to Jayne Hopper for putting her through that difficult interview.

Omelettes and eggs, as his mum would have said.

He's brought his appetite to the Plume of Feathers, and today as he opens the low door into the bar, he sees he's not alone. Three tables of diners are already eating, two of whom, he notices, have had the good sense to order pasties.

As he's settling in on a bench seat under one of the windows, the landlady, Frankie Keast, goes by carrying more plates of food. On her way back to the kitchen, she stops by his table and smiles.

'Hello there, my lovely. Inspector Fox, as I recall.'

He smiles back. 'That's quite a memory you have there, Frankie.'

'I still have your card in my office. Is this an official call?'

'Partly. More a yearning for a pasty and a pint of Ferryman.'

'Ferryman's off, until I get a minute to go down the cellar and change it. I got Avocet on tap. I think you'd like that.'

'A pint of that, then.'

'Coming right up.'

While he's waiting for his lunch, he picks up the gallery catalogue from the seat beside him and skims through it, stopping at the page showing the view that he – and Jayne – identified as the knoll on the Hoppers' land. Did Daniel recognise it, too?

He leaves it open at the inside front cover.

Frankie brings over his beer – a golden liquid with a creamy head, and on the glass, the outline of a bird with a long, curved beak.

'That looks great,' he says. 'Listen, Frankie, I know you're busy, but can you just take a second to have a look at this?' He shows her the portrait photo of Simon Orchard, a side-on shot against a background of a dawn sky over sea. 'Do you recognise this man? Could he be the guy who came looking for Daniel Hopper?'

She looks, and hesitates, and Fox's heart begins to sink. But then she nods. 'Yeah, that's him. He used to come in with Danny before sometimes. I wasn't sure just for a minute because his hair's different there. What is he, then, some kind of artist?'

'He paints wildlife.'

'What, he gets paid for that, does he? Nice work if you can get it.'

FORTY-FIVE

Over the following two weeks, Fox returns to his other cases, struggling to temper his impatience at the delays with the information he needs.

The bank records arrive first. Having seen Orchard's place in the country, it's no surprise to Fox that the artist's very comfortably off; he holds high-value current and savings accounts, and a quartet of gold and platinum credit cards, only one regularly used and paid down to a zero balance at every month end. On a detective's salary, Fox has never had a prayer of being in such robust financial health.

His logical starting point is transactions around the date of Daniel's death, though in his heart he's pessimistic. Orchard's an intelligent man. If he had criminal intentions, he's likely either to have covered his tracks, or not to have left any in the first place.

Frankie Keast remembers Orchard ate and drank at the Plume of Feathers that evening, but it's too much to hope he paid his bill with a card.

Except he did. On the date of Daniel's death, there it is, a charge of £15.95 from the Plume of Feathers, Fordingley.

Mentally Fox punches the air.

The circumstantial evidence is building nicely, but Orchard's phone records – when they eventually arrive – are icing on the cake.

On the evening of Daniel's death, Orchard's phone pinged masts all the way from his home to Fordingley. With the credit card payment for his dinner, there's no question at all he was in the area.

The records show a number of calls that day, though no activity with Daniel's mobile. But there's a landline number Orchard called twice, the day before and the day of Daniel's death.

Fox doesn't recognise the number, so he rings it.

A woman answers. A voice he knows.

Jayne Hopper.

Fox is taken aback. 'Jayne?'

A pause before she speaks. She's recognised his voice too. 'Yes?'

'Jayne, it's Russell Fox, Devon and Cornwall Police. I'm sorry to bother you.'

'That's OK.'

'I'm ringing this number because it's come up in the course of an investigation. I'll be honest and say I wasn't expecting it to go through to you.'

'And yet here I am. Am I allowed to ask what this is in relation to?'

'You can ask.'

'Is it about my brother?'

'It is, yes.'

'You found this number somewhere.'

'We did, yes.'

'But you won't tell me where.'

Fox sighs. 'At the present time, that wouldn't be appropriate.'

'Well, I'm glad to be of help. Was there anything else?'

'I don't think so.'

'Goodbye, then,' says Jayne, and hangs up.

For a minute, Fox sits looking at his phone, wishing the call had gone better.

Then he pulls himself together, and considers the implications of this information.

Orchard called Daniel on the house phone.

It's too easy, these days, to forget that old technology is still very much in use. Daniel and Orchard became friends years ago. Their early communication would have been via landline.

And old habits die hard.

Fox could have asked for the landline data weeks ago, if only he'd thought of it. But if he were Orchard, he'd say he rang to speak to Jayne about their Bristol meeting, and a jury might believe him.

There has to be something more.

FORTY-SIX

Fake it until you make it, Marietta said.

Lily is making a special effort to appear to be everything she wants to be but doesn't feel she is, wearing make-up to appear fit and healthy, coordinated clothes to look organised, and a smile to show she's happy and well balanced.

Inside, she fears her neediness will come spilling out with the very first question.

Connor asks for Naomi Page, and the receptionist invites them to take a seat.

Lily sits beside Connor on a red sofa, staring at a wall of posters encouraging their first steps in adoption. The children in the photographs are all laughing. Lily wants to cry.

Naomi smiles and shakes their hands and asks how Lily's doing, and Lily tells her first lie by saying, 'Fine.' Naomi's office has a view of the backs of buildings and the entrance to an NCP car park. As Connor and Lily sit down, Naomi's making herself comfortable in her chair, positioning a patch-work cushion at her back.

'My sciatica's playing up,' she says. 'The doctor reckons I spend too long sitting on my backside, but with a caseload like mine, what can you do? Anyway, I'm so glad you guys have taken the plunge and come in to see us. Why don't I go first and tell you how it all works, and then I'm sure you're going to have a ton of questions.'

Connor and Lily listen to Naomi's explanation of the process: registration and background checks, training and assessment, child matching and approval panels.

'I know it all sounds daunting, but we're here to guide you every step of the way,' she concludes. 'We'd expect to be looking at about a year for the whole process, start to finish, though of course it could take longer for us to find the perfect child for you.'

'What if I get pregnant in the meantime?' asks Lily.

'Of course that does sometimes happen,' says Naomi. 'We do ask though that you stop any IVF or fertility treatments once you commit to taking the adoption route.'

Connor clears his throat. 'I have a question, and I feel really bad asking this, but it's been on my mind. What if I – what if we – don't love the child we get? What if it feels different to having our own baby?'

From Lily's face, Naomi sees he hasn't discussed this with her.

But she nods her understanding. 'That's a perfectly legitimate question, Connor, and a concern of many people considering this pathway. But the world is full of happy adoptive families, and we take every possible care to make sure you're a perfect match for whichever child we find for you. Doubts are totally normal, but life is full of risks. When are we ever one hundred per cent sure about anything we do?'

*   *   *

Outside, Connor takes Lily's hand, and leads her away from the adoption offices, through the town centre towards the park. Neither of them says much. Deep in thought, Lily's happy to be led.

Inside the park gates, a path winds among beds of spring flowers, tulips, narcissi, pink and yellow hyacinths.

'Where are we going?' asks Lily, and Connor answers by squeezing her hand.

He brings her to the bandstand. Before they were married, they came here on occasional summer afternoons to listen to the brass band playing under the wrought-iron Victorian gazebo, wandering on down to the river when the concert was done. Whatever happened, wonders Lily, to the carefree couple they were back then?

Connor leads her up the steps to stand under the pinnacle of the ornate roof. Turning to face her, he puts his hands on her waist, and kisses her.

When they break apart, arms round his neck she asks, 'What was that for?'

'Can't a man kiss his wife when he wants to?'

'You've got something to say.'

Connor sighs, and bends to touch his forehead against hers. 'You know me too well. Do you still love me, Lily?'

Her eyes search his. 'Of course I do. What kind of a question is that?'

'Because I'm thinking you and me have got forgotten. Sometimes I think I'm just a means to an end, a convenient sperm donor for your project to make us parents.'

She pulls away from him. '*My* project? I thought you wanted a baby?'

He shakes his head. 'Not at any price, Lily. Not at the price of us. You're the love of my life, but I feel I'm losing you to someone who doesn't even exist, who might never exist. That's a tough battle for a man to fight, me against your fantasy child.'

'I can't believe you're saying this.'

Connor grips her hands. 'Please listen to me, sweetheart. Babies are wonderful things, and we're going to have one, someday. I promise you that. Even if we have to jump through all those hoops that woman just told us about, with police checks and references and night classes. But that's not how I want it to be. I want it to be *our* baby, born out of our love. You have to remember you're barely thirty years old. We have time, Lily. Plenty of time. You've just got yourself into the most screwed-up mess, and it's sucking you down, it's sucking *us* down. We need to breathe, take a break and relax. Forget about being parents, and remember how to be interesting people. Please. No more baby-fixation for a while. Let's have a holiday, climb a couple of mountains, raft a few rivers. We could have a real adventure, get leaner and fitter, take care of ourselves in every possible way. I need you to give us a big, long rest from all this craziness, this worry. We need to heal us, or we'll be no kind of family to bring a baby into. Do you understand me?'

For a long moment, Lily looks at him. When she opens her mouth to speak, he puts a gentle finger on her lips to silence her. 'No arguments. This is an ultimatum, from a man who loves his wife and wants to save his marriage.'

Now she looks troubled. 'Are things as bad as that?'

He nods. 'They're getting that way, yes. I need much more

out of life than what we have at the moment. I want fun and laughter and things to look forward to that aren't buggies and nappies and your menstrual cycle. I know it's hard for you, but I want you to try really, really hard to put babies to the back of the queue. For a while at least. Because I want us to fall in love again. I want to rediscover the woman I married, if she still wants me.'

'But what—'

He stops her with a shake of his head. 'There's only one question here. Does the woman I married still want me?'

'She absolutely does,' says Lily, and he folds her into his arms.

FORTY-SEVEN

For once in Fox's career, the powers that be are keen to meet with him.

He outlines what he's got: Orchard in Fordingley on the night of Daniel's death; an appointment with Daniel's sister that same evening he didn't show up for; calls around that time to Bleak Tor. And all this within a short time frame from Daniel possibly recognising the sketch of the spinney on his land.

As for motive, Fox suggests, Orchard's a man with a national reputation and a very comfortable lifestyle. Hardly likely he'd easily give up all that – and his freedom – to go down in history as a child-killer.

'The problem is, though, Russ,' says the superintendent, 'pretty much everything you've got is circumstantial.'

The man's known for being exceedingly cautious, but Fox has to admit that he's right.

But to his surprise, the chief inspector takes Fox's side.

'I think we've got enough here to justify an interview under caution,' he says. 'I'd like to hear his explanation for being in Fordingley when he was supposed to be in Bristol.'

'Fetch him in, then, and let's hear what he's got to say,' says the doubting superintendent. 'Let's hope he clams up and goes no comment. If he does that, I'll agree there's something there, and that's the time maybe – only maybe – we should be thinking about warrants.'

Fox can tell by the quality of his Bond Street pinstripe suit that Simon Orchard's lawyer will be expensive. As they take their seats, Budd gives Fox a look which says she's clocked it too, and is pleased they're off to a good start. Interviewees with nothing to hide usually come alone or with a local brief.

The downside is, the lawyer will need to be seen to earn his money, and that means they can look forward to plenty of interruptions in the course of their questioning.

Orchard's doing a poor job of feigning nonchalance, sitting well back in his chair, legs stretched out in front of him under the table. His clothes – beige chinos, a fresh-out-of-the-box white shirt and a gold-buttoned navy blazer – are oddly formal for this setting, and Fox wonders whether he's dressed for this meeting, or whether he's planning on going on somewhere else when they're done. As he smiles a welcome, he studies Orchard's face for signs of strain, but he looks as if he's had a good night's sleep. But then Orchard picks up his plastic cup and gives himself away: a barely detectable tremble in his hand makes tiny ripples in his coffee.

Once again, Budd does the niceties, the welcome introductions and the thanks for coming in, reciting Orchard's rights and setting the recorder going.

'We just have a few questions for you today, Simon,' says

Fox. 'Can I ask you about your relationship with Daniel Hopper?'

Orchard's eyes move sideways to his lawyer, who gives a nod which is barely more than a lowering of his chin.

'Dan?' asks Orchard. 'We were friends.'

'Good friends, close friends?'

'Casual friends.'

'And what about his sister, Jayne Hopper?'

Orchard folds his arms across his chest, and glances again at his lawyer, who remains still. 'What about her?'

'What's the nature of your relationship with her?'

'Do I have to answer that?' he asks the lawyer, and the lawyer shakes his head.

'That's personal,' says Orchard.

'Can you tell me where you were on the night of Daniel's death?' asks Fox, and states the date so Orchard won't have to ask him.

Orchard glances at the lawyer, who raises his chin.

And Orchard says, 'No comment.'

On Easter Sunday, Alice's daughters have brought her flowers.

In St Just's churchyard, the daffodils are at their best, brightening the afternoon with their glorious yellow. The rain, thankfully, has cleared, though the grass is sodden and muddy, and water still drips onto the pathway through the rusted holes in the porch roof guttering.

The gathering at the graveside is small. Lily's wearing a pink and white dress, and looks pretty with her hair done in curls. Marietta has chosen an outfit in green, and when the sun catches it, her red hair shines like copper. Connor looks

343

handsome in a suit, and Adam – in a rare attempt at formal wear – has borrowed a navy pea jacket to go with a shirt and indigo jeans.

Reverend Kate Northcott says a few words, and the sisters step forward. The urn they've chosen is painted with butterflies, and together they lower it into the earth, into the same ground where their brother lies.

Lily lays a bouquet of white roses against Baby Michael's headstone. Beside it, Marietta places a white chocolate Easter egg with Michael's name written in blue icing.

Once the gifts are laid, there's nothing else to be done. Alice's name will not be carved in stone; she'll lie here anonymously, in no danger from ill-wishers if her identity as Michael's mother should become public.

Marietta and Lily hug.

As the party leaves the graveside, the sexton steps out from the shadows by the graveyard wall. Putting his shovel to the loose earth, he begins the burying of Alice's remains.

FORTY-EIGHT

After Simon Orchard's decision to go no comment in his interview, it's a matter of straightforward formalities to get a search warrant for his home.

Fox takes his own car, leading the team across country, following his satnav from the A-roads down the country lanes. He doesn't remember the way well, but recalls a landmark, an old-fashioned phone box before the final right turn.

At Otterburn Cottage, parking is an issue. Fox takes the only off-street spot, and walks back to speak to the other drivers, asking them to wait while he checks the lie of the land.

Orchard's standing in the doorway of his studio, his stance unwelcoming. As Fox approaches, the tightness in Orchard's jaw warns him the man's on a short fuse.

'I see you brought the heavy mob,' says Orchard. 'I hope for your sake you have a warrant.'

'I do.' Fox holds out a sheet of paper headed with the crest of a magistrate's office, unsurprised when Orchard snatches it from his hand. 'That's your copy, all dated and signed. If you have a preference on where you'd like us to start, please say, but usually they begin in the main residence, which is to say, the house. And I'd advise you to supply us with keys if needed, because forced entry can cause significant damage. I imagine you put in a lot of hours painting those tulips on the front door.'

Orchard digs in his pocket and produces a bunch of keys. 'Tell them not to make a mess.'

'Unfortunately house searches tend to be messy procedures. I'll get them started, then you and I can have a word.'

As Fox walks into the barn, he wonders how long the transformation has taken, whether it's been in the last few hours, or whether it's been a gradual process, a slow dismantling and packing-away of his work. Either way, it suggests to him that Orchard's preparing to flee. Lucky they've arrived in time; another twenty-four hours, and they might have been too late.

He signals to the uniformed PC he's brought with him to stand by the door.

'Reinforcements?' asks Orchard. 'You're a much younger man than I am, Mr Fox. I'm flattered you feel the need.'

'PC Tate is here as a witness,' says Fox, 'for your protection, as much as mine.'

He looks around the gallery, and sees almost everything's gone. The painted aviary he admired when he was last here is stacked as individual canvases against the wall. The high table where Orchard worked – which Fox remembers filled with the tools of creativity – is all but empty except for a glass jar of brushes and pens.

And three framed pictures, laying face down at the table's far end.

'Are you going away?' asks Fox. 'Or moving out? You seem to have been very busy.'

'My plans are none of your business,' snaps Orchard. 'Make your search, and get off my property. I don't know what you think you're looking for, but whatever it is, you won't find it.'

'Do you mind if I sit down?' Not waiting for an answer, Fox climbs up on one of the stools pushed under the table. 'Will you join me? We may be here a while.'

With a sigh, Orchard does so, seating himself on a similar stool before the three inverted pictures.

'You do not have to say anything,' says Fox, 'but it may harm your defence if you do not mention when questioned something which you later rely on in court. Anything you do say may be given in evidence.'

Orchard laughs. 'I see, it's like that, is it? In that case, I shall just sit here and keep my mouth shut.'

'Shall I take that to mean you're offering me no comment?'

Orchard spreads his hands in a gesture of openness. 'I don't believe I've anything of interest to tell you, especially since I've no idea why you're here. But put your questions, and let's see.'

'Where were you on the night of Daniel Hopper's death?' asks Fox. 'Because your phone records and your credit card statement tell me you were in Fordingley, at the Plume of Feathers, asking after Daniel.'

For a split second, Orchard appears less confident, but his supercilious smile quickly returns.

'Credit cards and phone records, the treacherous electronic servants of modern policing,' he says, snidely. 'We've all seen *Crimewatch*, Mr Fox. Wouldn't a man with criminal intent have paid for his dinner with cash? Unless, of course, he'd had a momentary lapse and forgotten to stop at an ATM, for which he would berate himself, but would have had no choice but to use his card. I suppose it could have happened that way. Possibly.'

Fox hesitates, unsure if Orchard's making an admission. He presses on. 'Why did you want to speak to Daniel?'

Orchard gives an exaggerated shrug. 'Why shouldn't I wish to speak to my friend? I was in the district and thought he might be at the Feathers, so I called in on the off-chance of catching him and buying him a pint. I didn't see him, though. I ate dinner by myself – as you have already diligently ascertained through my credit card statement – and drove myself home.'

'What were you doing in the Fordingley area?'

'I hardly remember. Painting, I expect. It's what I do for a living, as you may have noticed.'

'Can anyone vouch for your being there?'

'Where? At the pub? The bar staff, possibly.'

'I meant more generally. Can anyone vouch for you being in that area, before you went to the pub?'

'I doubt it. Why should I need anyone to vouch for me?'

'Because I'm wondering,' says Fox, 'why you were in Fordingley when you had arranged to meet Daniel's sister that evening in Bristol.'

Orchard throws his head back, and for long moments stares up into the barn's ancient rafters. Fox waits. When Orchard lowers his head again, Fox is surprised to see he's smiling.

'I declare myself run to ground,' he says. 'Checkmate, game over. I have to say I think you've played a blinder, Mr Fox, an absolute blinder. You're anxious to know about Dan, and

I see no reason now not to tell you. He threatened me, so I was going to threaten him.'

'In what way did he threaten you?'

'As you surmised, he recognised the view of his land at the gallery exhibition, as did you. Such an insignificant little drawing, I don't even remember doing it. I suppose it must have been in the days when I was making a study of the hares at Bleak Tor. I spent a lot of time in the copse up there. The trees were good cover, and with the wind in the right direction, the hares had no idea I was there. It was the cover that made me think of it when I needed somewhere to dispose of the mess I made over Alice's baby.'

By the door, the constable is very still.

'He was your baby, too,' says Fox. 'Your son.'

'He was a screaming brat,' says Orchard. 'The two girls were disruptive, though we managed to offload them after a while. But the baby never stopped crying, night and day, on and on and on. Alice promised me he'd be no trouble, but how's a man supposed to work, to create, with that kind of racket? And Alice did nothing but weep and complain, and tell me I was a bad father. I wasn't cut out for fatherhood, and I'd told her so from the beginning. I gave her fair warning. In the end I said he had to go.'

'Where did he have to go? Where could she have taken him?'

'Anywhere but here. Home to her mother's and her other offspring, I didn't care, though she hadn't actually told her mother she was pregnant. Probably too soon after Rob, and I assume she didn't want to appear a slut. I had an exhibition coming up, a London gallery that was a bit of a coup. Peter

Doig was showing there, and Hockney. Did you know that Hockney did landscapes? Needless to say, I was desperate to finish my pieces, but I couldn't think, I couldn't work at all. And Alice wasn't well, she wasn't coping. More and more she was making demands, asking me to feed him, hold him, change him. I suspect she intended to invoke my paternal instincts, but all she did was provoke my temper. I had an idea one day to put a nip of whisky in his milk, see if that would shut him up. That was what my mother always used to do with me when I was playing up, a drop of gin in my bedtime cocoa. And it worked. Oh my God, yes indeed, it worked.'

'A nip? How big a nip?'

'A good measure. I was being generous. I was sleep-deprived, the same as she was. You might say in my defence I didn't know what I was doing. He slept. We all slept. Three of us went to sleep, but only two of us woke up.'

A sigh rises and falls in Fox's chest, releasing a breath he didn't even know he was holding. After all these years, he has the confession he hardly dared hope for. Head bowed, he allows himself a minute to let realisation take root.

But there are more questions to be answered, if only Orchard will keep talking. 'And when the baby didn't wake, what then?'

Orchard seems happy to go on. 'Well, of course Alice became hysterical. She was prone to hysterics anyway, but on this occasion she was impossible. I dealt with her before I dealt with the baby. How I dealt with him, I think you already know. Sad to say my efforts to destroy the evidence were not one hundred per cent successful.'

'Why didn't you report his death?'

Orchard considers. 'I saw no need. His birth wasn't registered, and the world would never miss him. I felt certain Alice would soon get over it, and have the sense to be glad that he was gone, since she certainly didn't have the means to take care of him, struggling as she already was with the girls. And if I reported it, my actions could have been misconstrued. You might have questioned my intentions, whether I only wanted him to sleep or whether I was aiming for a more long-term solution. On that, I could not possibly comment.'

'And what about Daniel?'

'Dan? A good soul, but a little lacking in brainpower. He was a bit of a lummox, to be quite frank, and he couldn't see the sense in keeping quiet. And he was diabetic. That made him vulnerable.'

Fox frowns. 'Vulnerable in what way?'

'Let me show you.' Orchard reaches out to the jar in front of him, and from among the pencils and brushes, pulls out what Fox assumes is a purple gel pen.

He removes the cap. 'An insulin pen. Dan was reliant on gadgets like this, so reliant he kept a few in the fridge, but they're easy enough to come by, off the internet. It was a life-saving drug to him, but he was still vulnerable to overdose. So I thought I'd pay him a visit. I hoped to find him in the pub, encourage him to drink a little more than was good for him to help the process along, maybe provoke a natural crisis. I missed him, but I wasn't worried. I knew he'd be home alone, because I'd arranged for Jayne to be warming a king-sized hotel bed in Bristol, hotly anticipating a last-chance erotic encounter. Poor Jayne. I have some regrets there, actually, that I never rescheduled. She was certainly eager, if you know what I mean.'

Fox feels the fingers of his right hand curling, clenching into a fist, and hides it under the table out of Orchard's sight.

But Jayne Hopper's forgotten, and Orchard's interest is back on the insulin pen.

'Ingenious little device. You see the needle, here? A single emergency shot in the arm, like so . . .'

Before Fox realises what's happening, Orchard's stuck the needle into his own bicep, in the same area as the puncture mark on Daniel Hopper's body. Fox moves fast to try and swipe the pen from his hand, but he hears the click as Orchard presses the plunger, and the shattering of glass as the jar of brushes is knocked to the floor.

Orchard is calm. 'Couldn't be easier. I've said all I have to say. Now if you'll excuse me, I shall make myself comfortable.'

'Tate, call an ambulance!' yells Fox.

'I'm afraid you'll have a long wait.' Orchard lies down on the battered leather sofa and arranges a cushion under his head. 'That's one of the downsides of country living.'

Orchard is right: forty minutes go by before Fox hears sirens in the lane, and by the time the paramedics arrive, Orchard's drifted away, lost in the depths of deep coma.

When the ambulance has driven away, Fox sits on the stool at the end of the table, and turns over one of the three face-down pictures: an oystercatcher stepping through shallows, from the trio at Trelonie House. The backs of all three paintings have been prised off, and the oystercatcher was hiding a secret: a photograph of a much younger Simon Orchard cradling a newborn baby. Across the back of the photo, in heavy black ink, are the words *MEA CULPA*.

The pen he used to write them lies alongside.

Fox is no Latin scholar, but he's well enough schooled in the Catholic tradition to know the words' translation: *through my fault.*

At home that evening, at ten minutes after nine, Fox receives the call.

Simon Orchard has passed away.

FORTY-NINE

'Is that Inspector Fox?'

The voice on his phone – an older female – rings a distant bell, but no name has come up on his screen. He closes the window on his laptop to give the caller his full attention.

'Speaking.'

'I don't know if you'll remember me, Inspector. I came in to talk to you a little while ago. It's Barbara, Barbara Constant.'

Fox recalls her well: blonde hair, expensive jewellery, inquisitive disposition.

'Mrs Constant, hello. Of course I remember you. How are you?'

'I'm well, thank you. I'm wondering if you can confirm for me something I've just read in the local newspaper, regarding the artist Simon Orchard.'

Fox decides to proceed with caution. A woman like Barbara Constant might easily be enquiring after the details of what seems to her an intriguing death.

'What would that be?'

'I wonder if you can confirm for me that he has actually died.'

Since it's in the newspaper, Fox has no hesitation in confirming that it's so.

'I just wanted to be absolutely sure before I said anything. Sometimes they print such rubbish, don't they? It's hard to know what's real and what they're making up. Anyway, I'm happy to take your word, and that being the case, I wonder if you might be able to come and see me? It's the most stupid thing, but I've turned my ankle and I'm not able to get about much at the moment. There's something I want to tell you regarding the Baby Michael case.'

Fox isn't ready to explain the case is closed. As he remembers, Mrs Constant doesn't live far away.

'Of course,' he says. 'If you'll let me have the address, I'll call in on my way home.'

At first glance, the address Barbara Constant has given him chimes with what he expects from her: a large house on a semi-suburban street of grandiose properties, probably all built originally as homes for post-war industrialists. But when he drives between the stone gateposts, he finds the frontage divided into numbered parking bays. He reverses into the single space reserved for visitors.

By the front door, he reads the names against the buzzers for four flats, and finds *Constant* beside number three. When he presses, for long moments there's no reply, and he presses again.

A hesitant voice says, 'Hello?' and Fox announces his name and rank.

The buzzer sounds, and he steps inside.

The skeleton of the industrialist's house is still there, in the oak-banistered staircase leading to the upper floor and the embellished cornices around the hall's high ceiling. Fox thinks of pathologist Felix Lindner's beautiful home, and how this house must once have been its equal, plush-carpeted and opulent. But the carpets are long gone, replaced with fake-floorboard vinyl discoloured by the passing of many feet, and the banister's scratched and in need of fresh varnish. Two fire doors are labelled flats one and two. Fox heads upstairs, and knocks at the door of number three.

Barbara Constant invites him into what used to be an attractive bedroom, with a bay window and a view over a park bounded by imposing beech trees. The room's proportions have been spoiled by partitioning walls; through an open door, Fox sees a tiny kitchen. This room is now a living room, where almost every square centimetre is occupied by enough furniture to fill the original house – a French-style sofa, occasional tables, lamps, footstools, a writing desk, even a coal scuttle, though there's no fireplace he can see. There are too many chairs, all piled with books, newspapers and magazines, and on every possible piece of wall hang pictures and photographs, many of a younger Barbara dazzling in evening wear, on horseback, walking on moors with gun dogs. A bigger, better past has been crammed into this inadequate space, and plainly Barbara has refused to leave anything behind. Fox finds himself pitying her: in her own home, the carefully curated facade she presents to the world reveals itself to be a sham.

Physically, she's deteriorated in the few weeks since they met. Grey roots spoil the platinum blonde, and without make-up her skin has the ashy tone of old age. She's supporting herself on a stick with a carved handle, and her face is strained with pain.

'You'll have to forgive me being so slow.' She points to her left foot, which is heavily bandaged inside a man's tartan slipper. 'This wretched ankle is crippling me, and it doesn't seem to be getting any better. I shall give it a few more days before I insist on another X-ray. They said it isn't broken, but it's still horribly bruised, and it's keeping me awake at night. So I'm afraid I can't offer you coffee. It takes me too long to make.'

'I just had one at the station,' lies Fox. 'Would you like me to make you one?'

'That's very kind of you, but no. It goes straight through me, and then I'll be running to the loo, and that's another drama in itself. Do sit down, won't you?'

There's nowhere obvious for him to go. Barbara is heading for a clear space on the sofa alongside a side table with a full ashtray and a pack of cigarettes. Fox chooses a carver chair near the window, from which he removes a stack of books and sits down, waiting until Barbara has made herself comfortable. As she settles, he notices a moth hole in her sweater, where a foundation garment shows through.

'I'm a bit cramped in here, as you see,' she says, slightly breathless. 'After my divorce, it became apparent my husband had been very creative in offshoring his investments, so while he and his bimbo – she's hardly that, in truth; she's fifty if she's a day – enjoy the fruits of his duplicity, here I am in my little flat. Still, it suits me well enough. Or it did until I was incapacitated. Anyway, you'll be wondering why you're here, so I'd better come clean. You may be a teensy bit cross with me, but I didn't tell you all I might have done about that dreadful man.'

In spite of himself, Fox's eyebrows lift. 'You mean Simon Orchard.'

'I do mean him, and I'm not sorry he's no longer with us. When I heard the rumour that he was gone, I can't deny my heart gave a little flutter. If only Alice had been here to see the day. I wondered about her death, you know, whether after all these years he got her in the end.'

'I don't believe there's any possibility of that. What was it you didn't tell me, Barbara?'

She sighs, and looks out of the window towards the park. 'That day she brought the girls to me, it was because Marietta had a broken arm. He'd done it. That's what Alice told me. They'd just come from the hospital. A greenstick fracture, they call it. The poor thing had her little arm all done up in a cast.'

Fox frowns. 'Why didn't you tell me this before?'

'Alice begged me not to say anything. She said if I did and there was trouble, she'd pay for it. I knew what she meant. She always made excuses for him, claiming his artistic temperament made him sensitive, that he needed peace and quiet for his work and the children drove him mad. He said they were frightening the wildlife from the garden, so she'd arranged for her mother to have them when she came back off holiday. I know that kind of man – self-centred and egocentric. He wouldn't want her giving her attention to the children, so he'd be glad to see the back of them.'

'How did Marietta's arm get broken?'

'An accident, she said. Isn't that what they always say? Anyway, I asked her what would happen when the baby came along—'

'What baby?'

'She was obviously pregnant. I reminded her that babies have a tendency to cry, and she said it wouldn't be a problem because It was his and he'd be more patient with it than he was with Rob's children. I told her she was mad, but she said he was a genius and allowances must be made. And all the while he sat there with the engine running, tooting his horn and keen to be off, forcing her to leave her children, her trying not to cry and telling those tiny, distraught girls she'd be back for them tomorrow. She wasn't, of course. Their grandmother came to take them, as I told you.'

'Did you hear any more from Alice?'

'Oh yes, plenty more. I'm sorry, do you mind if I smoke? Wretched habit, I know.'

Fox doesn't mind. He kicked the habit himself many years before, but the pull of it has never left him, and he feels a pang of envy as Barbara lights up and inhales.

'The next I heard from her was a phone call. She rang from a phone box – back in the days when they still had phones in them. She was terribly upset, and asked if she could come and see me. To my discredit, I tried to put her off. We had something planned for the evening – some dinner, I suppose it was – and a tearful Alice didn't fit with those arrangements, but she was insistent, so I agreed. She asked if I'd mind lending her money if she took a taxi, and of course I didn't. Money was no problem to me then, and I thought if I gave her some she'd be gone all the quicker. But when she arrived . . . oh my Lord, poor Alice! As soon as I opened the door, she burst into the most heart-rending sobbing. I hurried her upstairs to the guest suite, and told Derek some story about her mother having died, then sat her down to find out what was going on. And the shock of hearing her baby was dead . . . I shall never forget it.'

Fox's face darkens. 'You knew the baby had died? Why on earth didn't you or she report it?'

Barbara draws on her cigarette, exhales and shakes her head. 'I never knew for certain how he died. I didn't want to know, and anyway she didn't seem clear herself. As far as I was concerned, having been party to her offloading the girls – which to this day I believe she did for their safety – it would have been down to him losing his temper when the little mite cried. Babies do cry, don't they, and the younger they are, the more they howl. You don't need much imagination . . . Well. She just said that he'd died, and Simon had told her she mustn't tell anyone, that he was going to take care of it. Of course she had become hysterical, at which point he slapped her and locked her screaming in some outhouse and drove off, whereupon she by her account broke down the outhouse door with a shovel to get out and find her child, who wasn't there. She wept and wept, telling me there was no trace of him at all, that everything was gone, his clothes and toys and blankets, nothing was left, as if he'd never been. So having no better idea, she grabbed her coat and shoved a few things in a shopping bag and what cash she could find in her handbag and set off walking in a daze, wringing her hands and weeping so more than one vehicle stopped to ask if she was all right. But she had her diary in her handbag, and at some point sense broke through into her disordered mind, and she found my number in the diary, and rang with the aim of asking my urgent advice on where to look for Simon and the baby.'

'Where was she when she rang?'

Barbara shakes her head again. 'She didn't seem to know, or to have much idea how long she'd been walking, whether it was minutes or hours. So I told her to ring one of the numbers in the phone box – taxi firms used to do that, didn't they, post their numbers in those places – and try and describe where she was.'

'What happened then?'

'She moved into our spare room for the best part of a week. I got the doctor to come to her, and he gave her sedatives so she could sleep. I told him there'd been a death in the family, and he was happy to prescribe on that basis.'

'But you still didn't call the police?'

'No.'

'Why?'

Barbara stubs out her cigarette. 'She'd been with us two or three days when the story broke about Baby Michael. Straight away I thought Simon was the man you should be looking for, and more than once I put on my coat to go to the police station and say so.

'But Alice was so afraid of him, she made me afraid of him too. I didn't dare tell her about poor Michael at that point, what he'd done to him. I thought she'd lose her mind completely if she thought it was her baby. What mother wouldn't, after all? But somehow she found out – maybe she heard it on Derek's radio, or on the TV from downstairs – and she let me know she knew. And she seemed surprisingly calm about it. Maybe that came from knowing his fate, knowing there was no more to be done, that the worst had come to pass.

'At that point, I suggested we should go to the police

together, safety in numbers as it were, but she clutched my arm and told me how cruel he could be, how afraid she was for her girls. They were living with her mother, and he knew where that was. I talked about police protection, and said that once he was caught, the danger would be over, but she didn't believe me. She said he'd talk his way out of it, that he had the gift of the gab.

'Anyway, it became a moot point. He arrived one morning out of the blue, cool as a cucumber, and said he'd come to take her home to her mother's. I suppose he knew any relationship between them was over – how could it not be? – but by driving her home to Selmouth, he'd have plenty of time to persuade her what their story was going to be. She packed up her things meekly enough, told me she'd be in touch and got in the car. He closed the door for her as if he was some kind of gentleman, then walked back to where I was standing in the doorway, and leaned towards me as if he was going to kiss me on the cheek. But he didn't kiss me. He hissed in my ear – that's the only word I can use, he hissed – that if I said anything to anyone, ever, he'd kill them all. Before or since, I've never again felt the sensation, but my blood ran cold to hear those words.'

'And do you think he meant them?'

Barbara looks Fox straight in the eye. 'He killed Baby Michael and tried to dispose of his body in the most horrible way. Would you have doubted that he meant it?'

Fox wouldn't. 'What happened after that?'

'I kept my silence, for Alice's sake and the girls'. I heard nothing from her for a while, but the following Christmas I had a card with a little scribble inside that suggested it would be nice to meet up. So we did. We met for a pub lunch. I thought we'd be talking about how to get Simon Orchard arrested, but the moment I went close to that subject, she stopped me and said, "Simon says if I say anything to anyone, he'll say it was me and I'll go to prison and lose my girls. I couldn't let them go into care." When I pressed her and asked her what he'd say was her, she said, "I don't want to talk about it, Barbara." And she never did again, or at least not to me. So you see, I carried that burden with her for over twenty years, and I don't mind telling you, it's grown heavy, and I'm very glad at last to be able to put it down.'

Fox doesn't know what to say. A silence grows between them.

'Am I allowed to ask how he died?' she says, at last.

It's not his business to say, but he does so anyway. 'He committed suicide.'

She gives a hollow laugh. 'Did his conscience torment him to it in the end, then?'

Fox shakes his head. 'I'm sorry, Barbara, I don't believe it did. He knew we were coming for him for another offence, and I don't think he could face the indignity of prison. That's only a personal view, of course.'

'That would be Simon. Was it something serious?'

'Yes.'

'Did he kill someone else?'

'There was a connection to Baby Michael. That's all I'm at liberty to say.'

Barbara nods. 'I tell myself my silence helped keep the three of them safe, but Alice never got over it. Do you know she started wearing black that year, and I never again saw her wear anything else. She went into perpetual mourning for her baby.'

'She visited him sometimes, in the churchyard where he's buried.'

'I'm glad to hear it.'

'Her daughters have had her ashes interred there with him.'

'I suppose they thought it best.'

'In difficult circumstances,' says Fox.

'The circumstances were difficult for me too.' Barbara reaches for another cigarette. 'Shall I tell you what made it hardest for me? She made me a part of that sorry story the day she came to me for shelter, and forced me into that unholy pact, her and me and him together. And yet in all the years I kept their secret, she never once said thank you. She wanted it never to be mentioned, never aired or exposed or to see the light of day. I suppose she thought I was just getting on with my life, but you don't get on with your life with any kind of freedom hiding a secret like that. Ever after it was always on my mind, and it cast a shadow over everything I did. I lost my bubbly disposition, which was the part of me Derek most loved, so it set the rot in our marriage, and left me where you see me now, facing old age alone. If she had just picked up the phone and acknowledged what I did for her before she took her own life, I think I'd find that easier to bear.'

'You were a true friend to them all.'

But Barbara shakes her head. 'I was an accomplice in the concealment of a heinous crime. And all I have to hope for, Inspector, is that when my time comes, the Almighty will see fit to grant me absolution.'

FIFTY

Fox heads for the same car park he used on his previous visit to Selmouth, but with the early seasonal visitors already in town, it takes much longer to find himself a space.

The wind off the sea is cold. At least it isn't raining.

He takes the same uphill walk through the quaint back streets, remembering that the last time he came this way, his mind was full of questions. Now, he's bringing answers.

Detected, offender deceased.

Someone has lavished care on Trelonie House, cutting back the sprawling creeper, fixing the lopsided gate. The window frames have been painted, and the moss is gone from the roof, so the cottage appears welcoming, the kind of home where a happy family might live.

A *For Sale* sign pokes out from the lavender bushes.

Marietta's smiling when she answers the door. By her feet, Josie's wagging her tail. Marietta invites Fox inside, and he makes his way into the lounge past a stack of packing cases already sealed with brown tape. Lily's waiting on the sofa.

Fox accepts an offer of coffee, and sits down in an armchair, looking round at what he remembers as a cluttered room, seeing it's been stripped almost bare, though the gold carriage clock still ticks on the mantelpiece.

Marietta hands him his coffee, and takes a seat next to her sister. Josie jumps up and squeezes in between them, her head on Marietta's lap.

'Looks like you're on the move,' says Fox.

'Just me,' says Marietta. 'The house sale should go through next week. I'm going travelling for a while with my boyfriend.' She strokes the dog's ear. 'And Josie's coming too, of course.'

'I envy you,' says Fox. 'I always wanted to do that, just take off and go wherever the road takes you.'

'We're not going too far to begin with,' says Marietta. 'We decided to start close to home. Lily's family tree research identified some relatives we've never met, so for better or worse, Adam and I are paying them a visit. At least some good came out of her DNA test.'

'I'm glad to hear it.' Fox takes a sip of his coffee. 'And that leads me to my reason for being here today. I'm sure you've already worked out that it's not just a social call.'

'We had our suspicions,' says Lily. 'Does that mean you have news?'

'Yes. You may regard it as a positive, as closure, but I'm afraid you may find it upsetting, in part. We've identified Michael's killer.'

Seconds of silence go by, before Lily grips Marietta's hand and whispers, 'She didn't do it, I know she didn't.'

Fox shakes his head. 'Your mother was innocent, Lily. Of the killing, at least.'

'I knew it,' says Lily, but her obvious relief suggests to Fox she wasn't sure.

'Thank God,' says Marietta. 'Oh my God, you have no idea . . . We didn't want to believe it, but how could we help but think it was a possibility, with the circumstances as they were? And with what she did, it seemed to point to her being guilty. We tried to keep faith in her, but there was always a chink of doubt, and how could we have lived with that? So thank you, thank you for letting us know.'

'Who was it, then?' asks Lily. 'You will tell us, won't you? Will there be a trial? Will we have to be there?'

'There'll be no trial,' says Fox. 'You'll be spared that, at least. I'm afraid your brother's killer was the man you knew as your uncle, Simon Orchard.'

'Uncle Simon?' Lily appears baffled. 'I don't understand. Why would he have done that?'

'He was your brother's father,' explains Fox, carefully. 'According to our sources, he and your mother were in a relationship for a while after your father died.'

'Sources? What sources?' demands Lily. 'I don't think that's right. He was just a family friend.'

Fox looks at Lily, and sees in her the same resistance he's seen many times before in people confronted by difficult truths about those they love: violent sons, addicted daughters, predatory fathers. And in this case, a less-than-honest mother.

Marietta, though, is more open to the facts.

'Wait, Lily,' she says. 'Let's hear what the inspector has to say.'

Fox is grateful for her intervention. 'Our DNA tests have proved conclusively that Simon Orchard was Michael's father, so I'm afraid a sexual relationship between him and your mother isn't in doubt. We also have a witness who knew them at that time, who's confirmed they were living together. I'm afraid the relationship wasn't always a happy one. I believe Orchard was a controlling man. Your mother may have suffered some abuse, as, I'm afraid, may you.'

'I don't think so,' says Lily. 'We'd have remembered.'

'We were very young, Lily,' says Marietta. 'Has Simon been arrested?'

'No,' says Fox. 'I have to tell you Simon Orchard is dead. He committed suicide.'

'Oh.' Both the sisters appear shocked, but it's Lily who asks, 'Not the same way as our mother?'

Fox shakes his head.

'Was it because you found him out?' asks Marietta.

Fox blinks away the scene that flashes in his mind: the smashing of a jar, Orchard walking calmly to the sofa to lie down and wait for the inevitable.

'Without a doubt, yes,' he says. 'I was there with a team to make a search of his property in relation to another death.'

'You were there when he died?' Marietta's face shows her concern. 'That's awful.'

'Whose death?' asks Lily.

Fox hesitates, wondering how much he should tell them. He decides they have a right to know. 'Your brother's case became difficult,' he says. 'It was looking impossible to prove who was actually responsible, but I stumbled on a connection between Orchard and the death of a man who was a witness at the time, Daniel Hopper.'

'I read about him on the internet,' says Marietta. 'Didn't he find Michael's body?'

'He did. It's my belief Daniel had worked out that Orchard

was the killer, and was about to report it to us. When Daniel died, the cause of his death was recorded as uncertain. He was diabetic, and prone to crises because of his illness. Orchard knew we were getting close to arresting him for Daniel's killing. His phone records put him in the area; there were searches relating to insulin overdoses on his laptop, and it was only a matter of time until we found them. The prospect of prison was too much for him, I suppose. There was every prospect that at his age, he'd end his life there.'

'We thought he was on our side,' says Lily, quietly.

'As I say, you are at least spared a trial,' says Fox. 'And Michael's case can at last be officially closed. By the way, Orchard had your watercolours at his studio.'

'We sold them to him in the end,' says Marietta. 'He seemed determined to have them, though we were reluctant to let them go. Our mother was very attached to them.'

Fox recalls the photograph of Orchard holding Baby Michael, now logged and filed away in the case's evidence files. Alice Ansley was right to value those pictures so highly; they hid a threat of exposure sufficient to ensure the safety of her and her daughters. But he sees no need to give them that part of the story, to tell them they grew up with an image of their brother's killer hanging by the front door.

'What will happen to the pictures now?' asks Marietta.

'I assume they'll form part of his estate, and be dealt with accordingly.' Fox takes a drink of his coffee, finding it cold. 'There's something else you should know. Do you remember Barbara Constant? Lily, you gave me her name after your mother's funeral.'

'I remember her, yes.'

'I believe you both owe her a debt of gratitude. She kept you safe when Orchard was becoming abusive towards you as children, and when Michael was killed she took your mother in and did her best to keep all of you from harm. At your mother's insistence, she stayed silent about what she knew for over two decades, despite a troubled conscience. Your mother persuaded her it was the right thing to do, for your sakes. I have to say I'm afraid I don't share that view.'

'You think Mum should have come forward?' asks Marietta.

'Absolutely I do, yes. Once you were of age, I think she should have spoken to us. If she had, Daniel Hopper would probably still be alive. But I accept that in these kind of cases, fear plays a huge part. I'm sure she believed she was still at risk from Orchard, even after all this time.'

'If you think about what happened to Daniel, she was right,' says Lily.

'You could all have been protected until an arrest was made. But that's all hindsight. Can I urge you to take the time to hear Barbara's story? I think she deserves at least that, and I know she'd thank you for it.'

'We will,' says Marietta. 'And we must thank you for all the work you've done on behalf of our family.'

Fox grimaces. 'Before you thank me, we should talk about what happens next. This isn't the end of the road, in fact in some ways it's only the beginning. Devon and Cornwall Police will be issuing a press release on Friday stating that the Baby Michael case has been solved. It will be of huge public interest both here and abroad.'

Their faces show exactly what he'd expect in anyone who sees an approaching maelstrom: anxiety and dismay.

'We'll be besieged,' says Lily.

'What can we do?' asks Marietta. 'What do you suggest?'

'As I see it, you have two choices,' says Fox. 'You can embrace it, approach a good PR agency and get them to handle it. You'll be offered money for exclusive access, and it's for you to decide what to do about that. But the press release won't be out for another three days. If I were in your shoes, I'd be using that time to get as far away from Selmouth as humanly possible.'

Fox shakes their hands as he leaves. In the entryway, the watercolours have left pale patches, faded relics on the wall.

He doesn't have to be there at Bleak Tor, but there's a bullet he needs to bite. By the time he arrives, the search team are packing up.

Fox knows one of the team leaders well, and wanders across the yard to have a word.

'How's it going, Andy? Do I need to get suited and booted?'

'Hey, Russ. Long time no see. No, don't worry about that, we're already done. Found what we were looking for easy as anything, dropped in the kitchen drain. Deliberate drop, for certain. You'd have to remove the cover to get it in there. The grille's cross-hatched.'

Lifting the horseshoe knocker, Fox has no idea what kind of welcome he'll receive. When Jayne Hopper answers the door, her face is impassive.

'Hello,' he says. 'Am I disturbing you?'

'What, with half a dozen police vans in the yard? Believe me, I was already well disturbed.'

'I'm sorry for the drama. But I just spoke to one of the lads and I have news, if you'd like to hear it.'

She looks at him expectantly.

'They've found Daniel's phone.'

'Where?'

'In a drain.'

'So he dropped it, then.'

Fox shakes his head. 'Not with that cover on the aperture. Someone hid it there.'

'Simon Orchard.'

'I believe so.'

'So what happens now, Inspector?'

'I can tell you the full story. Or I can offer you an apology for all the trouble you've been through, and never darken your door again.'

He's about to walk away when she says, 'I could make you a cup of coffee before you go. As long as you promise not to read me my rights.'

Fox smiles, and to his relief, Jayne smiles back.

'I absolutely promise,' he says, and she leads him inside.

FIFTY-ONE

Marietta and Lily lean on the windowsill of the bedroom they used to share, looking out on a view of rooftops under an overcast sky. If they bend hard to the left, they can glimpse a sliver of grey sea.

The room around them is empty. In the worn carpet are dimples where furniture used to stand, including their old bunk beds.

'This feels like the end of so many things,' says Lily. 'I've always thought in the back of my mind that if life went really wrong, I could come back here and be cared for, and now it won't be here anymore. I suppose it's the beginning of being a real grown-up.'

'Adulthood's vastly overrated.' Marietta touches a spot at the centre of the windowsill. 'Do you remember the music-box that used to be here?'

Lily does remember: a tiny ballerina in a pink tutu, who twirled and span on a mirrored dance floor to a tinkling rendition of Swan Lake. 'Mum used to say it was her best-ever present as a little girl. She gave it to us when I was eight, because we were both old enough to take care of it. And we did take care of it, didn't we?'

'The ballerina was so pretty,' Marietta recalls. 'I wanted to be like her, elegant and perfect.'

'Neither of us became ballerinas, though, did we? Do you think Mum was proud of us, Mari?'

Marietta's face becomes sad. 'Not of me, no. What have I done she would have been proud of?'

'You've grown up beautiful and strong and adventurous. You'd probably still be living in Colombia if I hadn't made you come back.'

One phone call changed everything. Those sultry Latin days seem light years away.

'I thought you were being hysterical,' admits Marietta, 'and I'm sorry.' For so many things, she thinks. For not being there, for taking so long to realise she was on the wrong path. What's changed most, is her.

'This time tomorrow, where will you be?' asks Lily.

'Not far away. Somewhere in Devon, probably.'

'We'll be halfway to Scotland,' says Lily. 'Bakewell, so not quite halfway. We're staying there two nights.' She touches her eye, and Marietta wonders if she might cry. 'I feel we're being driven out.'

'We are. Not quite the legacy we expected, is it?'

A herring gull lands on a neighbour's roof, ash grey on white. The way it holds its head – alert, astute – reminds Marietta of the guillemot in their paintings.

'What do you make of it all, now we have the facts?'

Lily's silent for a few moments, until she says, 'If we're apologising for past behaviour, I'm sorry I was so stubborn. I didn't want to believe she could leave us that way, because I couldn't imagine ever leaving a child of mine. Now we know the full story, I think she felt she had no choice. If she'd told us what she was going to do, we'd have stopped her, and the police would have come for her eventually. I had the impression Inspector Fox wasn't ever going to give up. She was guilty on so many counts, wasn't she? She might easily have gone to jail.'

'She's left us with an unholy mess. I'm not surprised the house buyers pulled out.'

'We'll find someone else,' says Lily, 'when the initial frenzy has died down.'

'Do you think she was always unhappy?' asks Marietta. 'I'm worried that all the good times we had, for her it was all a facade.'

'I don't think so.' Lily smiles. 'Take it from one who knows, even the most miserable people on the planet sometimes have to take a day off.'

'Will we have to change our names, do you think? Get new identities?'

'Plastic surgery?' suggests Lily. 'I'd like a new nose. We'll have to see how it goes. Let's just make our joint statement today, and disappear until the dust settles.'

'If it ever settles. What about the offer from the *Sun*? Maybe we should grab it while we're hot.'

'What would we do with the money?'

'Charity. Holidays in Bermuda. Cosmetic surgery and a new home in the wild.' Marietta pauses. 'I'll really miss you.'

Lily steps forward to hug her. 'I'll miss you too. We'll see each other soon, won't we?'

'One hundred per cent,' says Marietta.

Lily looks round the room. 'No more sanctuary. Mari, I'm scared.'

'We'll be together,' says Marietta. 'Remember what they told us. No questions, just the statement and a few pictures and we're done.'

As they go downstairs, Lily asks, 'Do you think Mum realised what she was leaving for us? Do you think she knew how it would be?'

'I've thought about that. Maybe. I don't know. Don't think badly of her, Lily. She tried to do her best for us until she thought we didn't need her. Then I think she did what was best for her.'

In the lane outside, a taxi blows its horn.

'It'll be a strange new world for us out there,' says Marietta, putting on her jacket, 'but we're tough and strong and we have each other. Right?'

'Right,' says Lily. 'We're family. So, are we ready? Let's go.'

FIFTY-TWO

Friday, 5 p.m. Packing up, shutting down, signing off.

Fox is finishing the last of the digital paperwork for the Baby Michael case, finally putting the case to bed.

For such an achievement, he's feeling oddly flat.

'You OK, Russ?' Budd asks the question as she's tidying her desk for the weekend. 'You seem a bit out of sorts. What you need is a cheering pint.'

Before answering, he hesitates. 'Something on my mind about the case, that's all. I'll get over it.'

Budd's face shows her concern. 'Tell me.'

'Honestly? I think that article I got the paper to run about reopening the case was what pushed Alice Ansley into taking her own life. And I know it was designed to stir things up, but I didn't know what the fall-out would be.'

'We never do.'

'I didn't apologise to the family for that, and I think I should.'

Budd crosses the room, and sits down in front of Fox's desk. 'You know what this is? Methodology guilt. Clear-cut case. You're not responsible for the actions of an individual.'

'Maybe I am, though. Maybe she was thinking her death would kill it stone dead, take away any motivation Orchard had for coming anywhere near her and her girls.'

'They're not girls, Russ, they're adult women.'

'That's how we see them. But she was their mother, and mothers will do pretty much anything to protect their young.'

Budd nods. 'I agree, it could have been that, yes. Or it could have been that she couldn't face the notoriety, and the questions, and the end of life as she knew it. Maybe the burden she was carrying was already too heavy. You've no way of knowing what was in her mind. You did your job, and you did it brilliantly. And let me ask you this. If you had the time again, would you do it any differently?'

'I don't think I would, no.'

'So don't be so hard on yourself. You took the action you thought would best serve you in getting to a serious offender. Alice Ansley could have come forward any time in the last twenty-five years. She chose not to do so, same as she chose not to come and talk to you when she saw that piece in the paper. She could have done that, Russ. She did have other options.'

'I suppose you're right.'

'I am right, and don't you dare sit here brooding over things you had no control over. Come on, put your jacket on. It's Friday night, and one drink won't kill you. I'm buying.'

Budd's not much of a pub-goer, and an invitation from her is rare. And if he's honest, a pint might be just the thing to dissipate his mood.

'Where are you thinking?'

'George and Dragon?'

They do a decent pint of Doom Bar, and it's not too far to get a taxi home.

What the hell.

'OK, sounds good,' he says. 'Give me fifteen minutes to finish this, and I'll see you there.'

When Fox pushes open the lounge bar door, the room's all but empty, and there's no sign of Budd. An elderly couple at a corner table sit silent over lager and limes. At the fruit machine, a youth filthy with plaster dust is feeding in more coins.

Behind the bar, the landlord's loading Britvic juices into a fridge. When he sees Fox, he stands up slowly, pressing his hands into his painful lower back.

'All right, Russ?' he says. 'Haven't seen you in a while.'

'How are you doing, Sandy? I'll have a pint of Doom Bar, if it's on.'

'I think your lady's already got you one.' Sandy jerks his thumb towards a door still signed *Smoke Room*, though it's been years since anyone's smoked in there.

Fox walks past the youth at the fruit machine, and pulls open the smoke room door.

A cheer goes up. At the front of a crowd, Budd holds out a pint; almost everyone he knows, pretty much everybody in CID he's ever worked with, is standing behind her. Even the senior ranks are represented. Towards the back – the only one not smiling – is Liam Garrett.

The Chief Super comes forward, and claps Fox on the shoulder. 'Well done, Russ, outstanding. Very well done indeed.

'I just want to say,' he goes on, turning round to face the room in general, 'that Devon and Cornwall Police are lucky indeed to have an officer with tenacity and talent such as yours. To get a result after all these years in a high-profile case is a real feather in our caps. I think we can all be proud to have had you spearheading this investigation, and I'm sure you'd want me to thank on your behalf all the backroom staff, all our magnificent data specialists and forensics teams, everyone who's played a part. A fantastic result for us all. Raise your glasses, please, ladies and gentlemen. To Russ!'

'To Russ!'

Fox grins, and raises his own pint to his colleagues. The Doom Bar, when he tastes it, goes down like liquid gold.

Budd comes to join him. 'Well done, Russ. You really deserve this. Feels good to have a win, doesn't it?'

'Especially this one,' says Fox. 'The ambition of almost a lifetime.'

At the far end of the room, Liam Garrett slips out the back door.

FIFTY-THREE

Ivy's shelling peas picked from the garden, dropping the peas into a saucepan, the pods onto a copy of the local newspaper. Alice's picture was on the front page; Ivy cut out the article, and put it away in a drawer. The wireless is tuned to Radio 4, and she's waiting for the shipping forecast at three minutes past twelve. Even when the weather's calm, she enjoys listening to the forecast, but just as it begins, a heavy vehicle pulls up outside.

With its engine running, she can't hear what's being said. Abandoning the peas, she goes to the lounge window, lifting the lace curtain to look out.

Marietta's scrambling down from the passenger seat of a camper van, and by the time she's walked down the path, Ivy's waiting at the open door. Josie's followed Marietta, and jumps up to put her feet on Ivy's knees. Ivy bends down to rub her head.

'What in God's own name is that?' she asks, nodding towards the van.

'Adam and I are going travelling,' says Marietta. 'To get away for a while. Josie's coming too.'

'Ah, I told you she's your dog now,' says Ivy. 'You mind and take good care of her.'

'We will.'

Ivy straightens up. 'I saw you all over the news, you and your mum. I wasn't expecting that, truly I wasn't. All those years I knew her, and she never said a word to me. Makes you wonder, don't it, what other folks don't say.'

'It's all been a shock,' says Marietta. 'We had no idea.'

'I suppose it makes sense now, though, her walking off into the sea.'

Marietta looks at her. 'Not really. But it's what she decided to do.'

'And how's poor Lily taken it? Always the fragile one, she was.'

'She's getting through it. She and Connor have gone away, until it all blows over.'

'They'll be coming to Selmouth in droves, wanting a look at your house,' says Ivy. 'Good business for somebody. It's an ill wind, as they say.'

Marietta holds out a parcel wrapped in flowered paper. 'I brought you this. From me and Lily.'

'For me?'

'It's from Mum, really,' says Marietta. 'I think she would have wanted you to have it. Go on, open it.'

Ivy unwraps the parcel, and lifts the flaps of the cardboard box it contains.

Inside the box, wrapped in pink tissue paper, is Alice's carriage clock.

'Oh. I can't keep this.'

'Of course you can. I know you admired it.'

'I don't know what to say.'

'I'm afraid I've let it stop, but I know you'll keep it going. That's what Mum would want, to know it was still ticking away. You were a good friend to her, Ivy. It's no more than you deserve.'

'I shall treasure it,' says Ivy. 'I'll put it in pride of place. Aren't you coming in for a cuppa? Where are you off to, anyway?'

'Not too far, for now. Maybe Ilfracombe, or Appledore. We've got family there. We'll send you a postcard, won't we, Josie?'

'I should like that.'

'We'll see you when we get back.'

'You mind how you go.'

When the camper van has driven away, Ivy carries the clock into the living room. Fetching a duster and a pot of Brasso, she polishes away all the marks and fingerprints on the case; then, satisfied that the clock is looking its best, she gives the key a few turns, and sets it ticking on her mantelpiece.

EPILOGUE

Three years to the day after her death, Lily and Connor stand by the grave Alice shares with her son.

Lily's gained a little weight and has a touch of colour in her cheeks. In her bright summer dress, she looks happy and healthy. Connor has joined a running club and toned up. Lily tells him he looks better now than he did when she married him.

She's brought white roses as she always does, and lays them as a bouquet on the ground. Then, turning to Connor, she takes the blue-blanketed bundle from his arms.

'We've brought someone very special to meet you, Mum,' she says. 'This is your grandson. His name is Michael.'

ACKNOWLEDGEMENTS

During the writing of this book, I lost my long-term agent and mentor, Christopher Little. I owe him a huge debt of thanks; he stood by me and looked after my interests for many years, and is much missed. Thanks also to Emma and Jules at the Christopher Little Agency for their meticulous care – I couldn't have done it without them.

Thanks too to Cathryn Summerhayes for stepping into the breach, and I'm really looking forward to working with the Curtis Brown team.

Thanks to ex-DS Terry Parry for so patiently answering all my questions on police procedure, and to Peter Beirne, head of the Major Crime Review Team at Thames Valley Police, for his invaluable insight on the use of DNA in investigations.

I'm grateful as ever to Ken Fishwick for having the unending patience to meticulously check the manuscript.

Thanks are always due to my editor Toby Jones and his infallible eye for making the story stronger, and to all the team at Headline who turn the manuscript into a book.

And finally, thanks to Andy for always knowing when it's time to make a cup of tea.

Discover more gripping and emotional thrillers from Erin Kinsley . . .

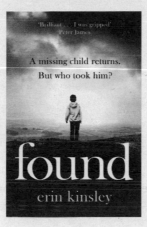

'Brilliant, utterly compelling, heart-wrenching . . .
I was gripped and loved it.'
PETER JAMES

A MISSING CHILD RETURNS. BUT WHO TOOK HIM?

When 11-year-old Evan vanishes without trace,
his parents are plunged into their worst nightmare.

Especially as the police, under massive pressure, have no answers.
But months later Evan is unexpectedly found, frightened and refusing
to speak. His loving family realise life will never be the same again

DI Naylor knows that unless those who took Evan are caught, other
children are in danger. And with Evan silent, she must race against time
to find those responsible . . .

Available to buy now

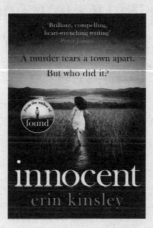

'Full of twists and turns . . . a gripping and compelling read you won't
want to put down'
HEAT

A MURDER TEARS A TOWN APART.
BUT WHO IS THE KILLER?

The pretty market town of Sterndale is a close-knit community where
everyone thinks they know everyone else. But at a lavish summer
wedding a local celebrity is discovered slumped in the gardens,
the victim of a violent assault that leads to a murder investigation.

As the police search for answers, suspicion and paranoia build –
and the lives of the locals are turned upside down. Secrets that
lurk beneath the pristine façade of Sterndale come to light
as detectives close in on the truth . . .

Available to buy now

HEADLINE

THRILLINGLY GOOD BOOKS
FROM CRIMINALLY
GOOD WRITERS

CRIME FILES BRINGS YOU THE LATEST RELEASES FROM TOP CRIME AND THRILLER AUTHORS.

SIGN UP ONLINE FOR OUR MONTHLY NEWSLETTER AND BE THE FIRST TO KNOW ABOUT OUR COMPETITIONS, NEW BOOKS AND MORE.